TOO GREAT A TEMPTATION ...

Eagle saw her coming, her red hair as bright as a beacon. He'd expected the intruders, but he'd never expected Kate Malone, brandishing a mop.

She was as noisy as a freight train, roaring through the night. Fearless, she stormed through the clinic.

Eagle watched her, amused. She was in no danger, for he'd kept watch all night. The clinic was empty.

"Come out," she said. "I know you're in here."

She poked the mop behind a stack of lumber and jabbed it into dark corners.

"Come out with your hands up and I might be generous."

Leaning forward with the moon impossibly bright upon her hair, she shaded her eyes, trying to see into the darkness.

The wanting of her pierced him like arrows, and watching, he knew it would always be so. She was in his blood, and the mere sight of her stirred him beyond imagining.

He stepped from the shadows, so close his thigh touched hers. She spun around, dropping the mop, her mouth round with surprise.

"Be generous, Kate," he said, reaching for her. . . .

Witch Dance

Peggy Webb

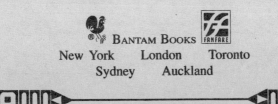

BANTAM BOOKS FANFARE

New York London Toronto
Sydney Auckland

WITCH DANCE

A Bantam Fanfare Book/August 1994

FANFARE *and the portrayal of a boxed "ff" are trademarks of Bantam Books,
a division of Bantam Doubleday Dell Publishing Group, Inc.*

ISBN 0-553-56057-3

Published simultaneously in the United States and Canada

*Bantam Books are published by Bantam Books, a division of Bantam
Doubleday Dell Publishing Group, Inc. Its trademark, consisting of the
words "Bantam Books" and the portrayal of a rooster, is Registered in U.S.
Patent and Trademark Office and in other countries. Marca Registrada.
Bantam Books, 1540 Broadway, New York, New York 10036.*

PRINTED IN THE UNITED STATES OF AMERICA

RAD 0 9 8 7 6 5 4 3 2 1

This book is dedicated
with love and gratitude to
JIM AND MARTHA JO PATTERSON

Prologue

The village lay snug under a blanket of snow, somnolent and peaceful in the early morning light as if it had never known violence. Kate Malone knew better. She stood on her front porch, clutching her coat high around her neck, shivering.

The previous day's fan mail had been slipped silently under the door of her clinic and still lay open on her bedside table. *Your tormentor watches you, pale face doctor witch. Repent or burn in hell.*

Coward. Hiding behind his mask of anonymity. She would never back down, for the lives of a people she had come to love were at stake. Threats of hell didn't scare her. She'd already been there . . . twice. And she'd survived both times.

Her boots sank into the snow as she started across her yard to the clinic. The cold air whipped her coat and set her adrenaline flowing. Five hours of sleep was not enough, but it was all she could allow herself. A dreadful sickness was stalking the Chickasaw children, and she was the only one who could save them.

With her head bent against the wind, Kate hurried along. Suddenly the wintry silence was rent by a sharp crackling sound. Kate froze. If it was her tormentor, she was fair game, for the nearest house was two miles away. There was nobody to hear her if she screamed.

She balled her hands into fists and took a karate stance, ready to fight. The sound came again, and a pine bough dumped its heavy burden at her feet.

"Nerves," she muttered, disgusted with herself. She couldn't afford a case of nerves.

She'd rammed her fists into her coat pockets and started forward once more, when another sound tore the silence . . . a high-pitched wail of terror. Fear bloomed in Kate's chest, and her own scream rose in her throat. The sound came again, shattering her nerves and the spell that bound her.

"Deborah!" Her head up, her heart riding high in her chest, Kate raced toward her clinic. The screaming had stopped, but a new terror presented itself. Smoke curled from the roof and an unearthly glow lit the windows.

"Please, God . . . please, God," she chanted as she ran, not knowing what she asked for, knowing only that prayer was necessary.

The toe of her boot caught on a root, and she toppled like a felled tree. Scrambling in the snow, praying and swearing at the same time, Kate lurched upright and started running once more. Snow clung to her lashes, blurring her vision. The acrid smell of smoke burned her nostrils.

She knew she was making progress, for she could hear the vicious crackle of wood catching fire, but the clinic seemed to be receding rather than advancing. Her lungs burned and her eyes stung.

There was movement behind the clinic, and she saw a shadowy form racing toward the cover of trees.

"The bastard, the dirty bastard."

Roots hidden in the snow threatened to trip her once more, but Kate fought for balance. When she finally reached the clinic, she was so weak with fatigue and fear, she leaned against the door. It was already warm from the fire inside.

Struggling against panic, Kate pushed it open. Smoke

billowed from the examining room in the back, filling the waiting room with a thick black cloud. She flung one arm over her nose, then dropped to all fours and crawled forward.

"Deborah!" she screamed. There was no answer except the hissing of flames.

The smoke was so thick, she couldn't see. Her head bumped into the receptionist's desk, setting stars in her eyes and sending the telephone flying. Disoriented, Kate crawled backward. Her foot connected with the bookshelf, and books cascaded around her.

Choking on smoke and sobs, she clawed her way out of the book pile and inched blindly toward what she hoped was the back of the clinic. Her hands landed in something slick. Splinters from the old wooden floor tore at her skin and ripped at her nails as she clawed for purchase. Her knees hit the slippery puddle and she sprawled forward.

Soft flesh cushioned her fall ... and luxuriant dark hair and the starched front of a nurse's uniform.

"Deborah," Kate called, terror reducing her voice to a scratchy whisper.

She levered herself onto her elbows, trying to see through the blanket of smoke. A burst of flame illuminated the room. Deborah Lightfoot lay in a pool of blood, her eyes staring blankly at Kate and her throat slit from ear to ear.

Keening like a wounded animal, Kate bent over her. She caught the wrist, knowing there would be no pulse, leaned her head against the chest, knowing there would be no heartbeat.

She was too late, too late.

"Deborah ... Deborah!" she screamed, trying to staunch the flow of blood with her scarf, refusing to believe death had claimed her best friend. "Dammit all to hell, I won't let you die. Not you too."

Tears streaked through the grime on her cheeks, and smoke stung her lungs as she abandoned the futile effort to stop the bleeding and pushed with all her strength against the silent heart. Suddenly the entire west wall went up in flames.

Stricken, Kate stared upward as the roof buckled and began a slow, fiery descent. She cradled her arms over her head and pressed her face into her dead friend's chest.

Eagle Mingo saw the flames as they leapt over the treetops. He urged his horse forward, refusing to give in to the terror that clawed his gut. If he'd been a praying man, he'd have called on the Great Spirit to spare him mercy and grace, but he'd ceased praying five years earlier, when he'd traded his heart and soul for a mantle of duty.

Angry tongues of fire licked the sky, and he leaned over his stallion's mane, coaxing him in the ancient language of his people. The phone call that had sent him flying through the early dawn on his horse still echoed through his mind.

"Mingo, I think Kate Malone may be in real danger. My sources believe the man who calls himself her tormentor is going to strike soon."

"Get some men over there," he had told Martin Black Elk, chief of the tribal police and lifelong friend. "I don't care whether she wants protection or not. Get them over there."

"I will. Soon as the first shift gets in here, I'll send a man to her place, but I don't know if it will do any good. She's about as easy to persuade as a wildcat."

"Tell her it's my orders."

"The last time I mentioned the governor's orders, she laughed in my face."

"I'll tell her, Martin. She won't dare laugh in mine." She might scratch his eyes out, but she wouldn't laugh.

Eagle had meant to wait until sunup, but some dark premonition had sent him flying to his stables in the predawn hours. In this weather his stallion was much more reliable than either his Corvette or his Jeep. It was one of the few remaining of its kind, a Chickasaw horse, bred for speed and endurance.

As he neared Kate's place he thought he heard a woman's scream, but with the pounding of hooves and the howling of wind, he couldn't be certain. Leaning low over his horse, he raced toward the blazing clinic.

"Deborah!" the woman screamed.

This time there was no mistaking the sound. It was Kate's voice . . . coming from somewhere inside the inferno.

"*Aiya!*" he urged his horse, bending low over its neck. "Go like the wind."

When they were close enough to feel the heat from the fire, his stallion balked. Eagle knew he would never survive the blaze on foot. He whipped off his jacket and tied it around the horse's head. Then he dug his heels into its flanks and the stallion vaulted through the wall of flame.

There were two bodies lying together on the floor, one with the long black hair of the Chickasaw and the other with hair the color of fire. Until that moment Eagle didn't know it was possible to breathe after your heart had stopped beating.

The ceiling above them buckled, sending flames shooting downward. Heat seared his leg and the flanks of his horse. The stallion whinnied, sidestepping. Eagle wrestled him under control.

There was movement on the floor, and Kate twisted her head upward. In the eerie glow of the blaze she stared at him with eyes widened by shock and terror. Deborah Lightfoot stared sightlessly at him with eyes gone glassy in death.

"Reach for me, Kate!" She didn't move. Eagle leaned far over the saddle. "In the name of all that's holy, *reach for me.*"

Tentatively she lifted her hand. He caught her arm and jerked her upright. Flames roared around them, and his stallion danced in place.

Counting on skills he'd learned as a child racing

across tribal lands, Eagle circled her waist and scooped her upward just as the roof gave way. He couldn't risk taking time to get her into the saddle. Holding her in an iron grip with her legs dangling over the side, he leaned low and urged his stallion forward. They leapt through the flames and into the dawn. The roof caved in behind them.

"Deborah." Kate sobbed as he pulled her into the saddle. Heat from the inferno still licked at their backs. Holding Kate against his chest, he leaned around her and jerked the coat off his stallion's head.

Kate clawed at his face. "Put me down, you savage. Deborah's back there."

"There's nothing you can do. Deborah's dead."

"I won't let her be." Tears streaked down her smoke-grimed face as she beat at his upper arms and shoulders. "Do you hear me? I won't let her die."

He wrapped one arm tightly around her chest, pinning her arms down, and with the other he guided the stallion into the woods behind the clinic.

Kate coughed and sputtered.

"Breathe, Kate. Breathe the fresh air."

Shivering violently, she sucked air into her starving lungs. Then, with a strength born of desperation, she struggled against him.

"I have to go to her. Let me down."

"It's too late."

"No! Damn you. It can't be too late."

Sobs and shivers racked her body as she fought him. The stallion pranced, skittish and ready to bolt.

"Stop it, Kate. You can't go back in there."

"How dare you decide other people's lives. Who made you God?" She drew back and her fist connected with bone. Tomorrow he'd have a black eye for his troubles.

He caught her right wrist, and she rammed his jaw with a left hook. "I don't want to have to hit you, Kate."

"You don't give a damn about her, do you?" Her chin

came up. "Hit me, almighty governor of the Chickasaw Nation."

Snow and cinders from the burning building swirled around them. She was nearing hysteria.

With the swiftness of his namesake, he bent down and crushed her mouth under his. Her lips were cold and tasted of smoke and tears.

For a moment she struggled, wild and fierce, then suddenly her arms stole around his neck.

And he knew that in five lonely years he'd never stopped loving her. He held her close, kissing her with the desperate knowledge that this time would be their last. The murmurs of pleasure he remembered so well started deep in her throat, a soft humming sound that set his blood on fire. He became primitive, savage, with one goal in mind, one need overriding all others—to possess Kate.

"Eagle . . . Eagle." Her voice was a broken plea, and he didn't know if it was a cry for release or a cry for mercy.

He died a little inside. Breaking his long silence with the Father Creator, he called upon that all-powerful deity to pull them both back from the precipice of hell. When he released Kate, she sagged against him, spent.

He cupped her face, and they stared at each other, linked by a passion that had survived five endless years and yet separated by duty and honor. Eagle wanted to shake his fists at the heavens and curse the day he was born. Kate's eyes mirrored his agony.

Slowly, he traced her lips with one finger. Kate flicked her tongue against his skin, but the searing touch was gone so swiftly, he might have been dreaming.

"I should have let you burn," he whispered.

"I wish you had."

BOOK I
The Eagle

The river cried out to her in a voice full of anguish,
And out of the waters rose a creature, magnificent and
  golden, splendid in all his glory.
The sun lay along his wings and its heat spread outward,
Reaching toward her with hands of flame,
Reaching even the places she held most secret,
Reaching . . . reaching . . .
Until at last it burned her heart.

1

Charleston, South Carolina
Summer 1989

She'd had her medical degree only three days when she realized it was not enough to please her father. Nothing was ever enough.

Sitting at the polished walnut table that had belonged to four generations of Malones, Kate watched him. U. S. Senator Mick Malone, the pride of Charleston, the hope of the South.

"This damned heat. A man can't think in this damned heat." Wiping his face with a perfectly pressed, perfectly white handkerchief, he looked at his wife as if the heat might be all her fault.

"I'll turn up the air-conditioning." Martha left her soup to get cold while she scurried from the room, careful to walk softly, careful not to call attention to herself.

Kate wanted to scream. Instead, she sipped her iced tea. Mick Malone concentrated on his soup.

The only sounds in the room were the tinkling of ice against crystal, the clink of silver against bone china, and the whirring of the ceiling fan. Beyond the French doors the setting sun was putting on a spectacular display, gilding the ocean and turning the Spanish moss dripping from the live oaks to gold lace.

Neither of them noticed.

"Martha still makes the best carrot soup in three counties," her father said when the silence got too uncomfortable. "You'd do well to learn."

"Yes, the soup's delicious," Kate said.

It was not the conversation she'd imagined. Three days before, standing in the line of medical school graduates waiting her turn to walk across the stage, she'd pictured her father saying, "I'm so proud of you. Top of your class. I knew you could do it."

She'd smile . . . modestly, of course; then he would put his arms around her and say, "I love you, Katie. I've always loved you."

What he had actually said that day was "If a school that charges this much tuition can't afford enough parking spaces, they ought to fire the administration and start all over."

Kate pushed her soup bowl away, her appetite gone.

"Is that better, dear?" Martha asked her husband as she slid back into her chair.

"It's too soon to tell."

"Maybe the fan's not turned on high." Martha rose halfway from her seat, glancing anxiously at the ceiling fan.

"Don't fidgit, Martha. It makes me nervous." Mick banged his glass onto the table. "Women!" he said, and that summed up his philosophy of life.

Kate shoved her chair back from the table and stood up.

"You're not excused," her father said.

She drew herself up to her full height, five feet ten inches, and every bit of it imposing. They faced each other from opposite ends of the table, father and daughter, so much alike, with eyes as green as the sea and hair the color of flame. Years and grief had lined Mick's face, but they'd done nothing to dim his hair.

He stared at his daughter with her square jaw so like his own. She had his temper too, and his stubbornness. Kate was a Malone through and through. Every now and then he looked at her and felt a little bit of hope . . .

but it always died as quickly as it came. She was a woman. She would never carry on the Malone name. She would never replace Charles and Brian.

The old pain settled around Mick's heart, sapping his strength, draining his energy.

Kate flattened her hands on the table and leaned toward him. "I'm a grown woman. I no longer need your permission."

"Katie Elizabeth!" Her mother's hands fluttered about as if she were swatting moths, then settled over her heart.

"And you don't either, Mother." With her head held high, Kate marched from the room.

"Mick . . . say something to her. Please."

"Let her go, Martha. She'll come to her senses."

She already had. About the time he'd told her she'd do well to learn to make soup.

Kate got her bags down from the top of the closet and began to pack. The first thing she put in was her winter coat. She'd heard the winters in Oklahoma were very cold.

Her suitcases were half full when she became aware of him standing in the doorway.

"And where might ye be goin', Katie."

When her father lapsed into an Irish lilt and called her Katie, she always lost her resolve. But not this time. Taking a deep breath, she faced him.

"I'm going to Oklahoma."

"What does Tulsa have that you can't find right here in Charleston?"

"I never said I was going to Tulsa."

"Where, then?"

So, finally he was inquiring about her plans. Did that mean he cared?

"I'm going to Chickasaw Tribal Lands."

"Do you hate me that much, Katie, that you'd squander a fine education off in the wilderness?"

Guilt. He'd always used guilt to manipulate her.

"I don't hate you, Father. I never hated you." Was it

a lie? She didn't know. "And it's not a wilderness. Dr. Colbert says it has a very fine hospital." He'd said other things too, the brilliant mixed-blood Chickasaw who had been her mentor during her student year at Massachusetts General. "You have talent, Kate, and a caring heart. There is a great need among my people for a doctor like you. You could make a *real* difference."

"You were going to practice right here in Charleston," her father said. "We had it all planned."

"No, you had it all planned. You never consulted me. You *told* me."

"You've let that savage corrupt your thinking."

"Dr. Clayton Colbert is not a savage. He's the finest endocrinologist in the nation."

They faced each other across the space that separated them—Kate beside her suitcase, Mick beside the door. Just once she wished he'd come close enough to touch her, come close enough to pat her cheek or take her hand and say, "Everything is going to be all right, Katie."

She waited, waited for the words she knew he would never say. Mick clenched his jaw and held his ground.

"My mind is made up," she said at last, "and there's nothing you can do or say to change it."

"If you do this thing, if you go off to this wild land and waste your talents on people who are not like us . . . you're no daughter of mine."

She'd never been a daughter of his, not since that awful day thirteen years earlier. Tears threatened to spill from her eyes, but she bit down on her lower lip, counting on the pain to keep her from showing any weakness in front of him.

"So be it," she said, and returned to her packing.

Mick watched her awhile longer, wishing he could take back his words. She had the same stiff-necked pride that had backed him into more corners than he cared to think about. Katie Elizabeth. His firstborn. He remembered the day she came into the world, red-faced, red-haired, and squalling. He'd thought she was the most beautiful thing in the whole universe. Still did. He'd planned to give her the sun and the moon, with all the stars thrown in for good measure.

And now look at them. They couldn't even be in the same room without quarreling.

"Is there something else you want to say?" His daughter looked at him the way she would a stranger.

"No. I've had my say."

He left her with her suitcases and her foolish notions. A good Bourbon whiskey was what he needed. The saints only knew how he managed to survive in a household full of women.

He was on his third whiskey when Martha tapped on his door.

"Don't just stand there with your mouth working like a fish," he bellowed. "Come on in."

He hated the way she scuttled about. Like a damned gray mouse. Her hair was gray too. And her face. Martha had let herself go since the boys had died.

"What did you say to her, Mick? She slammed out of the house like a cyclone."

"Don't take that accusing tone with me, Martha. Why is it that everything that goes wrong around here has to be my fault?"

"I'm not accusing you, Mick." She squeezed her hands together and looked down at her feet. The woman he married would have spit fire to be talked to like that. He guessed he ought to be ashamed of himself, but he wasn't. Shame couldn't bring back his sons. Nothing could bring them back.

"Well, Martha, you came in here . . . now speak up."

Martha went to the window and pulled the drapes. "Look at her out there, Mick, staring at the ocean."

"She always does that when she's upset. She'll come to her senses."

"It's not good for her to be out there all by herself." Martha squeezed her hands together.

"She's a grown woman . . . as she so succinctly told me at my own dinner table."

Martha stared out the window. Kate was walking along the beach now, taking long strides, her dress billowing around her legs and her hair lifting in the breeze that came off the ocean. Was she remembering? Martha wondered. What was she thinking? She never knew what her daughter was thinking these days. She never knew what *anybody* was thinking.

"She blames herself, you know."

"For God's sake, Martha, stop that damned whispering. Speak up so I can hear you."

"Nothing, Mick. It was nothing."

Martha left the room, then got her crocheting and worked until she heard Mick go to bed. When she heard his snores, she put down her needles and slipped out the back door. Kate was still by the water, sitting on the end of the pier, hugging her knees.

Martha squatted beside her and touched her hand almost shyly.

"Kate . . . honey."

Her daughter looked at her, dry-eyed. It was too late for tears. Far too late.

"I . . . don't know what to say to you, Katie."

The ocean lapped at the pier, and overhead a sea gull screamed at them. They reached for each other at the same time. Arms clinging, foreheads pressed together, they rocked in silent agony.

"It will be all right, Mother," Kate whispered. "Everything will be all right."

2

Brave words. She'd said brave words to her mother that night beside the ocean, then later, when she'd kissed her good-bye. "Don't worry, Mother. I'll be fine."

"He didn't mean what he said . . . I know he didn't."

It didn't matter anymore. Kate had Fitzgerald money from her mother's people, and Malone pride straight from her father. What more did she need?

They'd clung together a moment longer, then Kate had climbed into her car.

"Write to me," Martha said. "Let me know how you are."

How she was was scared to death and lonesome, as lonesome as she'd ever been in her life. Standing in a general store in Chickasaw Tribal Lands beside the hoop cheese, enduring the suspicious if not downright hostile stares of the locals, she wanted to run. Self-consciously she smoothed her shorts over her pale legs. She wished she'd taken advantage of the South Carolina sun the few days she'd been home. Then maybe she wouldn't stand out like an onion in a field of sunflowers.

"All right," she said to herself. "Just ask directions and then go home."

Home. Now, there was another thing. Home was no

longer an antebellum mansion in South Carolina; home was someplace she'd never seen in a strange land among strange people. She'd soon remedy that; she'd soon remedy a lot of things.

"May I help you?"

The young woman who spoke looked to be about nineteen, and she was exquisite, with luminous black hair that hung straight to her waist, skin the color of polished copper, and finely defined cheekbones.

"May I help you?" she asked again, smiling.

Kate could have wept at the sight of a smiling face.

"Yes, I seem to be lost." She held out the wrinkled map as if that explained her predicament.

"You're a visitor here, then?"

"No. Actually I've come to stay." More brave words, she thought as she held out her hand. "I'm Kate Malone, and I'll be practicing medicine here."

"A medicine woman?" The girl's dark eyes sparkled as she shook Kate's hand. "You don't look like a medicine woman."

Kate laughed. "What's a medicine woman supposed to look like?"

"Ancient as the hills with many lines of the crow's feet on her eyes and many hairs of gray in her head. You're too young and too beautiful. And your hair is as bright as the paintbrush that colors the land. Can I touch it?" Without waiting for permission, she reached out and rubbed a strand of Kate's hair between her fingers.

"The television shows women who color their hair from the bottles. Can you show me how to make my hair this color with a bottle?"

"I'm afraid not. I was born with red hair."

"And I was born with hair that looks like a horse's tail." The girl looked morose, then her face brightened. "But I'm smart, and I have many boyfriends."

Kate didn't doubt it for a minute. The young woman had so charmed her that she'd almost forgotten why she'd stopped at the store.

"Do you know where Dr. Clayton Colbert lives?"

"If I tell you, you'll only get lost again. Why don't I show you?"

"You'd do that for me?"

"Yes, but don't get the idea that I'm generous and kindhearted. I never do a favor without asking for one in return." The girl held out her hand once more. "I'm Deborah Lightfoot. Is it a deal?"

"It's a deal."

Later, streaking along behind the young woman's Jeep and trying her best to keep up, Kate figured she was breaking every tribal law on the books. Speeding . . . They were roaring along at ninety miles an hour. Noise pollution . . . Deborah's radio blared rock and roll loud enough to cause deafness. Destruction of property . . . She wasn't certain, but she thought Deborah had plowed down a fence post on that last curve they took.

It was a great relief when they finally arrived at their destination all in one piece.

"That was quite a ride, Deborah. I thought you were going to be my first patient."

"Are you not a daredevil?"

Kate looked at the mountains rising behind Dr. Colbert's house, listened to the calls of birds she couldn't identify and the far-off howling of an animal she didn't know, felt the gathering darkness across the vast, primeval land.

She was a stranger here, a white woman who knew neither the Chickasaw customs nor the Chickasaw culture. And yet she'd left everything that was familiar to her, not out of whim, not out of a temporary pique at her father, but out of her own great need. If she worked long enough and hard enough, if she saved enough lives single-handedly, without the aid of big hospitals and fancy equipment and big-name doctors, the bad dreams might go away and her father might forgive her.

"No, I'm not a daredevil," she said. Just a weak mortal with a mission.

"Welcome to Witch Dance," Deborah said, then

revved the engine till her Jeep was straining and shuddering like a stallion eager for the race.

Kate said good-bye, got her bags out of the car, and went inside to meet her mentor.

Charleston was another world away. Her life of atonement had begun.

3

Houston, Texas
Summer 1989

Eagle Mingo worked without a shirt, striding around the construction site with the intensity of a warrior and the proud bearing of a full-blood. Descendant of a long line of Chickasaw chieftains, including the great Opya Mingo, or Piomingo, as the history books called him, he carried the mark of his ancestors—high, finely defined cheekbones, fierce black eyes, and smooth bronze skin.

Marcus Rayburn kicked back in his swivel chair in the trailer that housed the temporary offices and watched the show. Brenda and Betty, the two secretaries, couldn't do their typing for gazing out the window, and Rosalind, the head bookkeeper, left her books so many times to go to the water cooler that Marcus got up a bet with Jim Clancy about when her next trip would be.

"Bet she won't last five minutes without coming to get some more water," Marcus said.

"Ten." Jim wadded the paper he was working on into a ball and tossed it into the garbage can. He missed, and the paper ball lay on the floor with a dozen others that had missed their mark.

"What d'you want to bet?"

"A cold beer."

"Make it two, and you're on."

Five minutes later the door to Rosalind's office opened and she sashayed out, fluffing up her hair and pursing her freshly painted lips.

"Thirsty, Roz?" Marcus said.

"It's this heat." Her face turned pink.

"Yeah, it's the heat all right," Jim said after her door closed behind her. "Body heat. Brought on by a pilgrimage to the Chickasaw shrine."

"I won," Marcus said. "Damn. It's going to be dull around here when he leaves."

"Yeah. No more swooning females."

"No more competition. Not that he ever notices. You'd think he was made of cast iron or something, the way he can resist temptation."

"Resist bait, you mean. The way the women go after him it's pure bait." Jim stood and stretched his long, bony frame. "I for one will be glad to see him go. He's giving the rest of us a bad name, working out there in the heat like a hired hand."

"I wish I could say he's all brawn and no brain, but my mama taught me never to tell a lie." Marcus got his hard hat off the top of his cluttered desk and rammed it onto his head. "Besides that, I like the guy. Best damned engineer I've ever seen. It's going to be a shame to lose him." He stalked toward the door. "Up and at 'em, Clancy. We've got a job to do here . . . if Mingo hasn't already finished it while we dawdled."

The trailer door banged behind them as they went out into the bright, hot Texas sun.

Eagle stood beside a stack of galvanized pipe and watched them come—Marcus with his wry wit and deep drawl, Jim with his easygoing ways and his locker-room humor. He was going to miss them.

"Ever think about puttin' on a shirt to make it easier on the females," Jim said, grinning.

"I like the feel of the sun on my skin."

"Yeah, well, if I let the sun on this skin, I'd look like a speckled egg."

"You do anyhow, Jim," Marcus said. "Hey, Mingo. Have you reconsidered?"

"No. I must go home."

"Witch Dance. That's a hell of a name for a town." Jim pulled off his hat and scratched his head. "What's it like?"

"Like no other place in the world."

Just hearing the name conjured up lovely images for Eagle, and such longing, he wished he could leave now instead of waiting until the following day. Indian paintbrush would be in bloom, and red-tailed hawks would be sailing the blue skies. The air would be so sweet and clear, a man could see the mountains and beyond. And the Blue River would be singing its ancient song. He could almost hear its music.

Witch Dance. He'd fished its streams, raced across its meadows, and hunted in its mountains. Witch Dance. A land of vast expanses and green sanctuaries and relentless beauty. It called to him across time and space, and in his heart he answered.

"Listen, pal," Marcus said, "if it's about pay, I've heard through the grapevine that old man Shamus would double your salary to get you to stay."

"This is not about pay," Eagle said. "It's about commitment."

His people needed him. When he'd left twelve years before to earn his engineering degree, he hadn't intended to stay away so long. But there had been so much to learn, so much he needed to know.

"You will return, my son?" his father had asked.

"I will return." He'd clasped his father's shoulders. "I won't let you down. Nor my people."

"There will be temptations."

There had been many temptations: easy money, big cities, fast women. But always Eagle had kept his vision before him. His people needed the prosperity and progressiveness of the new ways as well as the purity and strength of the old. They needed the modern roads he knew how to build and the strong bridges he could construct. They needed the hospitals and schools and banks and factories.

He could build them all. And he would ... on tribal lands for the benefit of his people.

"I can't argue with that, Mingo." Marcus clapped him on the shoulder as the five o'clock whistle sounded and workers on the construction site began their noisy leavetaking. "How about a farewell match at the old dartboard in Sally's Bar? Best three out of five. I need to redeem myself."

Eagle reached for his shirt, grinning. "Marcus, the thing I'm going to miss most about you is your eternal optimism."

"Prepare to lose your shirt, Marcus," Jim said.

"Does that mean you're going to bet against me?"

"I always put my money on the winner. Mingo hasn't lost a game yet. It's damned voodoo magic or something."

"It's the Chickasaw motto. Unconquered and unconquerable." Eagle was smiling when he said it, but Marcus and Jim didn't doubt for one minute that he meant every word he said.

Later that evening as Marcus consoled himself over his resounding defeat—he'd lost all five games—he saluted Eagle with his beer.

"My mama didn't raise no fools, and I can tell you one thing, I'd hate to get in a real battle with you."

"You'd lose, Eagle said.

Witch Dance

Eagle stood on the bluff with his arms lifted toward the sky. A red-tailed hawk arose screaming from his nest and bands of Indian paintbrush nodded their scarlet heads in the wind that swept across the plains. Below the ridge he could hear the music of the Blue River.

With his arms uplifted, he paid homage to four Beloved Things above—the clouds, the sun, the clear sky, and He who lives in the clear sky.

"Loak-Istohoollo-Aba," he chanted, addressing the Holy One above. "*Alail-o.*" The ancient words filled him with power, and he tipped his face upward so he could feel the welcome sun of his homeland. "I am come," he said. "I've come home."

All the years he'd been gone melted away, and he was once again a native son, fully, passionately in love with the land. Soon he would exchange his car for a Chickasaw horse so he could ride wild and free, feeling the wind on his face.

His mother would be waiting at home to greet him— and also his father, Winston Mingo, governor of the Chickasaw Nation. He'd see his twin brother, Cole, and Cole's wife and children whom he'd never met. His younger siblings, his beloved sister, Star, and his brother, Wolf, would be so grown-up, he'd hardly know them.

Eagle was eager to reunite with his family, but his most pressing need was to embrace the land, to bond once more with the mountains and the river and the sky that had spawned him.

Leaving his car parked on the ridge, he made his way down to the river. The lone hawk sailed low, calling its plaintive welcome. A cottontail rabbit scrambled out of the bushes, studied him with pink eyes and twitching nose, then disappeared over the horizon. In the distance the mountains watched him with silent majesty. The only sounds were the music of the animals and the music of the river.

He was alone, alone in the magnificent, far-reaching land he called his own.

The watchers were there again, standing on the hillside above the building site in a solemn, silent semicircle, their enmity evident in the set of their faces and the rigid lines of their bodies.

Kate put down her hammer and wiped her face with

a faded bandanna. Anxiously, she glanced at the intruders. Dr. Colbert poured two cups of water from the thermos and offered one to her.

"Don't worry about them, Kate. They'll get used to
you in time."

"How can I be their doctor if they hate me? How can
I cure their ailments if they won't even come near me?"

He laughed. "You've been here only a week; the clinic
is nothing more than a vision in our minds, and already
you're worried about the sick. Patience, Kate."

"You're always saying that to me."

"Could it be that you need to listen?"

"Who, me?" She did an elaborate pantomime of the
innocent, with widened eyes and rounded mouth. Then,
laughing, she sank onto the ground and crossed her
moccasined feet. Deborah at the general store had sold
her the moccasins. She'd tried to sell her a hat too, in-
sisting that Kate would burn her fair skin in this hot
country, but Kate loved the wind in her hair. There
would be no hats for her.

"You're too generous with me, Dr. Colbert. I'm not
sure that I have the temperament to carry on all this."
She waved her arms to encompass the clearing in the
trees, the studs that would soon be walls of a clinic, and
the watchers on the hill.

"I chose you for the job because you are perfect." As
always when they had these discussions about the
clinic, Clayton Colbert kept his darker motives hidden.
No one would be served by the truth—least of all, Kate
Malone.

She gazed at him with such luminous trust that he
had to turn his back.

"Why don't you take the rest of the day off?" He
busied himself by filling his carpenter's apron with
nails. Soon, *soon* he'd have to leave, or all his dreams
would go up in flames. "Go sight-seeing. Take a picnic.
It'll be good for your soul." And perhaps the salvation
of his own.

"Doctor's orders?" she teased.

"Doctor's orders."

She needed no further urging. A stop at the general store to buy wine and cheese, then a quick run to Dr. Colbert's house to rinse the sawdust off her face and put her purchases in a picnic basket, and she was all set to explore.

Soon she was striding along the wide open spaces, basket in hand. She scooped her hair off her neck with her free hand, then let it go flying about in the wind as she released it. White clouds were piled as high as cotton candy in a sky so relentlessly blue, it hurt her eyes. She'd brought her bird-watching book and her binoculars, but the thing she wanted to do most was get to know the land she now called home.

It was a beautiful land in a raw, exciting kind of way, and Kate was already in love with it. A wilderness, her father had called it. Well, it was *her* wilderness, far away from the jurisdiction of the senator from South Carolina.

She skipped along the way she had when she was fourteen and her two younger brothers thought she was the next best thing to buttered popcorn. Since there was no one around to cover their ears, she opened her mouth to sing . . . and that's when she saw the man in the river.

Mesmerized, she stood on the bluff, gazing down at him. It wasn't his nakedness that held her enthralled, but the sheer beauty of it, the glorious perfection.

He was standing with his face tipped skyward and his arms outstretched, every well-toned muscle and finely tuned sinew clearly delineated by the sun. The artist in her swooned, but the doctor in her exulted. He was a magnificent specimen, exuberantly male, passionately Chickasaw.

She didn't drop to her knees and try to hide behind the small scrub bushes, but stood tall on the bluff, watching him with unabashed pleasure. He looked as if he not only belonged to the land around him, but was a part of it.

He spoke strange and beautiful words in a powerful

voice that sent shivers down her spine, then waded
deep, where the water became swift and turbulent.

Unconsciously, Kate clenched her hands on the handle of the picnic basket. The water was chest-high on
him now. With one last look at the sky he plunged
under.

Kate held her breath, waiting, watching for him to re-
surface. Overhead, a large bird screamed. Hairs along
the back of Kate's neck stood on end.

"Come on," she whispered. "Come on." She shaded
her eyes, straining for a glimpse of his dark head rising
above the rushing river.

Could she have missed it? Was he too far downriver
for her to see?

Clutching her basket, she began to make her way
down the side of the bluff. There was still no sign of the
Chickasaw.

He'd gone under and he wasn't coming back up. Kate
began to run, blood roaring in her head . . . and memories filling her mind, always the memories.

*"Kate, Kate." A pair of hands clutched at her, glanced off
her swimsuit, then disappeared. She couldn't see. Wind and
rain whipped the ocean into a frenzy. Where were they?
Where were they?*

She must not panic. She must not. Brambles tore at
her shorts and scratched her legs as she raced down the
bluff.

"I'm coming," she screamed. "Hold on. I'm coming."

Her picnic basket hit the ground as she let go,
bounced once, then overturned.

*The sailboat was overturned. She couldn't get it to stay up-
right. The wind had been too strong . . . and the waves. She
fought the panic that made her arms and legs heavy. Couldn't
stop, couldn't stop swimming now. She had to find them.
Where were they?*

She was beside the river now. Sharp rocks bit into
her moccasins as she hit the shallows running. Hoping
the water was deep enough, praying she'd be strong

enough, she arched her body into a perfect bow and sliced the water.

There was no one to save him except her.

There was no one to save them except her. She was the oldest. She was responsible.

Swimming hard, she fought the water. She couldn't let it win. Not this time. She went under, searching, searching . . . and saw a leg.

"Brian," she screamed. Bubbles rose to the surface. "I've got you, Brian."

She couldn't hold on. He was struggling against her. She was losing him, losing him in the darkness and the rain and the winds that howled over the ocean.

"Stop!" Panic billowed through her as she fought to hold on to his leg. "Stop struggling, Brian. I have to save you . . . I have to save you."

Brian cried as he fought her, screamed as he clawed her face. She couldn't hold him. He was pulling her down. And where was Charles?

"Charles! Charles!" Tears streamed down her face, and water, so much water. She gasped for air. "Oh, God. I can't find Charles."

Hands grabbed her shoulders. Panic filled her, and such soul-searing agony, she wanted to die.

Charles was there now, and Brian, clinging to her, crying . . . Help me, Katie. Help me. Praying and crying, she swam. But which way was the shore? She couldn't see. Brian was pulling her under . . . and Charles was too heavy. They would all drown.

"No!" she screamed. "I won't let you die."

"I won't hurt you. Stop fighting."

"No. You can't die."

But they did. First Brian slipped away, his little face contorted as he called her name, his hair floating around his head like a pale halo. Then Charles. In slow motion he drifted, always beyond her reach, until at last she couldn't see him. She couldn't see either of them. The sea swallowed them, swallowed her brothers, then spit her out onto the cream-colored sand. She hadn't been strong enough. She hadn't been good enough.

She closed her eyes, wanting to die. Why hadn't she died?

Strong arms held her close. "Are you all right?"

That voice. It was the same one she'd heard moments earlier, the voice of thunder that beseeched the sky in a strange and wondrous tongue.

Coward that she was, she lay against his sun-warmed chest with her eyes shut. It was easier than looking into the face of the man she'd saved from the river.

"Are you all right?" he asked again as he lowered her to the ground. Oh, God, she remembered how he'd looked standing in the river, gloriously naked. He probably was a marathon swimmer who could take on the English Channel without ever getting winded, and here she was, wallowing around in his arms, getting goose bumps listening to his voice . . . and getting ideas besides.

"Of course I'm all right." She sat straight up, intending to act efficient and intelligent as befitted someone who had earned the right to be called doctor. But then she saw him close up. And she nearly swooned.

He was more man than she'd ever seen. And every gorgeous naked inch of him was within touching distance.

For all he seemed to care, he could have been bending over her in a Brooks Brothers suit.

"What impulse sent you into the river?" He squatted beside her with both hands on her shoulders, and she'd never felt skin as hot in her life.

"I thought you were drowning."

His laughter was deep and melodious, and as sensual as exotic music played in some dark corner of a dimly lit café where lovers embraced.

"I am Chickasaw," he said, as if that explained everything.

"Well, I'm human and I made a mistake." She pushed her wet hair away from her face. "Why can't you just admit you made a mistake, staying under the water so long, I thought you were going to drown?"

"You were watching me?"

"No . . . Yes . . ." His legs were powerful, heavily muscled, bent in such a way that the best parts of him were hidden. He leaned closer, intent on answers. How did he expect her to think straight with his leg touching hers like that? "Not deliberately," she said. "I was on a picnic. How did I know you'd be cavorting about in the river without any clothes on?"

He searched her face with eyes deep and black. Then he touched her cheeks, his strong hands exquisitely gentle.

"I'm sorry I ruined your picnic." Ever so tenderly his hands roamed over her face. Breathless, she sat beside the river, his willing captive. "You've scratched your face . . . here . . . and here."

Until that moment she hadn't known that every nerve in the body could tremble. Now she could attest to it as a medical fact.

". . . and your legs." He gave her legs the same tender attention he'd given her face. She would have sold her soul to feel his hands on her forever. "I have remedies for your injuries."

Oh, God. Would he kiss them and make them well? She almost said it.

"I can fix them. . . ." How? She could barely breathe. "I'm a doctor."

"You came to Tribal Lands to practice medicine?"

"You doubt my word?"

"No. Your commitment."

"Is it because I'm white that you think I'm not committed, or because I'm female?"

"Neither, *Wictonaye.*" In one fluid movement he stood before her, smiling.

And in that moment her world changed. Colors and light receded, faded until there was nothing except the bold Chickasaw with his glowing, polished skin and his seductive voice that obliterated every thought, every need except the most basic ... to die of love. Sitting on the hard ground, looking up at her nameless captor, she wanted to die in the throes of passion.

She stood on shaky, uncertain legs. Clenching her fists by her side, she faced him.

"If you're going to call me names, use English, please."

"*Wictonaye* ... wildcat."

"I've been called worse." Would God forgive her if she left right now? Would He give her the healing touch and allow her to save lives if she forgot about her lust and focused on her mission?

She spun around, then felt his hand on her arm.

"I've been rude. It's not my way."

"Nor mine." She grinned. "Except sometimes."

"You tried to save my life, and I don't know your name."

"Kate Malone."

"Thank you for saving my life, Kate Malone." His eyes sparkled with wicked glee. She'd never known a man of such boldness ... nor such appeal. "I'm Eagle Mingo."

"Next time you decide to play in the river, Eagle Mingo, be more careful. I might not be around to rescue you."

She marched toward the bluff, thinking it was a good exit, until he appeared beside her, still naked as sin and twice as tempting.

"You forgot your shoe." He held out one of her moccasins.

"Thanks." Lord, did he expect her to bend down and put it on with him standing there like that? She hobbled along, half shoeless.

"And your picnic basket." He scooped it off the ground and handed it to her. Then, damned if he didn't bow like some courtly knight in shining armor.

If she ever got home, she'd have to take an aspirin and go to bed. Doctor's orders.

"Good-bye. Enjoy your"—her eyes raked him from

head to toe, and she could feel her whole body getting hot—"swim."

She didn't know how she got up the bluff, but she didn't draw a good breath until she was safely at the top. He was still standing down there, looking up. She could feel his eyes on her.

Lest he think she was a total coward, she put on her other shoe, then turned and casually waved at him. At least she hoped it was casual.

Dammit all, he waved back. Facing full front. She might never recover.

"Did you enjoy your picnic?" Dr. Colbert asked when she got back.

"Hmmm." It was the best she could do.

"I'm glad. There are some wonderful sights around here."

"I'll say."

Dr. Colbert picked up her bird-watching book and thumbed through. "We have magnificent birds here too. You'll soon learn all their names."

All she needed to know was one name. The name of the most magnificent of them all. Eagle.

4

Home.

Eagle sat quietly on the redwood bench under a silver maple tree and took it all in. Nothing much had changed. The sprawling house with its wide verandas and tall windows was still the domain of Dovie Mingo. It had been Winston's wedding present to his wife. Built of cypress and glass with an eye for the view, it faced the mountains, which were stained pink and purple now by the setting sun. The house was grand in scale and built to endure because Winston had said that's how his love for Dovie was, magnificent and sweeping with an endurance that would last their lifetime and beyond to the Great Spirit world of Loak-Istohoollo-Aba.

The ravages of wind and rain and time had not dimmed the house's grandeur, and it sat now, weathered and graceful, in its wide sweep of pasture in the shadow of the mountains.

Through the open windows Eagle could hear the low, singing murmur of his mother's voice as she directed her two youngest children in the clean-up after their family meal.

"Not the pots too! Can't they wait until morning?" Star's wail of protest was tempered by the knowledge that she was engaged in a battle she would never win. "This is Eagle's first day home."

Eagle didn't hear Dovie's soft rebuke, only the firm tone of her voice. Then the unmistakable sound of his brother Wolf's laughter.

"Hey, sis, what's all the fuss about? You've got me."

They'd been mere children when he left, and now they were rowdy, raucous teens, full of the raw energy and the high, bright dreams of the young.

"I don't want you, toad breath," Star said.

"Yeah, well, that's what you've got till we finish these dishes. Shake a leg, squirt blossom, or we'll be here all night."

The argument in the kitchen was like the ones that had been waged years before. Nothing had changed except the names and the players. When Eagle was a teen, he and his brother Cole had been the ones bickering over the dishes. Dovie had always been a stickler for order. No matter what was taking place—weddings, births, homecomings, natural disasters—she always insisted that everything in the house be put in its proper place.

Eagle and Cole had thought they were doomed to carry on the chores forever, and had sat together in the barn loft, smoking a forbidden pipe and planning their revolt, when the unexpected had happened. At the age of forty-two Dovie had given birth to a baby girl.

"Who'd have thought the two of them were still *doing* it?" Cole said. He took a long draw on the purloined pipe, then passed it to his twin.

"I thought the equipment quit working when you got old." At the age of fourteen, Eagle considered anything over thirty ancient.

A year later, when Wolf was born, Dovie and Winston proved once again that everything was indeed in perfect working order, and that they enjoyed making it work.

Now a sophisticated fifteen, Cole and Eagle discussed this new turn of events over their first taste of alcohol—a bottle of cooking sherry clipped from their mother's kitchen cabinet.

"Papa's as bad as that old stallion," Cole said, and Eagle voiced his hearty agreement, but there was a certain element of awe and pride in their voices.

Remembering now, Eagle smiled. Judging by the evidence, Cole had inherited his father's prowess. His young wife, Anna, was ripe with child, and he already had two fine sons—Clint, secretive and stoic even at seven, and Bucky, exuberant and wild with the joy of childhood, racing around on his sturdy legs, defying his tender age of three by being as surefooted as one of the antelope that roamed the Arbuckle Mountains.

"Daddy! Daddy!" Bucky yelled as he raced around the yard. "Watch, Daddy!"

He lunged for the black Lab, and boy and dog went down in a heap. The Lab licked Bucky's face, then dog and boy were up and running again. It was hard to tell who was chasing whom.

"Watch, Daddy! Watch!"

With his arms held up toward the sun, the child spun round and round, ending in a dizzy tangle against Eagle's legs.

"Whoa, there." Laughing, Eagle lifted the child.

His nephew. Issue of the brother whose very soul was twined with his own. As the soft little arms went around his neck, there was a blooming in Eagle's heart . . . and something akin to envy.

"You're dizzy, little sport. Time to slow down."

"Daddy?" Bucky put his dimpled hands on either side of Eagle's face and cocked his head to one side.

"No. I'm Uncle Eagle."

"Unca Eaga?" Bucky puckered his brow and looked from Eagle to Cole, then back again.

Cole laughed at his son's puzzlement. "That's your uncle Eagle, son, the best man in Witch Dance besides your daddy. Give Uncle Eagle a kiss."

With the trust inherent in children, Bucky pressed his

rosy mouth against Eagle's, then squirmed out of his arms and gave chase to the dog once more.

" 'Bye, Unca Eaga," he yelled, his laughter lifting high and bright as a kite toward the fading sun.

"You should see your face," Cole said. "You look like you did that day you brought home the trophy for the debate team."

"I never knew that holding your own flesh and blood would feel like that."

"Remarkable, isn't it?" Cole wrapped his arm around his wife's thick waist. "It makes a man proud. Two sons already and another on the way."

Anna smiled at her husband, never daring to suggest that the child she carried might not be a son. She loved her tall, handsome husband with an adoration that bordered on worship and took every opportunity to show it.

If he let himself, Eagle could envy that too.

"Now that you're back, it won't take you long to catch up," Cole said.

Inseparable as children, Eagle and Cole had done everything together—ridden their first horse, climbed their first tree, bagged their first deer. They'd even broken their arms at the same time, the left ones, fractured when they'd fallen from the barn loft in an ignoble heap, drunk on their mother's cooking sherry.

"I'm afraid I'll have to leave you to carry on the family name," Eagle said. "At least for a while."

"You always were a visionary." Cole leaned down for Anna's kiss, then watched as she waddled off toward the house. "You build your bridges: I'll make sons."

Winston Mingo didn't miss a single nuance of the exchange between his sons, not Cole's triumph at having finally bested his twin brother at something, nor Eagle's sense of having sacrificed too much for his vision.

"Speaking of building, Dr. Colbert is building a new clinic." Winston said, watching his sons' reactions.

He'd been doing that a lot lately, watching, weighing, judging. Cole's expression darkened, and Winston shifted. Only part of his discomfort was due to Cole's reaction. No matter what he did these days, it seemed that he couldn't get comfortable. Dovie had sewed a cushion for his chair, even though he had told her the rain would ruin it. But she'd shushed him, and every morning he saw her checking the weather before she marched outside and arranged the bright red cushion in his favorite outdoor chair.

Eagle leaned forward, excited at the news . . . as Winston had hoped he'd be.

"He's moving back, then?" Eagle asked.

Clayton Colbert had left tribal lands twenty years earlier and had never come back except for summer vacations with his blue-blooded Bostonian wife.

"No, he's helping a young protégé of his, Kate Malone."

"A white woman," Cole said. "We don't need her."

Her skin was like lilies, creamy and cool to the touch. Eagle remembered it well. Too well.

"It seems to me that we need every clinic we can get," he said, ". . . and every doctor."

"We have a hospital." Anger curled through Cole like smoke.

"Only one," Winston reminded him. "And it's too far from Witch Dance for convenience."

"What does convenience matter if we lose sight of who we are? They've come here in droves with their white skin and their holier-than-thou attitudes. They've raped the land and corrupted our young, then gone back to their posh lives, convinced that they've done their duty on the *reservation*."

Twelve years had been too long to stay away. Eagle was seeing a brother he didn't know.

"How do you know Kate Malone is like that?" She'd been sobbing like a child when he carried her from the river, then was defiant as a wildcat when he'd questioned her commitment.

Kate Malone with hair bright beyond imagining. He'd wanted to touch it. Only the certain knowledge that doing so would be like crossing a bridge, then blowing it up behind him, had stilled Eagle's hand.

"Because she's not one of us," Cole said.

"Embracing new ideas and new people doesn't necessarily mean we must lose sight of the old ways."

"You sound awfully passionate for someone who hasn't been around in twelve years." Cole turned his fierce scrutiny toward Eagle. "Or is your defense personal?"

Having a twin was like having a second soul, a second conscience. Cole had always been able to ferret out his secrets. Though why he should keep his encounter with Kate secret was a mystery to him.

His silence damned him.

"You embrace her, Eagle. I have family duties." Cole stalked toward the house without looking back.

Disquieted, Eagle left his seat on the redwood picnic table and walked to the fence to look out over the pasture. The stallion that had been a gangly colt when he left flung up his head and flared his nostrils, catching Eagle's scent. Restless, the stallion trotted around the enclosure, his mane and tail flying out like flags as he increased his pace. In the last rays of the dying sun his polished coat gleamed as black as patent leather.

"He's magnificent," Eagle said as his father came up beside him.

"He's still yours. So are the three mares." Winston nodded toward a paint, a sorrel, and one beautiful mare so startlingly white, she looked like a ghost emerging from the shadows that gradually darkened the land.

Eagle whistled, never dreaming he'd get a response. The white mare whinnied, then tossed her mane and cantered to the fence.

"You remember me, don't you, Mahli?" Eagle stroked her silky muzzle."

"You always did have a way with horses."

"It's one of the things I missed most while I was away—the horses."

"Mahli will be receptive soon. If I were you, I'd breed her to the black."

Winston was not a man to speak about issues closest to his heart until he'd had time to let his instincts kick in. He talked instead of horses and ranching and Eagle's immediate plans.

"I'll take a few weeks off—perhaps the entire summer—before I open offices. The land is calling to me in a voice as seductive as a woman's." Eagle smiled. "I'm going to set up camp at the Blue River tonight."

"Dovie will be disappointed. She'd expected you to stay at the house, at least for a while."

"I'll make my peace with her."

"Good. I don't want to get on your mother's bad side." Winston smiled, recalling the many times he'd gotten on Dovie's bad side and ended up sleeping downstairs on the couch. His bones were too old and stiff for that now. Besides, he still liked the feel of Dovie's soft body curled against his. He slept better, somehow, just knowing she was there.

Winston studied his son. Some deep secret pleasure was hidden in his eyes.

"You know the woman ... Kate Malone?"

"Yes. Her clinic will benefit our people."

"She's not of our blood."

"You see too much, Father." Solemnly Eagle placed both hands on Winston's shoulders. "I am Chickasaw. I will never mix my blood."

Satisfied, Winston nodded. "May the Great Spirit guide you."

Eagle made his peace with his mother, then said good-bye to the rest of the family and rode off toward the shadowed mountains. The land was alive with scents and sounds. He rode bareback, the way he loved best, feeling himself one with the night-seeking creatures.

When he came close enough to hear the whisper of the river, he pitched camp. Although it was the middle of summer with heat rising from the earth and warm winds blowing across the land, he built a fire. There was something mystical about a fire, something powerful.

As his ancestors had done before him, Eagle opened himself to the fire so its strength could transfuse his soul. It was not a conscious move on his part, but an instinctive one. Myths and legends aside—and Eagle knew them all—there was a basic truth in the act of transfusion. A man's psyche was affected by his surroundings on levels he never dreamed. Beauty transfused harmony; ugliness, hatred. Nature transfused peace; mechanization, strife.

Stripped naked, Eagle paid homage to the four Beloved Things above in Muskogean, the ancient tongue of his people; then he spread his blanket under the stars, letting peace and harmony flow through him. Flames from his campfire leapt upward with a brightness that rivaled Kate Malone's hair.

The newly arrived medicine woman intruded so suddenly in his thoughts that desire caught him unaware. And he knew beyond a shadow of a doubt that she was nearby, that perhaps her nearness had led him to his campsite, and that she had already transfused his soul when he'd first touched her. When he'd carried her from the river.

He lay on the blanket, staring at the stars, with Kate Malone heating his blood like a flame.

The watchers had moved closer, a small, tight band of them, standing as silently as the trees that bordered the clinic. Dr. Clayton Colbert gave them no more than a passing glance.

It was the man on horseback who held his attention. Eagle Mingo.

Everybody in Witch Dance and for miles around knew him, firstborn of the Chickasaw Nation's governor, preceding Cole from the womb by mere seconds, dragging his reluctant brother by the heel, some said, emerging with a lusty war whoop that made every nurse on the maternity floor stop to listen. He'd been gone since he was eighteen, and twelve years had honed him to the lethal, keen edge of a knife blade.

Riding on his fine black stallion, he sliced into Clayton's consciousness and stayed there, striking sparks. Every nerve ending quivering, Clayton glanced at Kate. The lure of Eagle Mingo shone in her eyes. She stood motionless, the hammer hanging forgotten in her right hand, watching him as if destiny had come a-riding.

The black bile of despair clogged Clayton's throat. His grip tightened on his own hammer as Eagle dismounted and strode toward the lumber skeleton that would soon be a clinic.

"Kate." Eagle stood tall and magnificent before her.

She flushed as if he'd kissed her. The intimacy in his voice was more riveting than the most searing embrace she'd ever imagined.

"What brings you to the clinic?" she asked.

"I'm looking for the doctor."

"Any particular reason?"

"Yes. This." He held out a bouquet of Indian paintbrush, freshly plucked. "On behalf of my people, welcome to Witch Dance."

His skin drew hers like a magnet, and when she reached for the flowers, she couldn't let go.

"Thank you."

She had turned to liquid. Neither her hands nor her feet would move. Eagle closed her fingers around the fragile flower stems; then, stepping back, he nodded in the direction of the watchers.

"Are they causing trouble?"

"No. Only observing."

"I spoke with them. They're merely curious."

"I hope so."

"When they become accustomed to the idea of the clinic, they'll leave."

His bow was formal, but there was nothing remotely formal about his eyes. His burning gaze held Kate as her tongue flicked out and wet her bottom lip. Eagle watched as if he were guarding a recently staked gold claim.

Envy and despair rendered Clayton helpless. There was a low moan like an animal in pain. To his horror, he realized he'd made the sound. Not only that, but he'd shown his true colors to Eagle.

Clayton felt himself shriveling under Eagle's intense scrutiny. He wanted to trot off to his house like a whipped puppy and pee in the middle of the rug. Instead, he held his ground, returning the fierce stare with his head high.

They were like two proud bucks—one hoary with age, the other virile with youth—rutting after the same doe. The air was thick with challenge.

In a quicksilver shift Eagle nodded formally toward Clayton, then mounted his horse and galloped away.

The entire encounter couldn't have taken more than three minutes, but Clayton felt as if he'd been wading through quicksand for three hours. His hands shook as he poured himself a cup of water.

"You know him?" he said when he was finally calm enough to turn toward Kate. The glow of Eagle Mingo was still on her skin.

"I met him yesterday at the river."

She didn't elaborate, and he didn't dare ask.

"Well ... it's good that the governor's son approves of your being here." Blackguard. Liar. Clayton squashed the paper cup and water ran over his hands.

"Let me get you another." Kate laid her flowers on the sawhorse and gave them one last, lingering caress. Fresh envy slashed at Clayton.

"Your face is flushed." Kate's hands were cool when they touched his, cool and tender as the stems of flowers. "You've been working too hard. Sit over here and rest."

She led him to a shade tree with the same care he'd seen her lavish on the old people who populated the hospital wards. He wasn't old—sixty, with most of his hair and his body gone only slightly to fat—but he must seem ancient to her, abloom as she was with youth and lust.

His gut clenched again as she plopped down beside him and stretched out her bare legs, tanned now from the sun. Smiling, she patted his arm affectionately, as if he were an elderly uncle or a favorite pet.

God, how he hated it, that casual touch . . . and how he loved it. That was his burden to bear, his cardinal sin: He was in love with her.

His wife knew.

"Don't lie to me, Clayton," she'd said before he left. "You're not building this clinic because of altruism. You're building it so you can lure *her* to your side."

"I'm building a clinic to help my people."

"You had no people until you met me. And don't you ever forget it."

How could he? She never let him.

Sitting in the shade with the scent of Kate making his old sap rise, he thought of Melissa Sayers Colbert, the woman he'd left behind. Elegant, sophisticated, with the kind of cool beauty that drew second glances. Patron of the arts, chairman of numerous foundations, and benefactor to the underdog—including an outcast half-breed Chickasaw named Clayton Colbert. He owed his medical degree to her and his fancy Beacon Hill house and his chairmanship of the Department of Endocrinology.

He'd been a broken-down trick rider in a Wild West sideshow when she found him sleeping on a pier in Boston Harbor. Melissa Sayers of the Sayers Chocolate fortune had a habit of slumming in her chauffeured white stretch limousine.

She'd meant to give him a hot bath and a square meal and send him on his way. Then she'd discovered that cleaned up, he had the kind of sex appeal that was hard to resist.

Melissa Sayers didn't even try. For six months he'd lived in her penthouse surrounded by every luxury he'd ever imagined. Did he want a new suit? All he had to do was ask. A new car? No problem. All it cost him was a few hours of sexual performance, much like a trained tiger.

Later she'd discovered that he had a mind to match his body, and she'd decided to keep him. Permanently.

She gave him respectability and success, but the price was too high. In the end, it cost his dignity.

He felt a cool hand on his forehead.

"Are you all right, Dr. Colbert?"

Dr. Colbert. Not even Clayton. Kate saw him as her mentor, her friend, perhaps even a father figure. But he didn't dare put so much as a fatherly arm around her shoulder.

"I'm fine, Kate. I guess I need to rest."

"You shouldn't be working in this heat. I'll walk you to the house."

He was selfish enough to let her. Walking along in the drift of her perfume, feeling the brush of her thigh against his, was a simple pleasure he could steal without her ever knowing.

"I wonder if we should hire a crew to help with the building, Dr. Colbert?"

"You think I'm too old, Kate?"

"It's not that. The work will go faster and . . ." She flushed at her lie. "You're certainly not *old*, but perhaps you're too old to be working so hard in this heat."

"You never could lie well, Kate." He patted her cheek. It was the only familiarity he would allow himself. "Bear with me. This is something I must do alone."

"With my help," she corrected him.

"Yes. With your help."

The screen door banged shut behind her. Clayton's bedroom was cool and dark with the shades drawn. He sat in a chair with the leg he'd twisted in his trick riding days propped on a footstool.

Was it possible to buy back dignity?

The flowers lay scattered in the dirt, their stems broken and their petals crushed. In the white glare of the noonday sun they were an obscenity, delicate beauty deliberately destroyed, then left in the skeleton clinic like an omen.

Shading her eyes, Kate looked at the hillside. It was innocent and empty, as if the watchers had never been there.

Adrenaline pumped through her as reaction set in. The watchers had become the enemy. She wanted to run after them and throttle them for the wanton destruction of her property. Never mind that it was merely flowers. They were Eagle's gift, flowers he'd picked with his own hands.

Sawdust and lumber chips bit her skin as Kate knelt in the dirt and gathered up her flowers. Then she poured a cup of water and arranged them as tenderly as if they were hothouse roses. The bruised blossoms drooped over the edges of the cup.

Holding her damaged bouquet aloft, Kate shook her fist at the desolate hillside.

"You won't win, damn you. I won't let you win."

5

At the sound of footsteps in the hall, Deborah Lightfoot hid her book under the covers. It wouldn't do to let her father know she was reading when she was supposed to be sleeping. Pipe dreams, he called her books.

"A young woman should have her mind on finding a good husband and raising babies," he'd say when he caught her reading. "Not pipe dreams."

The novel was set in Vietnam during the sixties, and the heroine was a nurse of uncommon courage.

That's the kind of nurse Deborah would be. A nurse of uncommon courage. If she ever got to be one. Which was as likely as an antelope learning to fly.

Sighing, she pulled the sheet up under her chin and tucked the tiny flashlight she used when she read in the dark under her pillow. She let her breathing become even in case he checked on her.

Sometimes he did. Not that she minded. He'd done the best he could by them, by Deborah and her brother, Hal, but sometimes she wished he'd quit trying so hard.

The bedroom door next to hers creaked open, and she heard Hal's muttered oath as a chair banged against the wall. Deborah swept back her covers and tiptoed into her brother's room.

"What are you doing out so late?"

Hal whirled toward her, his long hair swinging over one dark eye. "You scared the devil out of me, Deborah. Don't you believe in knocking?"

"Why should I knock? Do you have something to hide?"

"None of your business."

Filled with a dread she couldn't name, Deborah flipped on the light switch. At fifteen, Hal was all arms and legs. He stood with his feet spread apart in fighting stance and his hands gathered into fists at his sides. Fresh scratches reddened the top of one hand.

"Have you been fighting?"

"Lay off. You're not my mother."

Maybe not. But she tried to be. She'd tried since she was seven years old and the mother they both adored was shot down in the general store like a rabid coyote, shot once in the throat and twice in the chest by a drug-crazed man who wanted the cash box.

Deborah never looked at the cash box without a sense of fear and revulsion, never touched it without wishing her mother had given it to the drug addict.

Brushing aside Hal's objections, Deborah examined his fist. "You have a splinter. Let me get a needle and take it out."

"Go to bed and leave me alone." Hal jerked his fist away.

Only a year ago they would sit up hours, talking to each other. What had happened to the sunny-natured brother she used to know?

"It will fester."

"Who gives a shit?"

"I do . . . and Father does."

"All he cares about is that damned store."

"That's not true."

Except partially. He *did* care about the store, cared so much that sometimes he failed to notice when Hal was three hours late getting home from school or when Deborah outgrew her dresses and wore them too tight and too short because she was afraid to ask for a new one. Money was scarce. If he couldn't afford to pay extra help at the store, how could he afford to keep her in the style of Juanita Beard or Cassandra Black Elk?

Not that she wanted to be either one of them. Juanita was stuck-up and Cassandra was silly.

"Are you in some kind of trouble, Hal?"

"Cool it, Deborah. Go to bed."

"You'd tell me if you were in trouble, wouldn't you?"

He looked down at the toe of the shoe he was scuffing on the floor, then shrugged his shoulders and grinned at her. It was a heart-melting smile that made her forget he'd been uncooperative and sullen only seconds earlier.

"Of course I'd tell you, Miss Deborah Fixitfoot." He held his hand out, palm up, and she placed hers over it, the way they used to when they were kids and made their pact, two against the world, Hal and Deborah, inseparable and unconquerable.

" 'Night, Hal." She kissed his cheek.

He jerked back, then gave her a sheepish grin. "I've outgrown that sissy stuff."

"Nobody ever outgrows the need for a good-night kiss."

"Sleep tight, sis," he said when she got to his door.

But she knew she wouldn't. Deborah crawled under the covers feeling ninety instead of nineteen.

Hal was keeping secrets, and she had nobody to tell.

The scream that ripped the air was pure rage.

Eagle's head came up as the sound tore through the morning once more. It was a woman's voice . . . coming from the direction of the clinic.

With water dripping from his face and shoulders, Eagle rose from the river's edge and raced toward his campsite, whistling for his stallion. His mount thundered toward him, and Eagle vaulted onto his back while the horse was still in motion.

Wind dried the river water from his skin and ruffled

his hair as he tore across the plains toward the clinic. He came upon it suddenly—the wanton devastation. What had once been a wall was now a heap of junk lumber, splintered and broken, with the sharp ends of nails glinting in the sun.

Kate Malone stood in the midst of the rubble, slinging broken boards with the force of a woman twice her size. Spots of anger rouged her cheeks.

"No ... dammit ... no! I won't quit!"

"Kate. What happened?" Eagle bolted from his horse.

"The bastards! The cowardly bastards." She prowled through the debris like an angry lioness, kicking at everything in her path. Her hair was loose and disheveled, as if she'd just arisen from bed. "They came in the night and did this."

She hefted a board, and a nail tore her tender skin from wrist to elbow. She was so mad, she didn't even notice.

Anger seared through Eagle. Not only had *his* people reduced Kate's dreams to a pile of rubble, but they had caused her harm. He reached for the board, but Kate pulled away.

"I want to help."

"I can do this myself. I don't need you."

"You're in shock. Let me see about your wound."

"I don't need you or any of your people."

With the swiftness of his namesake, Eagle captured her wrists and moved in on her, moved so close, their thighs touched, touched and retreated, then touched once more, trembling.

Long-held codes crumbled and resolve went spinning away like a tumbleweed before the wind. The temptation he'd avoided for twelve years was standing before him ... and he had no place to run.

Nor did he want to. Kate was like new wine in his blood: He was drunk with her.

In one easy movement he wrested the board from her hand and cupped her face.

"You need me, Kate."

"No," she whispered. "I don't need you."

"Yes . . ." He tangled his hands in her hair and with great deliberation pulled her close, so close he could see the tiny bursts of gold in the center of her eyes. Green eyes. Green eyes and clear skin that would burn easily in the sun, pale skin that would never have the rich copper tint of the Chickasaw.

None of it mattered now. Fate had sent her to him, and fate would not be denied.

He leaned down so that their lips were almost touching.

"You need me as much as I need you," he said.

And Kate knew he spoke the truth.

How much longer could she be brave with her dreams in rubble and this magnificent man seducing her in a voice that would make angels abandon their halos? He shone, golden and delicious, with the sun caught in droplets of moisture clinging to his bare chest.

Kate longed to lick them away one by one. She knew how his skin would taste, warm and musky as sin.

Her bones melted, and she leaned toward him, her vision forgotten in her quest to merge with the mighty Eagle, to be folded under him, to soar with him in swift splendor toward the heavens. A small sigh escaped her lips, and she breathed deeply.

Even the air was sweeter because he was a part of it.

"No," she said again, but she knew her protest was weak.

His laughter was pure seduction, wicked and knowing.

"Another time, another place, *Wictonaye*, and all your denials will vanish like wisps of smoke in a firestorm." He took her hand and led her to a clearing. "Come. I will tend your wounds."

She would have followed him to the gates of hell. No, through the very gates and into the inferno itself.

Even the suggestion that he tend her wounds was somehow erotic.

"I'm a doctor. I can tend my own wounds."

His eyes trapped hers as he traced the reddened path of the nail from elbow to wrist.

"To see such perfection marred is a desecration."

"You have a great bedside manner."

"You protest too much, Kate. Are you afraid of me?"

"No." She lied with her eyes sparking fire, and her chin jutted out. She was afraid of him all right. Not afraid that he would cause pain, but that he would cause ecstasy, so much ecstasy, she would lose her purpose.

"Even the brave are sometimes scared, *Wictonaye*."

Water touched her skin, and she realized that he'd found the thermos and a paper towel and was now washing her wounds. So powerful was her attraction that even when he left, she still felt his presence.

The water was soothing . . . and so was the touch of his hand upon her skin.

"In the ancient customs of my people, the eagle is invoked for healing." His voice flowed through her like warm honey. "They solicit him as he soars through the heavens to bring down refreshing things, to dart down quickly on wings of lightning and provide succor for the wounded."

He set aside the makeshift sponge without relinquishing his hold on her. Dark and deep with mysteries, he held her with his eyes as his hands continued their erotic massage.

"The eagle is the king of birds, prodigious in strength, swift of wing, majestic in stature . . . and so full of passion that he teaches all he loves to fly."

His eyes never left hers as he lifted her arm to his lips.

"*Waka ahina uno, iskunosi Wictonaye. Waka.*"

Heat seared her, but it wasn't the heat of skin against skin: It was the heat of desire burst full flower in a strange land with a man who spoke in a poetic and mesmerizing tongue.

"In English, please," she whispered.

"Fly with me, little wildcat. Fly."

His lips burned against her skin once more, and she trembled. It was not mere wanting that shook her, but something much more complex. He set off silent explosions under her skin, just where his fingers touched—and deeper, in secret places that had never known such primitive longing.

Already she was flying, flying irrevocably toward the golden Eagle who had risen from the river and forever captured her soul.

"Eagle," she whispered, and if he had given the word, she'd have spread herself in the dirt, as eager and open to him as a parched earth welcoming spring rain.

The passion that shimmered between them was almost palpable. Their senses were heightened so that even the air burned their skin.

Holding her captive with his dark eyes, Eagle cupped her face, then splayed his fingers through her hair.

"What magic do you possess, Kate ... what witchcraft that makes me burn with the wanting of you?"

"Do you burn, Eagle?

"Yes ... as you do. I feel the passion in your skin."

"It's the heat."

"No, *Wictonaye*. Your blood is hot with the same fever that rages through mine."

"I have a remedy for fever ... in my black bag."

"There is only one remedy for this fever, Kate. Only one."

Eagle leaned closer so that their bodies were partially joined—his legs pressed against hers, her shoulders bracketed by his arms, her nipples barely grazing his bare chest. And in that moment the whole world rearranged itself, ripped itself from familiar moorings, and came together in fresh configuration, reborn.

Kate knew the remedy ... and longed for it with the single-minded greed of a newborn seeking its mother's milk.

She threaded her fingers through his hair and was actually pulling him toward her lips when she heard echoes of her father's voice: *You'd do well to learn to make soup.*

She backed away from Eagle and scrambled to her feet.

"I don't know what you're trying to prove by riding around on that stallion, seducing women. . . ."

"Do I seduce you, Kate?"

"Damned right you seduce me, running around without your shirt." She shoved her hair back from her overheated face. "Don't you ever wear clothes?"

"I have no need of clothes, *Wictonaye*. I have nothing to hide." He was toying with her.

"Damn you, Eagle Mingo. I should have let you drown."

Even his laughter was seductive.

"But you didn't, Kate. You came to me in the river . . . as you will always come to me." He held out his hand. "Come, we have work to do."

Damned if she didn't take it. Would have fought anybody who told her to do otherwise, as a matter of fact.

They didn't speak again, but worked side by side, cleaning up the debris. Words weren't necessary between them: They communicated on a different level. And when the work was finished, Eagle mounted his stallion.

"The ones who did this will be punished, Kate."

"You're damned right. If I can ever find them, I'll see to it personally."

"If you are to be a medicine woman who serves my people, you will not engage yourself in this battle."

"You expect me to roll over and play dead?"

"Rolling over might be nice." His grin was pure sin. Then he sobered. "*I* will find them, Kate."

"How?"

"I am Eagle."

Without another word he wheeled his horse away and thundered across the plains. Kate felt as if she'd been snatched out of time and spun backward into a Wild West movie. Emotionally and physically drained, she leaned against the sawhorse, shading her eyes so she could catch one last fleeting glimpse of Eagle.

Even the sun conspired against her; it polished his bare skin so that he gleamed like a museum bronze. He *was* Eagle, commanding everything in his sight, including her.

"Kate Malone, you're in serious trouble."

She strained her eyes into the sunset until there was nothing left of Eagle to see except a pillar of dust blooming on the horizon.

He'd taken the coward's way out, not going to the clinic with her. Mild exhaustion, he'd said. Nothing to worry about.

If only she knew.

Clayton stood at the kitchen window and watched her coming. He'd watched out the window all day, watched *them*.

Already Eagle was in her blood; Clayton could tell by the way she walked, the spring in her steps, and the tight, seductive roll of her hips. Any minute now she'd be in the house, warm from the sun and hard work, ripe with lust. His nostrils quivered at the thought of the rich female smell of her.

When he heard the front door open, he beat a hasty retreat from the window and poured two cups of tea.

"I'm glad you weren't there today," she said, her voice preceding her into the room. "It was awful." Her hand brushed his when she reached for her tea. "Thanks. This is just what I need."

"What happened?" he asked, as if he didn't already know.

"Somebody destroyed the clinic." She tightened her grip on the teacup and jutted out her chin. "I'd like to find out who did it and beat the hell out of them."

Clayton's laughter provided the release he needed. He sat in the chair next to hers and took a sip of tea. He might be able to survive the summer after all.

"Aren't you going to tell me to have patience?" Kate grinned at him.

"Would it do any good?"

"No. I just hope you have some influence with the authorities. I'd hate to be burned at the stake."

"I don't think that's done anymore, Kate, even in Witch Dance."

They chuckled together, then Kate lifted her arm and raked her hair off her grimy forehead. That's when Clayton saw the scratch. When his fingers closed on her soft skin he almost lost control. Only years of medical training saved him.

"What happened to you?"

"Nothing to worry about. Just a scratch from a nail."

"Tetanus?"

"Up-to-date, Doctor."

"It needs cleansing and antibiotics."

"Eagle cleaned it."

Clayton stiffened. Eagle. Always Eagle.

"Well, I'm going to take care of it properly, then I'm prescribing a long hot bath, a good dinner, and bed for you, young lady. You've been working much too hard."

"Is it all right if I take the time to write a letter home, Doctor Dictator, sir?"

"The letter is okay, but no beating the hell out of anybody, no matter how much they deserve it."

"Aw, shucks. Foiled again." She grinned at him, stretching her long, tan legs.

He clenched his hands and balled them in his pockets.

"Promise me, Kate?"

"I promise."

He figured she had her fingers crossed behind her back when she said it. Kate was not the kind of woman to take adversity lying down.

After she left the kitchen, Clayton took a casserole out of the refrigerator and stuck it in the oven. Chicken and mushrooms with a white wine sauce. Whatever else happened to him while he was in Witch Dance, he would not go hungry. He'd learned cooking from Melissa's French chef.

It was one of the few things he excelled at. Cooking. Medicine. Sex.

He heard the sound of running water. Kate would be naked under the shower, young and naked and glorious. Her nipples would harden when the water touched them.

The casserole slipped from his hand and crashed to the floor. For a moment he gazed at the mess as if he were trying to figure out where it had come from.

Kate was singing in the shower now, singing in a bluesy, smoky voice, slightly off key.

Clayton got a dish towel and tried to kneel over the smashed dinner, but his erection got in the way.

With a sigh of resignation he went into his bathroom and locked the door. The casserole would have to wait.

6

Charleston, South Carolina

The letter lay open on the bedside table. Mick Malone skirted around it, trying not to notice. In the bathroom Martha was brushing her teeth, doing all that damned gargling he hated.

He balled his socks into a wad and rammed them into his shoes. He'd wear them again tomorrow if Martha didn't catch him. No sense in changing socks every day.

Martha turned on the shower, and he could hear the door banging shut as she climbed inside. She used to hum in the shower long ago, so long ago, he could hardly remember.

He glanced at the letter once more. Kate's signature stared up at him, bold as she'd always been. What would it hurt to look?

Dear Mother . . .

Mick's hands trembled.

Witch Dance is a beautiful land, and I'm busy and happy with my work. I don't want you to worry. I've made friends, and Dr. Colbert watches after me as if he were my father. I love you. Kate.

There was no sound except that of water cascading down the bathroom drain. Silently Mick replaced the letter on the bedside table, exactly as he'd found it.

He lay on his side of the bed, careful to leave enough room so Martha's legs wouldn't touch his. He closed his eyes and was soon breathing evenly, but his hands were clenched on top of the sheets.

7

Witch Dance

Anna Mingo liked to do her shopping on Saturday, especially when the weather was good. If she hurried with the grocery shopping, she always had time to go to her favorite store, the little needlepoint shop on the corner of Itawamba and East streets.

"Now, mind your manners, boys. No running around the store and *no* touching the merchandise."

"We'll be good, Mama," Clint said stoutly, though Anna had her serious doubts. Her oldest son probably would be good if Bucky didn't always get something started.

"I mean it, children."

They were still nodding their heads vigorously as she took both their hands and started across the street. She hurried along, thinking about the pink embroidery thread she wanted to buy and if she had enough money left over, the length of lace. Distracted, she almost didn't see the medicine woman until it was too late.

Kate Malone was crossing the street from the opposite side. Anna knew it had to be her, for no one else in Witch Dance had hair the color of the sunset and legs so long that she could walk as fast as a man.

Anna stopped dead in her tracks, and the medicine woman smiled directly at her.

"Why, hello there. What darling little boys."

Anguished, Anna let go of Clint and placed her hand over her stomach. The baby gave a vigorous kick.

Kate Malone stood in the middle of the street with an expectant smile on her face, waiting for an answer. It didn't seem right to turn away from her.

But Cole had been very specific, and Anna had absolute trust in her husband. Without a word to the medicine woman, she turned around and hurried back to her car.

"I thought we were going to the 'point shop, Mama."

"Hush, Clint."

Anna could still see the medicine woman, standing in the middle of the street. She looked as if she'd lost her best friend. Anna started the car and headed home, but for the first time in her marriage, she questioned Cole's judgment.

Kate watched the car drive away.

"I will not cry," she said, but she felt the tears gather anyhow.

The letter she'd sent her mother was nothing but a pack of lies. But how could it be otherwise? How could she tell her mother that the people she'd come to serve hated her so much they stomped her flowers into the ground, tore down the walls of her clinic, and passed to the other side of the street when she walked by?

In South Carolina everybody crossed streets to *get* to Kate, and in Virginia, where she'd gone to medical school, she was never without at least half a dozen invitations to go out for pizza and a beer. How could she say to her mother that she had only three friends in Witch Dance, and one of them had been so terrified of her father's censure that she'd almost refused a brochure about nursing school, and the other came and went on his black stallion as the mood struck him.

"If they think I'll leave, they've underestimated me. I'm a Malone. Nothing can stop me."

Having added talking to herself in the middle of the street to her list of sins, Kate marched across the street and into the ice cream shop with her head held high and a smile on her face.

Not only that, but she sat on a barstool at the counter and ordered the biggest banana split they had—even after the two people already there picked up their ice cream bowls and moved to a table. For good measure, she turned and gave them her best smile.

She'd never known it was so hard to smile with a lacerated heart.

That night they came to her in dreams. Charles and Brian came to her with their hands outstretched and their voices distorted by the water.

Help me. Help me, Katie.

The dream was always the same. They called to her and she couldn't answer. Weights held down her arms and legs, and a wide, watery expanse separated her from them. Her brothers.

Her fault.

"No!" she cried, her sleep-drugged voice as weak and mewling as a kitten's.

The covers were tangled around her legs like seaweed. She kicked frantically, trying to free herself. She had to get free.

"Kate?" Clayton stood in the doorway of her bedroom. "Are you all right?"

"Yes." Her hands trembled as she pushed her damp hair back from her forehead.

"Are you sure? Can I get you a glass of water . . . anything?"

"I'm fine. Just a bad dream."

"Well . . ." He lingered in the doorway, concerned.

"I'm okay. Really." She made herself smile at him.

His footsteps were soft, padded by the moccasins he wore as he crossed the room and stood beside her bed.

"Kate . . ." He reached toward her, wavered, then gently touched her forehead. His hands were damp against her skin. "Might as well make sure you don't have a fever."

"I've always heard the doctors are the biggest worrywarts of all when it comes to people they—" Premonition sent shivers along her spine. She'd never felt self-conscious around Dr. Colbert, but suddenly she was aware of the thin white cotton T-shirt that barely covered her bottom, of her naked legs and her tumbled hair.

". . . when it comes to family," she added briskly.

It was an awkward moment. He took a step back.

"You're almost family, Kate. Like a . . . daughter to me."

"Thanks."

"Well . . ."

His eyes were too bright. Kate wanted to pull the covers over herself, but that would only draw attention to her attire. More than that, it would indicate a lack of trust in him. Her dearest friend. Her trusted mentor. She wouldn't insult him in that manner.

"If you're sure you don't need anything . . . Good night, Kate."

Abruptly he wheeled away and was out the door before she could reply. Kate got out of bed and leaned against the windowsill. The walls of her clinic rose, ghostly, in the moonlight. It had taken four days to restore them. Four days of sweat and hard labor.

Without the watchers on the hill. Without Eagle.

Where was he?

Kate opened the window and let the night breeze cool her hot face. Prickles still danced along the back of her neck.

She tiptoed across the room and quietly closed her door. Then she turned the lock . . . feeling disloyal to Dr. Colbert. And somewhat silly.

Instead of going to bed and risking the dreams, she went back to the window. The yard was so bright, it might have been a South Carolina moon hanging in the

sky, a moon that rose up over the ocean and took its ir-
idescent glow from the waters.

Memories flooded her mind.

"Can't catch me ... can't catch me, Katie." Brian's hair
was silver as he raced along the edge of the water.

"I can too. I can do anything because I'm Daddy's girl."

Brian stuck out his tongue and raced off, his sturdy legs
spewing up sand. He didn't see the piece of driftwood in his
path. When Katie got to him, he had blood on his leg and he
was crying.

She sat cross-legged on the sand and pulled him onto her
lap.

"It hurts." Sniffling, he wrapped his arms around her neck.

"It's just a little blood ... see." She wiped it away with the
tail of her T-shirt.

Nobody would ask her where it came from. At thirteen, she
was already the neighborhood "doctor." Her patients ranged
from stray cats to baby birds fallen from their nests to an oc-
casional playmate who was not strong enough to withstand
her threats. "If you don't let me doctor you, I'll punch your
nose and really give you something to cry about," she'd tell
them.

"See," she told her five-year-old brother. "It's nothing but
a little ol' scratch."

He ran a chubby finger along his injury, then gave her a
watery smile. "Don't tell Daddy I cried."

"I won't."

"Promise?"

"Cross my heart and hope to die."

"An' Charles. Don't tell Charles. He'd laugh."

Ten-year-old Charles probably would. He prided himself on
being a man ... just like his father.

"I won't tell Charles."

Brian wrapped his arms around her neck and gave her a
kiss that left sand on her cheek.

"I love you best in all the world, Katie."

"I love you too, Bee Boy." It was the family pet name for
Brian, a name he'd given himself when he was first learning
to talk.

"Will you love me always, Katie?"

"Always."

"And take care of me forever and ever?"

"Forever and ever and ever."

He wiggled out of her lap and flew across the sand with his arms outstretched. "You can't catch me," he yelled, his joyous voice lifting on the wind.

A year later she'd broken her promise to Brian.

His forever lasted only six years.

Would nothing take the dreams away? Even wide awake she couldn't escape them, couldn't escape the guilt.

Kate pressed her hands against her face and felt tears. Angrily she wiped them away.

Dammit, she was in Tribal Lands for a fresh start. She leaned her elbows on the windowsill, determined to see nothing except the trees and the mountains.

And that's when she saw the horse and rider silhouetted against the moon. A man sat tall and majestic on a horse as black as the night.

"Eagle!"

His name ricocheted off the walls of her room, mocking her. She was so mesmerized by him that now she was seeing mirages. Rubbing her hands over her tired eyes, she glanced at the hillside once more. The horse and rider were gone.

She watched out the window awhile longer, letting her eyes adjust to the darkness. Nothing moved, nothing marred the horizon. And yet ... she was certain she'd seen them, the horse and rider so clearly outlined on the hillside.

Could it be an intruder come back to wreck the clinic once more?

"Over my dead body," she muttered.

Moving quickly, Kate pulled on a pair of jogging shorts; then she raced through the house, her bare feet scarcely touching the smooth wooden floors.

She'd been a long distance runner in her high school and college days. During her years in medical school she'd often relieved the tedium and stress by racing on the nearest track.

On her way out the back door she grabbed the first weapon she could get her hands on, the string mop hanging on a nail, still damp from scrubbing the kitchen floor. The Lord only knew what she would do with the mop, but she wasn't about to sit idly by while someone destroyed her work again.

Hiding wasn't her style.

Eagle saw her coming, her red hair as bright as a beacon. He'd expected the intruders, but he'd never expected Kate Malone, brandishing a mop.

She was as noisy as a freight train, roaring through the night with the mop held aloft. Fearless, she stormed through the clinic.

Eagle watched her, amused. She was in no danger, for he'd kept watch all night. The clinic was empty.

He knew the art of stillness. The years away from Witch Dance had not taken it from him, nor the ability to blend with the night, to be a part of it.

Kate passed so close, he could have reached out and touched her. Eagle stayed his hand. The touching would come. For now, watching was enough.

"Come out," she said. "I know you're in here."

She poked the mop behind a stack of lumber and jabbed it into dark corners.

"Come out with your hands up and I might be generous."

Leaning forward with the moon impossibly bright upon her hair and on the whiteness of her shirt, she shaded her eyes, trying to see into the darkness.

The wanting of her pierced him like arrows, and watching, he knew it would always be so. She was in his blood, and the mere sight of her stirred him beyond imagining.

He stepped from the shadows, so close his thigh touched hers. She spun around, dropping the mop, her mouth round with surprise. The knowledge of what they were to each other and what they would be sparked in their eyes.

"Be generous, Kate," he said, reaching for her.

She hesitated only a moment, then, surrendering, she wrapped herself around him, her arms circling his shoulders, her hands woven in his hair, her left leg pressed against his groin and her right curved around his leg.

"Where have you been?" she whispered.

He cupped her face. "Waiting for this."

Her sigh was as soft as prairie grasses bending before the wind.

Even before his lips touched hers he knew the honeyed taste of her, the warm, musky scent of her. It filled his nostrils and the pores of his skin. It raced through bone and sinew and blood, pounding with the insistent beat of war drums.

There was no need for words. Mouths joined, skin touching skin, they sank to their knees, weak and dying of the love-lust that consumed them. His hands were under her shirt, on her soft breasts, and hers massaged him through his well-worn jeans.

She made a soft, keening sound, like a wounded animal, and Eagle scooped her into his arms. He whistled once, twice. Out of the darkness came his black stallion. Kate was no burden to him as he mounted.

"I will not submit to these barbaric ways," Kate said even as she wrapped her arms around his chest.

"Submissive women bore me, *Wictonaye*." He bent close, his eyes challenging hers. Kate held his stare while night winds soughed softly about them. From far away came the cry of a coyote.

Still holding his gaze, Kate unlaced the leather thongs at the neck of his shirt, wet the tip of her finger with her tongue, then slowly traced his nipple.

"I will *never* submit," she whispered.

Smiling, Eagle dug his heels into the stallion's flanks. Thundering across the prairie with the wind in her hair, Kate existed in a state of being beyond time and light and knowledge.

All she knew was the sound of hoofbeats on the hard prairie floor and the swaying motion of the horse that rocked her in Eagle's arms.

Hal waited until the house was quiet, then climbed out the window. The minute his feet hit the ground he began to run. There was no need to look back. Nobody would pursue him. His father had been snoring like a downed buffalo when he left, and Deborah was out with one of her many boyfriends.

He'd be back long before she was, tucked safely in bed when she checked, as innocent as a newborn babe. Hal tipped back his head and laughed. A coyote in the hills answered him.

Hal wasn't scared. Nothing scared him. He had the power of the wolf.

His feet were swift and sure as he ran. He could outrun anybody in the Chickasaw Nation. Someday he would be a famous runner, earning lots of money, so everybody in Witch Dance would look at him driving by in his red Corvette and say, "There goes the luckiest man alive" instead of "Poor Hal."

He was sick of being Poor Hal, the boy whose mama got herself shot and whose daddy barely even knew he was alive.

Or maybe he'd prefer a black Corvette.

Wolf Man, he would call himself when he got famous. It would be a tribute to the great man who had shown him the future.

The Great One was waiting for him inside a small hut tucked in the foothills of the Arbuckle Mountains.

"You came." The man sitting on the dirt floor of the hut with his legs crossed nodded wisely. "It is good."

"Eagle is looking for you," Hal said, sitting opposite him and imitating the older man's posture.

"How long?"

"Four days now."

"The others?"

"They keep silent."

"Good. We will let the white medicine woman think peace has come to her clinic, then . . ." He made a slicing motion with his hands.

"I understand."

In the dim lights of the hut, the older man looked like a god as he reached into his pouch.

"To reward you for destroying the witch woman's work," he said, handing Hal a tiny packet.

Hal's palms dampened as he stuffed it into his pocket. He would save it for a time when he was alone in his room with no one to come and bother him.

"I have to go now."

"You will remember?" The older man made the slicing motion with his hands once more.

"I will remember."

He raced into the night, dreaming of fame and the kaleidoscopic journey he would take with the peyote.

They came suddenly upon his campsite. A blanket woven of all the colors of the sea lay upon the ground beside blackened embers from a recent fire, and the whisper of the river sang through the valley.

Eagle dismounted, taking Kate with him, and when he spread her upon the sea-colored blanket, she knew she would remember the moment always, the song of the river and brightness of his eyes as he undressed himself, then her. It was a slow unveiling, surprising considering the sexual frenzy that had brought them there.

Bending low, he touched her—touched her breasts, the soft down of her abdomen, the tiny indentation of her navel, the blue-veined skin inside her thighs. And all the while he chanted the strange beautiful words of his people.

He didn't have to speak English for her to understand. Eagle was speaking the language of love.

Breathless, she watched him. Every inch of her skin trembled under his inspection.

Levering himself over her, he gazed deep into her eyes.

"Say you want me, Kate."

"I want you, Eagle."

"Say you want me as I want you."

"I'm shameless. I would ride through an inferno to feel your arms around me. I would storm the very gates of hell to have you inside me, there"—she touched herself—"where I burn."

"*Waka ahina uno, iskunosi Wictonaye. Waka.*"

"Yes. Teach me, Eagle." She cupped his face. "Teach me to fly."

"Come." Taking her by the hands, he lifted her up so that they were facing each other, kneeling. "In the ancient traditions of my people, there is a ceremony lovers use so that they may know each other." He traced her lips with the tips of his fingers.

She closed her eyes, breathing in the dark, musky scent of him. Behind her, the mountains cast giant shadows while the river murmured its timeless song.

When Eagle withdrew his hands, she leaned toward him and raked the tips of her nails down his chest. "In the tradition of my people . . . we would long since have been joined together, panting on this blanket."

"Patience, *Wictonaye*." Smiling, he touched her breasts. "See what the waiting does." Her nipples, already peaked, turned hard as diamonds in his skilled hands.

He withdrew his touch once more. She was almost screaming with need.

"I've never had patience." She ran her hands over his chest. "If I had a weapon, I would take you at gunpoint."

"Will this do?" He pulled a lethal-looking knife from his belt and held it toward her, hilt first, the blade gleaming in the moonlight.

She traced the flat side of the blade, shivering at the

feel of the cold, deadly steel. Then, setting the knife aside, she scooted close to him, close enough so that their bodies touched from chest to knee. Lacing her arms around his neck, she bent down and slowly traced his lips with her tongue.

She felt the shiver run through him, then leaned back, smiling.

"So . . . mighty warrior. Teach me patience."

"We will begin"—he took a deep shuddering breath, then reached for her right hand—"like this." Slowly he laced their fingers together. His palm was warm and strong. "And then you will touch yourself"—he grazed her nipples with his fingertips—"like so, to indicate what you like."

"And you?"

"I will do likewise." He pressed his hand against the flat of his belly and ran it downward to circle his engorged flesh. Breathless, she watched the motion of his hand. "It is the mirror dance . . . an ancient and time-honored prelude to love."

With her eyes holding his, she touched herself, touched herself in all the places she wanted his hands, his lips, his tongue. She imagined him sliding through her slick, satiny passages, imagined the hard, heavy feel of him, the blessed friction that would both soothe and excite. Her breath sawed through her lungs, and her head fell back on a neck too limp to support its weight.

Her right hand clenched, tightened, and Eagle felt the shudder that racked her. His blood roared in his ears. She was ready for him now, wet with her own juices and ready for the final dance that would send them flying to the skies.

He loosened his hold on her hand, and slid his fingers slowly up the length of her arm, across the path of moonlight that gleamed on her bare shoulder and over her tender, blue-veined throat.

"Fly with me, *Wictonaye*."

"Yes . . . oh, yes," she whispered, reaching for him.

She was a lily stretched upon his Indian blanket, a

fallen flower offering her nectar to him. And he took it, took all of it, searing her with fingers and tongue until she was thrumming with need.

Humming low in her throat, a sound both musical and passionate, she rose from the blanket and bent over him. Her tongue made fire in his blood as her hair fell in a bright curtain across his groin.

And Eagle knew that her hair was the thing he would remember most about this night, her shining hair strewn across his dark skin like blood.

All the poetry in his soul spilled forth, and he whispered praises in the ancient tongue of his people, praises to her bright hair and her skin that was white as the wings of doves. Lowering her to the blanket, he covered her and together they soared.

Eagle and his *Wictonaye*.

8

She was totally without shame, lying on the Indian blanket in broad daylight, tangled with her lover. A pale pinkish glow lay on the land as the sun peeked over the mountain. In the early morning light his skin glowed, smooth and earth-colored. She knew how every inch of it looked, felt, tasted.

Kate bent down and pressed her tongue against the base of his throat. So fast she hardly saw him move, Eagle imprisoned her against his chest.

"I see the new dawn in the East, Kate. We must greet it properly."

"I have to go back before Dr. Colbert discovers I'm missing."

"He knows you're with me."

"No. I didn't tell him."

"He doesn't need to be told; he saw."

"When?"

"The day I brought you flowers."

Not only was she shameless, but now Dr. Colbert knew, and everything she'd worked for would go up in smoke. She'd go home in disgrace, and he'd find somebody who was *committed*.

And all because she couldn't control her libido.

"We won't do this again," she said.

"No." Eagle's eyes gleamed as he wound her hair around his fingers.

"No?" His ready agreement stung.

"No. Each time will be different. We will love in as many ways as there are stars in the sky."

"I'm telling you that I came here to practice medicine, and I won't let you interfere with that."

"Fate sent you to me. It's useless to argue with fate."

It was also useless to argue with Eagle. Especially when he was naked.

Kate sighed, leaning against him.

"Tell me about greeting the new dawn properly."

"Everything goes in a circle, Kate, and that circle is sacred. The new dawn of the East becomes the wisdom of sunset. The rain that comes down from Father Sky drenches Mother Earth, then returns as vapor." Eagle moved as he talked, running his hands through Kate's hair, gliding his tongue along her throat and down to her breasts.

"Someone will see," she whispered, but she was beyond caring.

He continued the erotic tongue bath as if he hadn't heard. She shivered as he licked the flat planes of her belly.

"In honor of nature's sacred circle, we will perform the medicine wheel." His tongue laved the skin of her inner thighs. Devilish lights twinkled in his eyes as he lifted his head to look at her. "I think you call it sixty-nine."

She didn't care what it was called, for she was already on the wheel, spinning round and round.

He heard them come in, just after dawn.

Standing in the shadows, Clayton watched as Eagle lifted Kate off his horse and kissed her. It was a kiss between lovers, a long, passionate embrace with their bodies melded and swaying together like two willows in the wind.

He watched. Imagining he was the one with his arms around her. Imagining it was his name she murmured in her low, love-sated voice.

Clayton couldn't turn away, even when Kate faced the window, even when she started into the house. He had to see her, had to see the flush of sex on her skin and the brightness of passion in her eyes.

His hands clenched into fists as she climbed the front porch steps. Even when she opened the front door, he couldn't turn away.

When she was inside the house, he slid behind the heavy drapery like a damned cowardly voyeur. Hiding in his own house.

She passed so close, he could have touched her. The smell of the fresh morning breezes and recent sex mingled with her own floral fragrance to create an intoxicating scent that almost brought Clayton to his knees. He clamped his bottom lip with his teeth to keep from giving himself away.

Her footsteps echoed across the wooden floor, then faded. Motionless, he stood behind the curtains with his mouth open in a silent scream of agony.

The door to her bedroom closed, and the house grew quiet. Clayton stood until he felt the rising sun warm his back; then he went into the kitchen and put on a pot of coffee.

It was only when he lifted the cup to his lips that he tasted his tears. He was just wiping them away when she came into the kitchen. Fresh and rosy from her bath. Bright-eyed. As if she hadn't spent the night in the arms of that savage.

"Good morning, Dr. Colbert." She pecked him on the cheek.

" 'Morning, Kate."

His hand tightened on the handle of the coffee cup as she walked to the refrigerator to get a glass of juice. Any faint hopes he'd harbored that Eagle wasn't good in bed were dashed: She walked like a woman fulfilled.

"It's a beautiful day, isn't it?"

"Yes." He cleared his throat. "I was thinking of a picnic—"

"Oh, Dr. Colbert—"

"Maybe down by the river," he said, hurrying on past the refusal he knew was inevitable. "We've worked every Saturday since you came. The change will do us both good."

"I promised Eagle. He called last night when you were in the shower." She flushed at her lie.

"Eagle?" As if he didn't know.

"Eagle Mingo. He's coming to take me riding."

As if he hadn't already taken her riding. All night long. Clayton was careful to set his coffee cup down without unnecessary noise and motion.

"The Mingos have fine stables," he said.

"I love riding." She pushed her hair back from her hot face. "I used to visit cousins up in Virginia and ride with the hounds. It's really a lovely way to relax."

What other lovely ways would they use to relax?

He might have made a complete fool of himself and asked if the sound of hoofbeats hadn't saved him. Kate flew to the window and drew the curtain aside.

Eagle Mingo—virile, handsome, young—came into view, riding a black stallion and leading a snow-white mare. He rode Indian-style, with nothing but bridle and blanket.

How could Clayton possibly hope to compete with him?

Kate raced to the door without even saying good-bye. Eagle dismounted and cupped his hands for her to swing onto the back of the mare. When she was seated, he slowly ran his hands the length of her leg.

Clayton didn't hear what he said, but he heard Kate's reply.

"I can hardly wait."

Moving swiftly, Clayton went into Kate's bedroom and lay upon her bed. Then he pulled the sheet that smelled like her over himself to cover his act of depravity.

* * *

"You ride like a Chickasaw, Kate."

"I feel like a Chickasaw. Wild and free." She gave a war whoop, then bent low over the mare's neck. "Race you!"

Hooves thundered over the prairie floor as Eagle took her challenge. The white mare was no match for the black stallion, but Eagle let her lead for a distance in order to enjoy the view. He enjoyed watching fine horsemanship, and Kate had a firm seat and a sure hand.

His eyes darkened, then he put troubling thoughts out of his mind.

"*Aiya*," he urged his mount, and soon he was beside Kate, reaching for her bridle. He drew the two horses to a stop beside a deep bend in the river. A stand of silver maple and elm created a natural shelter.

Scooping Kate into his arms, he waded into the river. When they were waist-deep, with the river soaking his jeans and the bottom of her shorts, he nudged her hair aside and whispered, "I'm in need of being rescued, Kate."

She cupped his face and looked into his eyes. "You're full-blood . . . all the way back to Piomingo."

"You've inquired?"

"Of Deborah Lightfoot. In a casual way."

"This is not casual, Kate."

"What is it?"

He unbuttoned her blouse, his fingers dark upon her creamy skin.

"Fate," he said.

All her years of study, all her lofty plans, even the deep schism between herself and her father, were nothing beside the reality of Eagle Mingo.

"Damn fate all to hell," she whispered, reaching for his zipper.

His jeans floated downstream and snagged on a tree branch over the river, and her shorts landed atop a large rock. Sleek as otters, they came together in the water. They rose and fell upon the waves, as skilled as the water creatures in their natural habitat. And when their need demanded a greater intimacy, Eagle carried her from the river and spread her upon a carpet of moss underneath the silver maples.

With fingers laced and eyes locked, he rode her until their cries mingled and joined his namesake circling the sky.

"You will come to me, Kate, at night, at my campsite beside the river." She lay still, watching his eyes. They were both beautiful and terrible, filled with passion and the desperate knowledge that they could never be more than lovers, stealing moments of glory in each other's arms.

"You will come on the white mare . . ."

"I won't . . ."

He put his hand over her lips. "Her name is Mahli. It means the wind."

The power of him flowed through his loins, still joined with hers, and made her tremble. He touched her as no man ever had, touched her in all the secret places of her body and in that shining place known as the soul. How could she deny him anything?

"I will come . . . but only because I *choose* to."

Smiling, he began to move in her once more.

As Kate spiraled upward, she thought it was appropriate that she would fly to him on the wind.

9

Anna's baby kicked inside her as if she already knew the sound of her father's voice. Anna placed her hand over her protruding stomach.

"Yes, my precious one. You know him, don't you, Mary Doe?"

She'd named her little girl, although she was careful not to use the name in front of Cole. He was thoroughly convinced that he'd fathered yet another son who would carry on the Mingo name.

Anna hid the tiny dress she was embroidering underneath the balls of yarn and the knitting needles in her sewing basket as Cole came through the door with Bucky riding on his shoulders. Clint trotted along beside Cole, swinging his daddy's hand.

"You should have seen them, Anna. Bucky's going to be a quarterback and Clint's going to be a fullback." Cole set Bucky on a kitchen stool, then patted Anna's stomach on the way to the refrigerator to pour four glasses of milk. "Pretty soon we're going to have our own football team."

"I saw you out the window. All three of you were marvelous."

"Drink your milk, sweetheart." Cole pulled out a

chair for her. "We want to make that little linebacker you're carrying big and strong."

She sank into the chair and lifted the glass to her lips. Anna knew the value of prenatal care. When Mary Doe was born, she'd have strong bones and a head start on growing fine, white teeth. She'd have Cole's straight nose and glorious cheekbones and Anna's full lips. Her little Mary Doe was going to be the most beautiful girl in Witch Dance.

Smiling a secret smile, Anna pictured herself and Mary Doe, mother and daughter, best friends, cuddled together in a room decorated with pink curtains and a frilly bedspread, talking girl talk. She'd tell her daughter to dream big dreams and not be afraid. She'd tell her that women could do anything men could. She might even use the new medicine woman as an example.

Mary Doe would have a wonderful life, full of encouragement and opportunity. She would know that she could be more than a wife and mother, or a secretary or a schoolteacher on the reservation.

Not that Anna was complaining. Her life was grand. She had her sons and a beautiful house on the ranch . . . and a magnificent husband. Cole was good to her. He loved her and pampered her and treated her with great respect. Sometimes, though, she wished he'd listen when she talked about her ambition.

"My wife has no need to be in politics and wear pants like a man," he'd say when she mentioned that she'd like to be on the school board. "My wife is too busy making babies."

And they were. Cole was an unselfish, caring lover, passionate about her, even in her third trimester of pregnancy. The night before, he'd brought her to a fast, hard climax with his tongue.

"Sweet *lhokomuk*," he murmured as she returned the favor. "My little nectar seeker."

Lhokomuk. Hummingbird. He'd first called her that the night they met at the drugstore in Ada, where she sold perfumes. He'd come to get a prescription filled for his little brother. She'd fallen instantly, madly in love. But Cole had taken longer. Three days longer, as a matter of fact, days he spent digging into her family tree.

She cringed to think what would have happened if her bloodline hadn't been pure. How could she have lived with a broken heart?

"Daddy, look. It's Uncle Eagle." Clint pointed out the window.

"Unca Eaga." Bucky flew across the room and pressed his nose against the windowpane. "On a big horse."

"Come on, Bucky. Let's go meet him."

Clint took his little brother by the hand, and they raced down the driveway toward their uncle.

Cole set his half-empty glass on the bar and wiped his mouth with the back of his hand. His face was set in terrible lines.

"Cole. Don't be too hard on him." Anna left her chair and put her hand over her husband's. "He's your brother. You love him."

"It's because I love him, Anna . . ."

"Invite him to dinner, Cole."

"He doesn't have time for dinner. He's too busy with *her*."

"He must have his reasons." She put an imploring hand on his arm as he strode toward the front door. "Just listen to him, Cole. Please."

Cole didn't like his wife to be upset, and more than that, he didn't like to be the cause. He snaked his arms around her and rested his cheek on her hair.

"*Lhokomuk*, sweet *lhokomuk*. If my brother weren't riding up the driveway, I'd make you forget about everything except me."

"You've already made me forget, my darling."

Cole kissed the top of her head, then put two fingers under her chin and lifted her face toward his.

"He's my brother, Anna. Nothing will ever change that."

She was smiling when he went through the door, exactly as he'd intended. He hadn't lied to her. He and Eagle had started in the womb together, and nothing would destroy that bond.

He stood beside petunia beds Anna had planted around their front porch, watching as Eagle dismounted and greeted Bucky and Clint. The reserve they'd first shown him quickly vanished, and now his boys cavorted with Eagle as if they'd known him forever.

"Catch, Unca Eaga." Bucky scooped up the football they'd been playing with and tossed it to his uncle.

Eagle caught the ball and raced without effort toward an imaginary goal line while his nephews yelled their encouragement.

"Go, Unca Eaga! Go!"

"Yeah, Uncle Eagle. Run for the touchdown."

His sons' voices faded as voices from the past echoed in Cole's mind.

"Ea-gle . . . Ea-gle . . . Ea-gle."

The crowd was on its feet, screaming for their favorite quarterback. Even in his football uniform and helmet, Eagle stood out from the other players. It might have been his habit of lifting his arms toward the sky as he entered the field, or perhaps it was the way he ran, without seeming to touch the ground.

With the roar of the crowd in his ears, Cole blocked for his brother. It didn't bother him that they weren't yelling his name. Teamwork. That's what winning a game required, and Cole would do anything to win the game.

Eagle would always be the hero, for he'd come from the womb first, bearing the mark of greatness on his thigh, a perfect print of the talons of his revered namesake.

Cole accepted Eagle's greatness, accepted the role he played in his brother's destiny: He was the prophet, the forerunner, the voice crying, "Make way. Make way."

Eagle glided over the goal line, then lifted both arms toward the sky.

"Ea-gle . . . Ea-gle . . . Ea-gle. . . ."

Cole was the first to offer his shoulder to carry his brother across the field in victory.

"You have fine sons, Cole."

Eagle's voice brought him back to the present.

"Yes. I have fine sons." He handed the bridle of the stallion to his oldest. "Clint, you and Bucky go down to the barn and take care of Uncle Eagle's horse."

"Can we ride, Daddy?"

Eagle nodded his assent, and Cole gave his boys a leg up.

"You've taught them well," Eagle said, admiring the way the boys handled the big black.

"I have. Bucky's a natural. Clint's more methodical and takes longer, but he never backs down from anything." Cole propped a foot on the porch railing and nodded toward a chair. Eagle glanced at the rocker as if it affronted him, then joined his brother. "We haven't seen much of you since you came home."

Ignoring the implied criticism, Eagle studied the ranch.

"You have a great place, Cole."

"Anna makes it beautiful and I make it successful."

Cole's idea of the proper order of things was not lost on Eagle, but again he refused to be lured into argument.

"Well, it *is* lovely. I'll tell her when we go inside."

Suddenly at a loss for words, Eagle watched Cole's horses canter around the perfectly kept paddocks. The silence between them grew heavy. Cole shifted his other foot to the railing.

"Is this a social call or a business call?"

"You always did get right to the point, Cole."

"And you didn't answer the question."

"It's not a social call."

"I didn't think so."

"Some of our people have been destroying Kate's clinic."

Not Dr. Colbert's clinic, but Kate's clinic. Cole's mouth tightened. The slip of his brother's lip was telling.

"Do you know anything about it, Cole?"

"Are you accusing me?"

"I'm not accusing you. Father said you'd been at the hunting cabin the last few days. I thought you might have seen something."

"What I've seen is almost too shameful to speak of." Cole's hands tightened into fists. "What I've seen makes me want to deny I have a brother."

Eagle willed himself to stillness. *Kate*. A thousand times he'd questioned his obsession with her; a hundred times he'd ridden the land and sighted the places that needed better roads and modern bridges. It was time, past time, to be about his life's work; but all it took was a glimpse of her hair or the sound of her voice, filled with the soft, seductive cadences of her native South Carolina, and he was her love slave, hungering to bury himself in her fragrant body.

Was it any wonder that his brother should question too?

"You judge me, Cole. You judge without knowing and without hearing."

"I've seen enough. She has led you astray, Eagle. With her bright hair and her white thighs she has made you forget who you are."

"I will never forget who I am. I am Eagle."

"She's a white woman. Would you have her bear pale-skinned sons who don't know a stallion from a jackass?"

"She will not bear my sons."

"How can you expect otherwise? You've rutted her like a damned bull. Every time you look at her, she opens her legs."

Eagle drew back his fist, wanting nothing more than to smash his brother's face. He pictured the satisfying crunch of bone against bone, the sharp sting of flesh battering flesh.

"Hit me, Eagle. That's what the white whore has brought us to. Brother against brother."

Every muscle in Eagle's body tensed, and his blood, hot for battle, roared in his ears. In the humming silence the brothers watched each other; then slowly Eagle lowered his fist.

"I'm ashamed that you spied."

"I didn't spy. I was riding by the river on the way to the hunting cabin. It didn't take a damned Philadelphia lawyer to figure out what was going on."

"You will not speak of her again."

"The whole village speaks of her, riding all over the countryside on your white mare ... with you at her side." A muscle in the side of Cole's jaw clenched and unclenched. From the distance came the sound of his boys' laughter as they streaked out of the barn toward the house. The back door slammed, and there was more giggling as Anna ordered hands and faces washed.

Softened, Cole put his hand on Eagle's shoulder. He wanted only what was best for his brother.

"Don't jeopardize everything you've worked for because of this woman."

"She will not turn me away from my visions." Eagle whistled for his stallion, then turned back to Cole. "She is necessary to me."

Love and anger, envy and admiration, mingled in Cole's breast as Eagle leapt on the stallion's back and galloped away.

He watched until his brother was out of sight, then went inside to join his wife and sons.

"Is Eagle staying for dinner?" Anna asked.

"No. He had other things on his mind."

Kate sat on the edge of the bed with her mother's letter open on her lap. It was a long, newsy letter telling about Dottie Brainbridge's new baby and Nancy Kellerman's wedding dress that was shipped all the way from Neiman's in Dallas and Barb Rothchild's operatic debut in Atlanta.

"Charleston has been full of tourists all summer long," Martha had written in her spidery hand, "and you know how your father hates tourists. I love them though. It perks one up to see the expectant look on their faces as they walk our cobblestone streets and sit under umbrellas, eating our famous pecan pie."

Kate had left the window open, and breezes stirred the blue curtains. Flapping, they looked like the broken wings of birds.

She wished she could see her mother's face, bright because the sight of strangers enjoying themselves made her happy.

"The cape jasmine beside the patio still blooms," Martha wrote. "It seems unwilling to acknowledge that summer is almost over."

Suddenly Kate was so lonesome for the smell of jasmine that she put her head between her hands and cried.

There was no one to hear, for Dr. Colbert had driven into Ada for lunch with friends. She gave vent to her tears until the far-off cry of a hawk reminded her of the many things she had to be grateful for in this strange and beautiful land.

She wiped her face and folded the letter. How silly of her to be crying over jasmine.

Perhaps it wasn't southern flowers she was lonesome for, but friends. In South Carolina she could pick up the phone and call any of a dozen numbers, and there would be somebody on the other end of the line who would come over and talk for hours about anything under the sun, or who would join Kate for a walk on the beach or a drive into town to catch a movie or go on a shopping spree or merely for a reprieve in the shade of a striped umbrella at an outdoor café, where they would sip iced tea with a sprig of mint.

Here people moved to the other side of the street at her approach, or stared at her as if she were an alien who had recently landed from another planet. Sometimes they whispered behind their hands when she approached on her white horse.

There was another thing. The horse.

She probably would never have taken it if he'd said it was a gift. And yet she hadn't put up much of a fight—

any fight at all, to tell the truth—about taking it so she could race all over the countryside just to be in his bed. Or on his blanket, as the case happened to be.

Bought for the price of a horse.

Her South Carolina friends would be shocked. Even her mother, indulgent as she was, might not approve.

She really ought to give the horse back. The bad part was that she didn't want to. The horse was her link to Eagle, and without Eagle she'd be desolate, a garden deprived of rain and sunlight, withering away in a sometimes-hostile land.

The mere thought of Eagle made her body go liquid. She wanted to race across the plains till she found him, then throw herself into his arms and have him do wonderful, exotic, erotic things to her in broad daylight.

The last time they were together—only six hours earlier, as a matter of fact, because she'd counted—he'd painted her face and breasts with vermilion and she'd painted him with cobalt. Remembering, shivers of pleasure ran through her. . . .

"You are Mother Earth." His fingers were slick with paint and warm with lust, and they left trails of shivers where vermilion stained her skin. "You are rich and ripe and receptive to the penetration of rain from Father Sky."

The blue paint pot was at her fingertips. Bending over Eagle with her hair brushing his chest, she caressed his face, spreading the blue paint, infusing him with the power of Father Sky. He caught her taut nipple between his lips and sucked deeply.

A spontaneous climax hit her so hard, she fell across his chest, crying out her pleasure.

"*Ihullo uno, iskunosi Wictonaye,*" he whispered, lifting her over his rigid flesh. "*Ihullo uno.* . . ."

It was hours later when she learned what he'd said. "Love me, little wildcat. Love me."

Remembering, she walked to the window and let the breeze cool her face.

Love. Oh, God, she couldn't be in love with Eagle

Mingo. Not after what Deborah had told her: "The Min-
goes trace their lineage all the way back to Chief
Piomingo. They *never* marry one who is not full-blood."

Besides that, there was her own work. How could she
save lives if she spent most of her time wallowing on
Eagle Mingo's blanket and the rest of her time thinking
about it?

No, she was obsessed. That was all.

The thing to do was find Deborah and plan a sight-
seeing trip to Ada. After all, it was the capital of the
Chickasaw Nation and she'd never even seen it. Then
she'd take Mahli back to Eagle and tell him the affair
was finished and they should both get on with their
work.

Altogether, it was a sensible plan.

Filled with purpose, Kate hurried to the small stable
behind Dr. Colbert's cottage, calling to the mare as she
went.

Mahli knew the sound of Kate's voice. The mare
tossed her mane and pranced in place and whinnied.

"You like me, old girl, don't you." Kate rubbed the
mare's soft nose. "Yes, you do."

The mare whinnied once more. It wasn't much in the
way of conversation, but it was about all Kate had.

She swung the Indian blanket on Mahli's back and
fastened the bridle. Then she led the horse outside and
vaulted on, Indian-style. Eagle had taught her many
things, most of them erotic, but some of them practical.

When she saw Deborah, the sensible plan went right
out of Kate's head. Deborah's once-sleek, beautiful hair
was a frizzy halo of reddish-purple around her lovely
face.

Ignoring the stares and whispers that followed her
down the crowded aisles of the general store, Kate hurried toward her friend.

"Just look at me." Smiling ruefully, Deborah grabbed
a handful of her hair and held it out for Kate's inspection. "I look like an Irish setter with a coat full of cock-
leburs."

"Who did that to you, Deborah?"

"I did. It all sounded so simple when I read the bottles. Bleach out the black and pour on the red. Then, presto! I'd look like the beautiful medicine woman."

Kate wanted to weep for the lost beauty of Deborah's hair. Instead, she said, "We'll go into Ada and find a good hair stylist who can fix you right up." Seeing the girl's crestfallen look, she added quickly, "My treat."

"You'd do that for me?"

"With pleasure. It will be small repayment for all you've done for me, Deborah."

Deborah gave Kate a broad smile. "Damned right. Only yesterday I told two old setting hens clucking about you and Eagle that it was none of their business. They huffed out without buying a thing, but I didn't care."

Deborah turned to look at herself in the small cracked mirror that hung behind the cash register. Her ugly face topped by wrecked hair stared back at her.

"Irish setters are beautiful," she said morosely. "This looks more like a fox's tail."

"I'm sure a good hairdresser will know what to do," Kate said. "Soon your hair will be as gorgeous as ever."

Deborah fought the tears that threatened. Kate was the kindest woman she knew, almost like a mother, except that she was far too young and beautiful. She had troubles enough of her own without Deborah wailing like a coyote over her silly hair.

"Thanks for the offer, but I'll just whack it all off and start over. Hair grows, you know."

Kate covered her disappointment by reaching for Deborah's hand.

"I understand," she said.

"My father ..."

"Shhh ... you don't have to explain."

"He found that material on nursing schools you brought me and he was awfully mad."

"I'm sorry, Deborah. I didn't mean to cause trouble for you."

Torn between loyalty to her father and her good
friend, Deborah tried to make amends.

"He's a good man. Really, he is. Not like everybody
else. They say you're a witch and Eagle is under your
spell."

"Nonsense. There's no such thing as witches and
spells." A flush heated Kate's neck. "Besides that, Eagle
Mingo is not the kind of man who falls under spells."

A romantic at heart, Deborah thought it only fitting
that the son of the governor should marry the most
beautiful woman in Witch Dance and the daughter of a
U. S. senator besides. A mating of royalty. Suddenly she
had a brilliant idea how she could accomplish that goal
and repay Kate for her kindness and friendship at the
same time.

"I have much experience with many boyfriends and
from reading novels where the nurse always gets the
doctor. I'll teach you how to make him fall under your
spell."

"Thanks, Deborah, but I think I'll pass." Kate lifted
her heavy hair off her neck. "My, it's hot in here."

Riveted, Deborah leaned forward and touched Kate's
skin just below the earlobe. Her finger came away red
and blue.

"That looks like war paint."

Kate flushed scarlet. Her mother had always warned
her to wash behind her ears. In her hasty bath, she'd
missed the telltale evidence of her night of passion with
Eagle.

She was saved by a commotion at the front of the
store. Eagle Mingo was galloping by on his black stallion, and the rush toward the windows emptied the
aisles of the store.

He sat tall and proud in the saddle with the wind in
his hair and the sun on his face.

Bewitched, bewitched, her mind whispered. But it
wasn't she who had bewitched Eagle; it was he who
had bewitched her.

Kate leaned against the counter, weak with wanting,

and as the sound of hoofbeats died away, she knew with absolute certainty that she couldn't return the horse and end the affair; that, in fact, she would take the first opportunity to mount the horse and fly through the darkness to Eagle.

Now and always.

Clayton heard her leave.

He lay in his bed, listening to her soft footsteps in the hall. The back door creaked on its hinges, and then the sound of hoofbeats filled the night.

Kate. Riding to meet her lover. Flying to him on the wind as she had every night for the past two weeks.

The nights were torture for Clayton, and the days even worse. Flashes of them came to him in short bursts of color and agony. Eagle on the clinic rooftop putting on shingles and Kate gazing up at him as if he were the sun. Eagle, his bare chest shining with sweat, bending while Kate poured water over his head. Eagle and Kate. Kate and Eagle. The secret smiles. The secret touches.

As if he couldn't see. As if he didn't know.

Rage filled him. He panted as he raced down the hall to her bedroom. Her nightshirt lay across the bed, where she'd tossed it in her haste. His lips curled back against his teeth as he snatched the shirt up. It made a small snapping sound as he stretched it tight. One more tug and it would rip apart.

Clayton closed his eyes, imagining the satisfaction of tearing her nightshirt to shreds. The smell of Kate filled his nostrils—the lotion she used to keep her hands soft, the shampoo that made her hair smell like flowers, the exotic musky scent that clung to her skin.

He fell to his knees and bent double with Kate's nightshirt pressed over his face. Moaning like a sick animal, he felt his semen spew.

Exhausted, he lay on the floor. From somewhere in the distance came the sounds of the night—an owl calling someone's name, a lone wolf howling at the moon,

the soft slapping sound of flesh against flesh. Kate and
Eagle tangled together in sweaty lovemaking.

Uncertain of what was real and what was imaginary,
Clayton finally lifted himself up. Signs of his degrada-
tion were everywhere, drying on Kate's nightshirt and
on the edge of the sheet she'd left hanging over the bed.
He stood on shaky legs.

Gathering her shirt and the sheets off the bed, he
headed for the washing machine. There would be plenty
of time to clean up before she returned.

Kate would never know, *must* never know.

"You're leaving?" Kate couldn't believe what she was
hearing. "You can't leave. The clinic's not finished, these
people don't trust me, and—" She'd suddenly run out
of reasons, all of them selfish. "I'll never make it without you. Never."

Clayton pushed aside his bowl of cereal, the decision
he'd made the previous night firm in his mind. He
longed to offer a shoulder to cry on, to touch her, but he
dared not.

"You'll be fine, Kate. You and Eagle will have that
clinic finished soon. Once the people see what a wonderful doctor you are, they'll flock to you. You'll have to
hire a guard at the door to keep order."

"Thank you for those sweet lies."

She came to him and put her arms around him. He
felt the shock of her touch all the way down to his toes.
Thank God her hips weren't touching his, or she'd
know exactly why he had to leave. He hoped she didn't
feel him trembling.

"I've been selfish to the core," she said, walking away.
"Of course I'll be all right. It's not as if everybody in this
town mistrusts me. I have Deborah . . . and Eagle."

"Yes. You have friends." Did his rage show? His jealousy? His lust?

"I never even asked why you're going. There's nothing wrong, I hope."

"No. A small family matter. Melissa is giving a benefit

dance for AIDS, and she needs my support." How easily the lie came to him. Melissa could plan and execute the liberation of a small besieged country without his help.

"Will you be back?"

"Of course. This is *our* clinic, Kate. Yours and mine. I'll help get it on its feet and running before I return to my practice in Boston."

"I wish you would decide to relocate . . . you and Melissa. We'd make a great team, Doc."

Yes, he thought. A great team. Working side by side. Sharing the day-to-day triumphs as well as the tragedies in a field they both loved.

And at night, sharing the same bed, sleeping between her thighs with the scent of her filling his nostrils.

He looked at her smiling face. Clearly, she respected him and enjoyed his company. Was there hope for him, after all?

"I'll be back, Kate." He patted her cheek, so soft, so fragrant. Surely he was due that much.

She covered his hand. "Thanks, Doc. You're like a father to me."

He kept his tears inside. Tomorrow on the plane back to Boston would be soon enough to cry.

10

Signs of approaching fall appeared in Witch Dance. A herd of antelope began their migration, and the fur of foxes, rabbits, and coyotes thickened. At night, when the stars hung low, winds blowing down from the Arbuckle Mountains brought chills and a promise of snow.

The two people sat huddled in front of the cabin with the moon a pale sliver in the cold sky and the shadow of the mountain hiding their faces. Hal and the Great One. Planning for the future of Witch Dance.

"Tonight," the Great One said.

"I'm ready."

"You know what to do?"

Hal nodded. He'd gone over the plans in his head a dozen times. Nothing could go wrong, for he had the power of the wolf and the power of the peyote stirring his blood.

"You've done well. Because of you, Witch Dance will soon be free of this tainted influence." The Great One put a hand on Hal's shoulder and he felt ten feet tall. "Go quickly now."

"Do you want me to report back to you?"

"No. I'll know when the deed is done."

The Great One sat in the doorway of the hut until Hal disappeared into the night. Then he built a small fire and sacrificed the fattest and finest portion from a loin of venison he'd kept inside. The fire flickered over his face as he danced slowly around it, calling upon the spirits to send down great things to his people and success for Hal's mission. His chants echoed off the walls of the mountains.

And from the distance there came an answer, the call of the screech owl. The man froze in mid-step. Shivers tingled along his spine.

The warning of the screech owl. Witches were about.

He snuffed his fire and went inside his hut. Then he pulled off his moccasins and left them upside down in the doorway to ward off the witches.

Eagle covered Kate with the blanket. She slept soundly under the stars, with one hand pressed under her cheek and one knee slightly bent. The delicate skin at the base of her throat and across the tops of her breasts was still flushed where he'd kissed her.

Softly he touched her hair, careful not to wake her. Even that small contact made him want her—the soft, shiny feel of her hair.

With the bright tendrils clinging to his fingers and the bright memory of their bodies joined making his blood sing, Eagle felt the cold winds blowing off the mountains, the cold winds of good-bye.

"You have bewitched me, Kate," he whispered as softly he kissed her hair and pulled the blanket close around her shoulders.

Kate didn't stir, even when he mounted his stallion and raced off into the darkness. Her sleep was peaceful and deep.

"You've made the dreams go away, Eagle," she'd told him.

Had it been only two weeks ago? It seemed like a lifetime, as if he and Kate had been together forever, would *be* together forever.

"What dreams?"

"The ones that have haunted me for years."

"Do you want to tell me about them?"

And she had. Leaning against his chest with the moisture from his tongue still drying upon her nipples, she'd told him of her brothers, of the small sailboat they'd taken into the waters, of the sudden storm and of her desperate search for them in the unyielding sea.

"I killed them."

"No. You had nothing to do with it, Kate. They were weighed on the path and made to be light."

"I can't excuse my negligence by saying it was an act of fate."

"The days appointed them were finished. There was nothing you could do to change that."

Her sleep had been peaceful after that, as it was now.

A hawk disturbed by his passing rose toward the night sky, and branches stirred by the wind off the mountains whispered secrets as he galloped toward the clinic. Summer was almost over, and the knowledge was heavy upon his heart.

Eagle drew his horse to a halt atop the hillside. The moon lay upon the clinic like a blessing. There was a sudden calm, as if even the wind dared not disturb his deep contemplation.

For weeks now there had been no hostile moves toward Kate and her work. She was euphoric, thinking the opposition dead, but Eagle knew better. Whoever was behind the hostilities was waiting his moment to strike.

Eagle watched with perfect stillness, watched and absorbed the grandeur of the land around him. There was too much beauty to mar a single moment of it with impatience.

From the opposite hillside came movement, a slight figure racing through the darkness as only a Chickasaw could, light and fleet and soundless. The runner stopped in front of the door of the clinic, where the moon shone brightest. In his hand was an ancient sacred musical instrument, and as he plucked the strings, he began to dance.

Chills raced along Eagle's spine and prickled the back of his neck, for he knew the ceremony. It was the *Keetla Ishto Hoollo*, a dance before the holy one designed to drive away witches.

Suddenly Eagle knew the enemy, knew his power and his motives, knew him without seeing him. Certainly it was not the slender boy dancing in the moonlight. He was hardly more than a child, and not capable of owning such an instrument, let alone understanding the significance of the dance.

No, the enemy was not the youth; the enemy was far more deadly. The enemy believed Kate to be a witch, and he would do everything in his power to stop her.

With the discordant sounds of the instrument and the muffled beat of moccasins ringing in his ears, Eagle descended toward the clinic. The young man was so lost in his task that he never heard Eagle's approach.

"I know you. You are the son of Lightfoot."

The boy dropped his instrument. "What the devil?"

"No, not the devil. But close."

Eagle dismounted and caught him around the back of the neck so swiftly that the boy had no time to run. A box of matches fell from his pocket.

Eagle ground it under his foot.

"You won't be needing those."

"Let go of me, you bastard." Hal had absolutely no hope of freeing himself, but he tried anyhow. He twisted and jerked, knowing that the iron grip of Eagle Mingo would hold him fast.

"You will take me to the one who commanded you to do this."

"It was all my idea."

"You speak with the *sente soolish*."

"And you speak like a savage."

"The *sente soolish*—the snake's tongue."

The boy spat in the dirt at Eagle's feet. "That's what

I think of your damned crazy talk and your damned
white witch woman."

Hal refused to cringe before the murderous rage in
Eagle's eyes. Eagle lifted him onto the stallion as if he
were a child. The arm holding him was as hard as a
band of steel. There was no possibility of escape.

"Tell me where he is," Eagle commanded. Hal remained stubbornly silent. The band of steel tightened
around his chest. "Tell me."

"In a cabin . . . east, at the foot of the Arbuckle Mountains."

As they thundered off into the darkness, Hal wished
he could die. He'd rather be shot down like his mother
than to face the disappointment and wrath of the Great
One.

"I've been expecting you." The Great One stood outside his hut dressed in full regalia. Streaks of dark um-
ber and bright vermilion decorated his face, and
pouches of various sizes hung on leather thongs around
his neck. In his right hand he carried a gourd rattle, and
in his left, the tailfeather of an eagle. Tools of his trade.
"When the screech owl called, I knew my mission
would fail."

The medicine man's face was old and lined with
many wrinkles, but his body was erect, and he held
himself proudly.

"I should have known it would be you." Eagle dismounted, taking the boy with him.

"Let the boy go home," the old shaman said.

"I don't want to go." Hal stuck out his chin. He could
still feel the power of the peyote working in his blood.

The Great One turned a stern face to him. "Go home.
I am the one he seeks. Without me you are nothing."

As soon as Eagle's grip loosened, Hal raced toward
home, the rebuke stinging in his ears. Someday he'd
show them. He'd show them all.

The medicine man turned toward his visitor. He
could feel the supremacy of his opponent. It was a

strong magic enhanced by noble visions and unselfish commitment. He was proud his opponent was worthy.

"The medicine woman has chosen her protector wisely."

"She didn't choose me; I chose her."

"Why?"

"Because I believe Witch Dance needs her."

"They don't need her; they have me."

"There is room for both of you. The old ways and the new should blend with harmony."

"What does she know of the curative powers of sarsaparilla and the root of the huckleberry? Can she find the black locust and the bear-wolf weed?"

"Her medicines are different."

"I have seen these medicines at the big hospital in Ada. I spit upon them." He spat on the ground.

Somewhere in the mountains around them a bobcat screamed.

"The medicine woman will stay in Witch Dance with or without your consent." Eagle waited long enough for the shaman to absorb the full import of his words. "I will tolerate no violence against her or her clinic. Nor will the governor."

"Winston knows?"

"I didn't think it necessary to tell him. I believe the three of us can work this out."

"Three?"

"You and me and the medicine woman."

"It will be as you say."

The Great One stood beside his hut and watched Eagle Mingo leave. Colds winds blew off the mountains, the winds of change.

11

The white witch woman was not afraid of him, even with his face painted.

The old shaman listened to her clear voice telling how she would cure the sick, and watched while the son of Mingo stood beside her, daring with his dark eyes that any harm should come to her. The Great One listened quietly and with respect, as if he intended to give his full cooperation.

"I want to work with you," Kate Malone said, "not against you."

And then she told of her experience in the big hospitals of the East and showed her degrees, hanging on the wall of the clinic that stunk of fresh paint. The shaman kept his face still. What did any of her credentials matter? She knew nothing of the *sinti abeka* that sets the stomach out of order nor the *iyaganaca abeka* that sends the patient out of his head and falling to the ground. And what could she, the white woman who spoke with the soft cadences of the South, know of the burning ghost disease, the *colop anatitci abeka*, that makes the feet swell and big blisters develop?

Filled with spiritous liquors, the medicine man listened, and listening, he dreamed. He dreamed of great

waters filled with terrible evil, and of the anguish of
women that rose up like birds scared from their nests.

In the midst of his dreams another woman entered
the clinic, breathless in her haste.

"Hal has run away ..." she said, not even noticing
the Great One. "He left this awful note." With her short,
terrible hair quivering like porcupine quills, the distraught young woman began to read. " 'Everybody in
Witch Dance can go straight to hell. When I come back
you'll all be sorry.' " Tears streamed down her face.
"What am I going to do? I *knew* something was wrong
... how can I ever tell Father?"

"Everything is going to be all right, Deborah," Kate
said.

"Come. I'll help you." Eagle took her arm and guided
her into one of the back rooms, but not before the Great
One had another vision.

Blood. So much blood, running red over the snow.

"Can I count on your cooperation?" Kate was asking.

"Practice your medicine with my blessing."

He left with the visions still swirling through his
head. There would be no further need for him to fight
Kate Malone. Not even his blessings could save her
from the dark course of fate.

12

Martha had left the invitation open on the hall table, where she knew Mick was bound to see it. She sat in the rocker on the sun porch with her hands folded in her lap and tried not to twitch as he walked in.

"Did you have a good day, dear?"

He loosened his tie and reached for the glass of lemonade she had waiting for him on the wicker table.

"That's a foolish question, Martha. It's hotter than hell out there. How could anybody have a good time in hell?"

I could, she wanted to reply. *If only you loved me.*

She didn't say that, of course. What good would it do? It would only stir up Mick's temper, and she was about to stir it up anyway, so why spoil the next few minutes?

"Glen Ellison called you about that new power plant—"

"Solid rocket booster plant, Martha. If you're going to tell something, get it right." Mick set his glass down so hard, the ice rattled. "Now I guess I'll have to spend all evening jawing with him on the damned telephone."

Martha's heart came up in her throat. Kate used to laugh when she'd say that.

"My heart's in my throat," she'd say.

"That's physically impossible, Mother," Katie would reply, laughing.

Oh, dear merciful Father. Her Katie.

Martha swallowed so her heart went back down to its rightful place. She had to be brave just this once for her Katie.

"Did you see the invitation on the hall table?" She sounded like a timid gray mouse. No wonder Mick no longer loved her.

"What invitation?"

She could tell by the way his face mottled that he was lying. He'd read Kate's invitation, just as he read all her letters when he thought nobody was looking.

Deep down, her Michael Malone was a wonderful man. Long ago, right after the boys died, and later after Katie left for medical school, Martha would plan how she would leave him. She wouldn't take a thing except the clothes on her back and enough money to get as far as her folks in Virginia.

She wouldn't even take the car, but would go on the bus, being frugal. She even planned what she'd say to him in her good-bye letter.

Dear Mick, I love you fiercely. Always have and always will. But I can't stand to live in this lonely prison you've shut me up in.

She never wrote the letter, of course, partially because she didn't want to leave behind as her last testament a sentence ending with a preposition. But mostly because she knew that deep, deep down Mick was a wonderful man.

"It's an invitation to the open house of her clinic in Witch Dance." She spoke all in a rush before she could lose her courage. "I've planned how we can go. Matilda can water the plants when she comes to clean, and Jim can take care of your insurance clients"—Mick looked like a peach pit with his face all bunched up and turning red—"that is, if you have any scheduled . . . not that

I would try to run your business . . ." Her voice trailed off, and she twisted her hands together.

Fidgeting. Knowing how Mick hated it.

"Hellfire and damnation." He leapt up so fast, his chair fell back against the polished Mexican tiles. "As if I didn't have enough to do without running off to some godforsaken land to sip tea with savages."

He left the room so fast that the soles of his shoes left scuff marks on the tiles. Martha stared at the black marks for a while.

Finally she got up to fetch a scrub brush and some good floor cleaner. Bent on her knees, she felt like a scrub woman . . . or a suppliant at early Mass.

She'd never wanted Mexican tiles in the first place.

13

The invitation lay open on Winston's desk.

Not wanting to think about all the ramifications of that simple piece of paper, he surveyed his office. Some governors in the past had opted for fine furnishings and rich appointments, but Winston had surrounded himself with simple things—a plain oak desk, neither fancy nor expensive, and the most basic, functional chairs.

Why should he sit in the lap of luxury while most of his people contented themselves with the basics? Basics were good enough for any man.

He picked up the invitation. It was a simple printed card, not engraved, not ostentatious, nothing that would call attention to the fact that Kate Malone was Virginia blueblood on her mother's side and the daughter of a fighting Irish senator.

The invitation was visible evidence that she was a smart woman. But then, Winston already knew that.

How else could she have held his eldest son enthralled for the better part of the summer?

"The Honorable Governor and Mrs. Winston Mingo," the card said.

Dovie wouldn't go, of course. He'd take the card home and show it to her, but she would ignore it as she'd chosen to ignore Eagle's involvement with the medicine woman all summer.

Once Winston had tried to talk to her about it, at the beginning of the summer, when the whole thing happened, when it was evident that Eagle had more on his mind than sleeping under the stars.

"Do you remember that summer I worked on a rig off the shore of Louisiana, Dovie?"

"I remember everything you ever did, Winston Mingo, including that business with the girl."

"Charlsie was her name, a lively, honeyed-talking, confection of a girl. She almost made me forget who I was. I never knew why except that there was a slow, sweet wildness in her. Do you suppose that's what has Eagle enthralled, that Kate Malone is wild at heart?"

"I suppose that you should feed the dog. And on your way out, water the petunias by the back door. If we don't get some rain soon, they're all going to die."

Remembering, Winston drummed his fingers on the invitation. No, Dovie would not go.

Would he?

He stuffed the invitation in the top drawer of his desk and walked toward the window. Halfway there, he reeled. Steadying himself on the edge of the bookshelves, he held on until his equilibrium returned.

A little dizzy spell. Probably inner-ear trouble. Dovie kept telling him that he was going to have to see a doctor.

There was no putting anything past Dovie. She knew everything . . . except what had happened the night before. As he lay beside her in their cherrywood double bed, he heard the owl call his name.

Boston

"If you go back to Witch Dance, you need not bother coming home. Ever again."

Melissa Sayers Colbert quivered with rage. Clayton

stood at the window with his back to her, rigid. Between them, the invitation lay on the table like an accusation.

"I won't have it," she continued. "Do you hear me, Clayton?"

"I hear you, Melissa." He didn't even turn around.

With her fists clenched, she wanted to scream. And then she realized she was already screaming, yelling like some common wife off the back streets of Boston. She forced herself to unclench her fists and take a moderate tone.

"Kate Malone used you to get what she wants, and now that she has it, do you think she's going to look twice at you?" Melissa hated the way he bowed his head, like a broken man. Where was the man she used to love, the sexy, spirited man who could do anything? The man she *still* loved?

"Please, Clayton . . . look at me." He turned slowly, still hunched over in his defeat. "Am I not enough for you?"

"Melissa . . . don't."

"You used to say you couldn't get enough of me . . . of this." She ripped aside her blouse. Buttons rolled onto the Oriental rug and the sound of tearing silk rent the silence. Her fingernails scored her tender skin as she grabbed her bra. It was nothing more than a delicate bit of lace, and it tore easily. Her breasts, still lush, swung free, the nipples proudly pointed.

She wet her fingers with her tongue and ran them around her nipples.

"For God's sake, Melissa . . ." Clayton jerked up her torn blouse and moved to cover her.

"Not this time, Clayton." She shoved his hands aside. "I won't let Kate Malone come between us this time."

Quickly, she knelt in front of him and opened his zipper. He was flaccid, but that didn't deter Melissa. She knew exactly what to do, exactly what he liked.

"Stop, Melissa . . . please. You're only humiliating us both."

She raked the tips of her long red fingernails over his

sensitive flesh. Power surged through her as he began to pulse in her hand.

Clayton tried to regain control, but his body betrayed him. Defeated, he stood in his richly appointed study in his fancy house and looked down at the top of his wife's head. Her mouth was warm and wet, and she made soft, catlike sounds of satisfaction.

A half-breed at stud. Bought and paid for with Melissa's money. Rage and semen spewed from him.

With the easy grace of a tigress she rose to face him. Even with her lipstick smeared she was very much in control.

"Did you think I'd let her win, Clayton?"

She didn't even pick up her torn clothes when she left the room. Rigid, Clayton stood in the wreckage, afraid to move lest he shatter.

There were no sounds in the house except the ticking of a clock that had belonged to the first Sayers to set foot in New England, and even that sound was discreet, as befitted anything connected to the Sayers name.

Without bothering to zip his pants, Clayton picked up the invitation and went to the Louis XIV desk. Sun poured through the French doors and warmed his cold skin.

He ran his hands across the invitation. The words blurred. Witch Dance Clinic. Dr. Kate Malone.

He closed his eyes, envisioning her bright hair and the intoxicating smell of her skin. Dr. Kate Malone, *his* Kate, with her future still before her.

Still clutching the invitation, he reached into the top right hand drawer of his desk. His fingers closed around the cold steel.

With slow deliberation he laid the gun on top of the desk.

"Nobody's coming."

"I'm here, Kate."

She was standing in the doorway of the clinic, looking at the empty road. Not a speck of dust marred the horizon. With Deborah's help she'd mailed a hundred invitations, and not a soul had come to the open house except Eagle.

She felt his hands on her shoulders. Gently but firmly he turned her around.

"What do you see?" he asked.

"A flower garden, thanks to you."

He had brought dozens of flowers, roses of every color and even white ginger, shipped from Hawaii. It was the closest thing to jasmine he could find, he'd said, knowing her love for the waxy, fragrant flower of the Deep South. Her mother had sent flowers too—purple violets with yellow throats—and had signed both their names, Mick and Martha. Dr. Colbert sent orchids, and Deborah had come early, while her father was still asleep, and brought a bouquet of Indian paintbrush she'd picked on the hillside. It was in a prominent place in the reception room.

A reception room without a receptionist. A clinic without patients. If she let herself, Kate could go into a blue funk.

"What else do you see?"

"Ice cream melting in paper cups I went all the way to Ada for, and cookies I burned with my own two hands in the oven from hell."

"Kate . . . Kate . . . what am I going to do with you?" Laughing, he hugged her hard. "You have a building you never thought would be finished, the most up-to-date equipment money can buy, a fine medical degree, and more grit than a grizzly bear. Eventually people will come to you for healing, Kate. Trust me."

"Oh, God, Eagle." She wrapped her arms around his chest and was suddenly bawling like a newborn baby.

"You're the best friend I've ever had . . . the *only* friend I have besides Deborah."

He held her close, rocking her in the cradle of his arms. His beautiful, passionate Kate. The woman his people shunned.

Didn't they know? Couldn't they see? Kate's clinic was the kind of progress needed in Witch Dance. Eagle believed in preserving the culture of his people, believed passionately, but he also understood that the little village would eventually die if it refused to move forward at all.

He smoothed her hair from her forehead and dried her tears with the tips of his fingers. His skin absorbed her tears, and he felt them in his own heart.

"They will come to accept you in time, Kate."

"How can you say that? After all they've done?"

"Good. Your spunk is back. Fight, Dr. Kate Malone. Fight for what you believe in."

"Is that what you do? Fight for what you believe in?" He tightened his hold while his silence screamed through the room. Kate pushed back the fear that threatened to defeat her. "I believe in you, Eagle Mingo, in the courage and wisdom of the man who defied his own people to help me build this clinic, in the essential goodness of the man who helped Deborah Lightfoot and her father face Hal's disappearance." She cupped his face and drew it close. "And I believe in us . . . in you and me together . . . on your blanket under the stars. . . ."

As he drew her hips into his, he wondered if there would ever be a time when Kate Malone would not bewitch him.

"How about on your examining table in your clinic, Dr. Malone? Don't you think it deserves a proper christening?"

"Eagle." With her hands tangled in his hair and her lips inches from his, she breathed his name.

Already they were flying.

* * *

Winston Mingo saw them through the window, his son with the white medicine woman. The fears he'd held at bay all summer came crashing around him. There was no mistaking that look.

Dr. Kate Malone was more to Eagle than a passing fancy, more than a summer affair. If he told Dovie, it would break her heart. And Cole . . .

Now Winston understood his son's concern, his anger. With trembling hands he opened the door and went inside. Without knocking. It was an open house, wasn't it?

The bells over the door tinkled, and Kate and his son moved apart. Without hurry. Without guilt.

Somehow that made Winston proud.

"I'm glad you came," Eagle told him. "Kate, this is my father, Winston Mingo."

"Governor, you honor me."

"Just Winston." Dovie would kill him. He might not tell her. "You have a fine clinic here, Dr. Malone."

"Just Kate, please." She smiled at him.

Kate Malone had everything his son admired—grace, courage, intelligence. And she was the most beautiful woman Winston had ever seen. Dovie would flail him alive for that too.

"Would you like a tour of the clinic?" she asked.

She showed him the modern equipment and talked enthusiastically about the need for accessible health care in Witch Dance.

"Will you stay with us, Kate?" he asked.

"Do you mean, am I committed or am I just passing through?"

"Yes."

"Eagle asked me that the day we met." Winston didn't miss the look that passed between them. "Yes, Governor, I'm here to stay."

Seeing the proud tilt of her head and the stubborn set of her chin, Winston never doubted for a minute that she would keep her word. A man could do worse than have grandchildren from such a woman.

Winston stayed for punch and cookies. And in that time, not a single person came through the door. He thought of the old medicine man who shook his gourds and waved his turkey feathers over the sick. He thought of all his people who had died because they refused to travel to Ada to the modern facilities there.

Eagle was right: There should be a way to blend the old ways with the new. When Winston took his leave, he had a new mission in mind, one he would carry through as quickly as possible . . . if he were not weighed on the path and found light.

The clinic bell was still ringing from Winston's exit when Eagle locked the door.

"Closed for the day," he said, reaching for Kate.

The sweet madness overtook them, and they reeled against the walls and rolled on the floor. Eagle's voice lifted and soared with the dark beauty of his native tongue. Impaled by him, impaled and dying the bright, exquisite death of passion, Kate knew that she would never hear his voice without wanting him.

"You will come to me tonight," he said even as they still lay tangled together.

"You could stay with me." *Forever*, she thought, pulling his face down to her aching breasts.

"The nights will soon be too cool to sleep under the stars."

"Will we sleep?" she said, laughing.

"Only if you wish."

He took her nipple deep into his mouth and began to move in her once more, and she knew that she would go to him, galloping through the night on Mahli, flying to him on the wind.

The first thing Kate heard when she returned from Eagle's campsite was the sound of the phone, ringing and ringing in the cold half-light of early morning. She drew Mahli to a halt, dismounted, and patted her neck.

"Wait here, old girl."

There was no need to tie the mare. Eagle had trained her well.

Kate took the steps at a run, the sound of the telephone setting her nerves jangling.

"Hello," she said, breathless. She placed her hand over her pounding heart.

The woman at the other end of the line was crying. "Kate, you have to come to Boston. Something terrible has happened. Clayton . . ."

The line went dead. Kate jiggled the receiver.

"What? Who is this?"

Her only answer was silence.

14

"Don't expect too much, Kate."

Exhausted from her long flight across the country, Kate stood in the hospital corridor and listened to Dr. Wayne Epsmith's report on Dr. Clayton Colbert.

"The bullet went in close to the heart. We've done what we can to repair the damage, but . . ." Wayne Epsmith shook his head.

"Is he going to die?"

"With this kind of damage, the odds are not in his favor, Kate. You know that."

As a doctor, she did. As Clayton Colbert's friend, she didn't want to know. She wanted to sit by his bedside and hold his slack hand and watch the machines do his breathing and hope that tomorrow everything would be better.

She wanted to believe in miracles.

"I'm sorry, Kate." Dr. Epsmith put his hand on Kate's shoulder. "I know how much Clayton meant to you."

He used the past tense. As if the bullet had already done its job.

She couldn't even say thank you for fear of breaking down. Her eyes were red and puffy, for she'd cried all the way from Oklahoma to the Hudson River. She'd barely been able to get from Logan Airport in one piece.

Inside the ICU cubicle, Clayton lay against the pillows, his face drained of the rich copper tints of his heritage. Kate stood silently by his side, not yet willing to make her presence known, wishing she could spare him this final humiliation: Her golden idol had turned to clay. The man she respected and revered above all others, the doctor who had taught her to save lives, had tried to take his own.

The previous night after the line had gone dead, she'd tried frantically to reach him. She called his house and got no answer. Then she called the hospital, expecting him to be on duty, expecting him to laugh and say the phone call was a sick prank.

Instead, she talked to Melissa Sayers Colbert. "He's asking for you, Kate. He keeps calling your name, over and over."

"Why? Why did he do it?"

"Because he loved"—Melissa became hysterical, sobbing and keening into the phone. Kate hung on to the receiver, her knuckles turning white—"me. It was me he loved. Clayton loved me."

"Of course he did, Mrs. Colbert. He always spoke of you in glowing terms."

"He did?"

"Yes. Always."

Now, looking down at his pale face, Kate whispered, "Why, Dr. Colbert? Why?"

His eyelids fluttered open. One hand lifted feebly toward her as he tried to focus his eyes.

"Ka—"

"Shhh. Don't talk. I'm here." She took his hand, scared by the cool, boneless feel of it.

He closed his eyes once more, and his chest heaved with his shallow breathing.

"I talked with your wife," Kate said. "She's right outside in the waiting room. She hasn't left your side since they brought you in." *Why? Why?*

"The . . . clinic . . ."

"It's wonderful. We had a beautiful open house." *Just the two of us, three counting the governor.*

"The house . . ."

"Don't worry about the house. I'm not much of a housekeeper, as you well know, but it's still in passable condition. I'll go on a real cleaning spree when I get home; then, when you come back to Witch Dance, that house will shine from top to bottom."

Clayton Colbert was dying, and she couldn't seem to stop her meaningless chatter. She was a doctor. She'd have to get used to death.

Brian and Charles floating away in the water came to her mind. *No.* She'd never get used to death.

"They're . . . yours, Kate. My will . . ." Clayton felt himself drifting away. He couldn't go. Not yet. He clung to Kate's hand. It was warm and full of strength. If he could just hang on, her energy would flow through him. "I want you . . ."

"Please, Dr. Colbert . . ."

". . . to have them."

Silent tears flowed down her cheeks, and Clayton knew: Kate loved him, loved him in the purest, most beautiful way.

He didn't have to die after all.

Melissa came in and kissed him. Her lips felt dry and cold. Beyond his wife's head he saw Kate, his beautiful Kate with hair like a halo.

"I love you," he said, but she didn't seem to hear.

"Flat line," someone said. Melissa flung herself across his chest, but he didn't feel a thing. He was already floating, floating toward the light that was as bright as his Kate's hair.

Melissa Sayers Colbert stood beside the open grave, watching Clayton being lowered into the ground, wretched and broken in her grief, holding tightly to the hand of the woman standing beside her. Leaves fluttered down from the oak tree and landed, golden, on the casket.

"Dr. Colbert would have liked that," Kate Malone murmured. "He always found beauty in nature."

Melissa didn't know. There were many things she
hadn't known about her husband, things she'd learned
from the woman beside her. Kate Malone.

Her nemesis. Her comforter.

He would have liked being buried in Witch Dance
with Muskogean words spoken for him, Kate had said,
but Melissa couldn't bear the thought of having him so
far away. She had to take comfort where she could get
it, and the familiar words of the Episcopal priest made
the sight of Clayton's bronze casket disappearing into
the dark hole bearable.

Keening in her agony, Melissa flung herself outward,
toward the grave. Kate's hands stayed her. Kate's arms
sustained her.

"Everything is going to be all right. Shhh ... everything is going to be all right."

But it wasn't. She'd killed her husband. She knew that
as surely as if she'd pulled the trigger. The scene in the
study replayed itself—Clayton with his head bowed, defeated, and she, oblivious of his pain, taking her pleasure any way she could get it.

"No," she whispered. "No."

Nothing in her life would ever be all right again.
Clayton was gone from her forever.

Without knowing she was in the arena, Kate Malone
had won. And even that didn't matter anymore.

"Will you take me home?" Melissa sounded as old
and tired as she felt. "I want to hear about Witch Dance.
I want to know what Clayton had for breakfast and
whether he read the paper in the morning or at night. I
want to know what he did when he was walking the
land, what he said, how he looked, how he acted. I want
to know everything about him." Oh, the wasted
months. The wasted years when she'd stayed behind in
Boston while he was roaming carefree over the land he
loved. "Make him live for me again, Kate ... please."

Kate took Dr. Colbert's widow to their Beacon Hill
house and told her every moment of Clayton's last summer. In doing so, she relived her own summer, the soar-

ing beauty of the land and the scorching passion of
Eagle Mingo. It all rolled over her like the tide, with the
same force, the same inevitability. The deep velvet
nights with the stars hanging so low, they burned the
skin. The muted mornings, as soft as pastel gowns,
stitched and laced and beaded with love rituals. The
thunder of horses' hooves in the bright indigo days with
the two of them racing along the river while the call of
the winged ones echoed off the hills.

Her summer had a name, and its name was love.

Wrapping her arms around herself, wishing they were
Eagle's arms, she leaned toward the fire. Melissa's voice
was nothing more than a muted counterpoint to her
thoughts.

Love. She was in love with Eagle Mingo.

Had he found her note on the clinic door? Did he
miss her as terribly as she missed him? Did he want her
as desperately?

"Clayton had a deep tribal affinity," Melissa was saying. "I guess I never realized that."

Kate knew someone else whose tribal affinity was even
stronger, someone whose very being shouted *Chickasaw*.

"I tried to make him over," Melissa continued. "I tried
to make him forget everything he ever believed in, everything that was Chickasaw."

Shivers skittered along Kate's spine. Could Eagle ever
forget he was a full-blood?

"In the end, I think that's what killed him. He could
never buy back the dignity I took away." Melissa covered
her face with her hands and began to sob. "If I could have
him back for one more day, one more hour . . ."

Speaking soothing words, Kate gave her hot tea and a
sedative and put her to bed. Then, exhausted both physically and emotionally, she leaned against the bedroom
door and closed her eyes. She needed about twelve
hours sleep and then a week to absorb all that had happened. But one need overrode all others: to see Eagle
and tell him she loved him.

15

Witch Dance

Winston couldn't find his way through the snowstorm. He kept stumbling and falling, and the wind was taking his breath away. An avalanche started high in the mountains and tumbled downward with terrifying speed. He took the full blow on his head.

"Winston ... Winston ..." Dovie was calling him from far away. "Wake up, honey. You're having a nightmare."

He struggled to sit up, and the avalanche knocked him back to the pillows.

"Winston!" Dovie's scream brought Wolf and Star running. "Call Cole," she yelled, jerking on her robe and slippers. "Find Eagle."

"What's the matter?" Wolf said.

"Something horrible is happening to your father."

Ada

The entire family gathered around Winston's hospital bed. That was the way he wanted it. IV tubes were hooked into his arms, and the left side of his face was drawn from the stroke, but he could still talk. Barely. And he still had his wits, or so the doctors said.

"You were lucky, Winston. Your cognitive abilities are still intact."

He'd need them for what he was about to do.

"My people are now without a leader." His speech was excruciatingly slow and slurred, but they all seemed to understand. Dovie squeezed his right hand, and he squeezed back. She understood what he was going to do. Many a night they'd lain side by side in their big bed discussing this very thing: the transfer of the Mingo mantle of duty.

"You'll be back in no time." Cole's eyes betrayed his lie. "A little medicine, a little therapy, and you'll be back in the governor's office, giving us all hell."

Mingo released Dovie and raised his hand for silence.

Star tried to muffle her sobs, and Wolf tried to look grown-up. His younger children were scared, but he wasn't about to give up and let them be without a father. No, he wasn't going to die, at least not anytime soon if the doctors could be trusted, but neither was he going to recover. Not entirely. Part of him was gone forever, the physical and emotional strength that would allow him to lead his nation.

"My firstborn will take my place." His eldest son's face was impassive. That was good. A leader's thoughts should not be discerned merely by the expression on his face.

Winston closed his eyes for a moment, gathering his strength. He had to get everything said now, in case the doctors were wrong.

"Both my oldest sons have great qualities, but only one of them will lead this nation." He held out his hand, palm up. "Eagle."

Cole's wife put her hand over his arm, and he smiled at her.

"It was fated from the beginning, Anna," Cole said.

An expectant hush fell on the room, and all eyes turned toward Eagle. With the perfect stillness in his face that Winston knew would soon become a trademark, Eagle moved toward the bed. Only his eyes betrayed his thoughts, his glittering, tragic eyes.

He took his father's hand, and in the ancient tongue of his people he accepted the terrible mantle of duty.

"It shall be as you wish. I am Eagle Mingo with the blood of my Chickasaw fathers for generations back to the great chieftain Piomingo flowing through my veins. I will serve my people and my nation with honor. And I will never waver in my duties."

Winston closed his eyes. He could rest now. The transfer of power was complete.

Eagle knew she would come to him beside the river. And so he waited, waited beside the mystical fire, letting the new gold of autumn leaves and the hurried rush of the river transfuse his soul.

He saw the white mare coming from a great distance. And when the moon showed its face from behind the cloud, he saw her hair, luminous as the flames warming his skin.

Naked, he stood with his arms outstretched. And she came to them without words, without preliminaries.

He held her with his hands pressed against the flat of her back and her curves fitted softly against his body. The night wind blew her hair against his cheek and her skirts against his leg. The look, the feel, the taste of her seeped through his skin and into his blood, and he knew that she was a part of him, would always be a part of him.

In that crystal moment he would have traded his soul to be with her forever.

He kissed her softly, as if it were the first kiss in creation, too new to be treated with anything except gentleness. And when she began to hum deep in her throat, he devoured her with lips and teeth and tongue.

"I couldn't wait to get back to you," she whispered. "I couldn't wait . . ."

Kate stepped out of her dress, and as it fell in a soft heap at her feet, the ceremonial leavetaking he'd

planned flew from his mind, borne away on the winds
of passion that swept over him. He took her down to his
blanket, and surrounded by her burning flesh he made
love in a firestorm of emotion, heaving against her with
a silent intensity that sought to obliterate everything in
the universe except their two bodies, melded and slick
and desperate.

The moon turned her skin to silver and the glow of
her entered into him, bone, sinew, and blood; and he
knew that as long as he lived, the memories of this
night would live too, a shining, untouchable core that
was Kate Malone.

Beside them, the river sang its timeless song and their
horses whinnied softly. Father Sky withheld his chilling
breezes, sending instead the warm breath of Indian
summer.

Eagle covered her until they lay at last with arms and
legs entwined, temporarily sated. He laced her fingers
tightly with his, and pressed their joined hands against
his heart. His pain leapt upward and outward, bearing
its unspeakable ugliness toward Kate so that she turned
to him, uneasy and not understanding why.

"Eagle?"

Her eyes were the color of the sea under storm, and
he knew that he would never again see them changing
as the seasons do, from the bright emerald of laughter
to the smoky gray of fear.

Silently he called upon the four Beloved Things
Above to give him comfort, but they hid their faces
from him and would not be found.

"Shhh." He touched her lips with his. "Now is not the
time for talking."

Now was the time for saying good-bye.

Eagle left the blanket. In his tent were two large sea-
shells and the feather of an eagle. Taking Kate gently by
the arms, he positioned her, kneeling, upon his blanket.

"Waka ahina uno, iskunosi Wictonaye." Facing her, he
knelt and cupped her face. *"Waka."*

"Oh, yes ..." She threaded her fingers in his hair. "Yes, my golden Eagle."

"Sexual fire is the magic of life," he said as he kindled a miniature fire in the largest seashell. "All the powers of the universe come together to create this magic, just as you and I will come together."

With the feather of his namesake he fanned the purifying smoke over their bodies. It curled around her thighs and drifted upward, ever upward, taking with it the power of the fire and the power of the eagle.

Kate's body went slack, and she reached for him. He caught her hands and held them tightly.

"A while yet, *Wictonaye*. This must be done with ceremony."

Sudden understanding made her weak. Braced against his hands, she leaned forward. Through the veil of smoke his face was unreadable, but nothing could hide the torment in his eyes.

"This is good-bye, isn't it, Eagle?"

"This is good-bye."

Kate held him fast. It was far, far too late for running away.

"Why?"

"While you were gone my father had a stroke."

She bit her lower lip to still her cry of despair.

"I am the oldest son, the chosen one." The smoke could not obscure the mark of the eagle on his thigh. "I will lead my people."

Love for him beat against her heart like tides seeking the shore, but she kept her feelings inside. From the beginning she'd known that Eagle could never belong to her.

"We had our summer, Eagle." His eyes burned into hers, and the smell of smoke became overwhelming. All the powers of the universe melded into a single explosion of sexual fire.

Kate and Eagle came together with such force that all the prairie became silent with awe. Even the winds stopped to watch and listen. In the dead calm there were no sounds except the anguished murmur of Mus-kogean. And when there were finally no ways left to say good-bye, the chosen one and his *Wictonaye* filled the night with their shattered cries.

They lay silent against each other, heaving. At last Eagle raised himself up and dipped the feather into the second seashell. The smell of lavender filled the air.

Kate didn't move as he caressed her body with the feather. The fragrant water beaded her nipples and pooled in the indentation of her navel. Shivers skittered along her skin when he touched the cool, wet feather between her thighs.

Their gazes locked, held.

"If you would say to me, 'Stay,' I would give up everything for you, Kate. Everything."

"How do you know I won't, Eagle? How do you know I won't get on my knees and beg you to stay?"

The feather brushed the blue-veined skin inside her thighs and behind her knees and in the arch of her foot. Sexual fires rekindled in Kate, but she held them inside.

"Because I know you, Kate. You're too proud to beg."

With Eagle bending over her, golden and delicious, and the scent of pheromones and lavender filling the air, Kate almost proved him wrong. In one graceful movement she stood to face him. Lifting her hair with one hand, she arched her back, offering her sweet wet juices to him.

"Not too proud for one last good-bye," she whispered.

He bracketed her hips, pulling her to him. The night was deep and watchful as he bade her a final farewell. When it was over, she knelt beside him, and, dipping the eagle feather into the lavender water, she cleansed his lips.

Her hand trembled when she laid the feather aside. That small weakness was the only one she'd allow herself.

"Good-bye, Eagle."

"Take Mahli, Kate. She's yours."

Three months earlier she would have refused the extravagant gift, but her summer among the Chickasaws had taught her that gifts were not to be rebuffed.

"I'll take good care of her, Eagle."

"She'll be receptive soon. I will breed her to the black. All I ask is for her colt."

"Of course. When Mahli is ready, I'll bring her to you." She took a small step back, severing herself from him by degrees. Already his face was a mask. Even his eyes were unreadable. The fire was gone from them, and they were as deep and black as the bottom of the sea.

Needing one last contact, she touched his lips lightly.

"You will be a great leader, Eagle Mingo."

"And you will be a great doctor, Kate Malone."

His warm skin made her fingers tingle, and she curled her hand into a fist as if she could capture a part of him and take it with her. Her dress lay upon his blanket, crushed and wrinkled.

Eagle's gaze never left her as she stepped into her clothes. She made herself walk away slowly, made herself ride away with dignity. Only when she was out of his sight did she set Mahli into a gallop. The wind caught her tears and flung them like dewdrops onto the prairie grasses.

At the campsite, Eagle walked down to the Blue River, and when he stood on the water's edge he lifted his fists to the sky and renounced Loak-Ishtohoollo-Aba.

16

By the time she reached home, Kate's dignity had begun to unravel. She brushed Mahli down and put her in the stable, then went into her house.

There was nothing to greet her except emptiness. The fire she'd lit when she got in from the airport was still glowing. In happier times Dr. Colbert would have been waiting for her with a cup of hot tea.

Maybe tea would make her feel better. She went into the kitchen, put the water on, and found a tea bag. Would tea cure unrequited love?

Oh, the big dreams she'd had flying home to Witch Dance. The kitchen blurred.

"Damn you, Eagle Mingo, I won't cry." The teakettle whistled, and Kate reached for her cup. Why hadn't he fought for her? What was so almighty important about being a full-blood? The cup slipped from her hand and crashed onto the kitchen floor.

Everything in her life was broken—her dreams, her family ties, her teacup. Reaching into the cabinet, she grabbed another cup.

"Why?" she yelled. "Why?" With one mighty burst she sent the cup flying across the kitchen. It crashed with a satisfying smack against the wall.

Katie Elizabeth, you're going to have to watch your temper.

Her father had said that to her when she was only five years old. Three little boys had come home with her from kindergarten, had eaten her cookies and played with her cat, and then they hadn't let her be a cowboy.

"Girls can't be cowboys," the biggest one had said. Larry Joe Higgens was his name, and Kate didn't like him to this day.

She'd put her hands on her hips and blessed him out, using every word she'd ever heard her father say. "Damnhell you, Larry Joe. Shitfart to good damnhell."

Big Mick Malone had taken her on his knee and chastised her for losing her temper. Then he'd kissed her curls and said she could be a cowboy; she could be anything she wanted to be.

Oh, Kate *did* miss her father.

She stepped through the shards of china and reached for the telephone. Her mother answered on the second ring.

"Katie? It's so good to hear from you."

"How are you, Mother?"

"Fine, just fine." When had Martha Malone ever admitted to anything else? "How are things with you?"

"I've had better days."

"Anything I can do, honey?"

Yes. You can kiss the hurt and make it go away.

"No ... it's just my period coming on. ... Is Daddy there?"

"He's ... I don't know. ... Let me check, okay?"

Kate heard Martha's footsteps tapping lightly against the wooden floor. It would be polished to a high sheen and smelling of lemon wax. Sun spilling through the beveled glass door would be casting a rainbow on the wall.

Suddenly homesick, Kate sank to the floor and cradled the phone against her shoulder.

"Who is it?" she heard her father shout. There was murmuring in the background, then Martha came back to the phone.

"He's not home yet ..." Martha's voice dropped to a whisper. "I'm sorry, Katie."

"Me too, Mother."

"Do you want me to tell him anything for you when he gets home?"

"No. Nothing."

What was there left to say? They'd said it all the day she'd left Charleston.

Kate got the broom and dustpan and cleaned up the mess in the kitchen.

She wished it were that easy to clean up the mess in her life.

Leaves fell from the trees and lay on the ground like colored confetti. Winds buffeted the wooden sign against the sides of the clinic.

Dressed in her white lab coat, Kate stood at the window, looking out. Even the watchers on the hill would have been a welcome relief from the tedium of emptiness.

Two weeks and no one had come. Her father had been right: She should have stayed in South Carolina with her own people.

But no, she had to do it her way. She had the stubborn Malone pride. And look where it had gotten her. She'd lost her father, her practice, her best friend ... and Eagle.

She pressed her hands to her temple. She couldn't bear to think of Eagle.

Dust rose from the road, and Kate strained her eyes into the distance. The car slowed as it approached the clinic. At last she was going to have a patient.

Kate grabbed her stethoscope and hung it around her neck, then stood waiting. The car came almost to a halt. An old Indian man leaned out the window and yelled something she couldn't hear; then the car picked up speed once more, moving away from her as fast as it could.

She stood at the window awhile longer, rigid with

shock and anger; then she flung her coat off, not caring that it landed on the floor. The packing boxes she'd used to move her equipment into the clinic were still in the back room. She ripped her blouse getting to them. Possessed of self-righteous fury, she jerked medical textbooks out of the bookshelves and flung them into boxes.

Sweat dampened her blouse and the edges of her hair.

"Kate?" Deborah stood in the doorway. Kate hadn't even heard her come in. "What are you doing?"

"I'm leaving."

"Leaving?" Deborah raced across the room and clutched her arm. "You can't leave. We need you."

"The people here don't need me, Deborah. They want nothing to do with me."

"*I* need you, Kate."

Quick guilt slashed Kate. She put her hand over Deborah's. "I'm sorry. I see no other way." Turning her back on her friend, she took an armload of books off the shelves and dumped them into a box.

Deborah watched quietly for a while, then she jerked books out of the boxes and began putting them back into shelves.

"You built this clinic in spite of what everybody said and did to you, and I'm not going to let you turn tail and run now just because nobody happens to be sick." Color flushed her dark cheeks as she swung on Kate. "Have you ever thought of that? Maybe everybody in Witch Dance is well. Maybe they don't need a doctor right now?"

Tears wet the corners of Deborah's eyes, then streamed down her cheeks. "Hal left and now you're leaving, and I'll be stuck forever at the general store, waiting for somebody to come along and take me away and give me babies."

All the steam went out of Kate. Of course she couldn't leave Witch Dance. The people needed her and she needed them.

"I'm afraid I let my Irish temper get the best of me, Deborah. Help me put these damned books back."

"What do you think I've been doing all this time? Whistling 'Yankee Doodle'?" Wiping her cheeks with the back of her hand, Deborah grinned.

They worked side by side, not talking, not needing to talk. When they had put the clinic back to rights, Kate made tea.

"Have you heard from Hal?" she asked.

"Once. He's working in a garage in Tulsa. They fix racing cars. I wish he'd come home. It's hard at the general store without him."

"You don't have to spend the rest of your life at the general store, Deborah. And you certainly don't have to depend on a man to set you free. Have you ever thought about leaving? I'm sure you could get into one of the good nursing schools. I'd help you prepare."

For a moment Deborah's face was alight with excitement, then she hid her expression over the teacup. "Eagle is very popular with the Tribal Legislature. They say he sometimes addresses them in the ancient tongue."

Kate understood only too well the mesmerizing power of Eagle's ancient tongue.

"All right. You don't want to talk about nursing school." Kate sipped her own tea. "*I* don't want to talk about Eagle."

"You could get him back, Kate. I know you could. They say women in Ada swoon in the streets when he walks by, but he never even looks at them."

"You shouldn't pay attention to the idle gossip of busybodies."

"Oh, pooh. Where's the fun if you can't repeat gossip?" Deborah's hair, grown to chin length, swung when she tossed her head. "Anyhow, someday I'm going to be old with nothing to do but scold my many grandchildren and entertain myself with titillating gossip. If you're not too busy making geriatric love with Eagle Mingo, I'll invite you over to listen."

Kate threw back her head and laughed. It was the first time she'd laughed in two weeks.

* * *

Eagle was building his house near the Blue River. Sitting atop the rafters that would soon be a roof, he could see his summer campsite and hear the river's music. How could a sound soothe and lacerate at the same time?

He worked without his shirt, enjoying the feel of the sun and the autumn breezes on his skin. In the paddock, his black stallion whinnied. A plume of dust on the horizon announced a visitor, arriving on horseback.

Shading his eyes, he watched into the distance. The white mare came into view, and then Kate's flaming hair. With nothing to give him strength except his own resources, he climbed down from the roof and waited.

Kate drew her mount to a halt a few feet from him and nodded her head in greeting. Neither her eyes nor her face betrayed her thoughts.

"Mahli is ready."

"Good. If you'll leave her here for a few days, I'll take you home."

"That won't be necessary. She's in standing heat. Once will be enough."

She dismounted and handed him the bridle, careful that their skin made no contact.

"You can wait in the shade. There's a thermos if you get thirsty."

"No. Mahli is mine. I'll go with you."

"It's not something you'll want to see."

"Don't treat me like a hothouse flower." She shoved her hair off her flushed face. "I'll decide what I should and should not see."

"As you wish."

How polite they were. Like strangers.

They walked side by side to the paddocks, not touching. The air around them was charged. Eagle felt the electric currents on his skin.

"How are things at the clinic?" he asked as if he didn't know, as if he hadn't driven by a dozen times and parked on the hillside to watch and wait.

"Is your inquiry official or personal, Governor?"

"Kate . . ."

"I'm here for one reason, Eagle—so your stallion can cover my mare. Let's get it over with."

His hands tightened on the reins. She wanted to get it over with, did she? He'd be only too glad to oblige.

"Wait here." He left her at the fence railing and led Mahli inside an empty paddock. He didn't dare turn his stallion loose with her until he was safely outside the fence. Already the big black was pawing the air.

Kate leaned over the fence, fascinated.

"Stand back, Kate."

Her quick Irish temper ignited. By all the saints, she was through being told what to do, especially by the man who found her good enough to bed but not good enough to wed.

"You may be governor of the Chickasaws, Eagle Mingo, but as you so clearly told me, I'm not Chickasaw." She tossed her head so that her red hair went flying around her face. "Don't tell me what to do."

"Stand back under your own power or under mine. Take your choice."

"I choose to stand right here."

They struck sparks off each other as their eyes met.

"My stallion is at stud. He'll be dangerous."

"Aren't they all?" She didn't budge an inch.

"You're an exasperating woman, Kate Malone."

Eagle unfastened Mahli's bridle and flung it over the railing, then he vaulted over and lifted Kate off her feet.

"Put me down."

He plunked her down without ceremony a few feet from the fence, but not before he'd paid a terrible price.

"You will stand here, and you will not move any closer." His jaw was clenched hard enough to break teeth.

"Barbarian."

Her chest heaved with anger, and her nipples pushing against the thin fabric of her shirt were hard. It took all his willpower to keep from throwing her onto the ground and taking her as fiercely as his stallion would cover her mare.

"*Wictonaye.*"

"Don't . . ." She held out one hand as if to ward him off.

"You're in no danger from me, Kate, only from my stallion."

He stalked off and let the big black into the paddock. The mare whinnied and exposed herself. Winking, the technique was appropriately called.

And so the mating ritual began.

Eagle stood a few feet apart from Kate, rigid. Every ragged, angry breath she took burned his lungs; every small movement she made jarred his bones.

In the paddock the stallion circled, snorting and sniffing. Mahli pranced, teasing him. Screaming, the stallion mounted, his front hooves flailing the air. Mahli sidestepped, and the stallion bit her neck.

"Stop them." Kate rushed toward Eagle and grabbed his arm. "For God's sake, stop them. He's going to kill her."

"He's holding her in place, Kate. It's natural."

Eagle balled his hands into fists and resisted the urge to cover Kate's hand with his own. She stood beside him, tense, her fingers hot coals upon his skin.

In the paddock, hooves pounded the ground and dust billowed with the fury of the mating. The stallion's triumphant scream went on and on.

"There's nothing natural about it. Stop them."

"No. Not until the stallion's seed is planted."

"If you don't stop them, I will."

He had her in his arms before she'd taken two steps.

"Put me down." She beat her fists against his chest.

"I'm taking you back to the clinic."

"I'll scream."

"Scream. There's no one to hear."

"Damn you, Eagle Mingo."

Her heart beat against his, and the wind blew her soft hair against his cheek. Wide-eyed, she stared at him, her lips slightly parted. He leaned close, so close, her warm, sweet breath mingled with his, so close, their lips were almost touching.

She wet her bottom lip with her tongue, and Eagle died inside. Slowly he set her on her feet.

"I am already damned."

The thunderstorm made her baby restless. Anna pressed her hand over her stomach and felt the hard kicks, as strong as either of her boys. She smiled. Her Mary Doe was going to be a tomboy.

"Are you sure you'll be all right, Anna." Cole hovered anxiously over her. "I don't have to go into Ada."

"Dovie needs you. It's too hard on her to drive Winston home in this rain."

"Eagle can go."

"Eagle needs to finish his house." Anna kissed her husband and shooed him out the door. "This little one is not due for another two weeks. If you're not back by then, I'll send the sheriff after you."

Cole was laughing when he left. Anna was pleased. All of them had much to laugh about these days. Winston was getting about with the aid of a walker; Eagle had forgotten the pale-skinned medicine woman, and soon another little Mingo would be coming into the world.

She went into the kitchen, humming, and began to assemble ingredients for gingerbread. From the den came the sounds of a Bugs Bunny cartoon and her sons' laughter. Anna rolled the dough onto her floured board, then reached under the cabinet for her cookie tin.

A pain doubled her over. She clutched her stomach, groaning. Another pain hit, and she felt the hot sluice of liquid between her thighs. The front of her dress stained red as blood ran down her legs and pooled on the kitchen floor.

"Cole! Cole!" she screamed.

"What is it, Mommy?" Her boys appeared at the door.

When they saw her, their faces crinkled in horror. "Mommy!"

"It's all right," she said, knowing it wasn't. "Run, catch Daddy."

Clint and Bucky raced toward the door, screaming for their father. A small eternity passed before they returned, an eternity in which her baby's secure world was being torn from her body.

"He's gone! Daddy's gone."

The children huddled around her skirts, staring down at the blood.

"What's wrong, Mommy," Clint whined.

"Your baby sister is trying to be born, and she needs you to help her. Bucky, go to the bathroom and get some towels. Clint, help me to your daddy's truck. We're going to Ada."

"How?" he asked, knowing his mother never drove.

"You can shift gears, and I'll hold it in the road."

Blood trailed behind her to the door. So much blood.

Eagle was atop his house, finishing the shingles, when he saw Cole's pickup truck weaving down the road. Alerted, he stood up and shaded his eyes. The truck was going at a snail's pace, veering sharply now.

Cole would never drive in such a manner, and Anna couldn't drive.

Anna.

Hammer and nails went flying as Eagle rushed down the ladder. He had his keys out before his feet touched the ground. The Jaguar burned rubber as he spun out of his driveway.

Cole's truck lurched toward an embankment and teetered there, on the edge. Eagle could see them now, Anna at the wheel with Clint's head close to hers. Bucky hung out the window.

"Anna!" The motor was still running as Eagle leapt from his car and raced toward them.

His brother's truck was awash in blood.

"Help me Eagle." Anna's voice was weak. "I must get to Ada."

Ada was too far. Both Anna and the baby would be dead before they could get there. Forcing back the terror that clawed at his gut, Eagle lifted her from the old truck.

"I'm here, Anna. Don't worry." Cole's boys looked at him like frightened little soldiers. "Bucky, Clint, hop in the back of my car."

They scrambled out of the truck, then sat up on their knees peering over the backseat. Eagle pushed the Jaguar to its maximum speed. Death rode shotgun.

He talked to reassure himself as much as Anna and the boys.

"You've done a good job taking care of your mother. When your little brother gets here . . ."

". . . sister," Anna said.

"When your little sister comes, she'll know how brave her brothers are."

"I b'ave," Bucky said while Clint nodded solemnly.

Blood puddled on the front seat. Eagle pressed the accelerator to the floor.

There was only one person who could help them now.

17

Kate's coffee sat on the edge of her desk getting cold as she wrote a letter to her mother. "Things are going well with me. My clinic has brought modern medicine to Witch Dance, and I expect to make a great contribution to the health and welfare of the Chickasaw Nation."

Lies. All lies.

She laid her pen aside and went to the window. The land was impossibly beautiful with high, clear skies untouched by pollution and tall, strong trees arrayed in as many colors as Joseph's coat. She pressed her forehead against the windowpane. The glass was cool against her skin.

According to Deborah, the old prognosticators were saying the winter would bring many snows. Still, no one said much of anything to Kate. It was almost as if she didn't exist.

She returned to her desk and picked up her pen once more. If she didn't have patients soon, she'd have to leave Witch Dance. Her money wouldn't last forever.

"Kate!"

At the sound of Eagle's voice, she dropped her pen. Something was terribly wrong. Eagle Mingo, the last of the great stoics, never raised his voice.

"*Kate!*" he yelled once more.

And suddenly he was there, standing in the doorway, holding a pregnant woman. Her blood covered his arms.

"Merciful God!" Shock riveted Kate to the floor.

"Help her, Kate."

Mentally she shook herself. If she didn't get a move on, her first patient was going to die. And along with her, the baby.

"This way." She ran ahead of Eagle, already planning how she would do the surgery without assistance. "Hurry. There's no time to lose."

Kate's hands shook as she scrubbed. On the table the woman groaned.

"The children," she whispered.

Two little boys stood in the doorway, clutching each other's hands and watching with rounded eyes.

"Take them out, Eagle," she said, working frantically as she talked. Time was running out. "There are coloring books in the reception room. When you get them settled, come straight back here." She found the vein, and inserted the needle. The woman would be asleep very quickly, and then Kate could save them.

Two lives in her hands. *Brian and Charles.*

No. Mother and baby. She was not in the ocean; she was in her clinic with a patient who had placenta previa.

Sweat poured off Kate's forehead. By all the saints, would she be equal to the task? She lifted her eyes to Eagle's.

"I need you," she whispered.

"I'll be right back."

She was only vaguely aware of his leaving. Time stood still as she worked.

"Don't you worry," she said. "I won't let you die. I *won't.*"

"Kate?"

Eagle stood in the doorway, his eyes and face tragic. "Scrub up, then get in that gown and mask and those gloves." She nodded toward the supply closet. "I'll need you to take the baby."

Thank God, he didn't ask questions.

Who was she, this pregnant woman? And why was Eagle carrying her?

"Her name is Anna Mingo," Eagle said as if he'd read her thoughts. Kate jerked her head toward him.

"My brother's wife," he explained. Over the mask, his eyes held hers.

God would surely strike her dead for the selfish, immoral thoughts she was having even while she tried to save lives.

"I'm going to save your brother's wife ... and his baby."

"I know you will, Kate. Your hands are skilled."

Hell was tame compared to the fires Eagle Mingo kindled. Kate kept her hands and mind functioning, even while her body went up in flames.

"Ready?" she asked.

"Yes."

She lifted the tiny, puckered baby from its mother's womb, and, trembling, held the infant toward Eagle.

"It's a girl," she whispered, unaware of the tears streaming down her face. "A perfect baby girl."

Eagle braced his hands under Kate's, and together they held the tiny miracle, a miracle that might have been theirs.

For a moment man, woman, and child were bonded by magic, and then reality intruded.

"Suction her while I suture the mother," Kate said.

"How?"

"That syringe with the bulb."

They worked side by side until the angry, mewling cry of the newborn rent the silence.

There was no basinet for the latest Mingo except a large box lined with towels. With her patient taken care of, Kate prepared the makeshift basinet, then tenderly cleaned the baby while Eagle held her.

All her maternal instincts came to the fore, and she

cooed softly to the newborn as she swaddled her in a clean towel.

"Yes, my precious, yes." There was tenderness in her voice and wonder in her face as she touched the tiny cheek. "You're a fighter, that's what you are." Kate counted the baby's fingers and inspected her toes. She ran her hands over the tiny rib cage, then lifted her face to Eagle.

"She's perfect," she whispered.

Two shiny tears traced down her cheeks. Aching with love and gratitude, Eagle reached toward Kate's glistening face. She stood in the humming silence, waiting.

To touch her would be to undo everything he'd worked for, everything he believed in. He let his hand drop and pretended to be busy arranging the baby's makeshift blanket.

"Will Anna be all right?"

"She'll be fine." Kate stepped apart, her face a mask of professionalism.

"You saved their lives. The Mingos won't forget you."

Nor would she forget them. Especially Eagle. Always, Eagle.

They put the baby in her box, then called the boys, who immediately fell in love with their baby sister. By the time Anna awoke, Cole had arrived, breathless and terror-stricken.

"You have a daughter, Cole," Anna whispered. "Her name is Mary Doe."

Cole kissed his wife and his baby, then took Kate's hand.

"I'll always be grateful to you."

Standing quietly in a corner, Eagle watched, remembering the sweet burden of the baby and the glow on Kate's face as she counted the tiny toes.

She glanced across the room, then slowly made her way to him.

"Thank you for helping, Eagle," she said.

"Do you need me for anything else, Kate?"

She stood before him like a long-stemmed rose, and

in that fragile crystal moment he hoped she would say, *Yes. Yes, Eagle Mingo. Stay.*

"No, Eagle," she said, as he'd known she would. Kate Malone was too proud to beg. "I don't need you."

The moment shattered with an almost audible tinkle.

Eagle left her quickly, going out the door without saying good-bye. He got into his car and drove away at a terrifying speed, never stopping until he came to the Blue River.

And when he stood on its banks he lifted his clenched fists to the sky.

"*Waka ahina uno, iskunosi Wictonaye,*" he cried. "*Waka.*"

His lonely cries echoed through the hills and came back to him as the howling of a wolf.

With arms outstretched he sank to his knees and hid his face against Mother Earth.

She received his tears, taking them deep into her bosom, where they would transfuse and be sent up to Father Sky. And in the winter when the winds blew cold and the snows piled in drifts over the prairies of Witch Dance, Kate would gaze at the brightest stars in the heavens, never knowing she was seeing the tears of Eagle.

BOOK II
The Witch Dance

Up from the waters rose a serpent, spewing his
  venom over the land,
And neither the hatchet nor the bow nor the cries of
  the people could break his back.
Stars fell from the sky like tears, and the lamentations of
  the women echoed over the land.
Two who were brave defied the death dance and were whirled
  away on the wind.

18

"Can't catch me . . . can't catch me," Bucky chanted as he ran.

"Can too . . . can too." Mary Doe was right behind him.

Nothing ever stopped his little sister. She could do anything a boy could . . . almost.

Bucky glanced over his shoulder. She was gaining on him, and if he didn't do something quickly, she was going to win. Surefooted as a mountain goat, he stepped onto the narrow footlog that crossed Witch Creek.

Mary Doe wouldn't dare follow him, because she was afraid of heights.

Beneath him, the water skipped over the pebbles. Brown leaves and a rusty tin can floated by. And one big fish, belly-up.

Halfway across, Bucky turned to stick out his tongue at Mary Doe.

"You think I'll let that old creek stop me, Bucky Mingo. Watch." Mary Doe rolled up her jeans and waded into the water.

"Mary Doe! Don't."

"I'm not going to let you win."

"Mama said don't play in the water. It's too cold."

"It's not cold . . . see?" Holding her nose, she plunged under.

Bucky felt his heart sink. Mary Doe was sure to win now. She could swim like a fish.

He ran as hard as he could across the log, but Mary Doe got to the other side first. She was waiting for him on the bank, wet and grinning.

"I won." Bucky could see a big gap where her front tooth was missing.

He'd worried when Mary Doe first got that hole in her smile, but Daddy had said when he was little his teeth fell out too. Not to worry, he'd said, they would grow back.

"I knew that all along," Bucky had told his daddy. "I was just checking to see if you did."

Of course he hadn't exactly remembered the details, but he certainly didn't remember looking as ugly as Mary Doe with that big old hole in her smile.

Now she stretched her mouth from ear to ear, grinning because she beat him.

"I'm telling," he said, feeling mean. "I'm telling you went swimming when it wasn't even summer."

Mary Doe stuck out her chin. Daddy always said she was the stubbornest of the bunch.

"If you tell, I'll beat you up," she said.

"You can't whip me. You're a sissy."

"Am not!"

"Are too!"

"Am not!"

"Bucky! Mary Doe! Stop that fussing and let's go." Clint climbed down from the tree, shoved his knife back into his pocket, and took their arms. High up in the tree, where he'd been sitting, a newly carved heart shone white against the bark. C.M. loves L.W., it said. "Nobody's going to tell anybody anything, understand?"

Clint looked as fierce as that old bobcat Bucky had seen up in the mountains the previous fall. He'd be glad when he got to be thirteen so he could boss everybody around.

They sneaked Mary Doe in the back of the house so Mama wouldn't see her wet clothes. Later, after they'd all gone to bed, Bucky was dreaming about running across Witch Creek, winning.

"Bucky . . . Bucky . . ." He opened one eye. Mary Doe was standing by his bed in her pajamas. "I don't feel so good."

"It's 'cause you got cold in the creek, Mary Doe. Hush up and go back to your own bed."

"No, I really don't."

She fell onto the floor and just lay there.

"Mary Doe," he whispered. She didn't respond. "Mary Doe." Bucky jumped out of bed and knelt beside his sister. She didn't move.

Suddenly he didn't feel too good either.

"Mama!" he yelled. "Daddy!"

His head got dizzy, and he felt the floor coming up to meet him.

All the beds in the clinic were occupied. Three years earlier, when Kate had added the six-bed unit to the clinic, she'd never dreamed it would have two people at one time, let alone six.

She moved from bed to bed, checking pulses, studying charts.

"Kate?" Deborah appeared in the doorway, her skin dark against the crisp white of her nurse's uniform. "It's the Mingo children."

"Pull their charts, Deborah. I'll be right there."

After Deborah left, Kate stood amid the white beds and pressed her hand over her heart. The Mingo children! Not them too.

"Everything is going to be all right," she assured Anna and Cole later as she examined the children, but in her heart she knew it wouldn't. All the signs were there. The yellow-hued skin and eyes, the fatigue, the brown-colored urine sample.

Viral hepatitis. The same as all six children in her clinic.

Something terrible was happening to the children of Witch Dance.

"They'll need total bedrest and medication. I'll move two more beds into the clinic."

"This outbreak of hepatitis is getting serious, isn't it, Kate?" Cole asked.

"Yes, it's getting serious." She patted his hand. "But don't you worry. I'll take good care of your children."

"You always have."

Five years before, he'd been her biggest critic. Now Cole Mingo was her biggest supporter—and had been since the night Mary Doe was born.

Working side by side with him, making room for two more beds, Kate remembered how he'd gone all over town, making amends.

"She saved the lives of my wife and my baby daughter," he'd told the townspeople one by one. "If it hadn't been for Dr. Kate Malone, they'd be dead."

First they made small concessions to her. Deborah's father started leaving the cash register and greeting her personally when she went into the general store. Women who had avoided her on the streets turned to smile and wave. Small gifts began to appear on her doorstep—a loaf of freshly baked bread, a pair of beaded moccasins, a chocolate cake. Then old Mrs. Martin, who owned the needlepoint shop, stopped her on the street one day and handed her a sampler. HOME SWEET HOME it said.

"Take it," she said, smiling her toothless smile. "It's yours."

And that was Kate's official welcome to Witch Dance . . . six months after she'd arrived.

The sampler still hung in the reception room of the clinic. Everybody who came in remarked how kind Mrs. Martin was to make it for Kate, and Mrs. Martin herself called attention to it if nobody else noticed.

"See that," she'd say, pointing a bony finger at the framed piece of needlework. "I did it for the medicine woman. I'm the first one in Witch Dance who ever did a thing for her." Then she'd point to the knots on her fingers and lean over to whoever happened to be sitting next to her. "See that. Arthritis. The medicine woman gives me magic pills made from sunshine to make it go away. Not many women with arthritis can make a stitch as good as Bethany Martin."

Kate treated their colds and their stomachaches and their headaches. And by the time Eagle Mingo was officially elected to replace his father as governor of the Chickasaw Nation, she was too busy to care.

Almost.

Sitting in front of the television, she'd watched him address the Tribal Legislature for the first time.

"We remember the greatness," he said. "We remember the ancient times when the rivers ran sweet and clear, and the verdant forests yielded up their game to us. We remember the swift bark canoes and the bison dances and the sacred fires. And remembering, we are proud."

With her bare feet tucked under her, Kate leaned toward the television, intent on Eagle's face. Even the poor reception couldn't mar the high, elegant cheekbones and the fierce eyes. Eagle Mingo was more than proud: He was noble.

"But we must not immerse ourselves in memories, or we will grow dull and stagnant. We must move forward. We must put all our intelligence and all our willpower to bear on merging old ways with new so that we go into the twenty-first century triumphant ... as we have always been triumphant."

Eagle paused to lift his fists upward. Kate held her breath, waiting.

"Unconquered and unconquerable!" he said.

The Chickasaw motto rang around the chambers, and the crowd roared.

"Eagle! Eagle! Eagle!"

The camera followed him as he left the podium and mingled with his people. They reached out to touch him, calling his name ... just as she had done once.

"Eagle," she whispered, but there was no one to hear.

The camera cut to a commercial, and Eagle was lost to her.

Kate huddled on the sofa and cried until she was too weak to move. Then she dried her tears and swore she'd never cry for him again.

She'd kept her word. She hadn't cried for him since, not even on those rare occasions when their paths had crossed.

"I'm scared," Mary Doe said, bringing her back to reality, and Kate moved toward her bed. "I want my Mama and Daddy."

"Shh, it's all right, sweetheart. I'm here." She pulled up a chair and sat by the little bed.

"Will they come back to get me?"

"Yes. They'll come back to get you."

"You won't leave, will you? I'm scared of the dark."

"No, my precious." She took the small, feverish hand. "I won't leave you."

Mary Doe's long eyelashes fluttered down to her pale cheeks, and soon she was fast asleep.

"Do you want me to stay tonight?" Deborah asked.

"No. You go home and get some rest." Kate surveyed the room. Eight little beds, all in a row. "I'll stay."

The bell over the front door tinkled when Deborah left. Kate made rounds, then ate a light snack and returned to Mary Doe's bedside. A sliver of a moon was riding high in the sky, and its pale glow fell across the child's face.

How still. Like death.

Shivers ran down Kate's spine, and she knew she had to be watchful. Death had beat her once. She wouldn't let it win again.

The moment Eagle had scrupulously avoided finally came. In seeing his beloved niece and nephew, he would at last see Kate Malone. Alone. Without the buffer of large crowds. Long after everyone had gone home, Eagle left his office in Ada and headed toward the clinic.

He found her sitting there, by the bedside, her hair
aflame in the moonlight. As he stood in the doorway,
the five years they'd been apart vanished, and he was
borne away by memories as vivid as yesterday.

As if she sensed his presence, she turned her head
slowly. At that moment he couldn't have said whether
the greater agony was in being with her or being apart.
Her eyes held his, burning, until he had to look away.

"Hello, Eagle." Her voice was neutral, as if they had
never held each other while they soared toward a black
and gold sky.

"Kate." He moved silently to the opposite side of his
niece's bed. "I heard about the children. How are they?"

"It's viral hepatitis."

He reached for Mary Doe's tiny hand. Wary, he and
Kate watched each other, connected by the still form
that lay between them. After five lonely years, finally
connected.

"So many beds," he said, mentally counting.

"It's approaching the epidemic stage." She talked to
him calmly, as if she didn't feel the heat, didn't see the
sparks. "Have you heard of any cases in Ada?"

"No. Apparently this disease is confined to Witch
Dance."

In the bed next to his sister, Bucky stirred.

"Uncle Eagle?"

"Yes, Bucky. It's me." He knelt beside his eight-year-
old nephew's bed and smoothed the dark hair back
from the child's flushed face. "How're you doing, pal?"

"Not too good . . . I'm scared."

"It's all right to be scared. Only the foolish are never
scared."

"I'm not foolish . . . but I did lie."

"About what?"

"'Bout swimming in the creek. Mama said not to."

"When I was a little boy about your age, I told a few
whoppers myself. And so did your daddy."

"Sure 'nuff?"

"Sure enough." Eagle smoothed the child's hair once more. "Now, you get some sleep. I'll be right here."

How natural he was with children, Kate thought. How wonderful. She hated him for taking that away from her, for denying her the joy of seeing his tender love for the children she would have borne.

Children she would never bear. And all because of him. Eagle Mingo had spoiled her for any other man.

And now, there he was, not six feet away from her, sexy and delicious, making her melt inside with the same quick, hot lust that overtook her the summer of 'eighty-nine. That still overtook her.

She hated him for that too.

"You don't have to stay," she said. "I'll be here."

"All night?"

"All night."

Memories of soft summer winds echoed through the clinic, and whispers of love words spoken in the ancient tongue. Kate's heart kicked hard against her ribs, and she stilled it with her hand.

"I'm staying," he said.

"As you wish." She turned away quickly, before he could see the flush that crept over her neck.

But Eagle saw, and seeing, he broke his long silence with Loak-Ishtohoollo-Aba. Silently he swore before that accursed deity that while he had breath in his body he would never set eyes on Kate Malone again.

Fear swept across Witch Dance like a prairie fire. The Great One smelled it in the Wind and felt it in his bones. At night, when he covered himself with the buffalo robe that had belonged to his fathers for generations back, he dreamed of death riding on a white horse. But its face remained hidden to him. He fasted for days, and finally, stripped naked and cleansed by the sacred fires that burned around him, he saw the face of death.

When the morning sun broke the sky, he arose from his fast and painted his face with the colors of the mountain cougar, infusing himself with the great strength of the Ghost Cat. Then he assembled his medicine pouches, and descended the mountain.

He was the only one who could conquer death.

The windows in the governor's office glowed pink with the setting sun, and soon a velvet darkness would descend on the land. In her clinic Kate would be bending over the tiny forms in their white beds.

Eagle gripped his pencil so hard, it snapped.

"That's all, Linda," he said, abruptly ending his dictation and throwing the broken pieces of the pencil into the garbage.

"Governor, I'm not leaving till we get this letter done. You said it had to go out today, and if I haven't gone blind as well as senile, the day is almost over." With her sensible shoes planted firmly together and her hands on her hips, Linda Running Deer faced him. "Besides that, I'm planning to leave early tomorrow so I can watch 'Days of Our Lives.' There's going to be a murder, and I want to see who does it."

Eagle suppressed his grin. Linda Running Deer had backed down drunks and drug addicts and thieves: She wasn't about to quaver before the governor. That's why he had hired her away from the chief of tribal police. Martin Black Elk had puffed and huffed about the best damned secretary in Ada being snatched from under his nose, but Eagle had known even then that Black Elk was secretly pleased. There was nothing Black Elk liked better than being considered a man of good taste, and he bragged far and wide that he had such good taste, he had to select the governor's secretary.

"Are you trying to tell me what to do, Linda?" He scowled, but only because he knew she'd be disappointed if he didn't. This was a game they played . . . and relished.

"Damned right, Governor. If I didn't keep you straight, you'd be as bad as old Raymond Lightfoot, sitting in that general store, not knowing sunup from sundown."

Linda plopped herself into her chair and whipped out her dictation pad. "What you need is a wife."

"What I need is a new secretary."

"I'm the only person in Ada who would put up with your dark moods, and don't you forget that. Now, do you want this letter to go out today or next year?"

He always let her have the last word; that, too, was part of their game. While he dictated, the sun disappeared and the cool darkness came down over the land.

After Linda had gone home, Eagle drove from Ada to his ranch in Witch Dance. The quiet pastures and peaceful mountains transfused his soul. As long as he had the land, he could survive. He became one with the night as he stood on his front porch and stared up at the sky.

Suddenly the telephone jarred the silence. Though the last thing he wanted to do was deal with someone else's problems, he couldn't let it ring without answering: His sense of duty was too well honed. He went inside and picked it up on the fourth ring.

"Eagle Mingo," he said.

"This is Deborah Lightfoot. Kate is going to kill me for calling you, but I think you should come to the clinic."

"What's wrong?"

"I know it's ridiculous to bother the governor with a problem like this, but the last time Kate had problems with the medicine man, you solved them."

"Can you be more specific, Deborah?" His muscles were bunched across his shoulders, and he felt as if a vise had suddenly squeezed his insides.

"He's been coming in here every day for the last three days, shaking his nasty old feathers and sprinkling his filthy potions over our patients. He and Kate are out in the reception room now, about ready to kill each other."

"I'll be right there."

"Don't tell her I called you."

"I promise."

He raced through the night on a black Chickasaw horse with a single white star on his forehead, firstborn of Kate's Mahli and Eagle's cherished black stallion, and as he rode he remembered the summer nights so long ago when he'd taken the same path. Desire curled through him like smoke, and with it the selfish pleasure of seeing Kate again, no matter what the reason.

When he arrived he could see her through the window, cool and professional-looking in her white lab coat. But there was nothing cool and professional about her eyes. As she faced off against the shaman, they smoldered with temper.

The bell over the door tinkled as Eagle entered the clinic. Kate whirled toward the sound.

"What is this?" she said. "An Indian powwow?"

It was only then that he saw her great fatigue. She had dark circles under her eyes, and her voice was ragged with exhaustion.

"I've come to help, Kate."

"I didn't ask for your help." She pushed her heavy hair away from her forehead. "I have a clinic full of sick children, and I don't need the leaders of the Chickasaw Nation to tell me how to do my job."

The old shaman faced Kate as erect as a war pole, and just as fierce. With his face painted the colors of the Ghost Cat, he looked like a man half his age. There was still power in his limbs and fire in his eyes. Whether Kate knew it or not, the Great One was not a man to alienate.

"Is Deborah inside with the children?" Eagle asked.

"Yes. Somebody has to be." Kate looked pointedly at the shaman. The eyes that stared back at her were full of enmity.

"Why don't we all sit down and have a cup of coffee?"

"Coffee? I don't want coffee. I want this man out of my clinic and away from my patients."

"I have had a vision," the shaman said. "The children of my people are dying. I have come to save them."

"By rubbing them with mutton grease and ashes? How can I keep a sterile environment if you bring that filthy stuff into my clinic? I will not tolerate it."

"Kate." Eagle touched her elbow, but she stepped away and faced him with her back ramrod-straight and her face stiff. "I'd like to talk to the shaman. Alone."

For a moment she looked as if she might protest; then she relented.

"Fine. But don't make any compromises on my behalf. This clinic is under my jurisdiction. He is *not* to interfere with my patients again."

Picking up her charts, Kate marched out of the reception room like a drum majorette in Macy's Thanksgiving Day parade. When she rounded the corner, her resolve failed, and she leaned against the wall with her hand against her throat.

Eagle was just on the other side of the door, formidable and delicious. Her pulse thrummed against her palm. Once he had touched her there, kissed her there. She could still feel his lips upon her skin.

Oh, God. How would she survive this second invasion of him?

She ran a hand over her tired face, then went into the clinic, where all her little patients lay in a quiet row.

"Any change?" she asked Deborah.

"None. You've been gone only thirty minutes, Kate."

"It seems like hours. Damned that old medicine man. I hope he sets his tail feathers on fire in one of his sacred rituals."

"Eagle will convince him to leave us alone."

Kate's eyes narrowed. "You called him, didn't you?"

"Somebody had to keep you out of trouble."

"Go home, Deborah, before I turn my Irish temper on you."

"You're exhausted, Kate. I can stay."

"No. It's my shift tonight." Besides, Eagle Mingo was in the clinic. She couldn't bear to see him, and she couldn't bear to walk away.

She gazed across the room at the little beds. "When all this is over, I think I'll ride through Witch Dance naked, screaming at the top of my lungs."

"Me too. Both of us deserve it." Deborah got her coat. "Good night, Kate."

" 'Night."

Kate was at the supply cabinet, doling out medicine, when Eagle entered the room. She didn't hear him so much as feel him. He still moved like a shadow, dark and silent and beautiful. She gripped the edge of the table to stop her hands from trembling.

She was too old and too wise now to cite fatigue or nerves as the cause. There was only one cause, and its name was Eagle.

"Kate." She turned to face him, holding the medicine tray between them. "The shaman will not be back . . ."

She didn't give him the satisfaction of asking how he'd accomplished what she couldn't in the last three days.

"Good," she said.

". . . unless the parents request him. The medicine man still carries great honor in our culture, Kate. I'm sure you can find a way to respect that and still care for your patients."

"What I'll find a way to do is make damned sure the parents don't request him. Not in my clinic."

"You haven't lost your spirit." His voice seduced her. *Damn you to hell, Eagle Mingo.*

"Did you think I would?"

"No." His fierce gaze pinned her to the spot, and he made love to her with his eyes. "I always loved that about you."

"Don't . . ." She wheeled away from him and started toward the beds, then, not wanting to appear cowardly, she turned back. "Bucky and Mary Doe will be glad to see you. There's no change in them."

"And the others?"

"I'm afraid for them."

"Only the foolish are never afraid."

"So you once said." She tipped her chin back, daring him to try to resurrect old memories.

"I've brought them something, if you think that's all right."

"Anything to brighten their day."

Moving quickly, she put distance between them. She could feel his movement across the room, as liquid as honey.

"Look, I brought you some magic," he said as he knelt beside his nephew's bed.

Kate's hand tightened on the medicine tray. *Always, Eagle brought magic.*

"How is it magic, Uncle Eagle?" Bucky asked.

"Hold it up to the moonlight, like this." He held the small round buckeye toward the light so its hard shiny surface glowed. "Then rub it and you'll remember all the good times you've ever had."

Her knuckles turned white. She didn't want to remember. Forcing herself to move slowly, she set down the medicine tray and escaped into the bathroom. Leaning against the door, she could still hear his voice as he moved from bed to bed, explaining the magic of the buckeye.

She closed her eyes and whispered, "Damn you, Eagle Mingo. Damn you."

Her face burned, and her body. *Coward.* Hiding in the bathroom. She couldn't hide forever.

Kate dashed cool water over her face, then hurried back to her duties. All her tiny patients were asleep except little Lolly Turner. She was clutching the buckeye in her frail fist when Kate approached her bed.

"I can't remember, Dr. Kate." Tears spilled from under her closed lids and rolled down her flushed cheeks. "I rubbed and rubbed . . . but I . . . can't remember."

"It's all right, sweetheart. I'll remember for you." Kate felt the pulse, weak and thready. Alarmed, she strapped on the cuff. Blood pressure ninety-seven over fifty and falling.

Lolly had been failing for the past three days. Kate pushed down the panic that threatened to swamp her. In all her seven years at Witch Dance, she'd never lost a patient except old Mrs. Weems, and she'd been ninety-seven. She didn't intend to start now.

"Remember the birthday party you had when you were five? Your daddy gave you a pony." A weak smile played around the child's pale blue lips.

Don't die, Lolly. Don't die.

"And remember that time you fell out of your tree house and got a cast on your leg and you had so many friends you asked me to put on a larger one so they could all sign it?"

I brought you into the world, precious child. I won't let you leave it.

Lolly's only response was a flutter of her eyelids. Kate tried to find her pulse, tried to find her pressure. Her vital signs were off the chart.

"And remember when you started school? You asked me if I had any pills that would make you remember the ABCs?" Kate talked rapidly. If she talked fast enough, she could keep death at bay. If she talked long enough, she could bring Lolly back.

Come back, Lolly. Please come back.

The buckeye fell from Lolly's lifeless hand and rolled across the floor. Swiftly and silently Eagle moved to her side.

Kate put the paddles to Lolly's chest. "Remember how you wanted to be a doctor, Lolly?" Flat line. "Come on. Remember!" Kate applied the paddles once more. "You have to remember."

Flat line.

Eagle put both hands on her shoulders.

"Kate . . . come away."

"I won't let her die," she said, applying the paddles once more.

"Kate . . . she's gone."

Fierce and defiant, she turned to him. "How do you know? You're not the doctor."

"It's no use, Kate. She's been weighed in the path and found light."

"She was just a child . . . she was just a child."

Wild with grief and defeat, Kate ran from the room.

In her office she crumpled into her chair. Eagle came in behind her and switched on the lights.

"I want the lights off," she said.

He flicked off the switch, and she huddled in her silent cocoon of blackness, feeling the electric presence of Eagle Mingo as he stood beside the door.

"Leave. I want to be alone."

"You need me, Kate."

"I stopped needing you a long time ago."

Her heart beat so hard, she could almost hear it in the silence of the room. For a small eternity he stood beside the door, and then he moved on the wings of eagles. His large shadow fell over her, and even in the blackness she was comforted.

"At least take this for your tears." He pulled a clean white handkerchief from his pocket and offered it without touching her.

"I'm not crying."

"Then allow me to stop all this water, for the Blue River has left its banks and is flooding your eyes." He knelt beside her and tenderly wiped her cheeks.

With his hands finally upon her, the thing she remembered most was not making love with the stars overhead, but swimming in the river naked with the sun on her face and Eagle sitting on a big rock, singing to her in Muskogean.

She let her tears flow freely, and, kneeling, he wiped them all away. And when she gave one final sniffle, he backed off, severing the fragile tie that bound them.

"Is the buckeye really magic?" she whispered.

"Only to those who believe."

She looked into his deep black eyes and saw only emptiness. Silently he folded the handkerchief and pressed it into her hands while the humming silence became a roar.

"In case you need it," he said, then turned quickly and left the room. The door closed softly behind him.

Kate slumped in her chair. Neither of them believed in magic anymore.

19

Fox squirrels and rabbits and deer were abundant in the mountains, hiding amid the fallen tree branches and the colored leaves, waiting for him to take his twenty-gauge shotgun and hunt them down.

But Clint had no heart for hunting. He had no heart for anything. His brother and sister were dreadfully sick, and he was well.

He felt guilty.

Home was not the same without Bucky and Mary Doe, and neither were his mother and father. Anna cried a lot and Cole was angry. They were in the kitchen now, fighting.

Clint tried not to hear. He pressed his hands over his ears, but the hateful words came to him anyhow.

"Three are already dead, Anna."

"I know . . . I know. Still, I think it would be wrong to get the medicine man."

"Kate Malone's medicine is not enough."

"His ways are old-fashioned, Cole."

"Hers aren't working."

"I will not have that dirty old shaman shaking gourd rattlers over my children!"

"Would you have them die? Would you, Anna?"

"No!"

His mother ran from the kitchen crying, and Clint raced upstairs to his room. He turned the music on really loud, but it didn't drown out the sound of his mother's grief.

Mick wiped tears from his eyes. One of them dropped on the letter. He tried to wipe it off before it smeared the ink, but he was too late.

"Dammit all to hell," he muttered. Now Martha would find out that he read Kate's letters.

Not that she didn't already know. Every time a letter came, she pussyfooted around the house, looking at him like a dying calf in a hailstorm, sighing and knitting. She'd knitted enough damned doilies to cover Texas. He hated the things, stuck on all the arms of the chairs, just waiting for him to knock them off on the floor or spill coffee or drop ashes on them.

When she'd run out of furniture arms, she framed the damned silly things and hung them all over the walls.

"Mick?"

He hastily stuffed the letter into his pocket. He'd take it to his office and pretend the maid threw it away.

"Are you ready, sweetheart? We don't want to be late to the opera."

Martha was dressed in a pink silk dress that made her skin look rosy, and she'd had something nice done to her hair. Every now and then, when he saw her like that, he was reminded what a beautiful woman she used to be. Still was, sometimes.

"In a minute," he said. He couldn't go to the damned opera with Kate's letter in his pocket. He unlocked his desk drawer and dropped it inside.

Her signature stared back at him.

Five years, and neither one of them had budged an inch. He'd started to give in and fly to New York the year before, when Martha went. On her little shopping spree, she'd said, as if he didn't have sense enough to know that she was going up there to meet Kate. Every

Thanksgiving they did the same thing, met in New York, while he stayed home and had pork and beans straight out of the can.

Not that he couldn't afford to go out to a fancy restaurant and buy a good rib eye. He wanted to punish them both; so he ate all his meals alone with the cat. When Martha got back, he'd always have lost three pounds, and she'd feel sorry for him and spend the next six weeks trying to make up for being gone.

Sneaking behind his back.

He locked the desk and joined Martha in the hall. The opera was *Madame Butterfly*. Katie Elizabeth loved Puccini. She should be here with them instead of out there in that godforsaken land.

"Kate would have loved this," Martha leaned over and whispered.

For a minute he started to ignore her, as he always did when she mentioned their daughter's name. Then he thought of all those little Indian children dying, and no one being there to comfort his Katie Elizabeth.

"Yes, she would," he said.

"Kate?" Hollow-eyed, Kate looked up from the medical records she was studying. Deborah set a cup of coffee on her desk, then slid into the chair opposite her.

"I'm staying tonight, Kate."

"No. I will. The Mingo children are desperately ill."

"You haven't slept in three days. If you don't get some rest, you won't be any good to any of them."

Kate's hands shook as she shoved aside the records and reached for the coffee.

"You're right. I have to get some rest." Her stomach clenched as the coffee hit it. She had to get some food as well. Fasting wasn't going to save her patients.

Nothing could save them. Four new cases, three dead already, and the Mingo children hanging on by a thread.

"What's happening here, Deborah? The symptoms say *hepatitis*, but my patients are *dying*. What am I missing?" She reached for her records, but Deborah put out a hand to stop her.

"Kate . . . leave it for tomorrow. Nurse's orders."

"Five years ago I never thought I'd hear you say that."

"Neither did I. It feels good." Deborah reached for Kate's coat. "Wear this. There's snow on the mountains, and the wind is cold enough to chill your blood."

"Call me if anything happens, Deborah. Anything."

"I will. Get a good night's rest, Kate."

Kate knew she wouldn't. Something terrible was stalking the Chickasaw children, and she wouldn't rest easy until she'd found the answer.

Cole lay rigid beside Anna, waiting for her breathing to become even. She tossed and turned, but he didn't reach for her as he always had. Their children stood between them.

"Cole?" Anna whispered, but he pretended to be asleep.

Somewhere in the darkness his children lay in their hospital beds, their little faces pinched with pain and their little arms hooked to tubes. The indignity of their condition rushed through Cole like a storm-swollen river.

Anna rolled back to her side of the bed. The clock in the hallway tolled three times. Would she ever sleep?

He counted off the minutes, each one jarring his nerves. Finally, her breathing became even.

Cole had learned the art of stealth as a child. No one heard him dress; no one saw him leave the ranch; no one saw him arrive at the clinic. Not even the nurse, Deborah. She was bent over papers in the office, her cap askew and her brow puckered in concentration.

"Daddy?"

He could barely hear Bucky's whisper as it rasped between the pitiful dry lips.

"Everything's going to be all right, son. Daddy's here now."

He was careful unhooking the tubes, careful lifting his precious children from their beds.

"Hold on to Daddy, now. I'm going to make everything all right."

They clung to him, his beloved Mary Doe and his stalwart little Bucky. Mary Doe whimpered and pressed her hot forehead into his chest.

"Daddy? Where are we going?" The wind caught Bucky's question and carried it off toward the mountains.

"Feel that, son? Feel the wind? See the stars and the moon?"

Bucky's nod was weak, and Mary Doe's arms were so frail. Fear gripped Cole. Was he doing the right thing? For a moment he stood poised between the clinic and the mountains, between the new ways and the old.

He could go either way. It was not too late to turn back. His feet were on the clinic path when Bucky spoke.

"I see the wishing star, Daddy . . . I wish I could ride my pony."

"We will ride and ride and ride, my son. We'll ride all the way to the stars."

Carrying his precious burdens, Cole mounted his horse and headed for the mountains.

Deborah filled her tray with medicine and made the predawn check of her patients. The minute she stepped through the doorway to the ward, she knew something was wrong. Hairs on the back of her neck prickled as she swept her gaze across the beds. Little Josh Traymore and his brother, Bert, were sleeping soundly, and in the bed next to them, Graham Black Elk dozed fitfully.

A dark cloud that had been threatening rain moved across the sky, and the moon came into view. Its rays illuminated the wrinkled sheets and the empty pillows on the two beds in the corner.

Horror clawed at Deborah's throat. She raced toward the beds, calling their names.

"Bucky. Mary Doe."

Calling and calling, knowing they wouldn't answer.

Her medicine tray fell to the floor with a crash, and she lurched against furniture on her race to the telephone. Who to call? Who to tell?

One person came vividly to mind, one man whose strength and wisdom she valued above all others.

He answered on the first ring with no traces of sleep in his voice.

"Eagle? This is Deborah Lightfoot. The Mingo children are missing."

"I'll be right there."

"What should I do?"

"Don't alarm anyone. Don't touch anything. Wait for me."

The wait seemed to be an eternity rather than the fifteen minutes the clock registered. When he finally walked into the clinic, she fell to pieces.

"It's all my fault." She covered her face with her hands and wept. "Kate wanted to stay and I sent her home."

"Stop it, Deborah." He took her shoulders and looked straight into her eyes. "Do you hear me? Nobody is at fault. Cole took the children."

"How do you know?"

"I read the signs outside."

"Why?"

"There's no time for questions now, Deborah. The important thing is to bring them back."

"They're so weak, Eagle. Hurry, please hurry before it's too late."

And Eagle, riding like the wind, tracking his brother toward a remote mountain cabin, had a vision of two tiny souls winging toward the stars.

Fear rode hard at his side.

Mary Doe was calling her name. Anna stirred in her sleep, then suddenly sat straight up in bed.

"I'm here, sweetheart. Mommy's here."

She reached out, but no little girl with dark pigtails and dirt smudges on her face raced into her arms.

And then she remembered.

Thunder roared in the hills and lightning flashed. Heavy with grief, Anna turned toward Cole's side of the bed, only to find it empty.

"Cole?" she whispered. She stepped into her house slippers and padded softly to the bathroom. "Cole?"

There was no answer.

The bathroom fixtures gleamed garishly in the harsh light. Anna leaned her head against the cool vanity mirror.

"Bucky," she whispered. "Mary Doe."

Nobody answered.

20

Sacred fires burned away the wintery winds. Even so, Cole shivered.

Between the sacred fires stood a long pole capped with eagle feathers, and in the line marked by the pole, two smaller wands, their tips painted red. From the upper tips of the small wands fluttered red ribbons, and from the lower tips, black.

In the midst of the sacred circle lay two blankets the color of fire, and upon the blankets lay his children. Still and colorless as death.

The ancient shaman danced slowly around, singing his chants and shaking his gourd rattle. The moon glistened on his bear-claw necklace, and winds caught the eagle feather, flapping it against the pole. The *Pishofa* ceremony had begun.

Filled with fear and hope, Cole closed his eyes. Smoke from the fires circled his head and the rhythm of the chant invaded his body. As he swayed, he felt the wings of the eagle enfold him and the spirituality of that sacred bird protect him.

"Great Spirit," he whispered. "I bring my children to You. I place them in Your loving arms and beg You to find them worthy."

Suddenly the sound of the gourd rattle ceased and the stillness of death fell upon the land. Without opening his eyes, Cole saw the souls of his children ascend toward the stars. He opened his mouth to scream his agony to the heavens.

Lurching upright, he swayed and felt the arms of his brother close around him.

"Cole?" Braced in Eagle's arms, Cole looked into his brother's tragic eyes. "It's over, Cole."

21

One figure stood apart on the windswept hill. The Mingo family gathered close, taking what comfort they could from one another; but Kate stood alone, her coat collar turned up against the chill and her hair whipping in the wind like the colored leaves that swirled around her feet.

Dark circles bruised the fair skin under her eyes and grief hollowed out her cheeks. Eagle ached for her; he ached for them all.

Anna swooned as the earth swallowed up the two tiny caskets. Cole, standing rigid at her side, would have let her fall if Eagle hadn't caught her.

"Everything is going to be all right, Anna," he said. Cole's black, empty stare turned his heart to ice, and Eagle wondered if anything would ever be right in the Mingo family again.

Dovie and Winston came to bear Anna away to the car. Clint, flanked by Wolf and Star, followed.

Cole stared down at the cold, raw earth.

"I killed them," he whispered.

"No, you didn't." Eagle put a comforting hand on his brother's arm. "You did what you thought was best."

"Anna says I killed her children."

"It's her grief talking. She doesn't mean that."

"She hates me."

"Anna loves you. Give her time, Cole. Give yourself time."

"Time for what, Eagle? Do you think time is going to bring back my children?" Cole's eyes were dry and hollow as he shook Eagle's hand off.

A sudden gust of wind howled through the cemetery, whipping the leaves to a demonic frenzy and snatching Kate's scarf. The bright blue silk landed at Cole's feet like an exotic bird. Mesmerized, he stared at the scarf, then he jerked his head back and fixed his glittering gaze on Kate.

"It's her." His jaw tensed so hard, corded veins stood out on his neck. With quick, jerky movements he picked up the scarf and twisted it round and round in his hand, then he started toward Kate, holding it like a garrote.

Eagle sprang toward his brother, wrapping his arms around Cole's chest.

"Let me go."

"Cole . . ." Rage gave his brother the strength of a buffalo. Eagle could barely restrain him. "Cole . . . get hold of yourself."

Watching them, Kate clutched her throat, white-faced.

Suddenly Cole slumped against Eagle, sobbing. "Help me, Eagle. Help me."

Supporting his brother's weight, Eagle half walked, half carried him to the car. Turning, he looked back at the lonely hill.

Kate had vanished.

She sat huddled in her clinic, still wearing her coat. Clumps of red earth clung to her shoes, and her cheeks felt chapped from the wind. Beyond her, in the room where three small patients still fought for their lives, Deborah moved softly, dispensing medicine and soothing words with equal skill.

"Kate?"

Eagle stood in the open doorway, and cold wind filled the room. In his hand was her silk scarf.

"I brought this back to you."

He laid it on her desk, watching her. She made no move to touch the scarf. Her strength was gone. She thought she might never move again.

"Are you all right, Kate?"

"I should ask that of you."

"The Mingos will survive."

And what of you? Will you survive? she wanted to ask, but what good would it do? She'd given up all claims to him five years earlier.

She rubbed her temples, trying to massage away the fatigue. Thinking was so hard.

"You did what you could, Kate. The Mingo family is grateful."

"Cole?"

"He's distraught with grief. He'll come to his senses."

Kate touched her scarf, touched it and felt the warmth from Eagle's hand lingering among the silk folds. Clenching it tightly in her fist, she leaned forward, her eyes alight with a crusader's zeal.

"I'm going to find out what killed them, Eagle. If it's the last thing I ever do."

A muscle ticked in the side of his jaw, and the look in his eyes set her skin aflame. Time stopped as they stared at each other, shattered by grief and hopeless passion.

"I hope your God is more generous than mine."

He left quickly without saying good-bye, and the agony of watching him go was as fresh as it had been the first time.

Kate dropped her weary head to her desktop, wondering where she'd ever find the strength and the courage to survive.

22

Mark Grant loved mysteries of all kinds. Murder mysteries were strewn around his office, and at least three of them sported bookmarks so he wouldn't lose his place.

"How can you read three books at a time?" Grayson Tyler had asked him the day before.

"The same way you can date three nurses at one time. It takes skill."

The mystery of the Bermuda triangle fascinated him, as well as the "big bang" and the various theories of creation. It was his love of puzzlement that led him to specialize in infectious diseases. Nothing in the field of medicine was more elusive and baffling than infectious diseases.

"Dr. Grant." His secretary's voice came over the intercom. "Dr. Malone is here."

"Give me two minutes, then send her in."

Dr. Kate Malone. He'd met her at a medical convention in San Diego four years earlier. Remembered her vividly, as a matter of fact. Gorgeous red hair. A figure to drive sane men crazy.

He'd swallowed the olive in his drink and nearly choked to death when she walked into the room. Grayson had banged him on the back and saved his life.

It took Mark all evening to finagle his way close enough to meet her. His face still turned red at the memory of the encounter.

"Did you wear that dress to drive all the men crazy, or is it just me you're after?" He slid onto the barstool beside her, feeling confident. He knew he wasn't much to look at, but plenty of girls had called his cowlick endearing and his prominent nose noble. Besides, he had personality. No sense in being modest about it.

"Neither, Doctor. I wore the dress because clothes are required at these functions."

"A pity."

"Hardly."

Nobody had ever called him an adonis, but he did lift weights at the gym and was nobody's slouch. The way she looked at him, though, he might as well have been leftover dog meat.

They weren't off to a good start, but, hey, nothing was ever perfect. He pressed on.

"Everybody gets a mite touchy at these conventions. What do you say we leave these medical types behind and stroll out onto the veranda. I hear the night air is very fresh in San Diego."

"That's not all that's fresh in San Diego."

She'd picked up her drink and left him sitting at the bar with the ice melting in his glass and his neck turning red.

And now she was in Ada, looking for his help.

Somebody up there liked him.

Mark scraped the potato chips and leftover ham sandwich into a napkin and dropped them into his desk drawer. No sense wasting good food. Then he smoothed down his cowlick. When he dropped his arm, he noticed his frayed cuff.

After he'd finished rolling up his sleeve, he started to the door. Then he noticed he had one sleeve up and one sleeve down. Matching sleeves. That was the ticket.

He rolled up the other sleeve and struck out for the

door once more. Then he changed his mind and scurried behind his desk.

Let Dr. Kate Malone find her own way through the door. She wouldn't find Dr. Mark Grant making a fool of himself over her this time.

The door opened, and she came through. Kate Malone looked like hell. *Beautiful* hell. She was thinner than he remembered, and her face was pinched with tension.

"Dr. Grant." Nothing wrong with her walk though. The way she glided along with those hips swiveling just right was enough to make a man forget his resolutions to play cool and hard to get. "The first thing I have to do is apologize."

"Apologize?"

"For San Diego." She pushed her hair back from her forehead in a gesture he found charming. But damned if he was going to be charmed by her. Blackhearted Mark. That's what he was going to be.

"I was rude to you," she added. "There was no excuse for my behavior."

"Why don't you try me? I like excuses."

"Would you believe a relationship gone bad?"

"With you? Not a chance."

"PMS?"

"Ah, a medical mystery. *That* I'll buy."

Kate Malone smiled and was transformed. Her green eyes sparkled and all the fatigue lines left her face.

Remaining hardhearted with her was going to be a pain in the ass.

"Now," he said, striving for the upper hand. "Tell me why you've come."

"My patients are dying from something that looks like hepatitis."

"How many?"

"Five out of eight."

Mark Grant whistled. The death rate from hepatitis was one percent.

"Cause of death?" he asked.

"Liver failure."

"You've started looking for a link among the victims?"

"The victims are little children." Her voice cracked, and for a moment he thought she was going to cry. Then she stiffened her shoulders and jutted out her chin. "My nurse and I have studied case histories extensively. So far, we've found nothing."

"You've done fieldwork?"

"That's why I've come to you. I want an expert, and they say you're the best."

"Yep. I'm the best." Mark didn't try to suppress his grin. "And you want me?" he asked, deliberately baiting her.

Kate was equal to the occasion.

"Something is killing the children of Witch Dance." She pushed her heavy hair away from her face once more. "Yes, Doctor . . . I want you."

He checked his right shirt-sleeve to see if the frayed end was showing, then fiddled with his pencil, letting her sweat. Vindictive, perhaps, but nobody ever said he was perfect.

"I wouldn't want to waste time driving from Ada to Witch Dance twice a day," he said.

"There's a guest bedroom in my cottage. You can stay with me."

"Dr. Malone, you've just made me an offer I can't refuse."

Mark Grant turned out to be a blessing in disguise. He breezed into her cottage like a cyclone, full of booming male noises and explosive laughter, and suddenly all the emptiness was swept away.

"You don't mind if I make myself at home," he said, not waiting for her permission, but dropping his bags in the middle of the floor and plopping onto her sofa. With the remote control he flipped the television to a sports channel, then grinned. "I always settle in with a beer and see what's happening in the sports world this time of day."

Thinking of her mother, and the way Martha scurried to wait on Mick hand and foot every time he came through the door, Kate drew herself up.

"I don't provide waitress service."

"I'm not as pampered as I look. Been waiting on myself since I was six years old. No mama and no daddy."

"You were an orphan?"

He struck a pose with his hand over his heart. "It brings 'em to tears every time." His grin showed two gold crowns. "Heck no. My parents were always off in some exotic part of the world. Left me to fend for myself at Grandma's mansion down in Atlanta. It took every waking moment to outwit the servants so I could enjoy the independence any six-year-old boy deserves."

He flipped off the television, then stood up to stretch. Kate suddenly realized how lonely she'd been. Just to have Mark taking up space in her house felt good. It felt damned good.

"Sit tight, Kate . . . you don't mind if I call you Kate, since we'll be living together?"

"No." She smiled. It was impossible not to with Mark Grant.

"I'll hustle us up some grub. We're going to need our strength."

"You cook too?"

"Best derned cook in three states. I bribed Grandma's chef."

"How?"

"Hid frogs in his stew pots till he gave in and let me watch."

She followed him into the kitchen and watched as he nosed around her cabinets and into her refrigerator. Another time, another man, Kate would have been appalled at such an invasion of her privacy. But it was not just any old time, and Mark was not just any old man. He was the man who might well save the lives of the children in Witch Dance.

Besides, she'd had enough privacy to last her a life-time.

"It will be a relief not to eat my own cooking."

"I know." He grinned over the pots and pans.

"Don't tell me. . . . Let me guess. You're clairvoyant too."

"I ate one of those chocolate chip cookies you brought to Sally Blaze's birthday party last year." Sally Blaze, the pharmacist in Ada who had become her friend over the years.

"I didn't see you there."

"You had already gone. I took one bite of that cookie and said to myself, 'It's a derned good thing I didn't marry that woman. I'd be a mere shadow of myself by now.' "

"Heaven forbid that you should be a shadow of yourself." She looked pointedly at his midsection.

He sucked it in. "Been meaning to hit the old barbells, but you know what a demanding bitch medicine is."

Kate made two cups of tea, then sat at the table while Mark moved around her kitchen. Humming. Her mother used to hum. *She* used to hum.

Maybe it was time to remember music once more.

The crushing sense of loss never left Anna, not for even the briefest second; but at least she was functional. Cole sat huddled over a bottle in dark rooms, first Bucky's bedroom, then Mary Doe's. Back and forth he went, alternating as the mood struck him.

Sighing, she watched out the window. Where was Clint? He'd been there only seconds earlier, tossing the ball in the air and catching it.

Panic seized her, and she raced to the door.

"Clint!" she called. There was no response, no dark head turned her way, and no gangly legs raced toward the house. *"Clint!"*

He stuck his head around the barn door.

"Mom?" Loping in his loose-jointed way, he came to her and touched her arm. "Is anything wrong?"

"No. Nothing. It's just—" Just that she couldn't bear for her only surviving child to be out of her sight.

Anna felt like a fool. Then she felt like crying, and she guessed a few tears leaked out, for her son wiped them away with his grimy hand.

"It's okay, Mom. I understand. Really, I do."

Only thirteen, and suddenly he was all grown-up. The sad thing was that he had to be. She was barely coping and Cole was not coping at all. Somebody in the family had to be strong.

"I'm sorry, Clint." She cupped his face. So handsome. So strong. So like Cole, it broke her heart to look at him. "It's going to get better. Just give me time."

"Sure, Mom . . . can I go now? I need to feed the horses."

She nodded, and then as he turned away, she called after him.

"Clint . . . thank you."

"That's what families are for."

Anna stood a moment on her front porch with the setting sun warming her face. It seemed like forever since she'd been in the sunshine. A breeze rustled through the dead leaves on her front lawn. She hadn't raked this year. The flower beds beside the front steps were full of weeds. She hadn't plucked weeds either.

There were lots of things she hadn't done lately. Anna went down the steps and knelt at her flower beds. With her hands in the dirt she saw Mary Doe, digging with her small spade.

"Not so deep, sweetheart," Anna said, laughing at her daughter's enthusiasm. "You don't have to dig all the way to China to plant flowers."

"These are special flowers, Mama, 'cause they're *mine*."

Mary Doe wiped her grimy hands across her face and down the front of her overalls, leaving streaks. Anna laughed again, remembering her visions of a daughter dressed in pink ruffles and lace.

A sob closed her throat, and Anna bent over her un-

kempt flower beds, her hands still clenched in the dirt.
Wrapped in her cocoon of beautiful, painful memories,
she didn't hear the sounds of the approaching car, nor
the footsteps.

"Anna?" Kate Malone was bending over her, her face
crinkled with concern. "Are you all right?"

Someday she would be. Maybe. But not right now.

"I can't seem to . . ." Anna stood up, groping like an
old woman. Kate took one arm, and a man Anna didn't
know took her other. "Thank you," she said, dusting off
her hands. "I must look a mess."

"You're fine." Kate's hand was warm upon her arm.
"Anna, this is Dr. Mark Grant. We'd like to talk to you
and Cole . . . about the children." Anna pressed her
trembling hands together. "If this is not a good time, we
can come back."

"No . . . no. Come in." Anna's house was as neglected
as her flower beds, but she couldn't worry about that
now. "I'm afraid Cole is . . . busy. What is it you wanted
to know?"

"We're trying to make sense of what happened. Hepatitis was not the killer; liver failure was. And we don't
know why."

"Mrs. Mingo." The man called Dr. Grant leaned forward in his chair. He had a kind and earnest face.
"We're trying to find a common thread. Do you remember any connection between your children and the others?"

"No. Nothing."

"Any parties they might have attended together?" he
said. "Any picnics? Any social outings of any kind?"

"No. The ranch is big. Clint and—" Anna's voice
cracked, and she thought she might cry again. Kate
reached over and covered her hand. "—Bucky and
Mary Doe kept pretty much to themselves."

"Was there anyplace special they played?" Kate said.

"Not that I know of."

"Any old water troughs?" Mark added. "Any lakes?
Any water at all?"

"No. Mostly they played in the yard or the pastures or the barn. It was too cold to go down to Witch Creek."

"Witch Creek?" Mark and Kate exchanged glances. "Had they ever played there?"

"All summer long. Mary Doe could swim like a fish, and Bucky was learning to dive. Clint always went along to watch them though. I didn't want them to . . . drown." A sob caught in her throat.

She covered her face with her hands, and her shoulders shook. The river of grief had to flow, no matter who witnessed it.

Anna felt Kate's arms around her, heard Mark leave the room, smelled the strong aroma of coffee when he returned.

The coffee made her feel better. So did the companionship.

She wondered what Cole would say if he knew Kate Malone was sitting in his den, drinking coffee.

The room was dark and smelled of stale liquor. But it still contained Bucky. Cole could see his son in the fishing poles and football posters hanging on the walls, in the books on horses and race cars lining the shelves, in the telescope that sat at the window, ready to bring the constellations down to earth.

A pair of Bucky's socks, wadded up and smelly, was just under the bed, and the sneakers and jeans and shirt he'd last been wearing were strewn across the floor.

Cole hadn't let Anna clean their rooms. Sometimes it seemed that if he closed his eyes and wished hard enough, they'd come back. Bucky and Mary Doe. His children. Bright-eyed and laughing.

The sound of a car intruded on Cole's solitude. He went to the window and looked out. Kate Malone was in his yard.

Rigid, Cole stood at the window, watched while Anna brought her inside, listened while she talked to his wife about finding a cause of death.

He knew the cause.

Cole didn't bother with a glass but drank straight from the bottle. Kate Malone's voice sounded like serpents hissing in his ears.

Or maybe it was the liquor. Had the whiskey turned to snakes? Did it speak with the *sente soolish*?

Covering his ears, Cole dropped the bottle. It crashed at his feet, sending whiskey and glass flying.

Cole gazed down at the mess. The room spun a moment, then righted itself. He had desecrated Bucky's room.

Hurrying, stumbling over his feet and the small furniture, Cole went into the bathroom for towels. On his knees he scrubbed at the wreckage. Hard. He didn't even notice when the broken glass cut his hand.

All he saw was the whiskey and the blood.

23

Melissa Sayers Colbert wore a plain black designer suit with a pearl and diamond choker that had been in her family for three generations. Her hair stylist had arranged her hair in a simple French twist. She sat with her legs demurely crossed at the ankles and her hands folded in her lap.

Folded and still. No fidgeting. Fidgeters didn't get out of The Towers.

The Towers. How she hated that name. As if she'd spent the last four and a half years at some great and glorious height instead of in a bare room that contained nothing she could use to cut her wrists or hang herself.

"You look good, Melissa." Dr. Marlin Houston looked like Buddha sitting behind his desk with his disgustingly fat belly and his bald head, but Melissa didn't tell him so. Her release depended on him.

"Thank you." *Keep it simple. Say nothing to tip him off.*

"You've made great progress these last three months." Dr. Houston folded his fat hands and propped them on his belly.

Clayton hadn't had an ounce of extra fat on his body. She remembered how he used to stand with his shoulders back and his hips jutted slightly forward so that he looked relaxed and arrogant at the same time.

Her hands began to tremble and she hid them behind her purse.

Don't think about Clayton until you get out.

"This is the most rewarding part of my job, Melissa. Signing the release." He wrote his signature with a flourish, then smiled at her. "I expect I'll be seeing your picture again in the society pages before too long."

"Perhaps." She let her own smile match his. Demure. Not triumphant. Not secretive.

"What are your immediate plans?"

"I thought I'd do a little traveling."

"Good. It's a great time of year to see the sights."

She knew Witch Dance had some beautiful sights. Clayton had talked about them enough so that she could picture them without ever setting foot on Tribal Lands. But it wasn't the sights she was going to see.

Back in her bare room she opened her purse and took out the cards. Then she spread them on the bed and counted them. Eight. One every Christmas and one every year on the anniversary of Clayton's death.

Although she knew them by heart, Melissa read them all again. Then she put them back in her purse and closed the snap.

Did that redheaded bitch think eight cards made up for stealing Clayton?

Kate and Mark worked tirelessly every day, searching medical records, questioning parents, and following false leads. And at night they fell into separate beds, exhausted. Finally the pieces of the puzzle fell into place.

All paths led to Witch Creek.

They left early Saturday morning, on horses. The creek was swollen with recent rains, its muddy waters overflowing the banks in some spots.

"Holy shit!" Mark said as two large carp landed at his feet, their bloated bodies ready to explode. He knelt quickly, studying the fish, then gazed out over the creek. Rusty cans and broken sticks floated by ... and other dead fish. "Pay dirt, Kate. Look at that."

Across the way the Witch Dance Tool and Die Plant spewed plumes of smoke into the air, running full tilt. The eight o'clock whistle rent the silence, and a large group of blue-shirted workers poured out the front door, while another large group went inside, changing shifts.

Quickly Mark and Kate gathered samples of the water. "What do you bet we find carbon tet?" he said.

Kate had a sudden vision of children playing in the water, laughing in the sunshine while the deadly solvent, carbon tetrachloride, was absorbed through their skin. It made perfect sense. And yet to find a factory guilty of pollution of that nature, either intentional or otherwise, would be politically and economically explosive.

"We can't know that yet."

"Until we do, this place had damned well better be off limits to everybody in Witch Dance. Who can do that, Kate?"

One man. Eagle Mingo.

"Monday I'll go and see the governor," she said.

Eagle watched for her out the window like a jealous lover. Kate's car stopped at the curb and Mark Grant helped her out. They stood close, too close for mere colleagues.

Anna had told him all about Mark, describing the young doctor in excruciating detail, right down to his boyish grin, never knowing that every word she uttered lacerated Eagle's soul.

Witch Dance was a small village where everybody's business was up for discussion, particularly the business of the governor's former lover. Eagle was ashamed of the way he had stationed himself beside the village gossips the past week, listening for the latest word on Kate. He became a regular at places he usually shunned, Graden's Pool Hall, Jimmy Running Bear's Bar.

"The medicine woman's found herself some new medicine," a man at the bar had said Saturday night. "A doctor with a great bedside manner." He slapped his hand on his knee, tickled at his own pathetic humor.

Depraved maniac that he was, Eagle picked up his beer and casually changed stools so he'd be closer.

"So I heard," the woman with him said. "My brother was coming off the night shift at the plant and saw them down at Witch Creek together. Kissing."

"Kissing? You don't say?"

"Well, he could have been mistaken, but he said it sure looked like it to him." She slugged back her drink. "Hell, he's staying right there in her house. I don't even have brains, and I've got that figured out."

"You got brains, honey, but they're not in your head."

"Where are they, Joe?"

"In the right place, Pearl."

The memory of that conversation still plagued Eagle. He'd released her five years before. What right did he have to know what she was doing now? Or to care?

"Dr. Malone is here," his secretary said over the intercom.

"Send her in." Eagle didn't have to freeze his face into a careful mask: It had been frozen for years. So had his heart.

"Hello, Kate."

"Eagle."

There was a brightness to her smile and a quickness to her step that hadn't been there before. Was Mark Grant responsible? Were the sleazy gossips right?

"As you know, I've been investigating the death of my patients."

He didn't pretend ignorance. He made it his business to know everything that went on in Tribal Lands. Kate, of all people, knew that about him.

"Yes." So far, so good. He sounded interested, yet cool and removed. As befitted a governor.

"Dr. Mark Grant is helping me."

How? Is he cooling your hot skin with his tongue? Do you fly with him as you did with me?

Waka ahina uno, iskunosi Wictonaye. Waka.

Her voice flowed over him like warm honey as she told him of their discoveries at Witch Creek ... and their suspicions.

"The area needs to be quarantined," she said.

"Even before the investigation is complete?"

"Yes. I'm not willing to take chances with the lives of children. Are you?"

The minute she asked the question, Kate was ashamed of herself. For the first time since she'd walked into the office, Eagle dropped his careful mask.

"Do you think I'll let more children die if I can prevent it?" Suddenly the thunderous rage went out of him, and he became businesslike once more. "If Witch Creek is polluted, as you and your colleague suspect, then the rest of the investigation will be the responsibility of this office."

"But—"

"I know you, Kate. I've seen you charge into battle with a mop."

Memories threatened to be her undoing.

Be generous, Kate, he said as she tangled herself around him like a morning glory vine.

She stood up. While she still could.

"I'm interested only in the medical aspect of this investigation, not the political. I'll do my job and you can do yours. Without me and my formidable mop."

Eagle watched until she was out the door, then he went back to the window and watched her walk all the way down to the street. She smiled when she saw Mark, smiled when he put his hands all over her, helping her into the car.

Eagle gripped the edge of the windowsill. It wasn't Kate's mop that was formidable. She was a powder keg and he was the match. Or was it the other way around?

Where would they go in Kate's red car? Back to her cottage to make love on her white sheets while the setting sun gilded her skin and turned her hair to flame?

Sitting at his desk, Eagle suddenly felt drained of all energy. Overwork was partially responsible. There was

more to do in his second term as governor than in his
first. More industries were discovering the advantages
of locating on Tribal Lands. Some of the legislators
wanted owners of gambling casinos to be allowed
building permits. There was an ongoing battle between
environmentalists and the manufacturers.

He went back to the window to see if he could catch
a glimpse of Kate's car. She was long since out of sight.

Foolish at his age to be watching out the window for
a woman he couldn't have.

He was not getting any younger. Perhaps his father
was right. It was time for him to be looking for a wife.

"I'm getting old," Winston had said. "I'd like to live
to see your issue, Eagle."

His issue. They would have to be full-blood, of
course. Mentally he ran down his list of full-blood
women. Most of them were already married, and the
others were far too young. Only one woman came to
mind. She was lovely, intelligent, and single. A perfect
candidate to bear his *issue*.

Everything in Eagle recoiled at the idea. Visions of his
future came to him, a future empty of love and devoid
of children. A brilliant image of Kate flashed into his
mind, Kate, with the wind and the sun in her hair, galloping across the prairie on Mahli.

He'd sacrificed his love for the good of the Chickasaw
Nation. Surely he could sacrifice his pride for the sake
of family.

With his jaw set in steely determination, he picked up
the phone and dialed. Never let it be said that Eagle
Mingo had destroyed the sacred lineage.

"Hello?" The female voice at the other end of the line
was full of life and spirit.

"This is Eagle Mingo," he said, committing himself to
a course of action that would forever rip asunder the
fragile ties that still bound him to Kate Malone.

24

Deborah hated keeping secrets. More than that, she hated feeling like a traitor. Actually, she hadn't betrayed anybody, not yet anyhow; but she was certainly tempted. Oh, how she was tempted.

"Deborah . . ." Kate came up behind her, and she nearly dropped the chart she was working on. "You're as jumpy as a cat today. Is anything wrong?"

"No." Now she was a liar too. "Just the excitement of sending all our patients home."

"Not all of them, Deborah."

The pain in Kate's voice nearly broke her heart. She put an arm around her best friend's shoulders.

"Three survived. Just remember that."

"I'm trying."

"While you're at it, think how many lives you've saved by finding out about the carbon tet in Witch Creek."

"It's not over yet. And anyhow, I didn't do it alone. Mark helped."

"Are you going to the benefit dance for the Chickasaw Cultural Center with him?"

"How did you know he'd asked?"

"I have eyes and ears, Kate, and they rarely ever fail me, especially when I've been eavesdropping." Kate

laughed. "You should go. It's time to move on beyond . . ."

"Eagle?"

"Yes." Deborah felt her face flame. Was she trying to
help her best friend, or was her advice self-serving? She
turned quickly toward the coffeepot.

"What's the matter with you, Deborah?"

"Nothing's the matter with me."

"Oh, yeah? Since when have you started turning your
back instead of looking me straight in the eye and telling me exactly what I should do? I no longer fall apart
at the mention of Eagle Mingo's name."

The cup slipped from Deborah's hand, sending hot
coffee and glass shards across the floor. She and Kate
reached for paper towels at the same time. Deborah
stepped back, redfaced.

Sudden comprehension dawned on Kate.

"*You're* the one who is upset. What's going on?"

"I didn't mean to tell you."

"Tell me what?"

"Eagle asked me to the dance. . . . But, Kate, I said no.
I would never betray my best friend."

Had the earth stopped spinning? Kate wondered. Was
that why she felt off balance?

"Why on earth did you say no? He's single; you're single. He's full-blood; you're full-blood. It's a perfect match."

"I can't do that to you, Kate."

"It's over between us. It's *been* over."

"You wouldn't be upset if I said yes?"

"Of course not." Not upset. Crazed was more like it.
Kate was crazy with rage and jealousy and pain. Maybe
she needed a psychiatrist.

Or a good stiff belt of whiskey. That's the way Mick
Malone faced all his problems. Maybe she was her father's daughter after all.

"Call him back and accept." She was saying that with
a smile? Was Deborah fooled?

"I will . . . if you're sure . . . oh, my gosh, Eagle
Mingo. He has to be the catch of the century." She gave

Kate a quick, sympathetic look. "Not that I can catch him. I mean . . ."

Kate forced a laugh.

"Of course you can catch him. You're a beautiful, desirable woman. Any man would have to be a fool not to want you. And believe me, Eagle Mingo is no fool."

Waka ahina uno, iskunosi Wictonaye. Waka.

By all the saints, she was going to make a fool of herself in front of Deborah.

"Look," Kate said. "I'm going to take off early. You'll have the clinic all to yourself. Don't wait till you get home. Call him from here."

"You're sure?"

"I'm absolutely, positively certain."

Of course she was certain. That's why she was on her third glass of whiskey. Hell, why stop with the third glass? Why not take the whole bottle?

With the bottle clutched in her hand, Kate attempted to rise from her chair. The kitchen wavered, then tilted. She caught the edge of the table.

"Whoopsy-daisy." Hanging on to both table and bottle, she waited for the room to stop spinning. Finally, it did, but the furniture wouldn't stand still. She held on to it anyhow, crossing the kitchen inch by inch, then navigating the treacherous den. The damned furniture kept coming up to meet her.

Her shins would be black and blue tomorrow. If there was a tomorrow.

Collapsed in an ignoble heap on the sofa, Kate contemplated the level of liquor in the bottle. There was still plenty to provide total oblivion.

She tipped the bottle up and felt the sting as the whiskey hit her throat. The front door banged open with such a racket that Kate nearly fell off the couch.

"Whoops!" With parts of her on the floor and parts of her on the couch, she giggled. "Damned treasherous furnishure."

"Holy cow." Mark stared at her, dumbstruck, then he began to laugh. "You're totally smashed."

"Nope. Didn't shmash a thing." She waved the bottle at him. "Wan' a drink?"

"Don't mind if I do." He helped her up and propped her on the sofa, then sat down beside her. "What's the occasion?"

"Shelebrashun."

"You heard already?" He took a swig. "Eagle's going to nail those bastards to the wall if he finds out they deliberately dumped carbon tet into Witch Creek."

"Too busy danshing."

"Who is?"

"The governor."

"I see." He saw far more than she was telling. Everybody in Tribal Lands knew that Kate Malone had once been the governor's woman. Mark set the bottle aside and gently pulled Kate to her feet. "No sense in letting anybody get ahead of us. May I have this dance, Dr. Kate Malone?"

"Shertainly."

"I dance a mean tango. Ever tango?"

"Tangled with Eagle . . . long time ago."

"If you had tangled with me, I'd never have let you go."

"Damn shtraight."

She swayed, and he braced her with both arms around her waist. Merciful saints, she felt good. Everything would be perfect if they had music.

He began to hum.

"Love-ly. What ish it?"

" 'Moon over Miami.' It's the only song I know well. I have to change the rhythm a little bit to make it right for the tango, but, what the heck, I'm a multitalented guy." Grinning down at her, he watched the play of firelight in her hair. "I guess you've noticed by now," he added, hoping she had.

Kate didn't answer, but leaned heavily against him with her face pressed in the open neck of his shirt. Her breath was warm against his skin, warm and erotic. Suddenly he felt the moist tip of her tongue.

"Hungry, Kate?"

"For you." She put her hand in the opening of his shirt and splayed her fingers against his skin. "Wan' chou."

Mark did a quick conscience check, and discovered to his surprise that he had one. He wondered if he wrestled with it long enough whether he could overcome it.

"Now," she murmured. " 'Side the fire . . . the mishtical fire."

Tears slid down her cheeks and burned his skin, and he knew it wasn't he that Kate wanted, but another, a man who spoke in the dark, honeyed tongue of his ancestors.

"I want you too, babe, but you'd never respect me in the morning." She was crying outright now, her tears wetting the front of his shirt. "It's all right, Kate."

He picked her up as if she were a child and carried her into her bedroom.

"Wait right here," he said when he laid her on the bed, though she was in no condition to go anywhere.

Her bathroom smelled like her, light floral fragrances blended with an exotic musky scent. Leaning against the lavatory, he looked at his pinched face in the mirror.

"Dr. Grant, you noble son of a bitch, you deserve a medal for this . . . or a head examination."

He found a pink washcloth, wet it with cold water, then tenderly washed her face.

"Feels good." She caught his hand and guided it down her throat. "Don't shtop."

"If I don't stop now, I never will." The bedsprings creaked when he stood up. "I would get you out of those clothes, Kate, but there's only so much temptation a man in my condition can bear."

"What condition?"

"I'll tell you about it tomorrow . . . when you're sober." Pausing in the doorway, he looked back at her, disheveled and dewy with desire. For somebody else. "That is . . . if you still want to hear about it."

Softly, he closed her door.

25

Hal Lightfoot was proud of his office. Only twenty and already he was an executive.

He balled a wad of paper and hurled it overhanded toward the wastebasket. It landed on the floor with the other wads of paper.

When he got up, the old swivel chair squeaked and threatened to topple. He kicked it with his steel-toed boots and sent it flying into the wall. The rusty rollers on the bottom made a scratch against the painted concrete walls, but nobody would ever see. Nobody cared.

The basement was his domain. So what if his office was a forgotten closet he'd cleaned out and furnished with castoffs he'd rescued from the garbage heap? And what if his title was one he'd made up? Maintenance engineer. It sounded a hell of a lot better than janitor.

Besides, he knew things, things that would advance him quickly up the corporate ladder.

If he played his cards right.

He gathered his dust mops and rags and was headed up the stairs, when a scene outside the basement window caught his attention. The governor and Lacey Wainwright were standing beside the garbage heap, which was exactly the place they belonged. In Hal's opinion, all the big-shot bastards who thought they were better than everybody else belonged right out there on the garbage heap.

He couldn't hear what they were saying, but it didn't take a genius to figure it out. Everybody knew about the scandal Kate Malone had stirred up.

Now, there was a piece of work. That bitch had a lot coming to her, and she deserved every bit of it.

That pompous asshole Wainwright who thought he was such a hotshot manager would be telling the governor that he didn't have any idea how the rusty barrels got out there and leaked toxic waste into Witch Creek.

In a pig's eye.

And Mingo would look at him with those eyes blacker than the pits of hell and tell him he spoke with the *sente soolish*.

Hell, he could tell that Mingo a thing or two. And might have if he didn't still remember the humiliation of that summer night in front of Kate Malone's clinic. Hatred boiled in him at the thought of that meddling witch.

And Wainwright. He hated that piece of shit too. Driving around Tribal Lands in his gold Cadillac as if he owned the whole damned place. Chicago white trash was what he was.

Still, he could be useful to Hal. He fortified himself with peyote, then leaned against the wall until the thundering of the white buffalo was a distant echo.

As he went up the stairs with his mops and rags, Hal remembered a saying of his grandfather's: Be careful when you hunt for the rattlesnake that he does not find you before you find him, for the bite of the rattler is death.

Hal knew how to be careful.

Kate's head felt as big as a watermelon. Movement set off jackhammers behind her temples that caused her eyes to come unfocused.

"You've done it now, Katie Elizabeth," she said.

Her sins had caught up with her. She'd never make it
to the front porch for the morning paper, let alone to the
clinic. Picking up the phone, she dialed Deborah's
number. Even the distant ringing of the phone set off
minor explosions in her head. Fortunately she didn't
have to endure more than one ring.

"Deborah?"

"Why are you whispering, Kate?"

"Shhh. Not so loud." Thinking fast, she made an excuse. "Mark's still asleep."

Too late, she realized that Deborah would wonder
how a telephone conversation would awaken him unless they were in the same bedroom.

"Hmmm" was all Deborah said.

"Can you handle things by yourself today?"

"Certainly. If there's an emergency, I'll call you."

"Thanks."

Coward, she said to herself when she hung up. She
hadn't wanted to face Deborah today, hadn't wanted to
see the glow of Eagle Mingo in her eyes. The hangover
was merely a convenient excuse.

"You'll have to do better than this, Katie Elizabeth,"
she muttered as she slipped into her robe.

This was what living alone had reduced her to: talking to herself. And sounding like her father in the bargain.

Could that be a sign? Was somebody trying to tell her
it was time to get on with her life.

She might start by being more responsive to Mark
Grant. Blurred images came to her mind of herself lick-
ing his skin. By all the saints, had she actually done
that?

Holding her head together with the palms of her
hands and sheer willpower, she crept through the house
and onto the front porch to get the morning paper.
Bending sent her into such a swoon that she closed her
eyes. Reaching blindly, she encountered something soft
and sticky.

A dead bird lay on top of her newspaper, its neck broken and its wings ripped off.

Kate sank to her knees and stared at the bird, horrified. How did it get there? She didn't own a cat, and birds didn't fall out of trees in that condition.

She took the next leap in logic: Someone had put it there. But who? And why?

She felt the bile rising in her throat, and leaning over the porch railing, she heaved. The crisp early morning breezes cooled her forehead and blew some of the cobwebs from her mind.

She was being paranoid. There were plenty of stray cats in Witch Dance. She'd seen them nosing around the garbage cans behind the clinic.

"Poor little thing," she said, picking up the newspaper with the bird cradled inside.

A blood-smeared headline caught her eye. "Governor Closes Witch Dance Tool and Die Plant." Still kneeling, she read the rest of the story.

"Governor Mingo personally investigated claims that Witch Dance Tool and Die dumped toxic chemicals into the creek that runs behind their property. Plant manager Lacey Wainwright claims the toxic spills were accidental. At this printing the governor has closed the plant, but says the closure is temporary, pending further investigation.

"Clean-up efforts are under way, and until they are complete, the entire area around the plant is quarantined.

"Employees at the plant, angry at the shutdown and temporary loss of jobs, charged 'bleeding heart environmentalists' with scare tactics. Dr. Kate Malone along with Dr. Mark Grant discovered the toxic wastes that led to the closure of the plant."

A recent photo of Eagle accompanied the article. Kate stared at it, racked by visions of Deborah in his arms. Her lover and her best friend.

Was there any justice in the world?

Sighing, she folded the paper carefully around the

small broken bird and carried the bundle to the garbage can. When Mark asked, she'd say the paper boy forgot to deliver.

No need to mention the dead bird. There were other, more pressing things she wanted to talk about. Such as whether Mark Grant would do her the honor of escorting her to the dance at the Chickasaw Cultural Center.

Anna sat across the kitchen table from her husband and tried to carry the conversation by herself.

"I might take a job," she said.

Cole stared at her, silent. Clint's brows drew together as he watched his father, waiting. Then he forced a bright smile.

"That's great, Mom."

Still, nothing from Cole. Two months earlier he'd have wrapped his arms around her and cajoled her with endearing words. "I can't do without you at the ranch, Anna," he'd have said. "What would I do if my sweet hummingbird were not here?"

Two months earlier Bucky and Mary Doe had been alive. Anna wadded her napkin in her fist and tried not to cry.

"Eagle said I could work in his office. His secretary is swamped." Her husband stared right through her. "I know it's not much, but it's a start."

Cole picked up his knife and sliced his roast beef.

"Whatever you want to do, Anna. It's no concern to me."

"No concern to you? I'm your wife!"

The knife clanked against his plate, and his chair fell over as he stood up.

"Cole, where are you going?"

He didn't answer. His boots echoed on the polished wood floor as he made his way to the back door.

"Cole?"

Tears started in her eyes as she looked at her son.

"Clint . . . stop him."

"Let him go, Mother."

* * *

The sun had left the sky and the first stars were beginning to show. In the distance a lone wolf howled,
and the nighthawk answered. Cole listened to the night
music and waited for peace to invade his soul. But it
didn't come. Peace had eluded him for many moons
now.

Behind him the kitchen windows glowed. Anna
would still be sitting at the table. Thinking of the tears
in her eyes, he wavered, then resolutely he started to the
barn.

Cold winds bit his skin. He probably should go back
to get a coat, but the journey he had to take would not
be postponed, not even for ten minutes.

His mare whinnied when he entered the barn. They
hadn't ridden together in a long time, not since the
night he'd carried his children into the mountains.

Filled with purpose, he felt strength and power surge
through him. He put bridle and blanket on his mare,
then vaulted onto her back. Nothing could take away
his riding skills, not even alcohol.

Outside, the sky had darkened and the stars brightened. Lights were on inside Cole's house, and through
the window he saw his wife. Anna. Love of his life.
Keeper of his heart. Guardian of his soul.

Impatient, his mare whinnied. Cole dug his heels into
her flanks and raced down the road with the night wind
singing in his ears.

He had no soul.

That was his mission. To find his soul.

26

There was no doubt that Deborah Lightfoot was a beautiful woman. Her hair hung down her back like a bolt of black silk and her skin shone like polished copper. She was gentle, kindhearted, and intelligent. All the qualities a man would want in a woman.

Or a wife.

The vague dissatisfaction Eagle felt turned to full-blown unhappiness as he gazed across the room. Kate Malone was dancing in the arms of another man.

"I haven't had this much fun in years," Deborah said, and Eagle leaned down to catch her voice above the music. With Kate he hadn't had to bend so far. Her head had fit exactly on his shoulder.

"Do you love dancing?" Foolish question. She'd just admitted as much.

"Oh, yes. When I was a little girl I dreamed about being a ballerina. Of course, that was before I decided to be a cowboy."

"A cowgirl?"

"No. I wanted to be a cowboy. I'd be in pictures, of course, and for once I'd be on the winning side."

Deborah's laughter was infectious. Over the top of her head he saw Kate laugh at something Mark Grant had said. He pulled Deborah closer, determined to make the relationship work.

"Let's dance under the stars," he said, leading her toward the open French doors. On the patio he wouldn't have to see Kate and Mark Grant pressed together like a matching set of bookends.

"Sounds like a wonderfully romantic idea." Deborah smiled up at him. "I'm a sucker for romance, you know."

The trust in her eyes was absolute. He'd wrestle with his conscience tomorrow.

Mark Grant saw Kate's eyes darken when Eagle left the room, felt the tension that came into her shoulders and back, heard her soft intake of breath. All the grand plans he'd made suddenly came crashing down around his ears.

What a fool he'd been. Whistling while he dressed for the dance, thinking she'd finally noticed him. Picturing the two of them cuddled cheek to cheek on the dance floor, then later, tangled together in his bed. Or hers. Heck, they might not even make it home. They might end up in the backseat of his car.

Now, standing on the dance floor with his dreams vanished like dandelions in the wind, he found a shining nobility he hadn't known he had. Obviously it had been meant for some ancient knight in King Arthur's court and had missed its mark by several hundred years, but heck, he was smart. He'd grab whatever lifeline came his way.

"You know, Kate, I'm mighty glad you asked me to this shindig, but I don't want you to get the wrong idea."

She went still, watching his face.

"I mean . . . I'm as human as the next man. I'm not saying I wouldn't like to take you to bed and screw your socks off."

"I believe I was the one making that move."

"Yeah, well, you nearly succeeded." He grinned to

take the sting out of his words. "But a man has his rep-
utation to think of. Too many one-night stands, and they
won't let me wear white at the wedding."

"You're leaving, aren't you, Mark?"

"Going to Africa is leaving, Kate. Going to Ada just
means I won't be in your house. This business with the
children is nearly over. I can do what needs to be done
from Ada." He chucked her under the chin. "But heck,
kid, if you get hungry for my cooking, haul ass over
here and let me rustle up some grub. You might even
talk me into a movie."

"Do you know how wonderful you are?" Kate cupped
his face.

"Grandma told me that once."

Kate kissed him softly on the cheek. He held her close
for a moment, then stood back, pasting a false, silly grin
on his face.

"Thank you, Mark. For everything."

He put his arm around her waist and led her from the
dance floor, even pausing in the doorway so she could
take one last look at Eagle, silhouetted against the
French doors, dancing under the stars with Deborah.

Noble to the bitter end, Mark thought. He ought to
get some kind of humanitarian of the year award.

Melissa Colbert saw Kate leave. Standing at the
punch bowl, surrounded by people who weren't important to her, she gave a secret smile. The bitch had been
so busy rubbing herself all over that man she was with,
she hadn't even noticed the visitor from Boston. Which
was fine with Melissa. The element of surprise always
had its advantages.

She wondered if the man Kate was seducing this time
belonged to somebody else.

"We're glad you're here to continue Dr. Colbert's al-
truistic work." The speaker was Black something or
other. She'd already forgotten their names, but it didn't
matter. "Everybody around here loved Clayton."

At the mention of his name, a dark fog began to fall

over Melissa, descending first over her chest so that she felt smothered. Fighting panic, she searched the room, looking for something, anything, to hold back the darkness.

And that's when she saw him. He stood apart from the crowd, his handsome face dark and brooding, his stance relaxed and yet arrogant.

"Excuse me, please," she said.

The man assessed her boldly as she approached, his eyes hooded and wary. "Hello, foxy lady."

"Hello. I'm Melissa Sayers Colbert."

"A woman with three names has to be important."

"I am."

"I've been watching you across the room."

"And I've been watching you."

"Do you like what you see?"

"I'll have to reserve judgment on that." Melissa held out her hand, and he took it. She felt the heat of him all the way to her toes. Oh, she liked what she saw, liked it very much indeed.

"Where are we going, Miss Foxy Lady with Three Names?"

"Do you care?"

"No. As long as I get what I want."

Her long white limousine was waiting for them outside the door. She gave her chauffeur directions, then settled back against the white leather cushions.

A beautiful copper-colored hand pushed her skirt aside and slid inside her panties. She was already wet for him.

"My name is Hal Lightfoot," he said.

"It doesn't matter, dear boy."

He was young, so young. And so very necessary.

The first snows had already fallen in the mountains and lay glittering like sugar over the tops of the trees and the roof of the hut. Its pristine beauty disguised the treachery of the mountain peaks and the jagged rocks that lay like sharks in the depths of the canyons.

Traveling in the darkness, a lesser man than Cole might have lost his life. But Cole knew the land, knew how to survive its treacheries. Neither the bitter winds nor the freshly falling snow nor the distant screaming of the screech owl deterred him. The mountains called to him in voices of beauty and the stars bent low to give him light.

His horse stepped into a hole drifted over with snow, but Cole knew he wouldn't go down. Nothing could stop his quest.

The dark winds cried with the voices of the coyote and the bobcat, but onward Cole traveled, winding upward toward the shroud of mists that covered the tops of the mountain. The Great Spirit caught time in a dark velvet net and held it captive for the duration of Cole's journey. Day and night ceased. Hunger and pain no longer existed. There was nothing except the shrouded peaks and the need. The urgent need.

Suddenly out of the mists came a vision, an ancient Spirit Talker wrapped in the buffalo robes. His bear-claw necklace gleamed in the moonlight.

"I knew you would come," he said, holding out his hand. It was warm and soothing. "I've prepared for you."

Smells of smoke mingled with the fragrances of medicinal herbs inside the small hut. Cole sat upon a bright red blanket while the old shaman covered him with the skin of a buffalo. He drew the tattered edges close and inhaled the scent of mold.

"A few more suns and I will vanish from these mountains just as the council fires and the curling smoke from our lodge fires have vanished," the medicine man said. "Gone are the bark canoes and the thunder of buffalo and the songs of our women." A heady, pungent smell filled the air as the shaman puffed on his pipe.

"I have had a vision," he added. "In dreams filled with bending grasses and clear waters, the white buffalo came to me."

He passed the pipe to Cole, who drew the mind-freeing drug deep into his lungs. Closing his eyes, he heard the thunder of the hooves as the Great Divine Presence showed himself once more, emerging from the darkness as white as the snow itself.

"I, too, see the buffalo."

"It is good. It is a sign." They passed the pipe between them once more, in perfect understanding.

At peace at last, Cole lay upon his blanket and slept.

The beauty of being maintenance engineer was that he had access to the building even with the plant shut down, and nobody was ever surprised to see him with his mops and buckets. Outside the door marked MAN- AGER, Hal mopped the same spot over and over. In the old, thin-walled building, every word Lacey Wainwright uttered was as clear as if it were being broadcast over a microphone.

"Dammit all to hell, Bruce, we've got to stop Eagle Mingo."

"We can't stop Eagle Mingo. He's the governor, and in Chickasaw territory that translates as the law of the land."

Bruce Graden was second in command, a skinny, whining man who looked as if he couldn't run a public toilet, let alone a whole plant. What Wainwright needed was a real man, somebody with guts.

"He's getting too close." Wainwright smacked his fist against his desk. The blow reverberated in the hallway. "We can't let him find out that we deliberately dumped toxic waste into the creek. Have you got your story straight?"

"Yes ... but what would it cost to dispose of it correctly? I mean, it seems to me ... with the lives of children at stake and all—"

"Bullshit! Hog-tie me with a bunch of regulations, and I might as well kiss all my profit good-bye. We've got a gold mine out here, and I'm not going to let anybody destroy that. Nobody. Do you understand?"

"I understand." Bruce Graden headed for the door.

Bent over his mop, Hal did some serious scrubbing until Bruce was out of sight. Then he leaned his mop against the wall and slicked back his hair.

The rattlesnake hunt was over. It was time to move in for the kill.

Lacey Wainwright didn't look too happy to see him. That would all change in about five minutes.

"Mr. Wainwright, I'm Hal Lightfoot."

"I know who you are. What I don't know is what in the hell you want."

"What I want can wait. What I know is more important." He sat in the chair without asking. Lacey Wainwright was not the kind of man who appreciated timidity.

Wainwright bit off the end of a big cigar, then lit up and sat back, blowing smoke. "And what is it you think you know?"

"I don't think; I know. These walls have ears, and I've heard everything." He winked. "We both know how Witch Creek got polluted, don't we?"

Lacey's jaw clamped over his cigar as he sized up Hal.

"And you want money. Is that it?"

"No. I want a promotion. Executive assistant sounds good to me. I can lie and cheat and steal with a straight face and a clear conscience, and as far as I'm concerned, Eagle Mingo is a man who hasn't met his match."

Wainwright blew smoke rings in his direction. Hal didn't flinch.

"You've got balls. I like that."

Melissa Sayers Colbert had liked them too. But that was a bit of information Hal intended to keep to himself. At least for the time being.

"Do we have a deal?" he asked.

The chair creaked as Wainwright stood up. Taking another cigar from the teakwood box on his table, he passed it to Hal.

"Deal," he said.

* * *

Bruce Graden was not surprised to find the pink slip in his box. Wainwright didn't even do him the courtesy of firing him in person.

He cleaned out his desk, careful not to leave even a scrap of paper that would benefit his successor. The janitor, of all people. News like that traveled fast.

It took him until five o'clock to get his belongings neatly boxed and stored in the trunk of his car. Then, as if he were finishing an ordinary day, he punched out and drove home.

His telephone would be safe, at least for a while. But one phone call was all he needed. He looked up the number and dialed. It was answered on the first ring.

"Eagle Mingo here."

Bruce thanked his lucky stars for the governor's open-door policy that made him accessible, even in his own home.

"I know how the toxic chemicals got into Witch Creek."

"Who is this?"

"I'm afraid I can't tell you that, Governor." No one would ever know. And by tomorrow he'd be so long gone that no one would ever find him. "Will you listen to what I have to say?"

"I'm listening."

As Bruce Graden began to talk, he knew that he might be signing his own death warrant.

27

Kate settled into an easy chair with a cup of coffee, then switched on the ten o'clock news. A dark, angry face filled the screen, shouting, "Clip Eagle's wings."

Kate reached for the remote control to turn up the volume. Pickets milled around the governor's office, waving signs and screaming.

"Who will feed our children?"

"Who will buy our shoes?"

"Eagle Mingo, unfair to labor."

The camera panned the crowd, and Kate leaned forward, riveted. One dark man stood out in the crowd, a part of it and yet strangely remote from the bedlam.

The face was vaguely familiar, but before Kate could be certain, the camera had switched to Gracie Wood, reporter for ADTV. Bundled against the cold in a red wool coat and scarf, she stood outside the state house, holding a microphone in her gloved hands. Snow swirled around her.

"In what is perhaps the first unpopular decision of his career, Governor Eagle Mingo some weeks ago ordered the closing of the tool and die plant on Witch Creek. Rumors that the closure is permanent have fueled tempers and sparked the riots you see here at the state house.

The governor is in his office in conference with attorneys, and we're expecting him to emerge any minute."

In the background the picketers shouted, "We want jobs. We want jobs."

The camera panned back to Gracie Wood . . . and Eagle Mingo.

"Governor, the jobless are picketing your office. Would you care to comment?"

"I regret any hardships placed on the employees of the Witch Dance Tool and Die Plant, but I will not be moved by strong-arm tactics. The major concern of this office is cleaning up the toxic waste and ensuring that the tragic deaths that occurred this summer will never happen again."

"Are you filing charges against Witch Dance Tool and Die?"

"No comment."

"Two of the children were from your own family. Is that not correct, Governor?"

Stone Face, Eagle's political enemies called him. But there was nothing stony about his face now. Pain etched his features and flickered briefly in his eyes.

Kate couldn't bear to watch, couldn't bear to listen. Quickly she flipped the TV off, then went into the kitchen to find some food.

A head of wilted lettuce and two shriveled carrots stared back at her from the refrigerator. Though she had no appetite, she knew she had to eat. She couldn't keep up her pace without food. Rummaging in the crisper, she found two slices of ham left over from the days of Mark Grant.

What was he doing now? Did he miss her? Did anybody miss her?

A wave of loneliness struck her so hard, she leaned her head against the refrigerator. Loneliness and anguish. All those little children, all those little graves. And it wasn't over yet. Who knew how many children had played in Witch Creek, how many new cases would crop up over the next few months?

Sometimes she felt inadequate for the task she'd set for herself. She took two deep breaths to ward off the helpless, hopeless feeling.

"Snap out of it, Katie Elizabeth, or soon you're going to be having a pity party."

With her chin jutted out, she grabbed the ham and a jar of mayonnaise and marched to her bread box. Setting the ham on the kitchen counter, she lifted the lid. The jar of mayonnaise slid from her hand and crashed to the floor. Sticky goo spattered over her shoes, and a large shard of glass ricocheted off the floor and cut her leg.

Kate never noticed.

Inside the box lay a cloth doll with red hair. It's neck had been sliced and blood had been smeared on the front of its dress. With trembling hands Kate lifted the effigy. The blood was real . . . and the hair.

Violent shivers overtook her. Someone had been in her house, someone who hated her. Still holding the doll, she hugged herself hard to keep the shivers from becoming convulsions.

A glimpse of white at the bottom of the bread box caught her eye. Kate leaned over so she could read it without touching it.

You're next, witch.

The note was scrawled in blood.

Kate dropped the doll on top of the note and slammed the lid of the bread box shut. Outside her window a whippoorwill called. Or was it a signal of some kind? She knew that many of the Chickasaws were excellent at bird imitations.

The hair at the back of her neck stood on end. The darkness had eyes.

Moving methodically, she checked the locks on all the doors and windows and lowered all the shades. In the safety of her bedroom she sat huddled in the middle of the bed. Wind moaned around the eaves, and the old house creaked and groaned. Funny, how she'd never noticed the noises before. Now every one raised prickles on her skin.

Something clattered against the side of the house, and she jerked, covering her mouth with her hands. The banging noise came again. Tiptoeing, she peeked through the shade.

A loose shutter. She remembered now. Mark had noticed it last week.

In the growing darkness the objects in her room loomed large, took on a life of their own. Had she left her robe hanging on the chair like that? And her high-heeled shoes? She remembered kicking them off the day before, and now they sat side by side, perfectly aligned, like soldiers waiting to go to war.

The antique wardrobe in the corner was big enough to hide a full-grown man. Kate jerked the door open so hard, she set the clothes swinging on the rack. The silky skirts whispered against each other, then settled into place. She reached inside and felt into the dark recesses of the wardrobe.

Nothing there. She was letting herself get spooked.

She jerked up her pajamas and marched into the bathroom, careful to lock the door. Bathed and dressed for bed, she sat down at the vanity and reached for her hairbrush. It was not there.

Pushing away the panic that threatened, she began a methodical search. She had misplaced it. That was all. People with too much on their minds frequently misplaced things.

The hairbrush was nowhere in the bathroom, nowhere in the bedroom. At last, emotionally exhausted with the search, Kate turned back the covers. And there on her pillow was her hairbrush. It lay on a black silk cloth. All the hair had been carefully plucked from the bristles and arranged in a red circle upon the black silk.

Another white note was pinned to the silk: *Your tormentor sees all, knows all. Nothing is safe from me.*

Kate stifled the screams she felt welling in her throat. She felt violated.

Outside her window the mournful call of the whip-poorwill sounded once more. Moving swiftly and surely, Kate went to the wardrobe and took down a gun.

Someone wanted her dead, but she had no intention of being an easy target.

BOOK III
The Passage

When the land grew weary with strife,
The Great Spirit sent rains to wash away the blood
    and winds to blow away the anguish.
From the center of Father Sky came a bright light,
    shining on all the earth's people.
And into the light flew the Eagle, his great wings
    outstretched, protecting the pride and the spirit
    and the honor of a nation.

28

Martin Black Elk had been in police work for twenty-five years, serving the last ten as chief of tribal police, but he'd never seen tracks covered as well as those of the intruder who came into Dr. Kate Malone's house. Except for the things he'd meant to leave behind—the notes, the circle of hair, the black cloth, and the doll—there was nothing.

"Do you think you can find out who did this?"

The dark circles under her eyes were evidence of a sleepness night, but otherwise Dr. Malone looked as if she would personally deal with the next person who came to her house uninvited. Her voice was firm and her chin was high. She was packing a gun too. That was the first thing he'd noticed. She was some gutsy woman.

But then, he already knew that. She'd fought like a tiger to save his grandson's life. That's one reason he didn't mind giving up his Saturday morning.

"It's going to be hard, Dr. Malone. Whoever did it didn't leave me much to go on. I'd like a list of people you think might have a reason to do this."

"That list would include just about everybody in Witch Dance."

Martin stuffed the notebook back into his pocket. What she said was true. She'd had enemies from the day she started building the clinic, and there were people out of work at the tool and die plant who hated her.

"I'm going to do my best to find the perp. In the meantime, don't talk to the press. I'd like to keep this out of the papers."

"I have every confidence that you'll find him."

"For you, I'll move heaven and earth. I owe you for saving Graham."

"I did only what any other doctor would do."

"You went beyond the call of duty. A man doesn't forget things like that."

She pushed her hair back from her forehead, then shivered as she glanced at the evidence bag.

"It's probably a prank." She didn't look as if she believed what she was saying.

"I wouldn't count on it. Too much is happening in Witch Dance right now, and you've been right in the center. You've made enemies." He nodded at the gun on the end table beside the sofa. "Do you know how to use that thing?"

"Right now I know enough to hit the side of a barn, but when I've finished practicing, I'll be able to give you a run for your money."

"I don't doubt it." Black Elk gathered the evidence in bags and headed for the door. "Call me if anything else turns up, Kate."

"You bet."

"And, Kate . . . be careful."

When Black Elk got back to his office, he examined the evidence once more. The circle of hair was the most disturbing, and the most telling. The sacred circle. The medicine wheel. What goes around comes around. Kate's would-be assailant was out for revenge . . . and he knew the Chickasaw culture.

Unconquered and unconquerable.

Whoever was after her wouldn't stop until he got what he wanted . . . and he wanted Kate Malone dead.

* * *

Twelve empty soup cans were lined up on the fence posts behind Kate's cottage. Standing with her feet apart and the gun in both hands, she squinted one eye and took aim. The loud report made her ears ring and sent a crow squawking toward the sky.

She opened her eye and counted the cans. Twelve.

"Damn," she said.

She shifted her stance and took aim once more. The bullet twanged against the steel trough, and water spurted out the hole.

"Hell's bells. Who could do anything with this damned coat on."

She jerked off her coat, tossed it across the fence, then resumed her position.

In quick succession she got off four shots. All the cans were standing.

"If you think I'm giving up, you're sadly mistaken."

This is what being scared had reduced her to: talking to tin cans. She reloaded her gun and took aim at the carrot soup can. It hadn't been fit to eat. Maybe her father had been right when he'd said she ought to learn to make carrot soup.

"Prepare to die," she said, then with both eyes open she squeezed off a shot.

The twang of a solid hit rang in the still, cold air as the carrot soup can became airborne.

Mick Malone would have celebrated with a good Cuban cigar. But then . . . Mick Malone wasn't around to see her triumph.

With her jaw set, Kate stood back and took aim at the pea soup.

The watcher on the hillside smiled, knowing his time was about to come.

Shameless. That's what she was.

Only her second date with Eagle Mingo, and already Deborah was trying to maneuver him toward bed. She was succeeding too. Partially.

He hadn't sounded too enthusiastic about a Saturday horseback ride, though she knew that was one of his favorite pastimes; but he hadn't declined either. She guessed that was a good sign.

And now, windswept, chilled, and surfeited with racing, she was making her way into his house. If rumor could be trusted, he considered his house off limits to women. Some said he eased his sexual ache with a woman in Tulsa, but others said he hadn't had a woman since Kate Malone, that he was celibate, like some kind of priest worshipping at her shrine.

"Are you cold?" he asked.

"Yes."

He bent to stoke the fire. She'd hoped for something else. Moving close, she held her hands out to the blaze. The heat from the fire warmed her skin, but it couldn't compare to the sexual heat that warmed her body.

Eagle glanced up, and Deborah held her breath under his solemn regard. Without changing expression he reached for her. She went into his arms in slow motion, wondering, now that she had come this far, how she would ever fight the ghost of Kate Malone.

She'd had many beaus in her time, but she'd never been kissed by an expert like Eagle Mingo. If his heart was not in the kiss, she couldn't tell. Nor did she want to. All she wanted was to be swept on the wave of sensation all the way to his bed.

Heady with love and excitement, she was only vaguely aware of having her blouse unbuttoned, barely conscious of being led away from the fire and down the hall. But suddenly she saw his bed, and she knew she was in the inner sanctum, a place where no woman had been allowed.

"This is not love, Deborah," he said as he moved them inexorably toward the bed.

"I know."

"It will never be love."

"I don't care."

He would never know how she lied. Love was a

beautiful dream she'd had once, but like all dreams, it faded in the light of reality. She was twenty-six years old, and every night she still went to her cramped little room at the back of the general store. When morning came, she woke up to the quarrelsome voice of a father who hardly ever remembered her name.

He needed to be in a nursing home, but her salary at the clinic wouldn't stretch far enough to add those expenses, and Hal was no help at all. She rarely ever saw him, and when he did come to visit, he was distant and unapproachable. The brother she'd once known and loved was filled with subterranean darknesses that Deborah didn't dare explore.

Even if Eagle Mingo wouldn't be the love of her life, he would be her way out. Sighing, Deborah stretched upon his bed, bartering her body for freedom. The red light from his telephone answering machine cast a ruby glow across her cheek.

Cupping her face, Eagle bent toward her. With his warm breath fanning her cheek and his lips only inches away, he tensed. The light on his answering machine beckoned.

Without a word he snaked out his hand and punched the message button.

"Eagle, I just thought you needed to know ..." The voice of Black Elk, chief of tribal police, filled the room. Deborah closed her eyes, trying to shut out reality.

"Somebody is trying to kill Kate Malone."

Eagle grabbed the phone and punched Black Elk's number. Holding her blouse together over her naked breasts, Deborah sat up, listening to one side of a brief, clipped conversation.

"This is Eagle. What's happened to Kate?" His back was rigid with tension.

"When?" Deborah heard his long, shuddering breath. "Do you know who did it?"

Black Elk's reply was a muted, distant murmuring, and when it ceased, Eagle replaced the phone. In the screaming silence Deborah held her breath. Finally, he turned to her.

"I'm sorry, Deborah."

She sat on the bed, watching him leave. His footsteps echoed down the hall and through the den. Still clutching her blouse, she heard the front door slam, then the distant pounding of horse's hooves.

Humiliation came over her, and on its heels a deep, creeping shame. Her best friend's life was threatened, and she hadn't even asked any questions. The shame stayed with her while she buttoned her blouse and mounted her horse. By the time she got home, her humiliation was beginning to abate. But not the shame. It would be with her always, a black thread woven into the fabric of her life.

"Deborah, is that you?" Her father was having a lucid moment.

"Will you find my bow? I have to go out and kill an elk. The children are hungry."

"Yes, Father, I'll find your bow. But first, let me make you a nice bowl of soup."

Outside her window the sun painted the earth pink and gold, and in her imagination Deborah heard the thundering hooves of a black stallion racing across the prairie.

Eagle, going to Kate.

He heard the shots long before he reached her house. Leaning low, Eagle urged his stallion to a gallop.

Another shot rang out just as he topped the hillside. Below him Kate was silhouetted against the sun, coat off, red hair blowing in the wind. And in her hand was a Smith and Wesson .38. Eagle pulled his mount to a halt, then sat on the hillside, watching, as relief washed through him.

She got off two quick shots, and two tin cans kicked into the air. Eagle smiled for the first time in months.

"Go, Heloa," he said to his mount. *Heloa.* Thunder. Issue of Kate's Mahli and Eagle's black stallion. A magnificent product of an explosive mating.

Kate heard him coming. She turned to him with the gun in her hand and a big unlit cigar in her mouth. Her face registered neither shock nor surprise. And certainly not welcome.

"Got a light?" she said.

Eagle dismounted and held a match to her cigar. It was man-size, a big Cuban variety that would stink to high heaven.

The end of the tip glowed as she took a draw. Her eyes watered and her face turned slightly green, but she didn't back down. Watching him, she took another draw.

"You've taken up smoking, I see."

"Yep. Today. Went all the way to Ada for these things." She flicked an ash his way. "And you've taken up prying."

"I'm not prying."

"Then why are you here?"

"Black Elk called me."

"He asked you to come?"

"No. That was my idea. I came to assure myself of your safety."

"As you can see, I'm perfectly fine, Governor." She took another draw on the cigar, then blew a smoke ring his way. "Leave."

The smoke curled around them, and in that veil of intimacy the physical impact of Kate screamed along Eagle's nerve endings. He moved then, as swift and sure as his namesake, closing in on her until their thighs were touching. With one hand he took the cigar from her mouth and with the other he cupped her chin.

"I will leave when I'm satisfied that you're safe, and not before." He could feel the shivers that rippled through her, and a selfish side of him exulted, glad she wasn't immune to him, as she pretended.

"Come," he said, sliding his arm around her shoulder.

She dragged her heels, resisting him.

"Where do you think you're taking me?"

"To your house."

"Savage! Do you think all you have to do is show up on my doorstep and I'll invite you into my bed?"

"As enticing as that sounds, I have no intention of going to your bed. I want to see where the intruder was."

Kate felt her face flame, but she wasn't about to admit her embarrassing mistake.

"Black Elk has already investigated."

"You can come under your own power, or under mine."

Remembering how he'd manhandled her the last time he said that, she jerked her arm free and stalked ahead of him to her cottage. It was high time to go in anyhow. She'd been out with her gun all day, and she was freezing to death.

"This is an exercise in futility," she grumbled, mostly to have the last word. "I don't know what you think you'll see that Black Elk didn't."

What he saw was her red silk gown tossed carelessly across the tumbled covers of her bed. The languid, exotic sweetness of her perfume permeated the air. Riveted, he stood in her bedroom, breathing in the fragrance, absorbing it into his lungs and his skin.

"This is where he left the circle of hair?" A redundant question, he knew, but he had to say something to break the spell.

"Yes."

Did she feel it too? The insidious sexual heat that moved about the room like a living thing? If he didn't leave, he'd break every vow he'd made, destroy everything he believed in.

He quickly inspected her windows, then moved out into the hall, where the air didn't conspire against him. He'd found nothing in Kate Malone's house except the past.

"I'm sending someone to guard you," he said when he finally made it back to her front door.

"I'll send him right back."

"These threats are serious, Kate."

"I understand the serious nature of the threats. What

I don't understand is how you have the nerve to tell me what to do." Angry and frustrated almost beyond endurance, Kate shoved her hand through her heavy hair. "This is my life. I make the decisions."

"I want to ensure your safety."

"No one is ever completely safe. It's the nature of the world we live in. And I won't give whoever is tampering with my life the satisfaction of seeing me hiding behind some muscle-bound goon sent over by the governor."

In spite of her stubbornness, Eagle couldn't hold back his smile.

"I hadn't planned to send a muscle-bound goon; I had planned to send Gloria Running Deer of the tribal police."

"No."

She stood framed against the front door with the moonlight pouring over her hair and her skin, exotic and deceptively fragile. And he knew then the price he'd have to pay for marriage without love and passion—the memory of a woman who would steal every shred of life and joy and emotion until he was nothing more than an empty shell.

"Kate . . ." he said, raising his hand as if he might reach for her.

"No." She stepped back, out of his reach, forever out of his reach. "Go to Deborah. . . ."

Something must have registered on his face—shock, surprise, despair—though he sought desperately to appear unmoved.

"Don't you think she talks to me?" Kate said. "Don't you think I hear her sighs and see the glow in her face when she speaks your name?"

The vast gulf of silence threatened to swallow them, and they stared at each other, bleak.

"Go to her," Kate whispered. "And don't you *dare* break her heart."

"I have no intention of breaking her heart."

He left her standing in her doorway. Alone. As he was alone.

29

Alone on the hillside, he watched Eagle leave.

Soon. Soon.

He began to sweat in spite of the cold wind. Drawing his coat close around his face, he waited in the shelter of the silver maples until the sound of hoofbeats was merely a faint echo in the distance. Lights flicked on and off in the small cottage, showing Kate Malone's progress through her house.

She didn't stay long in the kitchen. She never did. Next she sat a short time in her den. Probably reading a book. Watching, he'd learned her habits. Television shows didn't interest her. Only the books. Fiction titles with bookmarks sticking out and the fat medical texts she brought home from the clinic.

Rage came over him, a red, boiling rage that made his hands tighten into fists. In the dark he held out one of his hands and studied his fist. It was big and solid as a rock, capable of smashing through the white witch woman's fragile bones.

He could feel how it would be, the soft cushion of flesh, then the tender female bones cracking under the pressure of his fists. Sweating now in earnest, he started from his hiding place, intent upon smashing the witch woman until she was nothing but a bloody mess.

But, wait . . .

He'd been told . . . First she must suffer.

Forcing himself to remain calm, he waited in the darkness until she went into her bath. The stealth of foxes descended on him, and he stole into the night, silent and deadly, leaving no traces of himself for those who would keep him from his purpose.

Silently he laughed at the locks on her doors and windows. Would the white witch woman keep him out? Easier to keep out the north wind.

Steam from the bathroom seeped under the door and fogged the mirrors in her bedroom. He stood in the midst of the steam, listening to the sounds of her in the shower—the rush of water down the drain, the thump as she dropped her soap, the soft sound of her muttered curse.

Power filled him. He stole silently through her bathroom door, then stood in the steam and watched through the glass shower door as she lifted her right arm and drew her washcloth around her breast and down her rib cage.

Such a slender rib cage. It would crack like the tender branch of a sapling.

Watching her amused him, but he had other, more important things to do. He eased toward the door, and suddenly her head snapped up.

"Who's there?" she called.

Rivulets of moisture ran down his face as he stood in the steam. Hidden. Invincible.

"Is anyone there?"

He held his breath as she reached toward the faucets. If she discovered him now, he'd have to kill her.

A pity. It was too early for death.

"Nerves," she muttered, changing her mind.

As the water cascaded around her, he slipped from the bath and into her bedroom. It didn't take him long to do what he had to do.

Afterward, he stole into the night and let the darkness swallow him. She would never see him now.

Watching. Waiting.

Wrapped in her bath towel, Kate reached for the gun on her bathroom vanity. How sad to carry a weapon even to her bath. And yet, she'd be foolish not to.

Someone was after her.

Involuntarily she shivered. Some malevolent presence hovered, as if her enemy had been there, in the bathroom with her.

That was a silly notion, of course. No one would be that bold. Or that foolish.

Still holding her gun, she pushed open her bedroom door. The scream started in her soul and pushed its way past her constricted throat.

Her red silk gown had been ripped to shreds and scattered about the bedroom. Jagged red ribbons hung from the curtain rods and the lampshades and the bed posts. Bits of red dangled from the doorknob and the back of her chair and the top of her armoire.

She clamped her free hand over her mouth to stop the screaming. Then with the gun held firmly in both hands she advanced into the room.

Light from a lamp fell across her vanity, and on the mirror was a message. *The time is at hand, witch.* Steam from the bathroom had made the lipstick run, so that it looked like blood.

Paralyzed, Kate stared at the words. Then her gaze moved downward. On the vanity was a single eagle feather, its tip dipped in blood.

30

"I think you should ask for protection, Kate."

"I won't."

Headlines screamed from the newspaper in Deborah's hand. "Dr. Malone Under Seige." Somebody had leaked every gory detail to the press, even to the shredded red gown.

Had Kate been wearing red silk when Eagle raced to her side? Quickly ashamed of her jealousy, Deborah made herself forget her own loveless plight and concentrate on the safety of her friend.

"Your damned stubborn pride is going to get you killed," she said.

"If I give in to that weakness, I've let him win. No . . . I won't accept protection."

Deborah turned slowly around.

"Accept?"

"Eagle offered." A heavy silence fell between them. Kate reached out her hand, then let it flutter to her side.

"I knew he came to you."

"That's all it was, Deborah, an offer for protection. Please believe me."

"I believe you."

The desperate will believe anything. Deborah had never

thought of herself in that way, had never imagined that she'd end up one of those women who clung to hope no matter how faint or false.

"I believe you because I *have* to," she added.

The alternative was too painful. All the books she'd read and all the dreams she'd dreamed were wrong. There was no pot of gold at the end of the rainbow, no wizard at the end of the yellow brick road, no shining knight in Camelot. There was only the stunning reality that life had no guarantees, not of health or happiness or even friends.

Seeing Kate now, knowing that Eagle had gone to her, not out of fear but out of love, Deborah made a bleak bargain with herself. She would sacrifice her dreams and her pride because she needed Eagle ... just as he needed her. She would be the full-blood receptacle for his seed and he would be her security. With him she'd have a home, children, position, and support for her father.

"Kate, no matter what happens, promise me one thing."

"Anything, Deborah."

"Always be my friend."

"Always."

They both got teary-eyed for a second; then Kate brushed at her tears, laughing.

"Look how maudlin we're getting. The next thing you know, we'll be bawling like newborn calves and there'll be nobody to look after our patients ... if we ever have another one."

"They'll soon be coming in with sore throats and runny noses and bellyaches." Her spirits restored, Deborah gave Kate an arch grin. "And if they don't, I'll put laxative in the cheese at the general store."

"Hey, it's good to see your sass back, woman."

"You don't look too bad yourself, Doc, with that grin spread all over your face."

"What do you say we close this joint down and drive into Ada? I could use some real food for a change."

"Only if you let me drive."

"There won't be a fence post standing between here and Ada."

"Live dangerously, Kate. You live only once."

"Is that an old Indian saying?"

"I think it's an invention of Hollywood."

Kate lined her arm with Deborah's and went out the door. For one afternoon she would forget her fear, and if she tried hard enough, her laughter might become real.

Melissa loved the feel of silk against her skin. She flung her hands over her head and arched her hips.

"Baby, you're hotter than a firecracker today." Hal drove into her with such force, she was already climaxing.

When the hard shudders stopped, she pulled him down to her breast and tangled her hands in his hair.

"Shhh. Don't talk. Make me scream."

He took her rigid nipple between his teeth. She'd taught him exactly what she liked. And he always did as he was told.

As he bit down on her, she felt the frenzy building. Power surged through her, and she knew that soon she would have it all . . . and Kate Malone would have nothing.

"Yes," she said, "oh, yes. Now!"

He began to pump once more, faster and faster, until she was screaming his name.

"Clayton! Clayton!"

Anna had learned to drive. As a matter of fact, she'd learned many things. Working in Eagle's office, her neglected social skills as well as her forgotten secretarial skills had returned, and with them a resurgence of well-being.

Her sister, who lived in California, was greatly supportive of her efforts, and was even urging Anna and her family to move out there.

"You could help me in my shop, Anna," she'd written in her latest letter. "You were always better with a needle than I. And anyhow, the change might do all of you good."

Change. That's what they all needed.

With her sister's letter in her handbag, Anna walked into her house, calling her husband's name.

"Cole?"

The house had the echoing emptiness of a deserted dwelling. On the hall table a note from Clint said he'd gone to his friend Michael's house to study algebra and wouldn't be back till after supper.

Anna drew a deep breath, steadying herself. She had to let go of the fear that something terrible would befall her only child every time he left home.

"Cole!"

Clutching Clint's note, she raced up the stairs and checked all the rooms. Resolve almost failed her in the doorway to Mary Doe's room. Then she pushed it open and stood with dust swirling around her. Late afternoon sun turned the spinning dust to gold, and as it brushed against her cheek, Anna thought Father Sky had sent Mary Doe down as an angel to give her comfort.

Her feet felt heavy as she walked into the room, and dust and tears clogged her throat. A film of dust lay over all the feminine things she'd bought for her daughter, who preferred frogs to frills.

It was time to clear the dust away. Past time. No matter what Cole said.

She called his name once more, and the echoing silence mocked her.

She hurried outside, filled with purpose. The sweet smell of hay tickled her nose as she pushed open the heavy barn doors. Cole stood in the center of the barn, pitching hay. He didn't even look up, but his mare whinnied a greeting from her stall.

"I was looking for you in the house."

Cole stared at her as if she were a stranger, or worse,

someone he had grown to hate. Anna shivered at the power of grief.

"I want to talk to you, Cole."

A wisp of hay drifted down from the loft and settled on his cheek. He continued pitching hay as if he hadn't heard her.

Rage built in Anna. A senseless disease had stolen her children, and now a senseless silence was stealing her husband.

"Dammit, Cole. Speak to me."

Slowly he turned to stare at her, his entire body rigid and unforgiving, as if she had personally been responsible for the death of their children.

"I can't go on like this." She launched herself at him, knocking the pitchfork from his hand. "Do you hear me, Cole? I can't go on this way."

He caught her upper arms to keep them both from falling. A muscle ticked in the side of his jaw, and his own rage was plainly stamped on his face.

She beat his chest with her balled-up fists. The mare whinnied and kicked the wall of her stall.

"You killed my children and now you're killing our marriage. You rotten sonofabitch bastard, I won't let you. Do you hear me? I won't let you." Tears streamed down her cheeks as she caught the lapels of his shirt. "Goddammit, I love you, Cole. I won't let you do this to us."

Desolate, she pressed her face into his chest and her tears soaked the front of his shirt. Softly, he touched her hair. Astonished, Anna looked up into the face of her husband.

"Sweet *lhokomuk*," he whispered. "My sweet *lhokomuk*."

Standing on tiptoe, she wrapped her arms around his neck and felt the blessed touch of his lips upon hers. She clung to him with the urgency of a parched desert wanderer who had suddenly discovered water.

"My darling . . . my love." As she swayed against him, the months of their discord vanished.

Locked together, they fell upon the sweet-smelling hay, desperate in their haste. With the hungry grunting of animals, they tore aside restraints until at last they were joined, legs tangled, hips melded, wild in the ancient rhythms they knew so well. There were no sweet words, no erotic meanderings, no tender caresses, only the hard straining of bodies too long denied.

If Anna missed the whispered love music of Muskogean and the slow-melting heat of kisses that started at the throat and went to the outer edges of her being, she wasn't about to say so. It was enough that Cole was in her, filling her with his hard flesh and the sweet semen that spewed from him like warm honey.

Afterward she lay in his arms, hoping for the soft love words she remembered so well. But he lay silently against the hay, holding her so tightly, she could barely breathe.

"Cole?" When he didn't answer, she lifted herself on her elbow and kissed his lips. "I love you, Cole."

His eyes were black pools, sucking her down until she was filled with his tragedy and his despair.

Winds moaned around the eaves and snow drifted through the cracks. Anna shivered, suddenly so cold, she had to bite her bottom lip to keep her teeth from chattering.

"I'm cold, Cole. Let's go inside."

They straightened their clothes, then went into the house, side by side, not touching. Inside the warm kitchen, where they'd made love against the refrigerator and on the floor and in the pantry, giggling like teenagers, Cole sat on a tall stool, as silent as the mountains. And Anna knew she was losing him. She put water on the stove for tea then, and stood in front of him, forcing him to look at her.

"Your loss is mine too, Cole. Your pain is mine." She might as well have been one of the kitchen appliances for all the notice he took. "Every day of my life I feel the emptiness ... and it hurts so much, I want to fall with my face to the ground and never get up."

"But I don't give in, Cole. I won't be defeated. I have my son and I have you." She caught both his hands. "Let's leave here. Let's go to California and make a fresh start."

Water boiled over, hissing like snakes in the quiet room. The front door banged open and Clint called, "Hey, anybody here? I'm home."

Cole squeezed her hand, then abruptly he released her and stood up.

"I'm sorry, Anna."

His footsteps echoed on the tile floor and the back door banged shut behind him.

"Hey, where's Dad going?"

"I don't know."

"He forgot his coat." Clint lifted Cole's leather jacket with the sheepskin lining off the coat rack.

"Maybe he'll be right back." Anna knew she was lying to herself.

Cole didn't come back, not even when all the stars left the sky and the snow came down so thick, she couldn't see the trees in her front yard.

Wrapped in his buffalo robe, the shaman stood in the doorway of his cabin and watched the snow cover the tops of the mountains. The north wind wailed his winter song, and the smoke from his pipe curled upward to join the wind. Out of the smoke and the snow came the white buffalo, charging across the mountaintops like thunder. With its dazzling white skin, it flashed by so quickly that he was temporarily blinded.

Feeling his way, the medicine man went inside and shut the door. He'd seen the sign. Soon the white witch would be driven from the land, and once more it would be filled with peace and light, its people begging for the return of the Great One.

Filled with power, he cast aside his robe and pipe and began the ancient dance of his ancestors.

* * *

Winds buffeted the barn door, and snow sifted through the cracks to cover the piles of hay like powdered sugar. Eagle leaned against the side of an empty stall with his arms wrapped around himself, not certain whether the cold he felt came from outside or whether it was a bone-deep malady destined to freeze his soul.

Anna had been in tears when she called him. Cole never touched her anymore, she said, spilling intimate secrets that Eagle had no right to hear. He took no interest in his son, none in her work, and he wouldn't even talk about moving to California for a fresh start.

"He can't seem to work through his grief, Eagle," she'd said. "I don't know what to do anymore. Please help me."

Cole stared at him with eyes as black as tar pits, showing nothing, neither love nor welcome.

"Anna sent for you," he said.

"I came to help," Eagle said, ashamed of himself. Anna shouldn't have had to call for help. He should have been there to offer. He'd failed his family.

"Get on your horse and leave."

In spite of his months of grieving, Cole still had the look of a man who could wrestle with the cougars that prowled the mountains and come out a winner.

"No. I won't leave. Not until you talk to me."

Cole turned his back and began to pour feed into a bucket.

"Let's talk about your family, Cole. Anna loves you, and Clint worships you. How can you turn your back on them? And what about our parents? They're old and needy."

Dovie cried over her lost grandchildren every day, and Winston, whose stroke had left him emotionally fragile, was unable to provide the kind of comfort and support she needed. Wolf and Star, away at school in Boston, had no idea what was happening to the family.

Yesterday, standing in Dovie's kitchen with a mug of

hot chocolate warming his hands, Eagle had listened to his mother's anguished ramblings.

"Remember when you were six years old and so sick . . ." She laced her hands tightly together across her lap. "How can you remember? You were almost dead . . . like our little Bucky and Mary Doe."

Her voice broke, then she pulled herself back together. "Cole sat by your bed the whole time, refusing to even come to the kitchen for meals. I had to bring his food on a tray."

Dovie reached a fragile, blue-veined hand toward Eagle, and he clasped it tightly. "He loves his family so. Why doesn't he come to see us now?"

If there were any mercy left in the universe, it would surely have rained down upon Dovie Mingo's head. She was good, a woman whose purity of heart should have kept her folded under the protective wings of the Great Spirit.

But Eagle knew there was no mercy. Sometimes there was not even justice. There was only courage.

"Your family needs you," he said.

"Go to hell." His brother didn't even turn around.

"You're a coward, Cole." Leaving his place by the stall, Eagle towered over his brother with his hands balled into fists. "You're a yellow-bellied coward!"

Cole launched himself upon his brother. His fists were hard and deadly. Eagle let himself become a punching bag, taking blow after blow in the stomach without flinching.

"Take that back."

"*Imilha!*" Eagle said. "Coward!"

Grunting with effort, Cole swung repeatedly, until finally he sagged. Eagle wrapped his arms around his brother, and together they fell upon the hay. Lying side by side, staring up at the silver sunlight sliding through the barn's rafters, the brothers drifted backward to a time when they could bend over the creek and see their twin reflections in the sweet water singing over the rocks, a time when dreams were as high and bright as the kites they flew on the March wind.

"Remember that dog I had?" Cole said. "Sally?"

"Sally was mine."

"Ours."

"She was the best squirrel dog in Witch Dance."

"They don't breed squirrel dogs like that anymore."

"No. They don't."

"Bucky loved dogs." Cole began to cry.

Eagle comforted his brother as if he were a child, and Cole's tears wet the front of his shirt. When the racking sobs ended, Eagle pulled him to his feet.

"There is a grief counselor in Ada you and Anna should see, Cole."

"No. No doctors."

"Do it for Anna, Cole. I'm going in the house and tell her to set up an appointment." Eagle started toward the barn door, then turned and held his hand out to his brother. "Coming?"

"Not yet. But soon, Eagle. Soon."

Eagle pulled his coat collar close as he walked through the snow. Lights beckoned from the windows of Cole's house, and inside he could see Anna, bent over her sewing with the graceful sweep of her hair hiding her face.

What would he tell her about her husband? That he didn't want anybody's help? That the dead were more important to him than the living?

She looked up and smiled when he entered the room. Eagle decided he would temper the truth with mercy.

When Kate saw the note slipped under her clinic door, she recoiled. Instinctively she pulled her coat collar close and swiveled her head, searching the area for intruders. It was only five o'clock, and shadows still lay on the land.

Was that movement behind the silver maple on the hillside? Kate shrank into the clinic doorway, partially hidden. A flurry in the nearby treetop made her jump.

Lifting her gaze, she saw an owl climbing toward the rising sun, beating its wings on the air.

"By all the saints, I'm going to have to do better than this."

If she didn't get control of herself, she'd be such a bundle of nerves that she'd be of no use as a doctor. She took a deep, steadying breath, then bent and picked up the note.

"Please help me, Doctor Kate. My husband won't let me bring Adam and Rachel to you. Come to them, please. They are very sick from the Witch Creek. Marjorie Kent."

Kate leaned against the door, weak. She'd thought the war was over, but it seemed she'd won only the first battle.

She grabbed her black bag and went into the stable to saddle Mahli. The Kents lived in back country. Her car would never get through the rough terrain, and her old mare would be hard pressed to make it.

"It's just you and me, old girl." Kate rubbed the mare's velvety nose. "I hate to ask you to do this, pal, but it's the only way."

Mahli whinnied and tossed her mane. A high-priced Thoroughbred would never have lasted as long as Mahli, but she was a Chickasaw horse, built for endurance as well as speed. Mahli's speed was no longer anything to brag about, but she would go until she dropped in her tracks.

Kate set a sedate pace, saving Mahli's strength for the rough terrain near the Kent place. Cold winds whipped her hair and reddened her cheeks, but Kate was oblivious of the weather. She was remembering summer winds and summer stars and Eagle Mingo waiting on a rainbow-colored blanket.

You will come to me, he'd said, and she had, riding the back of her mare as pale as moonlight.

When Mahli was gone, her last fragile tie to Eagle would be dead. Kate shivered, chilled to the bone by wind and memories.

At the foot of the Arbuckle Mountains, Mahli balked. The road leading upward was hardly more than a faint trail through huge bolders and thick scrub brush.

"Come on, girl." Leaning low, Kate rubbed Mahli's neck. "You can do it."

Mahli started upward, gingerly finding her footing among the rocks. Clouds obscured the sun, and thunder rumbled like the distant beat of war drums. A flock of ravens, black as night, rose upward, crying their discontent.

Mahli sidestepped, her ears flattened. Shivers ran through Kate once more, and she glanced over her shoulder. Was someone hiding behind the rocks, or was it merely a shadow? Suddenly she wished she hadn't come alone. There was nothing for miles around except rocks and scrub brush and patches of trees. She could vanish, and it would be days before anyone found her.

Instinctively she reached toward the black bag hanging from her saddle. It contained more than medical supplies; inside was her .38 Smith and Wesson.

Behind the rocks, the man laughed without sound. Did the white witch woman think he was afraid of her gun?

Thunder crashed, closer now, and jagged lightning streaked across a sky as gray as death. As the man lifted his face upward, the awesome power of Father Sky filled him and a vision of the sacred circle almost blinded him. First the darkness, then the light. First the storm, then the calm. Out of the gray skies would emerge a rainbow whose light would fall upon the land until all the people knew, and knowing, they would remember, and remembering, they would sing. Their songs would lift upward on the wings of eagles, and bending down, he would hear them and be blessed. He, the avenger.

Kate's horse turned into the dark pathway of trees, and the man knew where she was going. There was only one family who lived at the end of that trail, and Kate Malone was taking the long way around.

Clinging to the sheer face of huge rocks, the man climbed. Almost, he could spread wings and fly like the eagle.

Below him, the witch woman's skin glowed in the dark woods, as white as death.

Lacey Wainwright was fit to be tied. His lawyer sat in a fat chair across from Lacey's desk, talking nothing but pure bullshit, and that rat-faced little pipsqueak he'd hired to cover up all this mess was nowhere to be found.

He punched the intercom and bellowed to his secretary, "Get Hal Lightfoot in here."

"I'm sorry, sir. Hal is out."

"Well, when he comes *in*, you tell him his ass is fired."

The overpriced lawyer cleared his throat and adjusted his glasses. Paper-shuffling sonofabitch. Didn't they ever bring good news?

"Now, about this class action suit against Witch Dance Tool and Die ... the parents are charging wrongful death as well as intentional infliction of emotional distress."

"I'm not interested in what a bunch of disgruntled Indians have to say. What I want to know is what you're going to do about it?" It was all that Kate Malone's fault. If she'd kept her nose out of his business, he'd be kicked back in his chair right now, smoking a cigar and dreaming about a vacation to the Bahamas. Hell, he'd even be willing to go to New Jersey. Anywhere would be better than this stinking rat hole.

"I'm not certain you understand the seriousness of this charge—"

"I don't have to understand. That's what I'm paying you for. Now, what in the hell are you going to do about it?"

"There is a procedure I will follow, of course. I will put together an irrefutable body of evidence proving that there was absolutely no intention on the part of Witch

Dance Tool and Die to dump toxic chemicals into Witch Creek." The skinny lawyer leaned toward Lacey with his squinty eyes watering. He looked like a damned long-necked, nearsighted turkey. "You *do* have company policies listing correct methods of disposal, don't you?"

He had policies running out the wazoo, thanks to that damned nosy governor. It had cost him a fucking fortune to clean up Witch Creek, and he'd had to put every damned move he made on paper.

"Hal Lightfoot's got all of that."

"The man you just fired?"

"Don't you know a joke when you hear one? Hal Lightfoot is my right-hand man. When he gets back, he'll explain everything to you."

Lacey clamped down on his cigar. Hal had better explain everything. If he didn't, he'd be back in the basement so quick, his head would swim.

Marjorie Kent was a large woman with a sweet smile, a tendency toward hives, and rheumatoid arthritis. Kate had been treating her for three years, and now Marjorie stood in the doorway, wringing her hands.

Kate looped Mahli's bridle over the porch railing.

"I thought I'd never get here. How are the children, Marjorie?"

"I shouldn't have asked you to come." Marjorie glanced anxiously over her shoulder.

"Nonsense. You know I'm always willing to make a house call." Kate unhooked her medical bag and strode toward the porch steps. She was cold and glad to be out of the woods. The smoke coming from Marjorie's chimney was the best thing she'd seen all day.

"Maybe it would be best if you just go on back."

"Marjorie, what's wrong?"

Marjorie glanced over her shoulder once more, and that's when Kate heard it, the distinctive sound of the gourd rattle.

"You called in the shaman?"

"No. My husband did." Marjorie continued to block the doorway. "The medicine man just arrived."

"It's all right, Marjorie." Kate put a hand on the woman's arm. "The shaman and I understand each other. I'll cause no trouble."

Reluctantly, the woman stood aside. The room was dark and smoky, with all the blinds drawn and the ancient chimney malfunctioning. Rachel and Adam lay on quilted pallets in the middle of the floor, and Kate's old nemesis danced slowly around them, waving his rattle and chanting in a singsong voice.

Even without checking, Kate knew that her worst fears had come true: Witch Creek had not yet claimed all its victims. Fever burned in the eyes of the children, and a faint yellow cast tinged their skin.

She hoped it was not too late. Approaching the shaman, she tried for the right combination of authority and cooperation.

"I came to help," she said.

The shaman continued to dance as if he had not heard her.

"*Oo'ole*," he chanted, invoking the eagle to dart down as quick as lightning and hide his children in the protective lee of his wings.

"I have powerful medicine," Kate said, refusing to give up.

The shaman was so old, the whites of his eyes were yellow, and when he turned his face toward her, Kate had the sensation of looking into the eyes of a snake. Pure venom radiated from him.

She tightened her hold on her medicine bag. The lives of children were at stake: She would not back down.

"For many years you have provided healing for these people, but you are like the great oak tree whose dry leaves rattle on dead branches. I am a sapling, strong and fresh, with new ways of healing in my magic bag." Kate entreated him with her right hand extended, palm up. "Let the circle spin itself out to completion."

His eyes glittered with hatred and confusion as he

stopped his chanting. He glanced from Kate to Marjorie, then lifted his face toward the ceiling and invoked his deity in a tragic voice.

Chills ran along Kate's spine. On the pallets, the children drew rasping breaths. If they didn't get help soon, it would be too late for them.

But Kate dared not step into the shaman's sacred circle. Finally his terrible voice faded, and the old shaman tucked his gourd rattle into the folds of his buffalo robe and slipped out the door.

Kneeling beside the children, Kate said a prayer to her own God that she would be equal to the task ahead.

Hidden among the trees, the avenger saw her leave. She'd been in the house a long time, and she was mounting her white mare with the black medicine bag clutched in one hand.

"It won't be long now," the man thought. Or did he say it aloud? He must have, for the hawk circling above his head suddenly darted upward.

The slow clip-clop of the horse's hooves echoed off the rocks. With her head slightly bent, the white witch woman appeared drained of all energy. An overhanging tree branch caught the sleeve of her coat, and she didn't even brush it away, but instead let it take hold and tug until the forward momentum of her horse pulled her loose. Moving along on a parallel course high above her, the avenger saw the ragged hole torn by the tree limb.

A pity. He liked his opponent fiery, at the top of her form.

Had the children died? Another sin to add to the witch woman's long list of transgressions.

Briefly the trees hid her, and then she came into view once more, holding on to a saddle horn tilted slightly to the left. The rocks beneath her horse's hooves were cold and gray and deadly. Kate swayed a little as the horse rounded a treacherous curve.

Empowered, the avenger stood on the rocks and lifted

his hands toward the heavens. As if the Great Spirit had been waiting for his signal, Mahli's girth snapped.

"Whoa," the witch woman screamed. "Whoa, Mahli."

But it was too late. Nothing could stop her headlong plunge toward the ground. Nothing could cushion her fall against the rocks. Nothing and no one.

She lay with her left foot at a crazy angle and her arms outflung, as if at the last minute she'd tried to call upon her own gods to save her. Beside her, the black bag was open, its contents spilling onto the ground.

Mahli stood watch for a long while, her saddle hanging sideways and her bridle dragging the ground. She whinnied softly, then flattened her ears as if she were waiting for her mistress's voice to tell her what to do.

The white witch woman's skin glowed like death.

High above her, the avenger opened himself for a vision—fires leaping into the sky, burning away the darkness until there was nothing left except light.

With the stealth of a night creature he left his watch on the rocks. Below him the witch woman lay broken, her powers forever ended.

31

Winston Mingo sat beside the fire, wrapped in a woven blanket while Eagle stood with his arm propped on the mantel. Even in repose he looked tense, wired for action. Winston sometimes wondered if he'd made a mistake when he named his oldest son his successor.

It was not a question of what was good for the nation: Eagle had done a magnificent job as leader of the Chickasaws. But had the mantle of duty been the undoing of his soul? To the casual observer he was a powerful, intelligent man in his prime. But to a father he was a haunted man, a man who hid his bleak heart behind a stern face and careful manners.

Winston rocked back and forth, letting the rhythm of the rush-bottomed rocking chair and the flicker of firelight comfort him. He was like the largest limb on the old tree outside his window, dried up and withered. Soon he would fall to the ground and become a part of Mother Earth so other, greener branches could grow in his place.

The time had come to speak truth.

"My days are slipping away."

"The doctors say you have many good years left.

With patience and therapy you'll regain some of your strength."

"I no longer have the luxury of patience."

The thunder outside punctuated Winston's statement. Fierce and terrible, it roared over the mountains and threatened the valley.

"There's a bad storm coming." Winston never changed topics without a reason, and now he was finished with the old one and no amount of persuasion could make him return to it.

Eagle looked out the window. Already rain was beginning to fall, not the soft, warm rain of summer, but a hard-driving rain that would turn to sleet as the night drew near and the temperature dropped.

"In weather like this a man should be in front of his own fire with his wife and children."

Eagle let the remark slide. Winston eased the blanket closer around his shoulders. He wasn't finished with his son yet. Not by a long shot.

"What are your intentions concerning Deborah Lightfoot?"

One of the things Winston liked best about old age was that old men didn't have to be subtle. He watched the changing emotions on his son's face, and he knew with a father's certainty that the white woman was still in Eagle's blood.

For a moment Eagle bowed his head and stared into the fire. When he looked up, his face was filled with resignation and resolution.

"She will bear my name and my children."

"It is good. She is full-blood."

"Yes, she is full-blood."

"You will court her properly, then tell her of this soon?"

A spear of white lightning split the sky, and rain lashed against the windowpanes. North wind moaned around the eaves and rattled the shutters.

"I have no time for courtship. I'm going to tell her tonight. The marriage will be quick and painless."

Winston thought of Dovie and of how he sometimes could still get hard just thinking of her soft body lying next to his. He was filled with sorrow for his son, but he kept his tears inside.

"May the Great Spirit be with you, my son."

Cold winds entered the house when Eagle left, and Winston pulled his blanket closer. His son was virile and passionate. Soon he'd have grandbabies on both knees to keep him warm.

When Eagle had been eleven years old he took every chance he could to visit Luther Mattox. Luther would grin his toothless smile and say, "Pull up a chair, young sprout. I know just what you want." Then he would unlock the glass door of a cabinet and take out the most exquisite knife Eagle had ever seen. It had a curved six-inch blade of the finest steel and a handle made from the horn of a deer. Luther had carved the handle and set turquoise and coral in the niches.

Eagle wanted that knife more than anything in the world. He wanted it so badly, he'd have done almost anything to have it. At home he volunteered for jobs he didn't have to do, even girl chores like mopping the floor. He did things without being told, such as taking a bath and doing his homework and turning the lights out at ten. Hope sang through him like the sweet waters of the Blue River. His birthday was coming up, and he knew he'd get the knife with the carved bone handle and the beautiful stones.

When the big day arrived, his father handed him a package. It was exactly the right size, long enough for the six-inch blade and the handle that fit perfectly in the palm of his hand. He was so nervous opening the package that his hands were sweaty.

Inside was a knife, an ordinary knife with a straight blade and a plain handle. He tested the shiny steel blade and found it good, hefted the weight of the knife and found it true.

"This is exactly what I need," he'd told his parents, all

the while still wanting the knife with the curved blade and the dazzling stones.

That was how Eagle felt as he drove home in the rain to call Deborah Lightfoot. She was good and true, but still he wanted the woman he couldn't have, the woman with the white skin and the dazzling hair.

Deborah was at the clinic, and answered on the first ring.

"This is Eagle. I have something of great importance to discuss with you." A compromise. A business proposition. He'd have told Winston without being asked, for the decision had been made long ago, the day he'd stood at his window and watched Kate drive away with Mark Grant. "Are you free tonight?"

In his single-minded pursuit of ensuring the family dynasty, was he robbing Deborah of love? Feeling like a thief, he waited for her answer.

"Eagle . . ." She sounded rushed and breathless. "I'm so glad you called . . . I was going to call you . . . I didn't know what else to do. . . ."

"Deborah, slow down. What's wrong?"

"It's Kate . . ."

Was it possible to die of fear and still be standing upright, talking into the telephone?

"What about her, Deborah?"

"She hasn't been here all day."

"Maybe she's on a house call. Is her car there?"

"It's still in the garage."

"What about her horse?"

"I don't know. Mahli's so old, I didn't think about checking. I'll do that now."

"There's no need for you to get out in this weather when I'm only a few minutes away. I'll be right—"

"Eagle!" Deborah's scream raised hairs on the back of his neck. "It's Mahli . . ."

"Kate? What about Kate?"

"The saddle is empty."

* * *

This was the part of his job Martin hated most, searching for the victim. Standing in Kate's stable, he inspected the saddle once more. The girth had been cut; there was no doubt about it. Martin ground out his cigarette and pulled up the collar of his rain slicker. The weather was a bitch. Tracking Kate Malone would be next to impossible. And the chances of finding her were even worse.

"How long did you say she's been missing?"

Deborah Lightfoot looked as if she might faint. That's all he needed, a swooning woman.

"I came in at six this morning, and she wasn't here."

"Shit."

Deborah glanced out at the sleet, coming down in thick sheets now, rattling hard against the stable's tin roof. They were both thinking the same thing: If Kate Malone was out there somewhere, injured, how would she survive the weather?

"You have to find her," Deborah said.

"How long ago did you say Eagle left?"

"About an hour ago. Do you think he can find her?"

"If anybody can, it's Eagle Mingo. Let's just pray he's not too late."

Hidden by trees, the avenger stood atop the hill above Kate's clinic and peered through the heavy sleet. There was no mistaking the black stallion or its rider.

Eagle. The man of legend.

With the power of the Great Spirit hovering like wings over his shoulders.

With the valor of his namesake and the heart of a dove.

With the mark of the mighty warrior bird on his thigh.

The avenger flung himself facedown on the ground, stretching his arms to embrace Mother Earth. In the prostrate position he sought a vision. He waited for the thundering approach of the white buffalo and for the magic circle of life and light.

He waited and waited. But nothing came except the pounding of horse's hooves as Eagle set out in search of Kate Malone.

Streaked with mud and shivering, the avenger left his watch above the clinic.

All hopes of finding Kate's trail had vanished. Heavy sleet obscured his vision as Eagle sat on his horse and tried to decide which direction to go. When he'd left Kate's stable, he'd been able to follow her trail for a short while. The ground near the clinic was protected by trees, and although the hoofprints were faint, they were still clear enough for him to know that she had headed west.

West lay the bluffs that had been scarlet with Indian paintbrush all summer, and the Blue River, swollen and threatening to overflow its banks. West lay the Arbuckle Mountains, their peaks hidden under a blanket of snow.

He'd come as far as the river, and now he had a choice to make. If he followed the course of the river, he would come to several small ranches, all of them owned by people who had at one time or another been Kate's patients. If he veered instead toward the mountains, he would come to the treacherous trail leading to the remote Kent cabin. Because of the weather, the trail would be even more dangerous.

Restless, his stallion pawed the ground, waiting for Eagle to make a decision. He dismounted and searched for clues, any tiny shred of evidence that would help him locate Kate. He found nothing, just as he'd known he would.

Nothing could help him now except his instincts— and perhaps divine intervention. Eagle lifted his head toward the heavy gray sky. It would be dark soon. High in the mountains, a wolf howled.

Eagle raised his fists to the sky.

"Loak-Ishtohoollo-Aba," he cried. But the Great Spirit wouldn't be moved by false piety. He hid His face from Eagle and would not be found.

Eagle mounted his impatient stallion and began to
follow the meandering path of the river. Suddenly he
veered his mount and changed course toward the distant mountains. They rose silently out of the mists of
sleet and shadow, calling to him in urgent voices disguised as the howling of the wolf.

He pushed his mount as hard as he dared, mindful of
the slick rocks and the sheer three-hundred-foot drop on
his right. Darkness covered the mountains, and the urgent howling of the wolf sounded closer.

Around a treacherous curve the stallion's foot
disloged a rock that started a slide. The horse reared,
screaming, white Eagle fought for control. In the ravine,
the falling rocks echoed like thunder.

Flattened against the stallion's back, Eagle used the
ancient tongue of his people to bring the horse under
control; then he dismounted and led his stallion around
the rock slide.

His foot touched something soft, something that
didn't belong on the mountain. Eagle knelt down and
picked it up. Kate's medical bag. Groping in the dark,
he found her scattered supplies and her gun . . . and the
rock covered with blood. Chance had led him there, and
a miracle had protected the evidence. An overhanging
shelf of rock had kept it safe and dry during the storm.

"Kate," he called, on his knees, searching for her, his
hands covered with blood. *"Kate!"*

Her name echoed back to him from the mountains.
And then, out of the darkness, came another sound, a
bone-chilling sound that froze Eagle's soul—the fren-
zied cry of wild animals smelling fresh blood.

Eagle pulled his rifle from its scabbard and followed
the howling of wolves.

32

She crouched in the shallow cave, watching the glowing yellow eyes. The wolves stared back at her. Their demonic howls pierced through the gray fog of pain and hunger that threatened to overcome her, and the stench of their hot breaths filled her rocky shelter.

Kate ran her hands over the floor of the cave, searching for the only weapon she had, the scalpel that had fallen out of her medical bag. Her hands closed around the steel, and she forced herself to an upright position. She hadn't survived a fall from her horse and a day in freezing rains only to be eaten by wolves.

"Just try to come and get me, you bastards."

The yellow eyes grew bigger. Six of them. The wolves were closing in.

Her hands were so cold, she could hardly feel her fingers, and she wondered if anybody would ever find her bones.

"Stop it, Kate Malone. You're going to survive."

A wave of dizziness caught her, and for a moment the yellow eyes faded. She bit down on her lip hard enough to draw blood. If she blacked out now, she was as good as dead. She'd heard that the dying have moments of epiphany, though how anybody could know that was beyond her, since the dead couldn't talk. Instead of thinking about lofty moments such as the summer when she discovered love or the winter when she knew she would be a doctor, she pictured a lobster dinner with all the trimmings. Which all proved the theory of epiphany was hogwash, for if the howls of the wolves were indication, she was about to die.

"Get out of here, you mangy mutts," she yelled, though the sound that came out was more whimper than shout.

She hated that most of all: that she wouldn't die with her boots on and her gun blazing. With her cold hands gripped around the scalpel, she watched the wolves.

A shot rang out. Then another and another.

Was she hallucinating? Had she thought up so many rescue fantasies that she'd crossed permanently into fantasy land?

"*Aiya!*" The savage shout came out of the darkness—and the thundering of hooves. Eagle Mingo leapt from his stallion, and the wolves scattered, yelping.

"Kate!" he called.

"In here."

He knelt down and pulled her from the cave. His arms were strong and warm, and the good solid feel of him made her want to curl up and stay for the next few centuries.

"What took you so long?" she asked.

"Are you hurt?" He ran his hands over her face and neck, and even in her foggy condition she cursed the fates that he was only checking for injuries.

"I'm wet and hungry and mad as hell about falling off my horse, but other than a lump on my head, I'm in perfect condition."

"You didn't fall off your horse, Kate. Someone cut the girth."

"Where's my gun? I'll shoot the bastard."

Even cold and hurt and hungry, Kate could make him laugh. He held her close, absorbing her chill into his bones, and the laughter released the tension that had

been building in him from the moment he'd learned she
was missing.

How would he live without her? She made survival a
grace rather than a necessity. Once in a lifetime the fates
matched two people who were luminous together,
whose love brightened even the darkest moments of
their lives.

Holding Kate now, Eagle felt the glow that leapt from
her heart to his, and he wept silently, without tears. He
could hold her only long enough to keep her warm, and
then he had to let go.

"We'll never make it down the mountain tonight in
this weather," he said.

"I know. I couldn't even make it down in the daylight."

"My hunting cabin is not far. Can you ride, Kate?"

"Anything is better than slipping and sliding around
over these rocks, lost as a goose."

With Kate sitting in front of him, Eagle guided his
stallion into the woods. Once in that familiar and less-
treacherous territory, they moved swiftly, arriving at the
cabin shortly after midnight.

He wanted to carry Kate inside, but she would have
none of it.

"I'm not an invalid. Put me down."

"As you wish." He set her gently on her feet, but he
did hang on to her elbow. "I don't want you to fall
again," he said when she started to protest.

The cabin was spartan without being shabby. Furnished with the barest necessities, it might have been
something from another century except for the electric-
ity and running water. It had been unused for several
years, and most of the light bulbs were burned out. The
dim glow illuminated cobwebs on the ceiling and gave
the dust covers on the furniture the ethereal look of
ghosts.

Eagle took a woven blanket from the closet and
wrapped it around her shoulders.

"That feels wonderful," she said, and for a moment

he thought she was talking about his hands. She shivered as he stared down at her bruised and battered face.

Rage filled him that he no longer had the right to comfort her and warm her and love her—rage and a certain hopelessness.

"I look that bad, huh?" Kate said.

With his hands lingering on her shoulders, Eagle knew he was in trouble. He'd let his feelings show. Making his face a careful mask, he gathered an armful of dry logs from the bin and knelt beside the fireplace.

"There's a bath down the hall and dry clothes in the closet. I'll spread your blanket by the fire to keep you warm."

He felt her damp coat brush against his thigh, and looked up to see her watching him. Both of them were remembering other ways they'd kept warm.

"If you need anything during the night, all you have to do is call out. I'll be down the hall," he said.

"I won't need anything."

Even if she did, she wouldn't ask. He could see that in her eyes. He stoked the fire, ignoring the way her nearness sensitized his skin.

"In the morning I'll take you down the mountain."

"I could get down under my own power if I had my horse. Damn that Mahli for leaving me. Poor old soul. I guess she gave me up for dead." Kate stripped off her wet coat and flung it across a chair. "Whoever is after me should understand it's going to take more than a lump on the head to do me in."

Even after she left the room, he still felt as if she were standing beside him. He picked up the poker and viciously stoked the fire.

The man who had tried to kill her would pay.

Hal lay spread-eagle upon the bed while Melissa rubbed oil over his skin and the peyote made him bright and invincible.

"Your body is beautiful," she said, then bent over him with her hair touching his abdomen.

It didn't matter that she was more than twice his age or that she called him Clayton in the throes of passion. She knew exactly what she wanted and had the money to buy it. Besides that, she was sophisticated, influential, and a damned good lay.

Her mouth was soft and slick, and he felt the hot, tight coiling that signaled an explosive climax. But he knew how to hold back.

Suddenly she lifted her head and knelt over him like a great, sleek cat.

"Will you love me forever?" Even with her hair tangled in her eyes and her makeup smeared, she was still a striking woman.

"Baby, the way you give head, I'd be a fool not to."

Her eyes glittered as she raked her long red fingernails down his chest, scoring his skin deep enough to leave a trail of blood. The pain brought him such pleasure that he threw back his head and howled like a wolf trailing a bitch in heat.

"Say it." She sank her teeth into his male nipple. Jagged edges of pleasure ripped through him. "Say you love only me and that you'll never look at another woman as long as you live."

"I love only you, wild woman with three names, and I'll never look at another woman as long as I live."

He'd said the words only to placate her, but as she straddled him and took them both howling and screaming toward the darkest ends of the earth, he thought it might be so.

Visions swirled through his brain, and in them she was the white buffalo woman, and he was riding her toward the sun, riding until they fell into its blazing center and became flame.

She'd been dumped on her doorstep like a sack of coal. And then he'd sent an emissary to do his dirty work and salve his conscience. Well, Eagle Mingo could find some other way to make himself feel noble. Kate wasn't about to do his bidding just because he was governor of the Chickasaw Nation and somehow felt responsible for her.

"You can take her right back where she came from." Kate crossed her arms over her chest and tried to look commanding in spite of her dastardly headache and ugly bruises.

The chief of the tribal police stood at the bottom of her porch steps, shifting uncomfortably from one foot to the other, and in the car the woman he'd brought to protect Kate stared off into the mountains as if she wanted nothing to do with the confrontation.

"She has to stay here, Kate. Governor's orders."

Kate laughed. So he was in a governing mood now, was he?

That morning, when she'd awakened to find him sitting cross-legged beside her blanket, watching her, he'd looked more like a lover than a governor. And later, pressed close while his stallion brought them out of the mountains, she'd felt the tension in his body and his efforts to hold himself aloof.

She'd fought the same battle. What would have happened if he'd come inside her house instead of leaving her on the doorstep?

"Tell the governor I don't take his orders."

"Kate, be reasonable. What happened to you yesterday was no accident."

Poor Martin Black Elk looked so long-suffering that Kate felt sorry for him. She *was* being unreasonable. Her father's daughter. Whether Mick Malone wanted to think so or not.

"Martin, I'll be careful." She put her hand over his and smiled.

"Don't make any more house calls alone."

"I won't."

"Keep your doors and windows locked and call me if you see or hear anything suspicious."

"I will."

"Kate . . . I don't like this. Why don't you ask Deborah Lightfoot to come over and stay with you?"

"No. I won't expose her to danger."

"Won't you at least get a good guard dog?"

"I'll think about it. And in the meantime, I'm hanging on to my gun."

Martin started toward his car, then turned to issue one last warning.

"Be careful, Kate."

"I promise."

All the promises in the world couldn't protect Kate Malone. Martin dreaded telling the governor she'd turned down his protection.

"She did what?"

"She laughed."

Eagle stared out his window at the Arbuckle Mountains. Purple shadows softened them so that they appeared benign. Only he knew how close Kate had come to dying in their uncompromising grasp.

"It's not your fault, Martin. Do you have any idea who is doing this?"

"I don't have enough evidence to convict a skunk, but I believe he's Chickasaw."

"I think so too. He's covered his tracks too well to be anything but Indian."

"Hal Lightfoot seems the likeliest possibility. He ran track in school, he's young and full of vigor and venom. His hatred of Kate goes all the way back to that old business with the medicine man when she was building her clinic. I'm staking out his house."

That was one more secret Eagle would have to keep from Deborah Lightfoot, one more way he'd have to betray her.

"I think you should stake out the shaman as well. She took over his territory, and his hatred of her is well known."

"He's old."

"Don't let his age fool you. Any man who can survive alone in the mountains is not to be underestimated."

"I'll put a man on him. He's got connections with everybody on tribal lands. But my bet is still on Lightfoot."

"Have you thought of staking out the manager of the tool and die plant? And what about the employees? I know some of them are extremely bitter toward her. Maybe bitter enough to kill."

"Hell, why don't I stake out the whole damned Nation? Would that satisfy you, Governor?"

Eagle held up his right hand in the age-old gesture of peace.

"All right. I'm going. You do your job and I'll do mine."

Eagle squared his shoulders as he prepared to leave, as if he were adjusting them for the heavy burden he carried. Martin wasn't known for interfering in people's personal lives, but he couldn't sit still and watch a friend put himself through hell.

"Eagle . . . I know this is none of my business, but are you sure you're doing the right thing about Kate Malone. Any fool can see . . ."

"You're right. It's none of your business."

"All right. I asked for that. May the Great Spirit be with you, Eagle."

Eagle took the long way to Deborah's house, riding on horseback, stopping on the hillside above Kate's layout long enough to satisfy himself that she was safely inside. The clinic was dark, but all the lights in her house were on. He could see her silhouette through the kitchen window.

He circled her house, far enough back so he wouldn't be seen but close enough so he could see if anyone was lurking about. Winter winds soughed lightly through the trees and stars gentled the land. The beauty and tranquility were deceiving. Eagle could feel the danger shimmering in the air, and it seemed to him the danger had a name.

Something was hovering on the edge of his conscious mind, something vital, something he'd missed. Sitting in

the darkness watching the light shine on Kate's hair, he
tried to capture the elusive solution.

At last he turned away, the vision of Kate still in his
mind, turned away and headed to Deborah Lightfoot's
house. He was going to ask her to marry him.

He knew that he had failed. The witch woman was
still alive.

The avenger's hands shook as he punctured the
end of his finger. Blood spurted out and pooled on the
end of his steel blade. Carefully he laid the knife aside,
then took his quill pen and dipped it in the warm red
ink.

"Your tormentor watches you, white doctor witch."

His ink ran out too quickly, and he held his finger up
to the light and punched another hole. The smell of his
own blood mingled with the smells of winter—the
sharp odor of the frozen earth, the musk of dead leaves,
and the clean fragrance of the north wind.

He dipped the pen once more and finished his note.
Repent or burn in hell.

His blood soaked into the paper, then dried to a
brownish-red stain. He'd have to bury the note deep in
his coat pocket to keep it dry. Winters in Witch Dance
. . . dampness always seemed to be in the air, whether it
was snowing or not.

With the note securely hidden, he stepped outside. The
stars stared at him, malevolent eyes that saw every move
he made. He would have to be careful. The hounds of
hell were closing in on him. He could hear them baying
at his heels, feel their hot breaths fanning the back of his
neck.

The avenger checked the position of the stars. There
was time, time to race with the north wind to his destination.

All the lights were out at her place. The white witch
was sleeping. She never knew when he slipped the letter under the door of her clinic, pushing it all the way
inside so the weather wouldn't destroy it. She never

knew when he picked the lock on her back door and slid inside her house.

She was asleep on her side with her right hand under her cheek and her left hand stretched toward the gun on her bedside table. A path of moonlight fell across her pale neck.

How easy it would be to end it all now. Slide the blade across her tender flesh and watch her blood flow onto the pillow.

Steel whispered against leather as he pulled the knife from his scabbard. The pale-faced witch stirred, moaning in her sleep.

Fearless and invincible, the avenger waited. She settled back into her covers with a great sigh. The moonlight was on her cheek now, illuminating the bruises.

Death would be too kind to her. Suffering. That's what she needed. When he'd finished with her, she'd wish she were dead.

33

Hal Lightfoot was on the move.

His Jeep careened through the darkness like a drunken sailor on his first shore leave. Martin Black Elk was right behind him, guiding the unmarked car with his left hand and radioing with his right.

"He's headed your way," he said to the car staked along the Blue River. "Don't lose him."

It was hard not to be spotted driving along the back roads in Witch Dance, especially so late on a Saturday night. Sane folks were gathered in the bars, swapping stories and swilling beer or piled in front of their hearths eating popcorn and watching movies. But whoever said police work was sane? Black Elk just hoped his disguise worked. He felt like a fool with the baseball cap and his hair in a ponytail.

Even his wife Doris had teased him.

"Honey, if I didn't know you better, I'd say you had a cute young thing stashed somewhere."

"Doris, I'm too damned tired for cute young things. The old stuff's good enough for me." He nuzzled her neck and pinched her butt.

"Who are you calling old?" Doris punched his arm. "Get out of here, you horny devil."

Racing along in the dark, Martin was struck with
such longing to be in front of his own fire that he made
an instant bargain with himself to retire.

"As soon as I catch this aspiring killer," he muttered.

Hal swerved abruptly onto a gravel road, and, curs-
ing, Martin let him get a lead, then went in behind him.
Where in the shit was the little bastard going now?

Martin's car bucked in the rutted road, and tree limbs
scraped the paint off the sides. It was going to be in a
hell of a shape if he ever got out of the woods.

Abruptly he came into a clearing, and there was Hal
Lightfoot, propped against a tree, smoking a cigarette
and fondling a woman more than twice his age. With
her skirt hiked up, she was clinging to Hal like bubble
gum on a shoe sole.

"What in the hell are you doing out here?" Martin
asked.

"What does it look like?" Hal removed his left hand
from the woman's bra, then stepped in front of her, took
the cigarette out of his mouth, and blew a smoke ring
Martin's way.

"Too bad you made that long trip all the way from
town, Chief."

"You picked a mighty remote spot for that kind of
sport, Hal. Aren't you afraid you'll freeze your pecker
off?"

"Is that the business our tribal police are in now, pro-
tecting peckers?"

"Only when it looks like it's fixing to get him into
trouble."

"Hell, Chief, can't a man have a romp in the woods
without getting spied on? I know how to stay out of
trouble."

"See that you do."

Martin had no choice but to leave. Something nagged
at his brain, but he was too tired to give it much
thought. On the way back to town he radioed Hal's lo-
cation to the other stakeout car.

"Looks like all he's interested in tonight is getting

laid. Sooner or later he'll come out of the woods, and when he does, try not to lose him."

Bone-weary, Martin headed home. Halfway there, he knew what had been bothering him.

"Holy shit!" The radio crackled as he contacted his office. "Ray, get me everything you can find on Clayton Colbert's wife."

"How far back?"

"Hell, all the way back to her conception if you have to. Clayton Colbert shot himself, and now his widow's in the woods, screwing Hal Lightfoot. I want to know why."

"Will do. Chief, there's somebody here to see you. Won't talk to anybody but you. Says it's urgent."

Probably some little old lady with a stray cat up a tree.

"Tell them I'll be right there."

The station house visitor was a frightened woman, but she didn't have a stray cat up a tree. Her name was Marjorie Kent, and what she had to say made the hair on the back of Martin's neck stand on end.

"My husband overheard them, Chief, the medicine man and some man he didn't know."

"Did he see a face?"

"No."

"Could he tell anything about the size?"

"No, they were sitting down, smoking the pipe. It was dark, and the man's back was to him."

"Did they use any names?"

"No. Only 'the tormentor' and 'the avenger.' "

"Did either of them say anything to indicate that one of them might be the avenger?"

"They talked about him in abstract terms, as if he were some kind of god." Marjorie Kent twisted her hands in her lap. "I know this is all hard to believe."

"I believe you, Mrs. Kent."

"My husband didn't want me to come. He said it would only cause trouble. He was there to consult the

shaman about the children . . ." Her voice trailed off. "I
had to come here. I didn't know what else to do."

"You did the right thing, Mrs. Kent. You were very
brave to come all that way this time of night. . . . Smith,
take her into the break room and get her a cup of coffee."

Everything the woman had said confirmed tips from
his own sources. As soon as they were out the door,
Martin picked up the phone.

"Mingo, I believe Kate Malone may be in real danger.
The man who calls himself her tormentor plans to strike
soon."

It was still dark when Deborah slipped into the clinic.
Kate had no idea she'd come. In fact, Kate would be fu-
rious if she knew Deborah was out so early after the
long, horrible ordeal they'd endured the day before.

First, they'd discovered the note slipped under the
door of the clinic. "Your tormentor watches you, white
doctor witch. Repent or burn in hell." The words were
as clear to Deborah as if she were still seeing them.

And then there had been the magazines scattered
across the floor as if a great gust of wind had blown
them there. Strange that the man who alternately called
himself the tormentor and the avenger had done nothing more than trash a few magazines.

Did that mean he was tiring of his sick game?

Deborah walked briskly through the clinic, checking
to see if anything was out of place. After yesterday, she
wanted to spare Kate. Finding the note had been bad
enough, but seeing Deborah's engagement ring at the
same time must have been devastating.

Kate had tried to hide it, but Deborah knew. She'd
heard the gasp; she'd seen her face.

"Eagle and I are engaged." It was all Deborah could
think of to say.

"That's wonderful. I'm so happy for you." She'd recovered quickly, and her congratulations had been sincere. "You'll make a beautiful bride."

"Will you stand beside me, Kate?"

"You bet." The enthusiasm of her reply took the sting out of her slight hesitation. "I'd fight anybody who tried to take my place."

"Truly?"

"Truly. Now, let's get this place cleaned up and get our butts out of here. We have a house call to make."

Remembering, Deborah held her finger aloft so the diamond would catch the pale morning light. *Diamonds are forever.* Who had said that? And was it true?

There had been no sparks between them when Eagle had slipped the ring on her finger.

"With this ring, I pledge my loyalty to you, Deborah," he'd said.

What about love?

"You will bear my name and my children, and you will be protected always under the Mingo mantle of honor."

What about passion?

He'd kissed her and nothing more. Obviously he was saving his passion for the wedding bed. With the faint morning light filtering through the blinds and sparking on the diamond, Deborah tried to remember if there had been any passion in their kiss.

How sad that she had to wonder. And how silly to stand there, trying to remember.

Summoning up some cheer, she hummed as she tidied up the front room. There were no signs of yesterday's malicious mischief. That was good, for she and Kate must once again make the long journey to the Kent cabin to check on Adam and Rachel.

It had snowed on them the day before as they'd made their way up the mountain on horseback. Kate had been like a child at Christmas.

"Snow! Every winter when it comes, it's like seeing it for the first time." Kate caught the fat, cold flakes on her tongue, then, laughing, she turned to Deborah. "I used to write letters to Santa, asking him to bring snow to South Carolina."

"If you'd had to shovel the sidewalks when you were a kid, you wouldn't like it."

"Yes, I would."

"No, you wouldn't."

"Yes, I would."

They argued like children, then laughed themselves silly while the snow covered their tracks and the chill filtered through their coats and scarves. Laughter was the way they stayed sane for the ordeal ahead.

Witch Creek still demanded sacrifice. And it looked as if Rachel and Adam Kent would be the latest offerings. Kate worked with them all day long, tireless and determined.

"You're my hero," Deborah had said on the way home.

"Shucks, ma'am. You don't have to say that just because my eyes are puffy and my tail is dragging."

"No. I mean it. All these years, I've never told you how I feel. From the first day you came to Witch Dance, I wanted to be like you. You've always been my hero. And I don't care if you laugh at my terminology; I don't retract a word."

"I'm not laughing."

There had been tears in Kate's eyes when she guided her horse in close and took Deborah's hand, the one with the engagement ring.

"You're the best friend I've ever had, Deborah Lightfoot. The very best. Nothing will ever change that."

Standing in the clinic, Deborah twisted the ring on her finger. No, nothing could ever come between them. Not even the man they both loved.

She kissed the shining diamond, then started toward the back to get the medicine they'd need for the long journey to the Kent cabin. She was standing in the doorway with her hand on the light switch when she heard the noise. A small squeak, like someone easing across the floor.

"Who's there?" she called.

A hand closed over her mouth. Deborah tried to scream, but the hand muffled the sound. Twisting and thrashing, she caught a glimpse of a buckskin-covered arm as she was dragged into the back room.

His movements were swift and sure, like an athlete ... or a madman bent on murder. With one hand he stroked the side of her face.

"Don't be afraid."

His voice was smooth and silky, hypnotic, even sensual. Sweat broke out on Deborah, and the smell of fear filled the room.

"What a pity you got in the way."

Deborah rammed her right foot down hard on his. He didn't even grunt.

"Don't struggle. It will only make things worse."

Pale light seeped through the blinds, and somewhere in the woods behind the clinic an owl called. Sheer terror seized her. When her captor loosened one of his hands, she managed to twist herself halfway out of his grip.

The face that stared back at her was as familiar as her own.

"We all have our missions to perform, Deborah. Mine will soon be over."

Abruptly he released her; then with a smile both beautiful and terrible he tossed a match into a pile of rags. The smell of oil and smoke choked Deborah. Her scream filled the room and pushed against the walls.

Suddenly she realized she was free. With her mouth wide open she started to run. The blade of a knife flashed once, cutting off her scream.

34

Flames licked the sky and smoke curled upward as the clinic caved in upon itself. She tried to turn her head toward the inferno, but Eagle tightened his hold on her face, forcing her not to watch.

"It's over, Kate."

His voice mesmerized, and his hands upon her skin. Kate fought her way out of the sweet web of memories that threatened to steal her reason.

"No. It will never be over."

The fire crackled, its reflection wavering across the snow. And in that macabre dance, Eagle's eyes burned as hot as the flames.

"You're right. It will never be over." He wheeled his stallion away from the blaze, away from the cottage and the dark brooding trees that surrounded it. The wind caught Kate's hair and whipped it around her face.

"What are you doing?" she yelled.

"I'm taking you with me."

"Dammit, Eagle. You can't kidnap me."

He tightened his arms around her as his stallion thundered across the prairie. Plumes of snow spewed up from the hooves, and all around them the land was white and pure, as if they'd left the menace far behind in the black-

ened ruins of her clinic. Eagle pressed the stallion to a
speed that was reckless, daring, obsessive. She was forced
to cling to him to keep from falling off.

"Stop right now. I have to go back. Do you hear me,
Eagle? I have to go back!"

He rode, still silent, his body rigid and his eyes as
cold as the frozen earth. She balled her hands into fists
and battered his chest.

"Take me back," she said.

"Save your rage for the man who did this to Deborah."

Unbidden, her last image of her friend came, lying on
the clinic floor in a pool of blood. Beautiful Deborah,
with her sightless eyes staring at the ceiling. Her blood
was still on Kate's hands, would always be on her
hands.

Anguish stole her will, and she sagged against Eagle.

"Where are you taking me?"

He didn't answer, just glanced briefly at her with terrible eyes, then off again into the distance, as if he might
be planning to take her all the way to hell.

Grief and guilt battered her, and she doubled over
with the force of it. Her tears soaked the collar of Eagle's coat.

"We're home, Kate." He lifted her from the stallion
and cradled her as tenderly as if she were a child.

"It should have been me, Eagle. I should have been
the one in the clinic."

"No, Kate. It was fate."

"Damn fate. Damn fate all to hell." She battered
against him, barely seeing her target through her tears.
"It was me. I killed her."

"Stop it, Kate."

"I killed her with my damned Irish stubbornness and
stupid pride."

"Shhh." She felt his strong arms tighten around her,
felt his cheek resting against the top of her head. He began to speak in the fluid tongue of his fathers. Lulled by
the sound, lulled and somehow comforted, Kate drifted

out of her skin and stood apart to watch as the shell she'd left behind grieved.

Winds moaned around the eaves, and snowflakes the size of flower petals swirled past the window. A Sunday-morning quietness descended on the house, and from somewhere deep in the heart of the village, bells tolled, their melodic mournful notes echoing Kate's sorrow.

Where was Eagle's sorrow? Had he no feelings at all for the woman he'd intended to marry?

Just when Kate had condemned him as unfeeling, she felt his tears fall upon her hair. And she knew that she would no longer fight him ... at least for a little while.

When he released her and stepped back, there was no evidence of mourning in his face. He was as cold and implacable as chiseled stone.

"You will stay here, Kate."

She nodded, still too full of death and tears to speak.

"I'm sending my ranch foreman up to the house to guard you until Martin's men can get here."

Again she nodded, thinking that it felt good to let decisions be made for her for a change, and that she might drift along this way forever, nodding her head while the rest of the world performed its macabre dance.

In the doorway, Eagle hesitated, and then he said, "I'm going to find Deborah's killer."

Had she asked, or was it merely mental telepathy between two people who knew each other so well that words were unnecessary?

Eagle moved as he always did, without sound; and when he had gone, Kate made her way toward the sofa, one step at a time.

Charleston, South Carolina

The French doors were open to let in the afternoon breeze. Mick propped his feet on the footstool and sipped his iced tea while a news reporter barely as old as his tennis shoes told him what was happening in the world. Not that he cared too much. Old age and southern breezes did that to a man, made him so mellow, his world got small.

Outside, Martha was humming while she puttered in her rose beds. At dinner she'd told him that her peace rose would still be blooming at Christmas if she got very lucky.

Hell, Martha didn't need luck with flowers: She had a green thumb. Not that he was complaining. He liked the look and the smell of freshly cut flowers in the house. They added class.

Being the red-necked, brawling Irishman he was, he'd always envied class. Now that he was rich, he could afford to buy it.

The cute young thing on the television prattled on about riots and murder and mayhem. Mick took a long, cool drink of tea.

"And in Witch Dance today . . ."

Ice rattled against glass as Mick banged his drink onto the table. He snatched the remote control and turned up the volume.

". . . a young woman was murdered in the clinic of Dr. Kate Malone."

A band of fear squeezed his chest so hard, he thought he was having a heart attack.

"The victim, Deborah Lightfoot, was a nurse at the clinic, which was destroyed in the fire that swept through it in the predawn hours."

Mick's footstool overturned as he leapt out of his chair.

"Martha!" he yelled, grabbing for the phone.

"What is it, Mick?" She poked her head around the French doors.

"What's Kate's phone number?"

"You want Kate's phone number?" Dirt from the flower garden dribbled down the front of her dress as she put a gloved hand over her heart.

"Dammit, woman, are you going to stand there all evening gawking, or are you going to give it to me?"

Martha hurried into the room and pulled her address book from the middle drawer of the telephone table. Behind her, the television blared.

"On site at the Witch Dance fire is Governor Eagle Mingo. . . . Governor, do you have any suspects in the murder at Dr. Malone's clinic."

Martha dropped the telephone book. Wordless, she stared at the television while Mick picked up the book and dialed Kate. The phone rang and rang and rang. She could hear the faint electronic buzz, like a crazed bee that wouldn't hush.

She jumped when Mick banged the receiver down, then, weak-kneed, sank onto the floor beside the footstool. He was dialing again.

"This is Senator Mick Malone. Get me on the first plane to Ada, Oklahoma."

"Mick?" she said after he'd hung up.

"I'm going to bring Katie home."

Witch Dance

When Eagle came home, Kate was asleep on the sofa, curled in a ball, using her coat for a pillow. One shoe lay on the floor beside her and the other dangled from her foot.

A faint pink light filtered through the curtains, and a band of hot gold painted the sky just beyond the mountains.

Eagle knelt beside the sofa and gently traced the tearstains on Kate's cheek. She didn't even stir.

"I see the new dawn in the East, Kate," he whispered.

Once, they had greeted it properly, coupled together in the medicine wheel to celebrate the continuity of nature and the magic circle of life. Once, so many years before.

Kate breathed softly with her mouth slightly open.

Eagle slipped off her shoe, then covered her with his blanket and quietly walked away.

Some things were harder to endure than death.

Kate jarred suddenly awake with the frantic feeling of someone trying desperately to outrun danger. Disoriented, she stared at the Indian blanket covering her, then slowly she remembered the horror and where she was.

She swung her feet over the edge of the sofa and scrambled for her shoes. Her coat was wadded at the end of the sofa. Dressed, she felt like yesterday's laundry.

"Good morning, Kate."

Eagle was sitting beside the fire, drinking a cup of coffee and watching her with eyes as dark and pitiless as the bowels of hell.

"I didn't see you," she said.

"Obviously." He stood up slowly and gracefully, like one of the giant cats that prowled the mountains. "Going somewhere?"

"Yes." She started toward the door, then remembered that she was at his mercy for a ride home. "Can you lend me your car . . . or a horse?"

"You won't be needing either one, Kate. You're staying here."

"Like hell I am." Chin up and eyes blazing, she struck out for the door. He caught up with her in three easy strides. His face and hands were ruthless as he gripped her shoulder and spun her around.

"The killer is still on the loose, and you're the target. You will stay here until it's safe for you to leave."

"Make me."

"Don't think I can't . . . or won't."

Lesser men would have quailed under his stare, but she was fighting Irish. Nothing deterred her.

"If you think I'm going to knuckle under and do your bidding, you're sadly mistaken."

"I'm Chickasaw. Unconquered and unconquerable. Don't try me."

"And I'm Irish. We may not have a motto, but we've got damned fine tempers and the grit to go with them."

"You can do this the easy way or the hard way, Kate. Take your choice."

She tried to stare him down, tried to get past the iron control that masked his emotions. He remained implacable, and underneath her heavy coat she could feel the sweat of pure rage and certain defeat.

"What is the hard way, Eagle? Do you plan to tie me up and lock me in my room?"

"Do you plan to try me, Kate?"

"Don't think I won't."

They stared at each other, unmoved and unmovable, while a log on the fire burned in two and split with an audible crackle. The air was thick with challenge and the desire, lambent and intoxicating, that always smoldered between them when they were in the same room.

The doorbell rang, but even that sound could not bring them out of the spell that bound them. It rang again . . . and again, its insistent clanging no more to the two beside the fire than the annoying noise of a distant mosquito.

"Does nobody ever answer the door in this godforsaken place?"

Senator Mick Malone strode through the door, and cold air swirled in with him. The shock of seeing her father after so many years paled Kate's face.

For a moment Kate felt the way she always did when she saw him, as if she'd been caught stealing cookies when she'd been told a dozen times not to eat them and ruin her supper. Hard on the heels of her childish guilt came rage.

"You are on Tribal Lands in the house of the governor, Father. You owe him the courtesy of a polite greeting." She felt the loss as she stepped apart from Eagle. "Governor Mingo, this is my father, Senator Mick Malone."

The two men assessed each other like gladiators who found themselves by chance in the same arena.

"Governor," Mick said, nodding curtly.

"Senator. Please be seated." The great dignity that was as much a part of Eagle as his long black hair and his beaded elkskin boots came to the fore.

"Don't mind if I do. It's a hell of a long way from Charleston to Witch Dance."

He sank into his chair like an old man. The sight of his infirmities saddened Kate . . . and scared her. Mick Malone was supposed to be invincible.

"I'll get you some coffee, Senator." Eagle left the room as soundlessly as the snow that drifted in fat flakes beyond the window.

Kate sat in a chair opposite her father, and an uncomfortable silence descended over them. Sweat inched down the side of her face, and she wished she'd taken a chair away from the fire.

"How are ye, Katie Elizabeth?"

"Dirty, disheveled, grief stricken at the loss of my friend and my clinic. Other than that, I'm fine, Father." She wouldn't give Mick the satisfaction of seeing how hot she was by taking off her coat. "How's Mother?"

"She misses you, Katie."

What about you, Father? Do you ever miss me?

Kate stared at him, knowing she would never ask the question that pressed upon her mind.

"I'll call her today . . . reassure her."

"There won't be any need for long distance calls, Katie. I'm taking you home."

"I'm not going."

"I've already bought your ticket."

"Cash it in. I'm staying here."

"This is all the doings of that savage."

"Don't you dare speak of Eagle Mingo in those terms."

"I'll use any terms I by God please. Do you take me for some kind of fool? I saw the two of you together when I walked into this room."

Kate stood up, giving herself the advantage of towering over Mick as he sat in his chair.

"You should have knocked first."

"I practically tore the damned bell off the wall, ringing it." Mick stood up to face her, his shoulders squared like a boxer's. "Katie Elizabeth, get your things."

"I don't have any things, and I'm not about to be picked up and shuffled around like a mail order package."

Eagle came into the room as silently as he had left.

"Kate, go with him. It's best."

She whirled on Eagle. "Best for whom? Who the hell gives a damn who it's best for? Certainly not you, *Governor*." She fixed a fierce glare on her father. "Nor you, *Senator*." She jerked off her coat and flung it onto the sofa. "While both of you are bickering over my life, I have patients who are dying. As soon as I take a bath, I'm going to make a house call, with or without your permission, Eagle Mingo." She turned to her father. "As for you, you gave up parental rights the day you told me I was no daughter of yours."

The look on his face might have moved her if she'd had any heart left to move. But she was stripped bare of feeling, totally naked emotionally. The only thing that mattered now was the Chickasaw children.

"I'm staying in this land you call godforsaken with this man you call savage."

"Not while I have breath in my body," Mick said.

"She's made her decision, Senator."

Kate marched out with her head held high, leaving the fighting Irish senator and the unconquerable Chickasaw squared off before the fire. Her righteous indignation got her out of the room and down the hall. In the bathroom that held the masculine smells of Eagle, in the shower that held the spicy soap still damp from his bath, she leaned against the wall and wrapped her arms around herself until she could stop shaking.

From the den came the sound of their battle.

"She's made her decision, Senator. I will not allow you to go after her."

"I don't need your permission to go after my own daughter."

"This is my house."

"Why, you arrogant whippersnapper. Do you know who you're talking to? I'm a by God United States senator."

"You're on Tribal Lands, Senator. Your title and power are meaningless here."

Kate could picture Eagle, as formidable and unmovable as Arbuckle Mountain. But Mick Malone was neither impressed nor intimidated.

"You'll think Tribal Lands when I get through with you. I'll have the feds down here so fast, it'll make your head swim. When they get through investigating the fire at my daughter's clinic, we'll see who has power."

There was the sound of footsteps as Eagle crossed the room, probably showing her father the door. Then a long silence, and Mick's parting shot.

"You haven't heard the last of me."

Only when the door slammed did Kate realize she'd been gripping her arms so hard, she'd made red marks.

"Kate." She hadn't even heard his approach, and yet there was Eagle, standing just inches away from her, on the other side of the glass shower door. Kate squeezed her hands together to keep from putting them on the glass like a child would on a shop window holding a great confection.

"I'm sorry, Kate."

She could withstand his coldness, but his kindness was killing her.

"Don't take my decision to stay here personally."

"I don't."

"And don't think I'm going to make it easy for you . . . because I'm not."

"I'd be disappointed if you did, *Wictonaye*."

Was the slip accidental or deliberate? Her breathing fogged up the shower door, but still she could see him, too close, too tempting. The humming sound she used to make when she was curved into him on summer evenings under the stars started low in her throat, and she clamped her hand over her mouth.

What kind of woman was she? Wanting her best friend's fiancé only hours after Deborah's death?

Eagle's house was sprawling, most certainly with two baths and probably three. Why had she barreled down the hall to his?

"Kate . . . are you all right?"

What if she weren't? Would he come inside the shower and help her fog up the glass door?

"Uhm-mmm."

"When you've finished your bath, I'll take you home to get some of your things, and I'll go with you on your house calls."

"All right."

He stood on the other side of the glass door for a small eternity, then he left. It must have been five minutes after he left before Kate had recovered enough to turn on the shower.

The horses' hooves sank deep into the snow as they struggled up the mountainside, single file. Only the life-and-death struggle of two children could have forced Eagle to take Kate on such a journey.

He glanced behind to see how she was making the trip. She gave him a thumbs-up sign, but he could see the tension in her face and knew she must be remembering what had happened the last time she'd braved the mountain.

There was a certain waiting stillness upon the land, as if someone, somewhere, watched every move they made. A raven rose suddenly from its nest, sounding alarms, and Eagle glanced upward.

Did a shadow move, or was it his imagination? If he hadn't had Kate with him, he'd have investigated, but his primary purpose was to deliver her safely to the sick children.

When they entered the woods, he again was convinced that he was being watched. Strange that he wasn't picking up a sense of evil, but a sense that whoever was out there belonged to the land in the way that his ancestors had.

Eagle scanned the woods, but not so much as the movement of a leaf betrayed the watcher.

35

Charleston, South Carolina

For the first time in years, Martha stood up to her husband.

"I want to know about my daughter," she said.

"She's living with a savage. What more do you want to know, Martha?"

"How was she? Did she look all right? What did she say?"

Mick crushed his cigar in the ashtray and sat down in his chair with the newspaper. As far as he was concerned, the conversation was over.

Martha walked over to his chair and stood, waiting for him to notice her.

"Dammit, woman. What do you want? Can't you see I'm busy?"

"You've seen Katie Elizabeth for the first time in five years, and all you can say is 'She's living with a savage.' I never considered you heartless, Mick Malone, but I'm beginning to think that's exactly what you are. A heartless ... son of a you-know-what."

"Martha, I do believe you came close to cussing me." Mick almost grinned.

"I do believe I did."

Martha could hardly believe what she'd done.

Flushed with success and newfound courage, she took the paper from his hand.

"Now," she said. "Tell me what you said to my daughter and what she said to you. I want to know the truth."

Mick seemed to grow smaller as he scooted down in his chair.

"The truth is ugly, Martha."

"Yes, Mick. Sometimes it is." She sat on the footstool beside the chair and took his hand. "Tell me about Katie."

Witch Dance

Anna had grown to hate her husband. Almost.

Looking at him now, sitting at the head of the dinner table, she could pretend for a little while that everything was normal, that they still shared the same goals, the same bed.

"This roast beef is delicious, Anna," Dovie said.

"Thank you." Anna had no appetite for roast beef. Even the smell of it made her sick.

She felt Cole's eyes on her, and when she looked at him, he smiled.

Don't give me false hope, she wanted to scream. She'd invited his family over, hoping that their presence would restore some sense of balance and normality.

Cole's smile dashed all her plans. For a moment it was sincere, intimate, *real*. And then it became something else, something she didn't even want to think about.

"Eagle flaunts the pale-faced doctor," he said.

"I know of this." Winston had aged terribly in the past few months. Except for his piercing eyes and the deep voice, there were no signs of the powerful, robust man Anna had known.

"She lives with him," Dovie said.

"He protects her," Winston said. "Nothing more."

"Black Elk sent tribal police to do that," Dovie protested. "They are all around Eagle's ranch. Why can't they do their job at Dr. Malone's house?"

Anna wanted to throw dishes at her husband for bringing this contention to their family meal. Instead, she spooned in a mouthful of potatoes and tried to swallow them without gagging.

"She'll turn him away from everything he believes in," Cole said.

Clint shoved back his chair and ran from the room. Dovie started crying.

"Now look what you've done." Anna's rage and frustration boiled over. "If anyone is destroying this family, it's you."

Cole's face was thunderous as he stalked out of the room.

"We will all survive this trying time." Winston helped Dovie into her coat, then put his arms around Anna. "You're strong, my daughter. I'm proud of you."

She stood in the doorway until they were safely in their car, then she went into the bathroom she shared with her husband and lost her dinner.

Cole didn't even bother to ask why she was sick.

The long white limousine slid through the night as silently as a shadow. Behind its tinted windows Melissa stared at the cottage and the charred ruins of the clinic.

"Stop here," she told the driver.

As she stared into the darkness, the old rage built in her. Clayton had lived there ... with another woman. Melissa flattened her palms against the glass and imagined how it must have been, the two of them sharing meals that Clayton had cooked and laughing together ... laughing at her.

"You won't win this time."

At her signal, the chauffeur carried her back to her apartment in Ada. Inside, she dropped her purse somewhere in the vicinity of the entry hall and slid one arm

out of her mink coat so that it trailed along behind her
to the bathroom.

"Hurry, hurry," she whispered to herself. "He'll be
here soon."

Her hands shook as she untangled herself from her
coat, then reached into the back of the linen closet to
take out her supplies. When all the pots of paint were
spread upon the vanity, she stripped off her clothes and
stood naked in front of the mirror.

She dipped her finger into a paint pot, then drew
careful circles around her breasts.

"Ni'tak intaha," she whispered. "The days appointed
are finished."

She dipped her fingers again, then raked them down
her body from breastbone to pelvic bone. Her pupils di-
lated at the sight of so much red. Like blood.

Clayton would be proud of her. At the thought of her
lover, Melissa became almost frantic in her haste. Soon
he'd be with her and they would lie together on the silk
sheets sealed at the hips, sealed so tightly that nothing
could tear them apart.

The blue slash she painted across her cheeks wavered
off course, and the yellow she put on her lips got out of
line, but that didn't matter now. Nothing mattered except being ready for Clayton.

When she'd finished painting herself, she selected a
knife from the kitchen and lay down upon the bed.

"Soon, my darling," she whispered.

She heard his key in the lock and his footsteps as he
came into her bedroom. She turned herself so that the
bedside light could show her handiwork.

"My God," he whispered.

"Do you love me?" she asked.

He came to her swiftly, and knelt beside the bed.

"You know I do." He bent over her hand and pressed
it to his lips. "I love you, Melissa. I *really* love you."

"Will you do anything for me, Clayton?"

His beautiful skin glistened in the lamplight as he
stared at her.

"Will you?" she whispered.

He touched her breasts and his fingers came away red.

"Anything, my love."

Smiling, she put the knife in his hands.

Every movement Kate made vibrated through him like a bowstring turned loose after the arrow has been launched. Eagle's house had become a mine field. If he turned his head too quickly, he would catch her watching him in ways that set him aflame. If he wandered through the house in the middle of the night, he would glimpse her, struck with the same wanderlust, standing at the window with the moon washing her skin silver.

Now, sitting across the table from her, he was surprised to see that look on her face again. He lifted his coffee cup . . . carefully, as he did everything these days.

Kate picked up her cup with equal care.

"I'm going to the barn to check on Mahli," she said. "She hasn't looked good since . . ." Her voice trailed away.

"I'll go with you."

"I'm afraid she won't be with me much longer. I'd like to spend some time with her." Their eyes met. "Alone."

"After I check the barn, I'll leave you. One of the guards can escort you back to the house."

They walked side by side to the barn, not touching. The night was cold and clear, with stars shining down on the snow and reflecting their light in patches that looked like celestial stepping-stones.

Only a fool would try to penetrate the wall of guards around the governor's house on such a night.

"It's beautiful, isn't it?" Kate looked up at the sky.

"Yes." Her face and hair were surrounded by a nimbus.

Waka ahina uno, iskunosi Wictonaye. Waka.

As if she'd read his thoughts, she turned to him.

"We can never go back," she whispered.

"No. Never."

Silently, he held the barn door open. She went straight to the stall and stood with Mahli between them while he checked for signs of intruders. Nothing was out of place. The sweet smell of hay and the rich smell of loamy earth lulled and soothed, just as the stars had done.

"You're safe, Kate. Just call one of the guards when you're ready to come back."

"Yes, Governor." She saluted, then came out of the stall and curtsied. "Anything you say, Governor."

The irony of her submissive attitude made them both laugh, and the laughter somehow saved them. When he went back to his house, Eagle's spirits were almost light.

He got a file folder and sat in a chair by the window, facing the barn. At his request, Martin Black Elk furnished him with copies of every report regarding Kate's case. The latest was on Melissa Sayers Colbert, widow of suicide victim Dr. Clayton Colbert, with addresses in Boston and Ada, Oklahoma—socialite, heiress, and recently a patient at a mental institution.

A memory stirred in the back of his mind, a memory of the look on Clayton Colbert's face when Eagle had welcomed Kate to Witch Dance with a bouquet of Indian paintbrush. It had been the look of a man desperately, hopelessly, in love.

Revenge was a powerful motivation.

Suddenly the back of his neck prickled, and he turned slowly to the window. A curl of smoke rose from the barn, and the acrid smell of burning filled the air.

Paper scattered to the floor as he raced from the room.

"Kate!" he yelled. There was no answer except the crackle of flame shooting toward the sky.

Eagle almost stumbled over the bodies of the tribal policemen he'd left guarding the door. Kneeling quickly, he felt their pulse, then burst through the barn door.

Smoke billowed around him.

"*Kate!*"

"Over here." She was struggling to lead Mahli and Heloa through the flames. The black stallion reared, and his hooves smashed against the ground, cutting deep grooves.

"Let him go, Kate! He'll kill you."

"He'll burn, Eagle. They'll all burn."

Kate's voice had the high, bright edge of hysteria. Eagle had a flashback of Deborah lying in a pool of blood amid the blazing clinic.

Not again. He wouldn't let the avenger win again.

He jerked the reins away from her and carried her outside. The police guards had swarmed from their posts and formed a bucket brigade. In the distance the fire truck's siren wailed.

Eagle pulled the burliest guard out of the lineup and thrust Kate toward him.

"Don't let her out of your sight."

Inside the barn, his stallion was thrashing the air with his hooves. Mahli's nostrils flared as she screamed with terror. Smoke burned Eagle's eyes and lungs, and flame licked up the hay on its ruthless march toward the walls.

Calling on all his skills as a horseman, Eagle mounted Mahli's back and grabbed the stallion's reins. The horses leapt through the door, then raced with demonic speed across the pasture while Eagle tried to control their terror.

Behind him, fire trucks circled and water arced toward the blaze. Firemen swarmed into the adjacent stables to release stall gates, and Eagle's other horses catapulted into the night.

By the time he brought Mahli to a halt and returned to the scene, the fire was under control. Kate sat on a tree root, drinking coffee someone had brought to her while a policeman stood guard, and Martin Black Elk stalked around with his hands rammed into his pockets and a scowl on his face.

"We're damned lucky the fire trucks got here in time to save your barn," he said.

The barn was the least of Eagle's worries.

"I'm taking Kate out of here."

"Six guards, and still he got through." Black Elk shook his head.

"Did you find any signs at all?"

"None. Whoever did this is a genius ... or a madman. I'll send more men to guard your house."

"No. The only way I can protect Kate is to take her where no one will follow."

They left in the middle of the night after everyone had gone.

This time Kate hadn't questioned Eagle's judgment, hadn't even questioned where he was taking her. Riding a big bay from his stables, she kept pace with him. Snow had begun to fall once more, and it powdered their clothes and covered their trail as they traveled. She lost track of time, depending instead on Eagle, who possessed mysterious instincts that guided them through a world as white and silent as death.

They didn't stop until dawn. Eagle held up his right hand, and Kate drew her mount to a halt.

"We'll pitch camp here."

It was a desolate place, high in the mountains, where nothing moved except a lone eagle winging his audacious way toward the rising sun. Their campsite, tucked under the shelf of an enormous rock, provided a natural fortress and afforded them a panoramic view of the mountains.

They tended and sheltered the horses, then Kate fell exhausted into the tent, bundled into a sleeping bag with all her clothes on.

Eagle kept watch until the sun spilled its unforgiving light around them, and then he lay down beside Kate. No person, either genius or madman, would attack such a place in broad daylight.

He came fully alert, drawn by a compelling force from a deep, dreamless sleep. Rolling onto his side, Ea-

gle looked straight into the eyes of Kate Malone. Everything they'd ever been to each other shone in her green
eyes, burned there until his skin caught fire and there
was nothing he could do except try to put out the
flames.

Wordless, he held out his hand and she tumbled
down upon him, silky and fragrant, her body rich with
the mysteries he remembered so well. There was no
haste, for they were alone on the desolate mountain,
alone in the cold sunlight and the ice-bound canyons.

She had not changed in five years except for the
slight, more exotic ripeness of her body and the desperate edge to her desire. As he discovered her anew, he
wondered how he could have chosen the howling loneliness of honor and duty over the eternal renewal of
passion.

Fully sheathed in her, he lifted himself on his elbows
so he could read her face and eyes. Still as a cat, she
waited, her body trembling with the same carnal impatience as his. They stared at each other, breathless with
fear and wonder.

There was no turning back now. From the moment
he'd held out his hand, he had set them on a course that
would rock the mountains and shatter the very foundations of their lives.

"*Waka ahina uno, iskunosi Wictonaye,*" he whispered.
"*Waka.*"

Later, he would not remember who had moved first,
but that slight nudge of hip against hip, of flesh against
flesh, exploded through them like a thousand rivers un-
leashed and roaring through the canyons.

The sun climbed through the sky, gradually burning
away the blue, but they knew neither time nor place nor
hunger. For the two of them there was only discovery,
time and again, of the slow sweet death of passion and
the resurrection of fulfillment.

When bands of hot gold gilded the western mountaintops, Eagle spread Kate upon his blanket, arranging
her lush and languid limbs for a celebration of the

magic circle of life. Her lips closed around him as they began the slow spin on the medicine wheel that would take them through the sunset and into the gray edge of evening.

Afterward, sitting side by side, eating beef jerky and drinking tepid coffee from a thermos, they didn't speak of what had happened.

"I'm going to scout around, Kate." Eagle found her gun among her belongings and placed it in her hand. "Sit with your back to the wall and your gun aimed at the door. Shoot anything that tries to come through."

"How long will you be gone?"

"No more than an hour."

She reached out and touched his lips, once, softly.

"Be careful, Eagle."

Armed with his knife and his rifle, he left her there, sitting with her gun cocked and aimed at the tent door. The snow stretched clean and untouched around their campsite. Eagle fed the horses the sweet oats he'd packed, then set out to find the enemy.

All Eagle's senses came alert. The enemy was out there, not watching, but waiting somewhere in a dark lair, waiting like an animal who knows his prey is nearby.

The first sign was a broken branch, less than half a mile from the campsite. Eagle studied the surrounding area. Either through carelessness or overconfidence the avenger had not bothered to cover his trail. Snow had covered his tracks, but the trees and bushes held evidence of his passing. A thread had been snagged from his jeans. Low-lying limbs had been knocked clean of their burden of snow. Some of them were crooked and broken.

Eagle tracked, following the clear trail. Around the side of a huge boulder he stopped, rooted to the spot by fear and a terrible sense of forboding. Planted in the ground was the red war pole, and carved deep in the snow at its base was the perfect imprint of a man, lying spread-eagle with his face pressed to the earth.

The size and shape of his body were as familiar to Eagle as his own. Terror paralyzed him, and denial rose screaming through his throat. He bit his lip so hard, he tasted blood.

Kneeling, he placed his hand in the indentation, right where the man's hand had been. A perfect fit.

"No," he whispered. "No."

He leaned close, studying the imprint, touching to assure himself that he was not deceived. There, his high cheekbones had been. And there, his wide chest. There, his coat had been open so the ornate belt buckle could press the snow. There, the scabbard for his knife. And there, his soft beaded boots.

Suddenly Eagle's hand closed over a small object, a familiar Italian blue glass bead, ancient and cherished, twin to the ones that decorated his own boots. Clutching the bead in his hand, he shook his fist at the sky.

Eagle knew the avenger . . . his enemy . . . his brother.

"Kate. It's Eagle." He called her from a distance, and she put her gun down and met him outside the tent door.

The first thing she noticed was the red-painted pole in his hand. A sinking sense of dread spread through her, making her arms heavy and her legs limp.

"You found him?"

"No. Only signs."

Silently he planted the pole outside their tent, planted it so deep and so hard that its top whipped back and forth as if strong winds were shaking it. Kate's dread became a nameless terror. With one hand against her throat she moved toward the pole.

"Don't touch it." She stepped back, struck by the flat, deadly tone of his voice.

"What is it?"

"The war pole."

"What does it mean?"

"It means the avenger prepares to go into battle."

Looking at the ancient symbol, Kate understood that

she was not the avenger's target this time: It was Eagle. He would have to remove her protector to get to her, but more than that, he understood that killing Eagle would be the worst punishment he could mete upon her. It would kill her spirit and her soul.

"We won't speak of this again." Eagle's face was tragic, his eyes shattered, as if a giant hand had smashed all the light from them.

"No," she said, for no amount of argument and pleas would get him to turn his face from fate. Moving with purpose, she put her hands on either side of his face. "Come inside, where it's warm."

He was in her before the tent flap closed behind them. With her arms and legs wrapped around him and the snow from his clothing melting on her skin, she knew that whatever happened, she would have this—a wild winter mating on a desolate mountaintop that would sustain her for years to come, just as their summer affair of five years past had sustained her.

"Make me fly, Eagle," she whispered.

"*Waka, Wictonaye. Waka.*"

High above them, hidden by trees and boulders, the avenger arose naked from his tent. Leaving behind the steaming rocks that purified him, he dressed in buckskins and carefully painted his face. With the clay streaked on his nose and cheeks and forehead, he was as fierce as the bear, as agile as the panther, and as cunning as the fox, for he knew he must be all three in order to subdue the eagle.

He filled his war pipe with sumac leaves and tobacco, lighted it, and drew it deep into his lungs. The smoke circled his head, and the power of the warrior filled his body. When he had finished, he set the pipe aside and ate a sumptuous feast, one he had prepared with great care and hauled up the treacherous face of the mountain.

By the time the war feast was finished, the moon had risen. The avenger's long knife glittered in the dark, brighter than the stars that studded the black sky. He

swung it in a huge arc, then lunged at the war pole.
Metal clanged against wood, and a chunk of red fell to
the snow and lay there like blood. Again and again he
lunged, until sweat poured off his face and the pole was
riddled with gouges.

The imaginary song of women rose up to cheer his
victory. Bowing deeply to his audience, the avenger
sheathed his long knife, then began a slow circle around
the pole, taking up the victory song. The circles became
tighter and faster and the song louder, until the night
was filled with the chant of war.

Kate slept curved against him, exhausted from three
days of tension and lovemaking. With her hair spread
across his naked chest and her lips pressed against his
neck, he watched the first pale light of dawn filter
around the tent flap.

It was time. The enemy would be waiting for him,
honed to the sharpness of a steel blade by three days of
preparation ... and armed to kill.

Gently he disentangled Kate. Softly he kissed her
cheek and covered her. She would be safe. The red war
pole had made it perfectly clear what the order of battle
would be. First Eagle, then Kate.

He dressed lightly so clothes would not impede him.
His knife lay beside their pallet, its blade catching a
shaft of light. As Eagle took the knife up, he remembered the first one he'd owned, a twin to Cole's, and
how they'd raced around their backyard, whooping and
fending off the imaginary hordes that attacked them,
and how, later, they'd tumbled in a heap in the sunshine, laughing.

The sun would not shine on them today, and there
would be no laughter. Quietly he slipped from the tent,
going to meet his enemy.

His brother.

Cole stood on a bluff overlooking the Blue River, his
feet planted wide apart, his painted face fierce, and his

arms uplifted to the rising sun. He didn't have to turn around to know his brother was there; he felt it in his bones. It was as if the other half of himself had crawled beneath his skin.

"You've come," he said, turning.

"Yes. You knew I would."

Eagle was not painted for battle, and yet Cole knew he was ready. There was tension in the way he stood, raw strength held in check by the sheer force of his will.

"It will be like old times," Cole said. "Just the two of us."

"No, Cole. Not like old times." A sadness fell over Eagle as he held out his hand. "Come back with me. It's not too late."

"Never."

"I'll help you." Eagle moved closer. "Please let me help you, Cole."

Cole threw back his head, and the canyon walls tossed his laughter back into his face.

"Traitor! You with your white witch whore. Would you help me face a white man's justice, a white man's jail? I'd rather die!"

As swift as the eagle that circled the bluff, Cole's twin moved in on him. Exultation filled Cole, and beyond the horizon he saw the white buffalo thundering upward toward the rising sun. It burned a white hole in the sky, and the whiteness spread until it surrounded Cole, bathing him in purity and righteousness. And out of the great burning center came the voices of his children, crying to him for vengeance.

His knife arced upward as he pulled it from his sheath, and the sun glinted against the long blade. Soon it would be red with his brother's blood, and then the white witch would die and his children would cry no more.

Kate jarred awake and sat bolt upright. Eagle's side of the pallet was empty. Panic pushed at her chest. He would never have left her without a word except for one reason: he had gone to do battle with the avenger.

"Eagle," she called, knowing there would be no answer.

Her hands shook as she threw on her clothes. Scrambling on hands and knees, she looked outside the tent. Eagle had made no attempt to cover his tracks. She grabbed her gun and followed them, running. Snow sucked at her boots and cold winds burned her lungs.

Overhead, an eagle screamed at her, and voices drifted down from the bluff above.

"I won't fight you, Cole."

"Fight, damn you. Fight like a Chickasaw."

"*Eagle!*" she screamed.

Her feet slipped in the snow, and terror gripped her as she clawed her way up the side of the bluff.

"Stay back, Kate! Don't come any closer."

"*Fight! Fight for the witch woman!*"

Kate topped the bluff just as Cole's blade flashed toward Eagle's throat. He sidestepped and saw her, crouching with the gun in her hand.

"Kate! No!"

Cole took advantage of the diversion, and in one swift move he had Eagle on the ground, the long blade at his throat.

"You're too easy, brother. Has the witch woman stolen your powers?"

Kate leveled her gun at his back, but her hands were shaking so badly, she couldn't hold it still. What if he moved suddenly and she killed Eagle? What if she didn't miss and killed Eagle's brother?

Eagle caught Cole's wrist and forced the knife away. Panting, they struggled. The brothers were evenly matched, and it seemed they might stay on the bluff forever, locked in mortal combat.

Holding back her screams, Kate lowered her gun and leaned against a rock, sick with fear and regret. She'd set brother against brother.

With a mighty heave Eagle shoved Cole aside, then

rolled into a crouch, his knife still sheathed. Cole glanced from his brother to his brother's woman. His blade made slow, menacing circles in the air.

"Who will it be, Eagle? You or the witch woman?"

Kate hardly saw the movement of Eagle's hand, but suddenly his blade flashed in the sun. Cole lunged at him. Steel clashed against steel.

She couldn't watch, and yet she dared not turn away. Kate covered her mouth with her hands. But some small sound must have escaped, for Eagle turned toward her, leaving himself vulnerable.

Cole's knife slashed his buckskin shirt, and the blood bloomed from his chest.

"*No!*" Kate screamed. "*Stop it!*"

With terrible face and eyes Eagle lifted his knife and scored along the side of his brother's cheek. Cole's laughter filled the canyon, and Kate covered her ears against its madness.

Their battle raged while the sun climbed upward, and slowly it brought them to the edge of the cliff.

"Give up," Eagle said.

"Never."

"You can't win against me."

The truth was so obvious that even Cole could see. Panting, he lowered his knife. Fierce and protective love glittered in Eagle's face as he held out his hand.

"Come with me. I'll get help for you."

For a moment the madness left Cole's eyes.

"Come," Eagle said once more, softly.

"To live forever in a place that has no sun? Kill me," he begged. "Put your knife to my throat and let me die with honor."

Wind and snow swirled around them as the brothers faced each other.

"Are you a coward?" Cole screamed. "*Kill me.*"

An eagle soared above them, its screams echoing Cole's. Eagle's hand tightened on his knife. Anguish filled his face as he hesitated. Then slowly, ever so slowly, he lifted the blade.

"No!" Kate screamed. "Don't let him do this to you."

Cole turned toward Kate, and for a moment she saw the kindhearted, loving man who had once been her friend and her champion.

"I never meant to do harm," he whispered. His eyes swung back to his brother. "I love you . . ." He took one backward step. "*Eagle!*"

His plaintive cry echoed off the canyon walls. For an instant, shock and horror held Kate in place, and then she was running, running toward Eagle and wrapping her arms around his chest.

Together they looked over the precipice. Cole lay at the bottom of the ravine, his neck at a crazy angle and his left leg folded underneath his broken body. Already the falling snow was beginning to cover him.

"It's over," Eagle said.

His face was terrible as he led her away, as frozen as the blanket of ice that would soon cover his brother.

"Yes, it's over," she said, knowing it was so, for Cole would always be between them, lying at the bottom of the ravine.

36

Martin Black Elk twirled his pencil in his hand as he listened to the governor's story.

"You have proof of all this?"

"None," Eagle said. "Only suspicions."

"Did Cole confess to Deborah's murder? Did he confess to ransacking Kate's house and burning her clinic?"

"No."

"Then I have nothing to go on."

Black Elk picked up Deborah Lightfoot's file and scrawled "Unsolved" across the front.

"What about her family?"

"Her father doesn't even know she's dead, and if her brother is capable of grief at all, it's enough without wondering whether a dead man killed his sister." Black Elk put a hand on Eagle's shoulder. "I'm sorry about your brother. I can't make any promises, but we can try to retrieve the body."

"No. He belongs to the mountains. That's the way he would have wanted it."

Anna couldn't grieve for Cole. When her children had died, she'd wept for days, weeks, but she had no tears for the man who had died on the mountain.

An accident, Eagle had said. Was it only two weeks ago? Cole had slipped and fallen into the ravine while he was hunting.

At odd moments she thought about how it must have been, about the surprised look on his face when he tumbled to the rocks. Had he called her name? Had he thought of her at all?

Sweat broke out on her forehead, and she rushed to the bathroom, sick. She closed the door so the rest of Eagle's office staff couldn't hear. Holding the sides of the commode, she lost her breakfast.

When she washed her face, she saw herself in the mirror, gaunt, hollow-eyed, somebody she didn't even know. A wave of nausea overtook her again, and she bent like a willow sapling and leaned her forehead against the cool washbasin.

Was this her body's way of grieving for Cole? Suddenly she remembered him as he had been the last time he'd held her—tender, virile, loving. And she knew the truth.

She found Eagle in his office. Every time she looked at him, she remembered the way Cole had once been.

"Anna, come in." His smile didn't touch his eyes. He had been that way since the day he'd returned from the mountain.

"I need the rest of the day off, Eagle."

"Take as much time as you need, Anna. Is it anything I can help you with?"

He'd been a rock for her, settling Cole's financial affairs, arranging memorial services, seeing that the ranch continued to run smoothly. Like Anna, he'd shed no tears. But in unguarded moments she could see the grief etched in his face.

"Not this time. This is something I must do alone."

Anna drove carefully, avoiding the ice patches on the road. The sign on the clinic door said CLOSED. Anna knocked on the door anyway, and when she got no answer, she tapped on the windows.

"Anna?" Kate came from the direction of the stables.

Bits of hay clung to her parka and her tumbled red hair. "I'm sorry. I was saddling Mahli and didn't hear you." She folded Anna in her embrace, then stood back to gaze at her. "How are you?"

"I'm pregnant."

"You're sure?"

"Yes, I'm sure. I've counted back. Nine weeks."

"Come inside and let me make you a cup of tea."

Kate's kitchen was cozy and cheerful. A bouquet of dried paintbrush stood in a pottery pitcher and a small flower-garden quilt was tossed across the back of an antique wooden bench. Anna sat on the bench and folded her hands, waiting.

"I'm sorry I didn't come to the memorial services, Anna. But I thought it best, under the circumstances."

"Yes. It was best."

Kate sat beside her and handed her the tea. Steam rose from the cup and warmed Anna's cold face.

"I need your help, Kate," she said.

"I'll help you any way I can. You know that."

"I want an abortion."

Kate set her cup on the table and walked to the kitchen window. Outside, the winds howled against the eaves. Rigid, she watched the snow blowing across the road, and when she finally turned around, there were tears on her cheeks.

"I won't abort your baby, Anna."

"You said you would help!"

"I will . . . but not that way." She sat on the bench and took Anna's hand. "Have you thought this through? Do you know the psychological damage you'll inflict on yourself if you do this thing?"

"All my other children were conceived in love. I don't want this child. It was conceived in the barn, in the hay, like an animal." Anna pressed her hands over her abdomen, as if she could protect her child from the evil of its origins. "There was no love . . . only madness."

"Are you sure?" Kate remembered Cole's lucid moment on the mountaintop, his whispered apology. "Cole was a wonderful man who loved his children so much, he couldn't handle their death. Once, you loved him."

Anna's hands tightened over her womb as she remembered the tender look on Cole's face when he'd planted his seed, and the way he'd called her his sweet hummingbird. At long last she laid her head on her folded arms and cried for her husband.

Kate got tissues from the bathroom, then reheated the tea.

"If the ranch holds too many painful memories for you, you can stay here, rent free."

"You're leaving?" Anna asked.

"Yes. I'm going home."

Anna didn't try to dissuade her. She understood only too well that Witch Dance could hold no hope for Kate Malone.

"I have a sister in California," Anna said. "She has a guest cottage by the sea and a little shop that sells embroidered children's clothes. I can work with her, and I think the change will be good for Clint."

"And the baby?"

She placed her hands protectively over her womb. "The baby too."

Kate stared straight ahead as she rode, for she'd said good-bye to the land the day she'd returned from the mountaintop. When Eagle's ranch came into view, she steeled herself to feel nothing, but instead she felt the flying sensation of making love to him under the stars and the uninhibited joy of riding bareback with him across the prairies. There, to her left, she'd first seen him in the river, naked, and later they'd cavorted in the water like lusty otters. And on the mountain she'd felt the snow from his clothes melt upon her skin, just as he had melted upon her skin and was there, still, a part of her that would be there always, even though an ancient culture and a thousand miles separated them.

He was standing beside his corral fence with the setting sun at his back. He was beautiful, perfect. How could she ever leave him?

She dismounted, and he shaded his eyes so he could see her better. He used to say the sun turned her hair to flame. Did it still, and did he notice?

"I came to give Mahli back to you." Why didn't he say something? "I'm leaving Witch Dance."

The sun blazed over them, red and gold, as she waited for him to beg her not to go. Waited for the impossible.

In the distance, the taxi she'd called earlier came up the road, spewing snow from its back tires. Eagle's expression never changed as he reached for Mahli's reins. He didn't even ask where she was going.

"I wish you well, Kate."

The taxi driver honked the horn, and Kate left Eagle without looking back. In the end, love had not been enough.

37

All the lights in Melissa's bedroom were pink so that the imperfections of her body were softened and the faint lines in her face were invisible. Even the scar on her wrist barely showed. Spread gracefully across the sheets, she watched every move he made, watched as if her life depended on whether he went toward the bed or the door.

Hal marveled at the power he had over her . . . and at her power over him. He approached the bed naked and kissed the inside of her wrist, where she'd slashed herself so his blood could mingle with hers.

"I am Chickasaw now," she said.

"Yes." Sometimes a lie was kinder than the truth, and Hal suddenly understood part of her power over him: He wanted to be kind to her.

She touched the small scar on his wrist. "Your blood flows through me and mine through you. You can never leave me." Tears started in her eyes. "Promise you'll never leave me, Clayton."

"I'll never leave you." His hands trembled as he brushed the tears from her eyes. There were no lies in him now, for what he felt was too powerful for lies. He loved this woman against all reason, and he would do whatever it took to keep her ... even become another man.

"You won't let them take me back?" she whispered.

"No. I won't let them take you back."

Somewhere in Boston was the place she dreaded, a place called The Towers that would bend her will and break her spirit until she became docile and ordinary. Dipping his fingers into the paint pot, Hal adorned himself with the blue of Father Sky, then drew a long path from her breasts to her thighs. As he followed the path, he knew that he'd been destined for greatness, and all the paths he'd followed had led to this softly lit bedroom, where Melissa Sayers Colbert flowed beneath him like the Blue River, turbulent and quixotic. With a triumphant Chickasaw victory chant he fell into the river, deeper and deeper until he was drowning.

"Clayton!" she screamed. "Clayton!"

"They'll never take you from me, Melissa." The river sucked at him once more, and he closed his eyes, riding the waves. "Never!"

38

Charleston, South Carolina

Kate rode along the edge of the water bareback with her knees hugging the Appaloosa and her hair blowing free. Along the beach, lights left over from Christmas glittered on the rooftops of cottages, and in a few of the windows artificial Christmas trees still shimmered with tinsel and glass ornaments.

"Go, Osi."

The big Appaloosa responded like his namesake, galloping so fast over the sand, he seemed to be flying. She'd bought him when she first came back to Charleston, bought him on impulse one Saturday after she'd cried all through *Dances with Wolves* at the matinee. Some sense of fate had prompted her to name him Eagle.

That or insanity.

She slowed the stallion as she approached the cove where the boating accident had occurred so many years before, and for a moment she thought she heard the sound of crying. Brian and Charles and Deborah and all the children of Witch Dance, crying out for her to save them.

Suddenly she felt the chill of the January wind and wished she'd worn a jacket. She untied the sweater that hung around her neck and stuck her arms through the sleeves.

The sound of crying came to her once more, borne on the wind. Osi whinnied softly, sidestepping.

"Whoa, boy. There's nothing here except memories."

The crying became a whimpering, and out from behind the dunes crawled a puppy, its reddish-brown fur bedraggled and its ribs poking like sticks underneath its skin. Kate dismounted and scooped the shivering mongrel into her arms.

"You poor little thing."

The shivering stopped momentarily as he looked up at her with soulful dark eyes.

"Don't you worry about a thing. I'm not going to leave you here to die."

She mounted the Appaloosa, then headed to her cottage. It was remote from the beachfront, set back among hundred-year-old live-oak trees hanging with Spanish moss that swept the ground.

In her stable Kate found a box for the puppy and set him in a nest of hay while she tended Osi. By the time she left the stable, stars had sprung out in the heavens, glittering through the ghostly branches of the trees as if they'd been thrown there by a careless hand. Her mother's long white Cadillac was parked in her driveway, and Martha was waiting for her on the front porch.

"What in the world are you bringing home now?"

"I found him abandoned on the beach. His name is Coahoma."

"Coahoma?" Martha followed Kate inside the cottage and sat on the sofa with her brown pumps planted carefully together and her hands folded in her lap.

"It's Muskogean. It means 'red panther.' " Busy with the puppy, Kate heard her mother's sigh. But Martha wouldn't say anything; she was far too civilized to start a quarrel over Kate's penchant for everything Chickasaw.

"I was hoping you might come over for dinner on Friday."

"I'm on duty at the hospital."

"Saturday, then?"

"I don't think so, Mother."

"Katie . . . you've been home over a month now. With the new year and all, I thought . . ." She let her voice trail off, and sat looking at her feet.

"Does Dad know you're inviting me over?"

Martha pulled a lace-edged handkerchief from her purse and swiped at an imaginary speck of dust on her skirt. Then she folded the handkerchief into a perfect square and tucked it back into her bag.

"He's as stubborn as a post oak, Katie. Just like you. Not budging an inch, even after I hung the glass ball with your name on it on our Christmas tree." Martha sank back onto the cushions with her hand over her heart, as if it had taken her last ounce of energy to be so plainspoken with her willful daughter.

Kate glanced at her own tree left over from Christmas, a spindly little pine that nobody else had wanted. It stood in the corner of the room, waiting to be planted, its roots wrapped in burlap and one single string of popcorn hanging limply in its branches. Kate remembered how she'd celebrated Christmas, taking every shift she could at the hospital, then at the last possible minute driving back to her empty cottage. On her way there she'd seen a tree vendor standing on his lot, still trying to sell his one last pitiful tree. She'd bought it, out of sympathy rather than any holiday spirit; and then when she got home she couldn't bear the thought of going to bed, so she'd sat up most the night, watching old movies and eating popcorn, then finally stringing the leftovers so the tree wouldn't look so forlorn.

"We're quite a pair, aren't we?" Kate grinned at her mother, hoping humor would dispel the gloom settling in the room like a fog rolling in from the sea; but seeing Martha's obvious distress, she relented.

"All right, Mother. I'll be there Saturday . . . but I'm not making any promises."

* * *

Martha was thankful Katie had come early so that the two of them had a little quiet time together before Mick got home. He went to his office come hell, high water, or holidays. She supposed she should have told him their daughter was coming for dinner, but she thought the surprise of seeing her combined with the spirit of the new year might soften him a little.

She did wish Katie hadn't brought the dog though. It might complicate things a bit.

"I see you've made Dad's favorite cranberry salad."

"It wouldn't be a company meal without it."

"He knows I'm coming?"

Martha bustled about the kitchen, ignoring her daughter's question. "Katie, would you hand me that spatula? I can't seem to get this icing to stay on the cake."

"Martha!" Mick burst suddenly upon the peaceful room like a big bear somebody had let out of his cage. Martha wished that sometimes he'd walk in nice and easy and say *hello*. What was wrong with just saying *hello*?

He stopped short when he saw his daughter. For a moment they stared at each other like perfect strangers, and Martha was afraid one or the other of them would turn around and walk out the door.

Katie was the first to break the silence.

"Happy New Year, Dad."

"Same to ye, Katie." He looked as if might be about to walk over and put his arm around her, but suddenly he turned back to Martha, all red-faced and blustery. "What in the hell is that damned dog doing in my living room?"

A red flush came into Katie's cheeks, and Martha saw the effort she made to hold her temper in check.

"It's my dog."

Martha pressed her hand over her heart just thinking about the confrontations Mick used to have with Katie. Wouldn't you think he'd be so glad to have her safe at home that he'd moderate his opinions?

But what did she know? Mick was a senator and Katie was a doctor, while she was just a rich little girl who'd grown into a rich old woman whose husband didn't love her and whose daughter didn't understand her.

"I'm too old to clean up dog piss," he said.

"Now, Mick," Martha said. Anxious. Lord, why did she always have to sound anxious?

"He's trained." Kate was nearly as tall as her father, and when she was mad she looked taller. "And even if Coahoma *did* wet the floors, it would be Mother cleaning it up. Not you."

"*Coahoma!* It's not enough that you went off and lived with that savage. Now we have to listen to you calling your dog Indian names."

"You don't have to listen." Kate wheeled around and marched from the kitchen, her color and her chin high.

"It's a by God miracle she didn't come back carrying a half-breed child." Mick poured himself a scotch on the rocks. "She's driving me to drink."

Martha's hands trembled as she dropped her dirty spatula into the sink. She didn't even bother turning on the water.

"No, Mick. You're the one who's doing the driving. You're driving our daughter right out of our lives. . . ." Was she actually saying those things? The stunned look on Mick's face told her she was, and that furthermore, he was listening. "And I'm going with her."

She left the kitchen, but when she got outside she thought about the spatula and almost went back in. Once the icing dried on the blade, it would be like cement.

"Martha . . . come back here!"

She could hear Katie in the living room, collecting Coahoma and his toys.

Martha set her face toward the front hallway. Let *Mick* clean the spatula for a change. Resolute, she went through the front door, even slamming it behind her. Outside, she climbed into Katie's car and waited.

She'd worry about clothes tomorrow.

39

Witch Dance

The old shaman had been dead for days when they found him. He was frozen cross-legged on the floor of his mountaintop cabin with his eyes wide open and a look of shock on his face as if death had surprised him. His tattered buffalo-skin robe was wrapped around him, but it had done nothing to keep out the cold. The door banged on its hinges and snow lay in drifts on the cabin floor.

At the direction of Governor Mingo, he was buried in the ancient ways, in a sitting position, his head anointed with oil, his face painted red and facing the east. Eagle stood with the mourners in a circle around the grave, knowing that what he witnessed was more than the burial of a revered medicine man: He was watching the passing of the old ways. As the songs of lamentation rose toward Father Sky, he heard the whisper of birch-bark canoes through still waters, saw the great painted warriors thundering across the plains on their Chicka-saw horses, smelled the smoke from the council fires. He clung to the archetypal memories as if he could im-plant them in the hearts and minds of a nation by the force of his own will.

Around him, the mourners were not only oblivious of

his struggle but eager to be away from a ceremony that obviously made them uncomfortable. Soon they would put aside their ancient funeral songs and climb into their modern cars to return to their houses, where Oprah exposed the sins of a nation on television and the whiskey bottle waited under the kitchen sink to help them forget their defeat.

The old ways were gone. His heart fell to the ground and mourned.

Del Mar, California

Eagle hardly recognized his sister-in-law.

"You shouldn't have come all this way ... but I'm glad you did." Anna lay against the covers with her hands folded protectively over her bulging womb. She'd changed her long hair to a short modern style, and her lips and eyes were painted like the California women he'd glimpsed on the streets.

She was beautiful, a woman he hardly knew until she smiled. And then she became the Anna he'd known when Cole had first brought her into the family—warm, animated, and approachable.

"I'm glad too." He took her hand. "How are you, Anna?"

"Fine. Wonderful, really." She laughed. "Except for being flat on my back. My sister shouldn't have called you."

The call had come unexpectedly, not to his home but to his office, where he'd been standing at the window, watching the last snow of the season sputter against the sidewalks and melt into slick puddles. "Anna has been in the hospital," her sister had said. "The pregnancy has made her very sick." Shocking news considering that the few notes Anna had written since she and Clint moved had been brief and cheerful, telling him nothing really about their life in California. He'd caught the next plane out, and as was his way, had gone straight to the best source for information.

"The doctor assured me that you and the babies are going to be all right," he said.

"Twin girls. Can you believe it?"

"Cole's children."

Anna said nothing, but smoothed the covers, obviously flustered.

"He really loved you, Anna. Always. Even during the bad times."

Her glance slid away from his. "How are Dovie and Winston?"

"They send their love. They wanted to come, but Dad's health is too fragile and Mom won't go anywhere without him."

"Tell them I said hello."

Suddenly Eagle ran out of things to say. Embroidered curtains fluttered at the open window, and the sound of waves filled the silence. Anna tried to hide her discomfort by reaching to her bedside table for a sip of water.

The table was a frivolous piece of furniture—French, Eagle thought. There was nothing of her former life in the room, no Indian pottery, no colorful woven rugs, none of the western prints Cole had loved. Everything surrounding her was new and generic. It might have belonged to any woman anywhere in the United States.

There was the sound of a car door, and then footsteps in the hallway.

"Anna." A tall man with blond hair and thick glasses came into the room.

The first thing Eagle noticed was that the man had come into the house without a key, and the second was that he went straight to Anna's bed without even noticing she had a visitor.

"How are you, darling?" he said, bending to kiss her on the lips.

"Larry . . . we have a visitor. My brother-in-law from Oklahoma."

The man Anna called Larry turned, not at all flustered at having been caught kissing Cole's wife.

"Hello. I'm Larry Carnathan." He stuck out his hand. "You're Eagle Mingo."

"Yes." His handshake was firm and his gaze unwavering as Eagle assessed him. Self-assured. Determined. Not a man to be taken lightly, Eagle decided.

"You've come a long way to see Anna. Why don't I leave you two alone?"

"You don't have to leave, Larry." Anna thrust her chin out as if she dared Eagle to contradict her.

"I won't go far. Just to the kitchen to make us all a pot of coffee."

They heard his footsteps disappearing down the hall. In the humming silence, Anna fidgeted with the covers.

"He's my sister's accountant," she said finally. "I met him when I first moved out here. He's been good to me."

"You and this man have made plans?"

"Yes. I'm going to marry him." Her chin came up. "I need a father for my children, but more than that, I love him."

"They have a father."

"Cole's dead, Eagle."

Eagle heard his brother's cry as he fell over the edge of the cliff. He wanted to shut his ears, but he couldn't. Cole's haunting cry had become the lamentation of a nation, falling over the edge of a cliff into oblivion.

"He lives through his children, Anna. They will carry on the Mingo name, the Mingo traditions."

"Clint will remain a Mingo if he wishes . . . he's old enough to choose. But my babies will be called Carnathan . . . like their adoptive father."

"They are Cole's children. If you do this, you desecrate the Mingo name."

"Cole desecrated the Mingo name."

The fearsome truth glittered in Anna's eyes, and Eagle understood that both he and Cole had vastly underestimated this woman.

"Didn't you think I'd guess?" she added. "Didn't you think I'd add up all his absences, his erratic behavior?"

"No one else knows . . ."

"No. Nor will they ever." Anna folded her hands over her vast abdomen. "I will tell the babies their tribal history, but I won't burden them with paralyzing traditions and a name they'll have to defend."

In the face of her implacable will, Eagle was defenseless.

"My father's spirit will never recover from this final blow."

"You underestimate Winston, Eagle. You always have."

There was a discreet knock. Larry Carnathan stuck his head around the door.

"Is anybody ready for coffee?"

Eagle knew that his response would set the course for the future. With the waiting stillness that had characterized his ancestors, he studied the man who would raise his brother's children, studied him, and saw his strength and his courage.

"Coffee sounds like a good idea," he said.

40

Charleston, South Carolina

Every morning Martha cooked bacon and eggs and bis-
cuits, in spite of what her daughter said about choles-
terol, and every evening Kate stopped on her way from
work to pick up some special treat for them, the Italian
ices they loved so well, or boiled peanuts from the vendor on the corner near the hospital.

Often now, her mother sang. And three days a week
she put on her striped cotton uniform and did volunteer
work at the hospital. Gray Ladies, they were called.

"How do you like being a Gray Lady, Mother?"

"I love it. But what do you suppose they'd call me if
I dyed my hair red?"

"They'd call you beautiful. Do it."

Restless, Kate went to the window. Soon it would be
spring. Though the lilacs weren't yet blooming, their
fragrance was already in the air, as if it had been borne
in from some exotic and faraway place on breezes drifting across the sea.

The news reporter on *Wake Up, Charleston* was giddy
with the sighting of a bluebird she'd seen on the way
to work. As Kate leaned on the windowsill, listening to
the woman's drawl, thick as molasses, she remembered the musical rhythms of Deborah's voice telling

her she should wear a hat in the sun, and the mesmerizing cadence of Eagle's voice as he wooed her in Muskogean.

"And now ... here's what's happening around the
nation," the woman on television intoned. "In Tupelo,
Mississippi, a new furniture market is opening, and in
Ada, Oklahoma, Governor Eagle Mingo announced the
opening of Native Arts, Incorporated, at the site of what
was once a tool and die plant."

Suddenly his voice was more than a memory; it filled
the room, flowing through Kate like the Blue River, until
she was full of the sound and the music of it.

"The new enterprise has two purposes," he said, "to
employ the people who need work as well as to pre-
serve and promote Chickasaw culture."

His face filled the screen, chiseled and so beautiful, it
took away Kate's ability to breathe. The camera panned
to woven baskets and hand-painted pottery, and the
honey-voiced Southerner waxed eloquent about the art;
but Kate still saw and heard Eagle. Only Eagle.

"Katie." She felt her mother's hand on her arm. "Are
you all right?"

"I'm fine."

"You remind me of the way I used to look forty years
ago when I knew Mick would be calling."

Kate walked toward a chair, keeping her eyes on the
television screen, although she knew that she'd seen the
last of Eagle Mingo. *Wake Up, Charleston* featured sound
bites, not in-depth reporting.

The cameras were panning across a zoo now, in Wash-
ington, D.C., honing in on the pandas.

"Mother, what are you going to do?"

"I thought I'd go down to the nursery and buy some
plants. Don't you think flower beds would look nice in
front of the cottage?"

"I'm not talking about today. I'm talking about the
next few months, the next few years."

"My future, you mean?" Martha laughed, then inspected her hands. "I don't know, Katie. I don't need the

money, but I realize I can't depend on you the rest of my life to keep me company and make all my decisions."

"Wasn't there anything you wanted to do? Any burning ambition you had when you were young?"

"Not like you. You're like Mick. Both of you always knew exactly what you wanted."

A long silence fell over them. Finally Martha went to the window and opened it wider to let in the breeze.

"I used to think I might like to be a concert pianist," she said almost timidly. "But my hands are too stiff now and my skills too rusty. It's far, far too late for those dreams."

"If I left, would you stay here? At the cottage?"

"You're leaving, aren't you, Katie?"

Until that moment Kate hadn't known it was so; but suddenly she understood that she had to leave, that the redemption she'd spent years trying to find had been inside her all along, waiting to be discovered. At last she forgave herself for the death of her brothers, the death of the Chickasaw children, and most of all, the death of Deborah.

"Yes, Mother. I'm leaving."

Martha untied her apron and began to tidy up the kitchen.

"Don't you worry a minute about me. I'll be fine. I might even go up to Virginia for a while to visit Cousin Clara. She's been after me to go to Europe with her."

"Dye your hair red first," Kate said, hugging her mother.

"I might just do that."

Kate turned her face to the open window, where birdsong drifted through on fresh breezes. Spring had come, and, with it, peace.

41

Witch Dance

The land was coming alive after a harsh winter. In the mountains, patches of snow still clung to the ground, shaded by enormous trees, but in the valley the grass sprang up fresh and green, and flowers threaded like colored ribbons along the edge of bluffs and the banks of the river.

High above the land where ravens nested and eaglets tested their wings on maiden flights, Eagle stood alone, staring into the ravine. There was no sign of violence now, only the quiet beauty of a land renewing itself. On the place where his brother had died, flowers grew, more vivid then the ones around them. An eaglet lost its confidence and landed among the blossoms, squawking.

"Fly, little one," Eagle said. "Fly."

And while he watched, the eaglet spread its wings and lifted upward, growing stronger and more beautiful as it flew toward the sun.

Eagle tipped his head back to watch the flight, and as he lifted his head toward Father Sky, he slowly lifted his arms.

"Loak-Isthtohoollo-Aba. *Alail-o*. I am come."

The eaglet bent its wings and swooped close, crying out ancient secrets to him, and the vision that had been in Eagle's mind all winter became so real, he could almost touch it.

Kate was riding Indian-style, sitting proud and erect the way he always remembered her. He lowered his arms and stood with his feet planted apart as the big Appaloosa topped the ridge and cantered close, stopping a few feet from him.

"Hello, Eagle."

His soul wept for her, and his heart cried out, but he stood apart, wrapped in dignity and the heavy mantle of duty.

"Hello, Kate."

She stared at him with eyes that held memories. Even across the distance his skin burned with her and he felt the warm, sweet melting of his flesh into hers. Her bottom lip trembled ever so slightly. She caught it between her teeth as she dismounted.

For a small eternity they faced each other, watching, waiting, wanting. Finally the eaglet swooped between them, its cry breaking the screaming silence. Kate turned abruptly and walked to the edge of the cliff.

He wanted to reach out to keep her from falling over the edge, wanted to cry out *Stop*. Instead, he remained as still as the carved mountains around him.

She stood at the edge of the cliff for a long time, and when she turned to him, there was a hint of tears in her eyes.

"Aren't you going to ask why I'm here?"

"Kate, you were never one to keep secrets. You'll tell me."

"Damn you, Eagle Mingo."

He smiled at the quick spots of color that came into her cheeks. Nothing about Kate Malone had changed. At least he had that.

"Why are you here?" he said.

"Because I knew you would be here, standing just as you were when I first saw you with your arms lifted to the sky. I knew those things, Eagle, because you are still here . . . inside me in ways that no man has ever been or ever will be." The hand she had spread over her heart clenched, catching the fabric of her blouse and drawing it tight across her breasts.

Eagle wanted to take the clenched hand and gently pull it apart, wanted to lift it up to his lips and taste the sweetness of her palm. The high mountain wind whipped her hair around her face. He could almost reach out and touch it, that bright hair of his visions, that silky, flaming mass that moved him in ways not even he could fathom.

One small movement. That's all it would take to send him flying across the space that separated them. If she had lifted her hand to hold back her hair, the sight of soft, blue-veined skin of her underarm would have been his undoing. If she had shifted her right foot, thrusting her hips forward ever so slightly in the provocative angle that used to drive him mad, he'd have covered her with wings that would carry them on a flight from which neither of them could ever return.

But she stood unmoving, her arms wrapped around herself as much to ward him off as to keep out the spring winds still chilly in the high mountains. The wind soughed between them, crying out for their isolation.

He opened his mouth to speak, though he didn't know what he would say. How could he bind her to him with words when he couldn't bind her to him with deeds?

"Please ... don't say anything, Eagle. If you call me *Wictonaye,* I'll lose my resolve. If you speak to me of flying, I'll spread myself on the ground at your feet and beg you to take me with you." She held up her palm. "No ... don't speak to me yet. I have to finish what I came to say."

He watched her silently, but his eyes spoke to her of love, and she turned her face away so she wouldn't see. His stallion pawed the ground, impatient, and hers whinnied, skittish.

"I'm going to rebuild my clinic as a memorial to Deborah, and I'm going to rebuild a life here in Witch Dance. A real one this time, Eagle."

Without him. Her stance and her stubborn chin made that perfectly clear. There would be no more summer affairs beside the Blue River, no more explosive matings in the mountains.

"The clinic will be a good thing. The old shaman is dead, and Witch Dance needs you."

Witch Dance needed her, she thought, but not Eagle. Governor Eagle Mingo would never need her.

She mounted her stallion in one fluid movement. The time had come to go.

He took a step forward, and for a moment she thought he meant to catch her bridle so she couldn't leave. But he stopped short of the Appaloosa.

"If I can help you in any way, let me know. The governor's office is always at your disposal."

"You can help me by staying away, Eagle." She tossed her hair and held her back erect. She would not ride away a defeated woman. "If any man ever rides up to my door again to carry me off on a horse, he'd damned well better mean it."

She wheeled her stallion away, wanting to shut out the sight of him quickly before she could change her mind.

"Kate!"

His voice was not a plea, but a command. She brought her mount to a halt and looked back at him over her shoulder. His eyes sucked her into him so that she went spinning away, caught forever on the medicine wheel.

She held her breath, waiting. At last he spoke.

"Good luck, Kate."

"I don't need luck; I plan to make my own."

The Appaloosa thundered off and disappeared down the side of the mountain. Kate could hardly see through the blur of her tears, but she sat tall and straight on her stallion in case Eagle Mingo had come to the top of the ridge to watch.

Alexandria, Virginia

Martha's suitcases lay open on the bed. Outside her open French doors she could hear Cousin Clara whistling as she walked toward the paddocks, where she would leave explicit and lengthy instructions for the care of her Thoroughbreds.

One last dress hung in the closet, waiting to be packed, a blue sequined gown that Clara had said made her look classy but available, like a woman who might be interested in a man but didn't necessarily need one. Martha took the dress off the hanger and held it against her body, then twisted around to see herself in the mirror.

She looked like what she was, an old woman trying to appear young.

"Silly old fool," she said. But she put the dress into the suitcase anyhow. No sense in going off to Europe half cocked, which was another of Clara's favorite sayings, one she'd used the day they went shopping together for their trip.

"Clara, you're going to corrupt me," Martha had said.

"It's high time somebody did."

Martha went through the French doors and stood on the balcony, watching her cousin. Clara strode through the paddocks like a woman who knew exactly where she was going and what she was going to do when she got there.

Martha envied that, Clara's sense of purpose. She herself still felt as if she were drifting around in a little boat in a big, scary sea. She wondered if she would ever be able to find any direction without Kate ... and without Mick.

At the thought of her husband, her hand flew over her heart, and she thought she might be turning into one of those women who suffered dizzy spells.

"Martha."

As if her thoughts had popped out of her head and become real, Mick stood in the center of the room next to her bed, where the blue sequined gown spilled out of the suitcase.

"Mick . . . I didn't hear you come in."

"I didn't mean to scare you. I'm sorry."

Mick Malone *apologizing*? Was the world coming to an end?

"You look good, Martha."

Suddenly she was glad that she'd dyed her hair red and that her dress was pink, and that her new shoes made her look three inches taller.

"Thank you, Mick."

He glanced at her suitcase, and then back at her, suddenly an old man, his bones shrunken too small for his skin and his bluster nothing more than a faint breeze.

"Are you going somewhere, Martha?"

Was she? Even with Mick standing in the room?

"Yes. Clara and I are taking a little jaunt to Europe."

He stood watching her while the grandfather clock in the hallway chimed the hour. Then slowly he moved across the room.

"Am I too late?"

Almost shyly he reached out and squeezed her hand. She wished he would tell her that he loved her, tell her that he was sorry for all the months and years of isolation. But it was enough that he had come.

"No, Mick. You're not too late."

Witch Dance

Indian paintbrush colored the hills and red-tailed hawks wheeled upward to the burning blue sky. Eagle rode hard, his long hair braided and blowing in the wind. Just the other side of the ridge, Kate's clinic stood under the trees with an OPEN sign on the door. He hadn't seen it, but he knew.

Governor Eagle Mingo knew everything ... except how to live with a broken heart.

He raced toward the Blue River and, stripped naked, swam until his arms were heavy. Lying on a rock, he let the sun dry his skin while the seductive music of the river called to him.

Kate. Kate.

He heard her name everywhere, in the voice of the river and the silence of the stars, in the new dawning of the east and the gentle sleeping of the west. At last, his skin warm from the sun, he rode toward his father's house.

Winston sat in his favorite chair under the trees, propped up by cushions and shelling peas from Dovie's garden.

"I thought you might come today," Winston said.

Today. An auspicious occasion. A turning point.

The wedding invitation lay open on Eagle's hall table, engraved with their names, Anna Mingo and Larry Carnathan.

Eagle dismounted and leaned against the trunk of a massive oak.

"Are you and Mother all right?"

Winston's black eyes could still pierce in spite of his age and his illness.

"What use is it to keep trying to fly with a broken wing?" Winston popped open the green pods and forced the peas out with his thumbnail. "The old ways are disappearing, Eagle. Nothing we can say or do will stop that." He cast the empty shell carefully into the open paper sack sitting beside his chair; then he studied his son. "Dovie and I are fine. How about you?"

"Kate lives and breathes no more than fifteen minutes away from my ranch, and I am separated from her by honor and duty and a tradition that I can no longer justify."

"Where is the honor if your heart shrivels within you? What is duty that it should steal your happiness?"

"Our nation . . . even our family is becoming homogenized."

"One man alone can't stop it." Winston reached for the peas, and concentrated as he popped them into the pottery bowl he held on his lap. "In my illness, I've had much time to think, and I've come to believe that courage is more important than blood."

The courage of a woman who rebuilt her clinic from ashes. Eagle pushed away from the tree and knelt beside his father's chair to help shell the peas.

". . . And that old blood can become stagnant if it's not mixed with new," Eagle added.

"You've given this much thought," Winston said.

"Yes. I was compelled to. The roots of my heart are forever entangled with Kate Malone's, and the strongest winds cannot separate us."

A breeze ruffled Winston's long gray hair as he silently performed the task that Dovie had set for him.

Eagle waited beside the chair, his hands moving among the peas and his heart already flying across the prairie.

"And what conclusions have you come to?" Winston asked finally.

"A wise leader can adopt the exigencies of modern society and yet retain tribal heritage."

"You are very wise, my son."

Kate escorted her patient to the door—Bethany Martin, her face shriveled like a prune and her hands curled under with the arthritis that constantly plagued her.

"I knew you'd be back." Bethany gave her a toothless grin, then pressed a box into her hands, its sides greasy from the cookies that were stacked inside.

"And how did you know that, Mrs. Martin? Are you taking up clairvoyance as well as needlepoint and cookie making?"

"Nope. Plain old common sense." She tapped Kate's chest with a knotty finger. "You've got a stout Chickasaw heart. You're unconquered and unconquerable."

"You bet your sweet boots, I am. Nobody's going to drive me out of Witch Dance again. Not ever."

Bethany giggled. "My boots are no longer young and sweet, but they still get me where I'm going."

Kate watched as the old woman climbed into her car, adjusted her hat, then set off in a cloud of dust.

Her first patient. And there would be many more.

When the dust settled, she tipped her face to the sky and the noonday sun fell over her like a benediction. There was a new warmth to the sun, a new welcome in the sky. Kate knew that she was finally home.

She had turned to go back inside her clinic, when she heard the thundering of horse's hooves. Shading her eyes, she looked into the distance.

Eagle Mingo rode into view.

He stopped at the top of the hill, backlit by the sun. Hope thrummed through her, but she stood still at the door, not yet trusting, not yet believing. On the hillside

Eagle dismounted and stood gazing down at her as if he, too, could neither trust nor believe.

Suddenly the silence was rent with the cry of an eagle. As the majestic bird spiraled upward, the sun lay along his wings and spread its heat outward, burning, until the glow touched their hearts.

Without taking his gaze from Kate, Eagle bent to gather a bouquet of Indian paintbrush. She reached behind her and turned the sign on the clinic door. CLOSED FOR THE DAY.

Eagle mounted his stallion, then, holding the flowers high as he might carry a banner of victory, he raced down the hill, riding hard, straight toward the clinic. Kate cast aside her white lab coat and started running, running to meet the future.

When the horse was even with her, Eagle dismounted. His eyes never left hers as he held out his hand.

"Waka ahina uno, iskunosi Wictonaye. Waka."

"Yes," she said, reaching out to him. His hand closed around hers.

"This time forever," he said.

Epilogue
The Eagle

*The river sang its timeless song, and out of its waters rose
   the Eagle, magnificent and golden.*
*The sun slanted along his wings and reached outward,
   spreading its warmth to the one who lay upon the colored
   blanket, touching her hair with fire.*
His heart. His soul. His mate.
*He glided downward softly, tenderly, folding her in his wings
   until he was lost in the deep womb that had
   nourished his sons.*

Acknowledgments

I want to thank the following people who so generously shared their time and talent with me during the writing of this book: Glenda Galvan, Chickasaw Nation, Ada, Oklahoma; Buddy Palmer, Julian Riley, and the staff of the Lee County Library, Tupelo, Mississippi, for sharing their knowledge of Chickasaw history; Dr. Charles Montgomery and Ruth Ann Wilson, R.N., Tupelo, for medical information; and Dr. Lynn Cox, All Animal Hospital, also of Tupelo, for unabashedly describing the mating ritual of horses.

A special thanks to Earl J. Cacho of Victorville, California, for allowing me to use his face on the cover. A renowned wildlife and western artist, Earl is from the Tarasco tribe of Michoacan, Mexico.

I've taken literary license with some of the magnificent Indian customs and legends, and I take full responsibility for any errors I might have made in portraying the sickness that stalked the Chickasaw children. In any event, I could not have written *Witch Dance* without the help of these wonderful people, and I am eternally grateful to them.

ABOUT THE AUTHOR

PEGGY WEBB, who holds an M.A. in English from the University of Mississippi, is the author of over twenty-five romance novels and over two hundred magazine humor columns for trade journals. She is very active in church and civic activities in her hometown of Tupelo, Mississippi, and often graces the stage of the community theater.